Praise for the novels of Jo McNally

Barefoot on a Starlit Night

"A fun read." —Harlequin Junkie

"Filled with tension ___ emotion, *Barefoot on a Starlit Night* is sure to please re___ contemporary romance."
—New Journal of Books

"If you are lookin___ el-good book with romance, laughs, and a guaranteed ___ h an author who writes with a practiced hand, then look no further than this book!"
—The Lit Bitch

Stealing Kisses in the Snow

"Readers will be charmed by this sweet, no-nonsense Christmas romance full of genuine emotion." —Publishers Weekly

Slow Dancing at Sunrise

"With witty characters and only a small amount of drama, *Slow Dancing at Sunrise* is an entertaining and charming story that will appeal to readers of small-town romances."
—Harlequin Junkie

JO McNALLY

When Sparks Fly

HQN

HQN®

ISBN-13: 978-1-335-91638-9

Recycling programs
for this product may
not exist in your area.

When Sparks Fly
Copyright © 2022 by Jo McNally

Lost in Love
Copyright © 2022 by Jo McNally

For questions and comments about the quality of this book,
please contact us at CustomerService@Harlequin.com.

HQN
22 Adelaide St. West, 41st Floor
Toronto, Ontario M5H 4E3, Canada
www.Harlequin.com

Printed and bound in Barcelona, Spain by CPI Black Print

CONTENTS

This book about friendship—truly ALL of my books to date—exists because of one person: my coach, my cheerleader, my agent, and, more importantly, my friend.

To Veronica, with so many thanks and much love.

WHEN SPARKS FLY

CHAPTER ONE

ZOEY HARTFORD HAD been called to the principal's office. Been a while since *that* happened. But here she was, sitting in a hard wooden armchair next to the thoroughly unrepentant reason for the call—her thirteen-year-old daughter, Hazel.

"Thanks for dressing up there, Mom." Hazel eyed Zoey's gray coveralls and the Hartford Fix-It cap that hid most of her dark hair. She'd had no intention of doing anything more than repairing Mrs. Franklin's central vacuum cleaner—located in a crawl space—when she'd left the house that morning.

"Excuse me for rushing straight here from a house call." She brushed her hands down the drab gray fabric. "That's what a good mom does when they get a call that their child has been involved in an—" she raised her fingers to form air quotes "—*altercation* at school. Besides, I can't take them off. I wore my It's Wine O'Clock Somewhere T-shirt this morning, and I don't think that would impress your principal."

Hazel snorted. "He'd probably like it. Rumor has it Mr. Sheffield keeps booze in his desk."

Zoey didn't answer. If she was in charge of several hundred middle schoolers, she'd probably keep booze in *her* desk, too.

Her coveralls were quite a contrast with her daughter's

colorful outfit. A fan of so-called *influencers* Zoey had never heard of, Hazel had belted a long purple shirt over a black top and leggings. Her bright green ankle boots were tied with lengths of sparkly purple lace. Hazel's dark hair was loose, with sleek waves that looked natural, but Zoey knew the girl spent a half hour creating that effect.

She had no idea how she'd ever produced this little fashionista with the wisecracking mouth. Well…to be fair, there was no doubt the smart mouth came straight from Zoey. She glanced at her watch.

"Where is this guy, anyway?"

Before Hazel could respond, Principal Ted Sheffield entered, nodding a greeting before taking his seat in the oversize chair behind his oversize desk. He'd clearly read one of those executive books that claimed large furniture made him seem more powerful. That was wasted on her and Hazel. Hartford women weren't easily intimidated.

"Okay…" Sheffield cleared his throat loudly, speaking to Zoey. "I assume Miss Carson in the front office filled you in on what transpired here this morning?"

Zoey gave him a thin smile. *Game on.* "Yes, she did. So did my daughter, by the way. I'm assuming she'll be getting an apology at some point?"

"I'm sorry?" He coughed, his face turning red. "I mean… I'm *not* sorry…um…who am I apologizing to? And for what?" Mr. Sheffield managed to regroup after a little huffing and puffing. "Mrs. Bennett, your daughter *punched* another student. We have a zero tolerance policy on violence here…"

"First, I am no longer Mrs. Bennett. I'm Miss Hartford." She'd dropped her ex's last name, with Hazel's blessing. "And secondly, Hazel only punched Micah after he snapped the back of her bra—my daughter's *underwear*—repeatedly."

Hazel groaned. "Please don't ever say the word *underwear* out loud again, I beg you."

"Well…yes." Sheffield nodded, still looking pained. "But your daughter should know that violence is never the answer."

"I'm pretty sure it's violence to harass a female student. Isn't there a zero tolerance against *that*, too?" She took a deep breath and blew it out slowly. She wasn't helping Hazel by escalating this. "Mr. Sheffield…oh, hell… *Ted*…" He'd only been two years ahead of her in high school. "I've taught Hazel to never accept nonconsensual touching from anyone. Ever. And I've taught her how to respond to it." She turned to Hazel, counting questions off on her fingers. "Did you use your words?"

"Uh…yeah." Hazel rolled her honey-colored eyes dramatically. "I told him to knock it off, but he kept doing it."

"Did you go to someone in authority so they could step in?"

Hazel tossed her hands in the air. "I *tried* to. I told the study hall monitor, Mrs. Bailey, but she told me to sit back down."

"So you defended yourself?"

"You bet your… I mean…yes, Mother, I did."

Zoey bit the inside of her cheek to keep from laughing at her daughter's sarcasm. She had to be the adult here. She turned back to Ted, with his giant desk and his giant chair.

"Are you suggesting my daughter shouldn't have defended herself?"

There was a beat of silence, and Zoey knew the tide had turned. Ted Sheffield knew it, too. They negotiated a one-day suspension for both Zoey *and* Micah Wilkins, the kid who couldn't keep his hands to himself. There was only a month left in the school year, but rules were rules. Suspension wasn't great, but the school's zero tolerance policies were well-known to students and parents. Ted called Micah's mother on the speakerphone and they all approved the plan. Tammy Wilkins laughed, saying her son's pride had been injured by Hazel's punch more than his nose had been.

She and Hazel rode home in silence. It had been an exhausting few months since moving into Dad's house in January, with its peeling paint and rusted folk art "sculptures" in the front lawn. She'd inherited the place when her father died unexpectedly last fall. Behind the house was the barn that housed the business she'd also inherited—Hartford Fix-It Shop. It wasn't until she'd parked Dad's small white pickup behind the house that Zoey spoke.

"I had your back in there, Hazel. I always will." She turned off the ignition. "But you and I both know that you had other options besides hauling off and punching Micah in the face. Just because the room monitor didn't listen didn't mean you couldn't have gone right to the principal's office. Or to another teacher."

Hazel rolled her eyes. One of these days those teenage eyes were going to roll right out of her daughter's head. "You're always telling me to fight if someone tries to mess with me."

"Yes, but *fight* doesn't mean literally using your fists." She unzipped her coveralls and sighed as the cool air swept over her. Springtime was in full swing in Rendezvous Falls, with Upstate New York temperatures bouncing between freezing cold one day to hot and humid like today. "I know it's been a bumpy year, but let's not make it worse by getting yourself expelled from school, m'kay?"

She understood why Hazel's reactions had been...edgier

than normal lately. The divorce. Chris getting engaged to someone new in a hot minute once it was finalized. Losing Hazel's grandfather—Zoey's dad. Selling the only home Hazel had known and moving into Zoey's dad's place—a solid old house, but in desperate need of updating. Add in the hormonal roller-coaster ride of Hazel's "tweenhood," and it had been a wild ride for both of them.

Zoey knew there was a limit to how far they could take this *Thelma and Louise* act of theirs before they reached a mountain of trouble. Zoey appreciated the honest relationship she'd developed with her daughter, but sometimes she forgot Hazel was still barely a teenager. She'd had to grow up much too fast since the divorce. As great as it was to feel like friends, Zoey was still the mom.

Hazel just shrugged. "Pop-pop taught me not to let boys get away with sh…" She caught herself. "With anything. He said *you* should have learned that, too."

Zoey winced. Dad had definitely been right about Chris. But she didn't want Hazel thinking every male member of the human species was the enemy.

"Look, boys can be jerks. But not *all* boys."

"Yeah, well…if I have the same luck finding jerks that you did…"

Zoey let out a sharp laugh, clutching her chest. "Ouch—direct hit! But your dad wasn't always a jerk… I mean, he *isn't* a jerk." *Be the responsible adult here.* "Your father is a good man."

He was just a lousy husband.

Hazel blinked away, staring through the window to the tired old place that was now their home. Rendezvous Falls was famous for its colorful Victorian houses, but this particular house hadn't been painted in over twenty years. Zoey reached over and took her daughter's hand.

"I know you're still mad at your dad because we had to sell the house. But I couldn't afford to buy him out, and what's-her-name didn't want to live there…"

"Genna. With a *G*." Hazel's flat tone mirrored her mother's thoughts perfectly.

"Right. Genna-with-a-*G* wanted them to have their own house. And that's…fair. We'll make this into our home, I promise. I told you that when we moved in, and I meant it. And this is *your* year, remember?"

Zoey had promised Hazel that this year was *Hazel's Year*. The girl had lost enough the year before. Zoey was determined to create something stable here that Hazel could rely on.

After a pause, Hazel flashed her a quick, brittle smile. "Sure it is, Mom."

Zoey sat back against the truck seat with a heavy sigh after Hazel went into the house. She didn't have the emotional energy to follow her. Instead, she pulled out her phone and texted her best friend.

Z: How much trouble would I be in if I locked Hazel in her room permanently?

She decided she should clarify.

Z: Or at least until she safely reaches adulthood without giving me a heart attack.

It only took a moment for the answering bubbles to appear.

M: Do you plan on feeding her?

She chuckled. Her friend knew laughter was exactly what she needed right now.

Z: I suppose.

The bubbles floated longer this time.

M: Even so, as your attorney, I advise against it.

M: The authorities frown on that sort of thing.

There was a pause, but she could see her friend was typing something else.

M: Is this a red wine or whiskey night?

She could definitely use one of their cocktail hours in the repair shop later.

Z: Hazel punched a boy in the face at school today.

The answer came swiftly.

M: Damn! Did he deserve it?

She grinned at the instant assumption that it must have been justified.

Z: Yup

M: Go Hazel! Whiskey night.

Z: For sure.

ATTORNEY MIKE MCKINNON stared at his phone for a moment, knowing what he had to do. Zoey would expect no less.

M: What kind of music do chiropractors like?

Z: I'm seriously afraid to ask.

Mike grinned.

M: Hip pop.

"What are you grinning about over there?" His twin sister, Mary, made a playful grab for his phone. She'd picked him up from the car dealership where he'd left his SUV to get new brakes. "Do you have a secret admirer or something?"

He didn't answer until after Zoey's reply appeared.

Z: GROAN! CU later

"No admirer, sis. Just Zoey."

"That was a pretty big smile for *just Zoey.*" She glanced over again, one eyebrow raised. "Oh, God, are you two…?"

"No! Hell, no!" He straightened in his seat and pretended to shudder. "Stop. She's basically family. I'd never…" Sure, there'd been a time, back in high school, when he *may* have wondered what it would be like to kiss Zoey. A girl who took shop class and wore nothing but jeans, flannel shirts and Doc Martens. A girl with a quick laugh and a sharp wit, tall and lean, with coffee-colored hair. But even then, he'd known he couldn't risk losing a friendship unlike any other he had.

The problem was, for the past few months he'd been

thinking about it again. What *would* it be like to kiss Zoey Hartford, now that she was no longer a girl? And no longer married? Over the past few months, every time she'd bent over to pick something up in the shop, he'd paid more attention to the inviting curves of her backside than to whatever she was saying. It was a new sensation, and he had no idea what to do about it. One thing he *did* know is that he couldn't tell his sister. *Or* Zoey. Their friendship was *still* too important to him. This attraction he was feeling was probably some odd phase—nothing more.

He turned in the seat to face Mary, knowing she'd use that weird twin connection to figure out if he was being honest or not. "Zoey got me through the worst year of my life by not tiptoeing around me like everyone else did after Becca died. She made me laugh when no one else was even trying." He thought of the late-night texts she'd sent, often linking to obscure news stories about Bigfoot sightings, or a video of giant fish jumping out of a river and hitting some guy sitting in his boat. Random nonsense to take his mind off the sudden emptiness of his life. "Now *she's* having a tough year, and I'm returning the favor."

Mary wrinkled her nose, keeping her eyes on the road. "Great—now I feel guilty for not doing more for her myself since that asshat Chris made her sell the house. How is our unofficial triplet?"

That's what their parents used to call Zoey when she was at their house as a child, which was often. When she was around, Mom said her kids went from twins to triplets.

"She's having a rough day today. Hazel punched a boy at school."

"Yikes." Mary pulled to the curb in front of Mike's house. "Did the boy deserve it?" He nodded and she chuckled. "Good for Hazel. I'll have to give Zoey a call. You sure you don't want to borrow our car instead of taking that hot rod of yours out before summer?"

"Nah." He opened the passenger door. "Summer's almost here, and it's supposed to be dry for a few days." He kept his dark green 1971 Mustang Mach 1 stored safely in his garage during the winter. Even in the summer, it only came out on sunny days.

Mike headed over to Zoey's after dinner. Her dad's old place was up on the hill above Rendezvous Falls. Rob Hartford had been an interesting guy. Blunt, but kind. Talented, but scattered in so many directions he'd never really capitalized on that talent. His tendency to get distracted left his property in a bit of a shambles.

Instead of the bright color combinations of most of the Victorian homes in Rendezvous Falls, the solid gray-blue paint scheme had been an act of defiance on Rob's part. Now it was faded to simply…gray. It made the whole place look sad. And then there were the works of so-called art in the front yard. Shovels and rakes and metal ductwork formed into shapes. "Sculpting" had been Rob's weirdest hobby. It gave the place character, that was for sure.

The lights in the workshop were on, and when he got out of his car, Mike could see Zoey inside. Her dark hair was tugged into a high messy knot held with a big plastic clip—the type that held bags of potato chips closed. Sure enough, a bag of chips sat open on the workbench. She wore a T-shirt that said something about wine. Zoey was bent over the bench in deep concentration. The woman was a whiz at machines, just like her dad. Even as a kid, she'd loved puzzles. That's how they'd started their friendship— with riddles. He pulled out his phone and started typing.

M: The more I take, the more I leave behind. What am I?

She glanced over at her phone, then smiled when she saw it was from him. Something pinched at his heart. Did she always smile like that when he texted her? Did her face always soften…tension easing in every line? He hoped so. But he didn't want to examine why. His phone pinged.

Z: I give up. Who are you?

M: Footsteps. Outside. With whiskey.

Zoey looked up at the door and waved him in. She didn't say anything, just turned to the cupboard and brought out a couple of red plastic cups. He pulled a barstool over to the bench, opposite where she sat.

This was the "shop night" routine. Drinks—alcoholic or otherwise—late in the evening while Zoey tinkered on repairs. Some nights they talked nonstop, solving all the problems of the world or laughing about the characters in *Ted Lasso*. Some nights he just sat in relative silence, watching her work. He wasn't sure what Zoey got from their shop nights, but he knew *he* got a dose of peace from it. No pretense. No secrets. No games. Just his best friend and a splash of whiskey.

They'd started this routine after his wife, Becca, was killed by a drunk driver three years ago. He couldn't stand being in his house alone, dealing with all the ghosts of dreams that would never come true. Zoey invited him to stop by one night. She was working for her dad then, tackling the smaller items like vacuum cleaners or sewing machines in the shop. And their shop nights became a habit.

Mike hadn't been kidding when he told Mary that Zoey had gotten him through that awful first year. They'd continued to meet once or twice a week. It wasn't anything formal—he'd just show up, and she'd pull out the plastic cups so they could enjoy a glass of the wine the Finger Lakes region was so famous for. Or something stronger. On hot summer nights, it might be an ice-cold soda from the antique vending machine she and her dad had refurbished together.

He opened the bottle of whiskey, holding it up for her approval.

"A bottle of Paddy's, courtesy of my cousin at the Shamrock." He grinned. "Bridget says hi."

Bridget ran the McKinnon family pub, the Purple Shamrock. All the cousins owned a portion, but Bridget was the majority owner and manager.

Zoey snorted. "Liar. You stole that bottle without telling her, didn't you?"

"Meh…" He shrugged. "I'll tell her eventually." He poured a splash in each cup, but she nudged hers.

"I think I need a double tonight."

He obliged, pouring until she waved him off. She told him about Hazel's adventures in school, and Zoey's meeting with Ted Sheffield. Mike thought about it. "It sounds like you did everything right. You made sure the punishment fit the crime…for both kids. You talked to Hazel about not punching first and asking questions later. So…" He nodded toward her cup. "Why the double tonight?"

Zoey's face fell. "She's growing up so damn fast, Mike. I swear it was just yesterday she was running around the house dressed like Cinderella and begging us for a coach and six white horses for her birthday." Zoey gave him a chagrined look. "I didn't always *understand* her fascination with all things sparkly, but I loved that she *believed* in it so much, you know? That innocence…" Her voice trailed off. "Now she's punching boys for grabbing her bra. When did she get old enough to *wear* a bra? And when did she grow up enough to have to deal with *boys*? My little princess has vanished. I don't know if I'm ready to deal with a teenager."

"Look, I can't help with parenting advice." Mike ignored the stab of pain the topic always brought. "But I *can* tell you that you can deal with anything. You're the fiercest woman I know, and your daughter's just like you. Except…frillier."

Zoey had never been one to care about clothes, especially as a kid. Not that she didn't ever dress up—he remembered the flowy blue dress she'd worn to Mary's wedding. The way it swirled when she'd chased after a then-toddler-sized Hazel.

After a long pause, Zoey took a swig of her drink and scrunched her face.

"Whew! I mean…it's good whiskey, but…whoa."

"Irish whiskey is for sipping, not gulping, knucklehead. This isn't that cheap swill we used to sneak under the school bleachers with Mary in high school."

Zoey picked up the red cup and extended her pinkie finger in the air with a grin and what he guessed was supposed to be an aristocratic accent.

"Well, excuse my lack of decorum, Mr. McKinnon. I'll try to keep our upper-crust surroundings in mind the next time we drink together." She wiggled her eyebrows as she looked around the shop. The walls were lined with pegboard, and there were machine parts and rubber belts and packages of filters hanging everywhere. It was good to see her smile return.

"I expect china cups and saucers next time." Then he snapped his fingers. "Oh, that reminds me! I haven't told you about my latest adventure with your godmother's book club pals."

"Oh no! What did Vickie and her geriatric gang do now?"

The Rendezvous Falls book club was a bunch of silver-haired delinquents who'd convinced themselves they were matchmakers. The only problem was…they were horrible at it. He'd been in their sights for a while now, and lately Zoey was, too.

"They set me up with Rachel Reynolds. The librarian at the college. They're determined to put me with every woman who works on that campus. It's like they think I have a college fetish or something." Brady College was a small private college sitting on the shore of Seneca Lake at the base of Main Street. It was the largest employer in the area.

"Wait…isn't Rachel the one who lives on her boat? She's kind of a recluse, right?"

"That's her. Lives on her boat with three cats and five hundred books."

"And you know about her cats and books because…?"

He leveled a get-real look at Zoey before draining his whiskey.

"Because I'm a gentleman and I walked her to her boat after dinner at the marina restaurant. It's like she's a hoarder, but only of books. On a boat. I'm surprised the thing still floats." He shrugged. "I couldn't tell if she was painfully shy or just really private. I did all the talking at dinner. I don't know what the book club was thinking."

Zoey laughed. "What are those sweary old people *ever* thinking? Vickie insists they put a lot of effort into this matchmaking project of theirs, but honestly it feels like they just throw darts at a list of all the single names in town and pray for a match." She picked up the miniature vise grip she'd been using and bent over the small motor in front of her. "Last week they suggested I go out with Matt Black. He's twelve years *younger* than me and lives with his mom! It's a miracle they haven't set you and I up with each other yet."

There was the slightest beat of silence before she looked up and started laughing. He joined her, but his laughter wasn't quite as convincing. He couldn't screw their friendship up by chasing some *feelings*. No matter how tempted he was.

CHAPTER TWO

ZOEY WAS HUNCHED over her coffee when Hazel came down for breakfast the next morning. Her daughter stopped in the doorway.

"Do you want me to get you a straw for that caffeine juice? Or maybe an IV?"

"Ha ha." Zoey straightened in her chair. Mornings were *not* her happy time. "I'm just trying to appreciate the complete magic bean experience—the way it swirls in my mug. The amazing aroma. The jolt when it hits my bloodstream. And before you ask, yes, it's organic fair-trade coffee. I won't let my caffeine addiction harm the planet."

"Good job, Mom." Zoey pulled a box of all-natural granola from the cupboard. Between saving the planet and eating organic foods, their grocery bill was probably double what it would be if Hazel wasn't such a passionate little activist. It was okay, though. Zoey was proud that her daughter cared enough to take a stand on global issues at such a young age. And Zoey kept a hidden stash of junk food out in the workshop for herself.

Hazel settled at the table with her cereal and a glass of juice and began her ritual of scrolling through her phone. Today's fashion was a colorful tie-dye T-shirt with a smiley face on it—apparently those were making a comeback—with baggy white capris and Roman-style sandals.

In both grade school and high school, Zoey had taken a

fair amount of grief from classmates about her denim and flannel wardrobe and her father's home with his so-called sculptures in the yard. Kids could be jerks, but the Mc-Kinnon twins always had her back. Mike and Mary were part of a well-known local family, with lots of cousins who also welcomed Zoey into their circle. Their grandmother, Maura McKinnon, would often have the family and all their stray friends come to her home on Sundays for a big meal after church.

Those noisy gatherings had been a revelation to Zoey, who was used to having a quiet meal with her dad at the little kitchen table, or more often, in front of the television, eating from TV tables. Her dad was a loving man, but in a quiet way. She knew he'd never intended to be raising a little girl on his own, but he'd done the best he could after her mom died so suddenly. She'd grown up following him around the shop and riding along on house calls, so it wasn't surprising that she'd developed the same interest in tinkering that he had.

Dad hadn't been much of a conversationalist but spending time with the McKinnons had given her all the conversation—and hugs and I-love-yous—that she'd needed.

"Earth to Mom?"

Zoey flinched. "What?"

"I've been talking, but you're in a fog. The magic beans aren't doing their thing yet, huh?"

"Sorry. I guess I am a bit hazy this morning." That extra glass of whiskey may not have been such a great idea last night. "What were you saying?"

"I was saying I need to be in the detention room by eight o'clock. I can't be late."

Zoey glanced at her watch and swore. "Okay, we're outta

here in five minutes." She drained her coffee and stood. "What are you going to do all day?"

"We have to do school-related stuff, so I'm going to catch up on homework, read a few chapters in my history textbook and work on my term paper for English."

Zoey nodded and turned away, heading to her bedroom to do something with her hair. But she stopped in the doorway, turning slowly.

"What do you mean by 'catch up on homework'? Are you *behind* on homework?"

"Out of my whole list, *those* words are the only ones you heard, huh?"

"That is not an answer."

Hazel's eyes rolled skyward. "I didn't do last night's homework because I knew I'd be able to do it today. *That's* what I meant. Okay, Momster?" Not Zoey's favorite nickname, but she was learning to choose her battles. Hazel stood. "If I'm late, they'll give me another day of suspension."

Zoey hurried up to her bedroom to grab a sweatshirt from the stack on her dresser. She checked to make sure it didn't say anything inappropriate, in case Principal Sheffield wanted to talk to her. She was safe—it was from The Spot Diner in town. It was a gift from her friend Evie, who had given it to her after Zoey and Chris split up. Evie had jokingly referred to it as a prize for the most tears shed into coffee cups that month.

Chris hadn't been happy when Zoey called him last night about Hazel's suspension. He was worried Hazel was getting too sassy for her own good, but Zoey reminded him that the school counselor had warned them that it was natural for children her age to "act out" a bit after a divorce. Hazel had to figure out her place in the new dynamic. Hav-

ing the divorce happen just as Hazel entered puberty made
it feel as though her daughter had gone from Barbie dolls
to bras overnight.

She was pretty sure Chris's new opinions on parenting were thanks to Genna-with-a-*G*, who had opinions on
lots of things. She didn't seem to be a bad person as far as
Zoey could tell. Just…opinionated. And Chris was still in
the glow of new love—Zoey tugged on her overalls—so
he was hanging on his new fiancée's every word.

"I'm in the truck, Momster!"

Zoey ground her teeth together, biting back her annoyance. Hazel was trying to get a reaction, and she wasn't
going to give it. She headed to the door, turning off all the
lights her daughter had ignored on her way out. Sure, Hazel
claimed to love the planet, but she was a teenager and there-
fore allergic to turning off light switches.

"*Mom!* Let's *go*!" Hazel had opened her window to call
out.

"Yeah, yeah, yeah." Zoey slid into the truck. She knew
Hazel preferred being seen in their red compact car, but
she had a house call today and needed the work vehicle.
"We're going."

She'd barely started to turn the truck around when Hazel
stopped her. "Do you have your work schedule with you?
All the parts you need? Did you pack your lunch?"

This kid was a better business manager than Zoey was.

"Parts are in the back. My schedule's in my tote bag,
along with my lunch."

"You know," Hazel said in a singsong voice, "I'm not
always going to be here to take care of you."

"What does *that* mean?" Chris and Genna-with-a-*G* had
made it clear Hazel was welcome to spend more time with
them in their shiny new house.

Hazel's eyebrows gathered together. "Um…it means I'll graduate high school eventually? Unless you're planning on locking me in my room, I'll be off to college somewhere and…you know…living my life. And you'll be here, conducting fashion crimes all on your own."

Zoey chuckled at Hazel's repetition of the threat *she'd* made to Mike the day before. "I've been advised that locking you up is against the law, so I guess I'll have to learn to live without you managing my every moment, or my wardrobe." A surprising pinch of emotion made her blink. "But let's not rush the clock, kid." Zoey pulled up in front of the school and tugged Hazel's ponytail before she hopped out. "Try to stay out of trouble today, okay?"

Hazel shrugged as she stood. "I don't start it, but I'll finish it if anyone…"

Zoey held up her hand. "Take the high road, Hazel. I can't get called off a job again, and you need to be in class." She pointed at her daughter. "I mean it. No more punching people."

"As a wise woman once said…" Hazel wagged her eyebrows playfully. "Yeah, yeah, yeah." She turned to jog into the school.

"Lord, give me strength," Zoey muttered as she pulled away from the curb. There were times when she wasn't sure if she should laugh or ground the kid.

Her first service call was at a waterfront property past Brady College. It was a new client for Hartford Fix-It, but it sounded like an easy enough job—a sink disposal wasn't working. Probably a clog—her guess was potato skins, but sometimes shrimp shells could cause the same problem. Both tended to congeal and get hung up in the trap below the disposal if it wasn't flushed out with enough water.

She was a little surprised they hadn't called a plumber,

until she noted the address—next door to her godmother Vickie Pendergast's home. Odds were Vickie had strong-armed her neighbor into using Hartford's Fix-It. Vickie was a force of nature, and one of Zoey's most ardent word-of-mouth advertisers in Rendezvous Falls.

She turned onto Main Street, noting the summer flower baskets had been hung on the old-fashioned lampposts. The downtown committee had clearly been busy getting the town ready for tourist season. It seemed a little early for the petunias and geraniums to appear. May was the start of the greening and blooming season, but snow—or at least frost—was still a real possibility. Upstate New York weather wasn't for the faint of heart.

Evie Hudson was sweeping the sidewalk in front of her family's diner, The Spot. Her newborn daughter, Evelyn, was strapped to her chest in a canvas carrier. Zoey tapped her horn and waved. Maybe she'd have time for a quick lunch later. Evie and her mom always had the best gossip.

A few minutes later, she parked the truck in front of a large, modern waterfront home. She grimaced at all the glass and stark edges. This stretch of Lake Road was more upscale than most neighborhoods in Rendezvous Falls, and the Victorian homes were closer to being actual mansions than the houses in town. But sometimes people bought them just for the waterfront property, and if they weren't from Rendezvous Falls—or had no appreciation for the style that made the town famous—they tore down the grand old home that stood there originally and built new. In this case, they'd built *new*-new. Modern new. No character new. Ugly new.

The stocky, bald man who answered the door seemed surprised. She'd been doing this long enough to recognize the look. Someone clearly wasn't expecting a woman re-pairperson. She plastered on her brightest smile.

"Hi! I'm Zoey Hartford. I'm here to look at a disposal?"

The man's mouth opened, then snapped shut before he finally spoke. "I'm Jack Nelson. You're the repairman?"

No, I'm his secretary...

She pointed to the patch on the cap she'd tucked her hair under. "I prefer repair*person*, but whatever works." She moved forward and he stepped aside to let her in. "Point me to your kitchen."

One lesson she'd learned was that it was better to get inside and get busy, rather than stand at the door defending herself. She followed Nelson to the kitchen. He was going to be a hoverer. And probably an armchair expert, too. It was tough for some men to admit to a woman that there was a "manly" household task they couldn't do. Like unclogging a disposal.

"It's not clogged," he assured her. "But the thing won't drain. It eventually empties, but it takes a long time."

It's definitely clogged.

She'd also learned not to argue before starting the job. It was a waste of time, especially with *manly men*. Instead, she took a quick peek inside the disposal with her penlight, then turned on the water and waited until it reached the top of the disposal. She hit the switch. The machine sounded fine, but the water wasn't going anywhere, that was for sure. The problem was in the trap beneath it. An awkward job to get to, but not complicated.

Jack cleared his throat. "Vickie Pendergast insisted your company could fix this, but if you can't, I understand..."

She ignored the not-so-subtle hint that she should give up and leave. Instead, she opened the lower cupboard and sat on the floor, her toolbox within reach.

"No worries, Mr. Nelson. I'll have this cleared in a jiffy."

She'd brought in a small black pail to catch the water, and slid it under the curved drainpipe.

"Call me Jack. You won't need a bucket," Jack said with a great deal of confidence. "It's not clogged."

"Well, I like to rule out the easy fixes first. The disposal itself looks and sounds fine, so let's take a quick look at the trap."

Which I know is clogged.

A few minutes later, Zoey's nose wrinkled as she pulled a gluey glob of potato skins—*nailed it!*—from the pipe directly under the disposal. She ran her rubber-gloved fingers around the inside of the PVC pipe to make sure she'd gotten it all, then reassembled everything. Before saying a word to Jack, she turned on the faucet. Water flowed freely before, during and *after* running the disposal.

He had a shocked smile on his face. "Well, I'll be damned. What was it?"

Zoey reached under the sink for the small pail, setting it on the counter. "Potato skins." Jack's cheeks flushed. She didn't want him to think it was some kind of *gotcha* moment, regardless of the slight pleasure she felt from being right. "It's a very common culprit. They're thin and small, but in any kind of quantity and without enough water pressure, they can create a ball big enough to clog a pipe." She smiled. "Let me guess… Mother's Day?"

His eyes went wide, as if she'd just pulled a rabbit out of her hat, then he nodded with a chagrined smile. "We had fifteen people here for leg of lamb and roast potatoes. I figured the disposal could handle the peels, though."

"It probably could, as long as you don't stuff them all in at once and you keep that water flowing for a minute or two *after* you turn the disposal off. Grinding it up isn't enough—you gotta wash the debris down the pipes." Zoey turned the disposal and faucet on and off a few times, then checked underneath to make sure everything was connected tightly with no leaks. She grabbed her invoice pad and handed a slip to Jack.

"That's it?"

She shrugged. "It's my minimum house call fee. I didn't really repair anything…just cleaned the pipe and put it back together."

He gave her a shrewd look before pulling out his checkbook. "You knew what was wrong from the minute you stepped in the kitchen, didn't you? How long have you been doing appliance repair?"

"Since I was five." She winked when he stopped writing and looked up. "I developed my fix-it gene early. I used to ride around with my dad all the time."

"Well, your number is the first one I'll call for appliance repairs, for sure."

Another man won over. And easier than some. The fact that she was careful not to rub his nose in it probably helped. She thanked him and headed out to the truck. Mike had helped her figure out how to navigate male customers without pissing them off, from mild skeptics like Jack Nelson to flat-out misogynists like that jerkwad Hal Comstock down near Watkins Glen.

When he was alive, Dad would have just hauled off and punched anyone he thought was hassling his daughter. That wouldn't be very good for business, so she couldn't go to him. But Mike, as angry as he'd get on her behalf for any grief she got, kept his cool and helped her be more proactive.

Hal Comstock had been rip-roaring drunk last year when she arrived at his home, and things had gone downhill from there. His wife tried to run interference while Zoey looked at their washing machine, but Hal's comments got more inappropriate by the minute. When Zoey went out to get a part from the truck, he'd followed her and suggested she was "stealing" a job from a man, called her a few names, then tried to intimidate her by standing so close she ended up with her back pressed to the side of the truck. At which point she'd kneed him hard in the balls and got out of there as fast as she could.

Shaken, she'd pulled over at a gas station and called Mike in tears of fury. He told her to stay put, and he was there in minutes. He listened to her story, made sure she was okay, then made a quick trip to the Comstock home. When he returned, he'd told Zoey not to worry about anything, then took her out for milkshakes and burgers the size of their heads. They'd ended up laughing over the disastrous day.

A few months passed before Mike admitted he'd barely avoided punching the guy. Instead, he'd told Comstock to never call Hartford Fix-It again, and to never utter a word about Zoey, good or bad. If Mike heard otherwise, he'd be back and make sure Hal regretted it.

It was clients like Comstock who were pushing Zoey toward jobs that allowed her to avoid going into strangers' homes. She was trying to pick up more commercial business, and she'd been doing more jobs for antiques dealers and collectors in the area. She was building a strong reputation for being able to rebuild small mechanicals like music boxes and clocks, and even a few larger items like vintage vending machines.

There was good money in it—more than there was in home appliances in this age of disposable electronics. Why repair something when you can get a new one at the nearest big-box store?

Zoey pulled her truck into the long driveway leading to a sprawling Victorian mansion on a waterfront lot. The home wasn't quite as brightly colored as some of the homes in town, but the closer Zoey got, the more colors and detailed paint schemes she could see. The house itself was a soft butter yellow. The spindles on the porch railings were grayish blue, but the top rails were a muted reddish-brown. The lacy gingerbread trim was a combination of pastels that must have taken the painters days to figure out. The overall effect, much like her godmother, Vickie, was unique and elegant.

The change in her business focus had been Mike's idea. He'd floated it after the Comstock incident, but became more insistent after her father died. He was worried about her. Or maybe he just didn't want to come running to her rescue all the time. No, she knew how much Mike cared. He'd do the same for Mary. Zoey was his extra sister—a twin and a spare, as his father liked to say. She was more family than friend. It was good to know Mike had her back.

She headed toward the pastel house, knowing she'd be facing an inquisition from Vickie. And probably news of some blind date the book club wanted to set up for her. She shook her head. She might need Mike to come to her rescue again.

CHAPTER THREE

VICKIE KNEW ZOEY might stop by after going to Jack Nelson's place, and she opened the front door before her goddaughter had even reached the top of the porch steps. She was curious to hear how the call went. Jack could be blunt at times, but he and his wife were good neighbors. The kind of neighbors who stopped by to bring Vickie's dock in from the water every fall and helped put it back every May. They'd been doing that for years, in exchange for nothing more than a couple cold beers and snacks on the back deck.

Zoey gave Vickie a smile—a good sign. Vickie stepped aside, swinging the door wide.

"I thought I might see you today. Coffee's on, and there's a bagel on the kitchen island."

"No tea and crumpets? I'm disappointed." Zoey patted Vickie's shoulder affectionately as she passed.

"The last time I tried tea and crumpets with you, you told me you'd rather have beer and pretzels." Vickie closed the door and followed Zoey to the sunlit kitchen. "You were twelve. And I had guests."

Zoey grabbed a mug of coffee from the marble-topped island and turned to face Vickie, one eyebrow arched high.

"Think about what you just said, Vicks." Vicky did her best not to grimace, knowing Zoey was just trying to get a rise out of her by using a nickname Vicky hated. "You invited a *twelve-year-old* to an adult ladies' luncheon where *actual* crumpets were being served." Zoey chuckled. "I still remember the looks on their faces when I came clumping in wearing my Doc Martens. I thought Marjorie Adams was going to pass out."

Vickie took a sip of her coffee. "Marjorie always had a big stick up her ass, God rest her soul."

"She never understood your efforts to make me into a…" Zoey stuck her nose in the air and her pinkie finger out dramatically as she held her cup high. Her voice slid into a prissy half-British accent. "…proper young lady of Rendezvous Falls."

Vickie took half a bagel and spread some strawberry-flavored cream cheese on it. Zoe did the same, but she used the "Everything" cream cheese—onion, garlic, pepper, basil and whatever else the manufacturer could find to toss in. Vickie was tempted to point out Zoey might render a client senseless with her breath later, but mentioning it would only encourage her stubborn goddaughter to eat more of the stuff. She shook her head as a swell of affection rose inside her. Zoey was the closest thing to a daughter she'd ever had.

"You are every bit a proper lady, my dear…whatever that means these days. Marjorie was hopelessly stuck in the age of those old black-and-white Hollywood movies where so-called *ladies* wore big hats and white gloves while they stabbed you in the back. I prefer my lady friends looking me right in the eye when they're trying to bury me."

"I'm not trying to bury you, Vickie, but I get what you're saying." Zoey's nose wrinkled as she set the bagel down after one small bite. "If I eat the rest of this, I'll be losing clients from here to Watkins Glen. Sorry for wasting it— the cream cheese smells so good, but it's a bad idea."

Vickie chuckled. "I'll eat it later, I'm sure. God, your

mom loved a fully loaded breakfast. Western omelets, everything bagels, onions galore in her scrambled eggs. I told her she was living dangerously, but she always said—" The memory caught up with her suddenly, making her melancholy decades later. She swallowed hard. "She said if one was going to be living, they may as well do it as dangerously as possible as long as they could."

"So bizarre how you two ever became friends. She was such a bohemian live wire and…" Zoey's cheeks flushed.

"And I'm such an uptight snob?" She knew it was how many people thought of her.

"That is *not* what I'm saying, and you know it. You're not a snob, but you…um…care about appearances more than some people do. People like my mom, from what I've heard."

"Oh, your mom *never* gave a damn what anyone thought about her." Zoey looked so much like her mother—tall and slender, with the same long dark hair and brown eyes. The heavy brows and long eyelashes. The boldness of her walk. But Zoey's air of confidence wasn't quite as authentic as Gloria's had been. She was smart and independent, running her own business and learning how to be a single mom, but there was an air of fragility to Zoey that Gloria never had. Probably because Zoey had lost her mother when she was only four years old.

An aneurism felled Gloria one morning as she cleaned up after breakfast. One minute she was talking to Rob about where they should go to dinner that weekend to celebrate their anniversary, and the next she was on the floor. Gone without warning at thirty-four. And just like that, the honorary title Vickie had accepted at Zoey's christening became a solemn responsibility—godmother.

"I know you met at the Rendezvous Falls Festival Committee, but how…"

"I've told you the story a hundred times," Vickie said. "I was married to Stanley Noor at the time." Stan was her first husband *and* first divorce. She didn't care that he was bisexual, but she *did* care that he was unfaithful on a regular basis with any man or woman who gave him the opportunity. "Gloria wanted to change the Halloween festival to a Ghostwalk event, and I thought that was ridiculous. Letting people wander all over town and telling them nonsensical legends… I thought the town would be a laughingstock. And I said that in the meeting." She could still recall that meeting, more than thirty years ago, and the ever so slight, but determined, narrowing of Gloria's eyes.

Gloria was new to Rendezvous Falls back then. She'd followed Rob there after they married. She didn't know anyone in town, but that didn't stop her from volunteering for the prestigious festival committee which oversaw the near-monthly festivals that brought tourist revenue to town.

"Yes, I know," Zoey said, munching on the plain bagel she'd spread just a bit of butter on. "You and Mom got into a shouting match in a meeting, and like some lovers' meet-cute in a movie, you became fast friends afterward."

"It wasn't a shouting match." Vickie sniffed. "I don't do public shouting matches. But your mom wouldn't back down an inch." She circled her hand in front of her stomach. "And she was out to here, pregnant with you."

Zoey gave her a wink. "Well, she got her way. *And* she was right. The Ghostwalk is still one of the biggest festivals every year."

"Yes it is." Vickie finished her bagel. "It's a perfect event for a town full of old houses. The stories were already there—we just had to collect them."

Zoey was looking out the French doors facing the water from the kitchen. "Oh, no—what happened out there?" She was pointing at the broken section of railing and a crushed corner on the deck.

"Ugh," Vickie answered, making a face. She hated messes and her back deck was nothing *but* a mess right now. "That storm we had last month brought down a huge limb from that maple tree. Luckily it missed the house, but it took out the whole corner of the deck. The tree guys finished cleaning up the debris last week." She joined Zoey at the door. "Gordon Lexiter is going to do the deck work… hopefully sooner rather than later. He was supposed to start this week, but as you can see, there's no sign of him yet."

She knew people thought she was too demanding, but how hard was it to be punctual?

"Gordy's a good guy," Zoey said. "You two went to school together, right?"

"He was a year behind me, but yes. It's not like we hung out in the same circles." Not that anyone knew of, at least. But there was that one night…

Zoey laughed. "I wasn't suggesting you were sweethearts or anything. Just that you're both locals, like me." Her phone let out a ping, and she pulled it out to check, then started laughing. "Mike and his stupid riddles." She responded, then groaned, turning the phone so Vickie could read the texts.

M: What's the opposite of a croissant?

Z: No clue

M: A happy uncle!

"You two have been trading jokes since you were kids." Vickie rolled her eyes. "After all these years, the jokes aren't getting any better."

"I can't argue that," Zoey answered. "And speaking of Mike…did you and your pals really set him up with Rachel the librarian? She lives on a boat that's lucky to be floating for all the books inside. What on earth made you think that was a good idea?"

Vickie let out a long sigh. That hadn't been the book club's greatest match. "We're running out of options for the man. Cecile said Rachel was a nice, quiet woman who was a little shy. Mike's a nice, quiet guy who never goes anywhere, so we thought maybe they could be a nice quiet couple *together*."

"I think your little gang of matchmakers should take a break where Mike is concerned. I know it's been three years since Becca died, but neither Mary nor I get the sense that he has any real interest in dating yet."

Vickie sighed again. "Well, you two would know. She's his twin and you may as well be. We just hate to see such a pleasant, handsome, successful man with no one by his side." She tipped her head and stared at Zoey. "You aren't interested…?"

"Oh, *hell*, no!" Zoey's face scrunched up. "We've known each other since third grade, and there's never been a hint of attraction between us." She leveled a look at Vickie. "Don't even think about it."

Vickie was facing the window, but she watched Zoey out of the corner of her eye, looking for any hidden spark of chemistry at the mention of dating Mike. But there was nothing. Too bad. She would have liked to see two of her favorite people together, but you couldn't force chemistry.

"And what about you? Are you ready for another match? Rick said there's a very nice associate professor at the college this semester. I hear he's a looker."

"And Rick couldn't get a date with him himself?"

"Apparently not." Vickie chuckled. "But he thinks the man might be open to female companionship."

Zoey hesitated. "I don't think so. Not yet, anyway. I made a vow to Hazel that this year would be about *her* needs. And…lay off Mike for a while, okay?"

Vickie held up her hands in surrender. She couldn't help wondering why *Zoey* was saying this instead of Mike, but maybe he'd asked her to.

"I'll tell the book club when we meet. If he's not ready, he's not ready."

Zoey looked at her phone and turned. "I gotta run. There's a washing machine in Penn Yan that needs my healing hands, and I have two vacuum cleaners at the shop to repair this afternoon. Thanks for recommending me to Jack Nelson, by the way. He was skeptical at first, but I think I won him over."

"I'm glad. Jack's a little crusty, but he's a good guy. He and his wife help me out once in a while."

"Help you with what? You know you can always call me if you need help."

"The Nelsons have been helping me for years, honey. If they can't help, I hire someone." She looked out at the crushed corner of the deck. She needed to call Gordon and put a fire under his ass. Again. "Although some hires are more reliable than others."

MIKE STARED ACROSS his desk at his two o'clock appointment. Who was also his grandmother. God save him from all the meddling old ladies in his life.

"Nana, why are you *really* here? We just redid your will last summer, and nothing has changed that I'm aware of."

Maura McKinnon's eyes narrowed on him. "What's changed, Michael, is that I apparently need to make an appointment if I want to see my grandson these days. How are you?"

He sat back in his chair. "I work at the pub every Friday night, Nana."

The Purple Shamrock was originally owned by Mike's great-grandfather, then Nana's husband took it on, and then her son, Patrick. And now Patrick's daughter, Bridget, and her husband Finn were running the place.

"And is your poor old grandmother supposed to go to the *pub* to see her grandson?"

Maura McKinnon had won a scary battle with breast cancer and was now looking more fit than ever. She wasn't anyone's poor anything.

"Knock off the Irish-Catholic guilt trip. What's really going on?"

"That's why you're such a good lawyer, Michael. You can read BS from a mile away. But you *have* been hard to pin down lately. You've missed two family dinners this month, and you weren't at the last business breakfast for the pub. Your cousins and I are worried about you."

He tapped his pen restlessly on the manila folder in front of him. She wasn't wrong. He loved his big Irish family, but lately he'd felt suffocated by all the noise and chaos and questions. So many questions.

How are you, Mike?

Met anyone lately, Mike?

Isn't that house getting lonely, Mike?

You know there's more to life than just business, right, Mike?

They meant well. They loved him and wanted him to be happy. But they seemed to have decided as a group that it was time for him to "move on." That after three years, he should be over losing his wife. That he couldn't possibly be happy alone.

Except…he *was* happy. Or at least *content*. And that was enough right now. His law office might not be the thrill-a-minute drama of some fictional TV lawyer defending people in criminal court. But he was proud of the work his little one-man office did. Mom and Dad still hadn't given up on convincing him to follow them to Albany, where Dad was raking in the big bucks as a lobbyist in the state capital. It seemed no one in his life wanted to accept that he was doing just fine.

"I don't know what people want from me, Nana." Mike raked his fingers through his hair, absently thinking to himself that he needed a haircut. "I'm tired of being everyone's *project*. Find Mike a date. Find Mike a fancier job. Find Mike a way to be—" he raised his fingers to make air quotes "—*old Mike* again."

His grandmother was quiet for a moment, her eyebrows gathering together.

"It's been—"

He held his hand up. "Do *not* tell me how long it's been since Becca was killed. I wake up every morning knowing *exactly* how long it's been." Thirty-five months and five days since the police came to his office with the news that left a gaping hole in his life—in his heart—that had never fully healed.

"I was trying to say it's been hard for me to see you withdrawing from the family." Nana's eyes softened. "I understand what you're saying about being a project, but it's only because—"

He cut her off again. "Because they love me. I know—" Nana sat up abruptly, shaking her finger in his direction. Even with his desk between them, he leaned back.

"Look," she started, her eyes narrowing. "You wanted me to lay off the guilt trip and tell you why I'm here, so... fine. Let me finish a flippin' sentence once in a while, and you might learn something." Her voice sharpened to the tone she used to use when he and Mary were children— usually right before she threatened them with a wooden spoon. "Yes, your sister and cousins love you. How awful for you, you poor thing. Over the past few months, you've gotten awfully prickly, you know. I don't need you to be your *old* self, but you being a jerk isn't going to work for anybody."

Mike's mouth fell open. "You think I've been a jerk?"

Her expression softened. "Let's call it borderline jerk for now." One corner of her mouth quirked up into a slanted, affectionate grin. "This all started after Bridget and Finn got married last fall. I know a wedding may have brought back some tough emotions for you—it's the first family wedding since Becca passed. But it seems to me that you're more...*restless*...than grieving."

His cousin, Bridget, once told him she was convinced their grandmother had second sight—the ability to read minds or foresee the future. He'd scoffed at her at the time, but right this moment? The hair on the back of his neck was on end. Nana had just nailed it. He *was* restless.

He didn't know why, or for what, but he'd been more on edge the past few months. Less willing to sit in an empty house. Less willing to be the subject of people's pitying eyes. But also less willing to be sent out on dates with women he had no interest in. Ready to move on, but having no idea how to do that, or who he was supposed to do it with.

"Nana, you're not wrong, but I don't know how to describe what I'm feeling. I mean... I *am* happy. Or at least..."

He acknowledged her skeptical look. "At least *satisfied*. I'm not *un*happy, you know? I like my job. I have a nice little house that's paid for and a fun little hot rod to drive. I have good friends, like Mark Hudson and Finn and Zoey." He straightened the papers on his desk and dropped his pen in the red Buffalo football mug he used as a penholder. "I'll never be *over* losing Becca, and I don't think I should be." He'd loved his wife, and expected to grow old with sweet, beautiful Becca at his side. "But I don't want to be alone forever, either. I just… I feel like I'm stuck. Like I'm waiting for something, but I have no idea what."

His grandmother watched him in silence. Her lips were pinched together, but more in deep thought than anger. "You're clearly at a crossroads. A threshold of some sort. I wish I had a better answer for you, Michael, but the solution won't be found in avoiding your family. Or snarling at them. If you don't like our questions, you can easily tell us to stop asking. No reason to beat around the bush in the McKinnon clan. You know that."

Oh, yes—he knew. His family didn't pull any punches.

Mike nodded. "And if I don't show up, can I expect more family members to be making appointments at my office in the future?"

Nana chuckled as she stood, and Mike scrambled to his feet. She gave him a wink as she turned to go. "This visit was your cousin Kelly's idea, and was approved by vote at the last pub-business breakfast meeting. So it's a safe bet there will be more appointments made if needed." She paused at the door. "Dinner is at three this Sunday."

"I'll be there, Nana."

She hadn't been gone twenty minutes when his sister, Mary, texted him.

MT: Nana says you folded like a house of cards.

He frowned.

MM: What else did she tell you?

He watched the floating bubbles, sure Nana wouldn't have shared their personal conversation.

MT: I was kidding! She just said you were coming this Sunday. But now I'm curious about what ELSE you said?

Mike should have known his twin was just poking at him. And he'd fallen for the trap. His phone pinged again.

MT: Mike? Should I be worried?

Uh-oh. He'd fired up Mary's twin sense.

MM: Everything's fine. I'm just busy. And tired. C U Sunday.

MT: You work too hard. You need a paralegal or something.

He repeated that he was fine and she replied with a rolled-eyes emoji. She might be right about the paralegal. He'd been thinking of hiring someone. The recent real estate boom had increased his workload substantially. Mary was right about the sleep, too. But that would have to wait. He'd already told Zoey he had a nice bottle of wine from his friend's winery.

Luke and Whitney Rutledge ran Falls Legend Winery on the hills above Rendezvous Falls. Falls Legend had become one of the premier small wineries in the area in recent years, once Luke and Whitney married and took over operations from her aunt Helen. Luke had stopped by the office that morning to discuss a potential lease contract for an adjoining vineyard and left a bottle of three-year-old pinot noir. There was no one Mike would rather share it with than Zoey.

The year after Becca died, Zoey had kept him going, and he'd tried to do the same for her after Chris left her last year. But now their friendship was…morphing. When they got together at the repair shop, it wasn't as much for support or relief as it was about just friendship. He didn't need to lean on Zoey—he simply enjoyed being with her. He looked forward to their time together.

He pulled his phone out of his pocket as he left the office at the end of the day and started typing.

M: What will a grape say if you step on it?

Within seconds, Zoey replied.

Z: Ouch?

M: It won't say anything…just let out a little wine.

Z: Hardy har har. Bring more than a little wine tonight, okay?

He frowned.

M: Bad day?

Z: Nothing specific. Hazel and I snarled at each other. Be warned…this house is a hormone hell today.

M: I'm trying to come up with a funny reply, but I have a feeling it could be dangerous.

Z: Very. Just bring the damn wine.

Mike grinned as he walked into his house. Zoey, Mary and he had grown up together, so Mike knew pretty much *everything* about Zoey, including how she was at that time of month. She and Mary's schedules had "synced" when they were inseparable teens, which had fascinated Mike at the time. It still did, to be honest. Mary and Zoey never shied away from talking girl stuff around him, and he'd never asked them to. Maybe because of the twin connection—it was natural for him to just know…everything. And frankly, knowing when the hormones were going to be raging ahead of time saved him a lot of grief through the years.

No, there weren't any secrets between him and Zoey. The two of them liked to brag that they were living proof that men and women really could be *just friends.* But he kept having those sneaking thoughts lately of wanting more.

Which meant he *was* keeping a secret—he couldn't tell her how he felt until he'd figured it out for himself. Telling her was bound to make things weird between them, and he didn't want that. He wasn't sure if his feelings were just because they were together so often and he was lonely, or if this was something more serious. Was Zoey simply a safe choice because he literally knew *everything* about her?

Or was she the most dangerous choice of all?

CHAPTER FOUR

"This is your weekend with your dad, Hazel. He's expecting you."

Zoey chewed the inside of her cheek. She sympathized with Hazel, but she had to do the right thing here. Just as soon as she figured out what that was. Hazel was supposed to be with Chris and Genna-with-a-*G* two weekends a month. Hazel had always been Daddy's Little Girl, but since the divorce, her role in her father's new life was uncertain. She didn't like going to the new house his girlfriend had insisted on, tearing Hazel away from the home she'd grown up in.

"Why should I have to abide by some contract the two of you came up with without my input? It's all so…mercenary." Hazel's eyes shimmered with tears. A lot of this was hormones. Zoey's hormones had her on edge, too. But she couldn't just dismiss her daughter's concerns.

"It's not *mercenary*. There's no monetary advantage for anyone whether you're at Dad's place or mine." Zoey looked around her daughter's bedroom. It was still a drab olive green—the same color her father had painted it twenty-some years ago. She'd promised Hazel they'd paint it, but it kept getting pushed off for other projects. Right on the heels of her guilt came the burning of tears in her eyes. Oh, yeah. She was hormonal for sure.

"But why should I have to go if I don't want to?" Hazel

sat on the edge of the bed next to the small duffel bag sitting open. "It's like you two are telling me what I'm supposed to feel. This weekend, I'm supposed to like Dad. Then next weekend, I'll like *you*. It's stupid."

Zoey crouched down on one knee in front of Hazel. She rested one hand on Hazel's leg, waiting for her to make eye contact. "I want you to like *both* of us. All the time. This…" She nodded at the duffel. "This is just…logistics. We're talking about where you're going to lay your head at night, not how you're supposed to feel. It's not easy for us, either, but your dad and I are doing the best we can."

Hazel rolled her eyes dramatically. "Really? 'Cause I'm the one who's always packing."

"If you'd start leaving stuff *there*, like I keep suggesting, you wouldn't need to pack so much. Dad's new house is your home, too. You are the center of *both* of our worlds." She gave Hazel's leg a squeeze. "You're lucky to have two parents who want you to feel loved no matter whose house you're in. You could be like Kimmy Wilkes, and how awful would *that* be?"

Lonnie and Donna Wilkes had divorced in rather spectacular fashion last year, just before Chris and Zoey split. Lonnie owned a car dealership in Watkins Glen, and Donna reportedly caught him with one of his saleswomen. In the back of a minivan. Testing the seats. Naked. She'd kicked him out of the house and changed the locks, promising he'd never see his daughter again. He took her to court, and boy, they redefined the term *airing dirty laundry*. Turned out Donna had a boyfriend herself. And Lonnie had a secret bank account the IRS was interested in. And Donna's boobs were fake. And Lonnie had had a tummy tuck. Every week brought a new revelation, and neither of them did a thing to shelter their twelve-year-old daughter from the fallout.

The poor girl's grades plummeted when kids started teasing her over the gossip.

Lonnie's parents finally stepped in and took Kimmy to Rochester to live with them. Sadly, it seemed Lonnie and Donna barely noticed she was gone—they were still too busy trying to one-up each other.

Hazel's eyes shimmered with tears. "I'm sorry, Mom. It's just…no matter how nice you and Dad try to be, you're still divorced. I have to tiptoe now and not play favorites and…"

"Oh, sweetie." Zoey rose to sit next to Hazel and pulled her into a tight hug. She tried her best not to let her own emotions interfere with her daughter's relationship with Chris, but right now she was *furious* with him for blowing up their little family. "It is *not* your job to keep Dad or I happy. It's your job to be a teenager." She pinched Hazel's ribs playfully. "This week you're a teenager who's also a massive bundle of hormones, but that's okay. They'll settle in a day or two and you'll feel like yourself again."

Hazel returned the hug, talking against Zoey's shoulder. "Is this *really* going to last my whole life? Being a woman is awful."

Zoey laughed. "Not quite your whole life, but for the next forty years or so. Sorry. Being a woman is *not* awful. Our bodies are incredible. The mood swings are…challenging." She cupped her daughter's face in her hands. "But it won't always feel so out of control. You won't be in puberty forever. You'll learn to know why you're getting emotional, and you'll learn how to control it…to a point. It's a lot easier when you embrace it instead of fighting it."

Hazel looked skeptical, then she blinked a few times and pulled away. Heaven forbid her strong-willed daughter give in to uncertainty for more than a minute.

"So you're saying I need to pack some tampons this

weekend? I don't know if there are any at his place. What if Dad sees them?"

Zoey pinched her lips together to keep from laughing. Chris had always hated shopping for feminine products. Thinking of him squirming if Hazel asked him to stock tampons gave her a perverse spark of pleasure—no sense denying it. "Your father is very aware that you are female. And since you're his daughter, he clearly understands how the reproductive system works. Don't be afraid to discuss it with him." She stood, grabbing a nearby pair of jeans and rolling them up before packing them in the small bag. "Don't ever be ashamed of something so natural."

In the blink of an eye her little girl was going to be a woman. In five years she'd graduate. Then college. Then off to live her life.

A FEW HOURS LATER, Zoey was telling Mike all about it. "I can't wrap my head around the idea that I could be a grandmother someday. Do I look like a grandmother to you?"

Mike was leaning back in the wooden chair her dad used to use. His feet were propped on a big box of vacuum cleaner belts, his red plastic cup resting on his stomach. He lifted it to take another sip of wine, shaking his head emphatically.

"I learned a very long time ago to never respond to a woman asking my opinion on how she looks."

"You're supposed to be my friend. My friend would be honest with me."

He huffed out a laugh. "Your friend *is* being honest. That question is a trap and I'm *honestly* not going to answer it. But I'll say this much…you'll make a terrific grandmother someday. You've done a great job with Hazel. I assume she ended up going to Chris's after all that?"

Zoey nodded, not sure why his casual compliment made her skin heat up the way it did. "After her little meltdown, she realized she had no real reason why she didn't want to go. I think it was a control thing—she felt like she didn't have enough choice in the matter. Add in a flood of estrogen, and panic briefly took over." She reached for her own cup of wine. "PMS is the ultimate loss of control, especially at that age. You open your mouth and it feels like someone else is doing the talking. It's a little like being possessed."

He chuckled. "Becca used to say the same thing. She'd swear she didn't mean the words that came out."

Zoey stared at him in surprise. He looked up and frowned.

"What?"

She was on unfamiliar ground here.

"I… I don't know. You usually have this little…catch… thing in your voice when you mention Becca. But just now, you sounded…normal." She set her cup down and refilled it, then slid the wine bottle toward Mike so he could do the same. "Are those memories getting easier?"

His forehead furrowed. "I was going to say *no*. But Nana and I were talking about it earlier today—how time dulls the edges eventually. She thinks I'm on a threshold of some kind."

Zoey stared down into her wine. Mike had been stuck for so long in this limbo of being afraid to be happy again. Grief was different for everyone, but he'd been punishing himself ever since Becca's accident. He had nothing to do with what happened. The driver had been drinking and claimed they were blinded by the sun when they came around the curve. But the car never should have been that far on to the shoulder where Becca was jogging. They were also speeding. Becca never had a chance, dying instantly.

"What kind of threshold?"

"That's the kicker." Mike sat up, bringing the front legs of the chair back down to the floor with a thud. "She has no idea, and neither do I. Is this me *moving on*, whatever the hell that means? Or is it just a hiccup and there's some giant cliff ahead of me?"

He'd been a broken man after Becca died. He and Becca had one of those fairy-tale marriages—two beautiful, successful, kind people who truly loved each other. But their fairy tale didn't have a happy ending. She was glad to see her friend beginning to move away from his grief.

Zoey picked up the small screwdriver and attached the base back on the upright vacuum cleaner standing upside down against the workbench. It was one of those massive all-plastic things that was like a Jenga puzzle to take apart and reassemble, but she'd managed to find the child's sock that had clogged the intake.

"I told Vickie to have the book club lay off sending you on dates. But maybe you *are* ready to meet someone?" For some reason, that idea weighed on her.

Mike frowned. "You told the book club biddies to stop setting me up? Why?"

"Did I overstep?" She'd thought she was doing him a favor, but maybe not.

"As if you ever could. It just surprised me. I thought you liked hearing about all the disaster dates."

She tightened the last screw and flipped the vacuum cleaner upright.

"I do."

As long as they're disasters. She froze. What a weird thing to think.

"And what about you?" he asked. "Any disaster dates coming up for you? Another go-round with Nate Benson?"

"Do you really want to taunt your hormonal friend with the memory of that handsy asshole?" She started to laugh. "And he was so *bad* at it that I almost felt sorry for the guy. I mean, groping is one thing, but he didn't even know *where* to grope. I know my boobs are small, but they're right there. They're not invisible!"

"Definitely not invisible." Mike's gaze stayed on her chest a fraction longer than absolutely necessary.

Huh. That's weird.

"How much wine have we had tonight?" She held up the bottle with an awkward laugh.

Mike ran his fingers through his hair in that way he did when he was agitated. "I didn't think any topic was off the table for us, but your boobs seem to be…" He closed his eyes, his cheeks going ruddy.

"Off the table? Yes, they are. Literally and figuratively."

It was a joke, but it fell flat. She kept trying to lighten the moment, but she was making it worse instead. She had no idea how to salvage it.

After a long silence, Mike finally gave a harsh laugh. "Jesus, Zoey. I don't know what happened just now, but…"

"I do. I'm supposed to be your pal. One of the boys. But I'm guessing you don't sit around and talk to the guys about periods or the size of your…" She was not making this any better. "…of your…um…parts."

Mike grew suddenly serious, walking around the workbench to where she stood. His eyes were dark and surprisingly solemn.

"You're *not* one of the boys. And you're far more than a pal, Zoey. I don't talk to the guys about *most* of the things you and I talk about—the silly stuff or the serious stuff. I never want that to change."

Why did he think he had to say that? Zoey didn't want

anything to change between her and Mike, either. She grinned and shoved his shoulder. It served two purposes—it broke the mood and got him a little farther away. She didn't mind having a serious conversation with Mike, but this felt different. His closeness was making her skin prickle with an unusual awareness of the man. As a man, not just a friend.

"Is there really any off-limit topic for us after all these years?" she asked, desperate to get things back to normal. "Good grief, we had chicken pox together. And we had that awful stomach bug together in middle school, remember? I was staying overnight with Mary, and the three of us spent the night fighting over the upstairs bathroom because your parents wouldn't let us use theirs!"

Mike laughed so hard it echoed in the small shop. "Oh, God, what a horrible night! I can't blame Mom and Dad for keeping us at a distance—we were *so* sick and it was *not* pretty."

Laughter made things feel right between them again. Mike patted her on the shoulder on their way out the door, and his hand lingered there.

"Never change, Zoey. I need you just like this. I need *us* just like this. It's important to me."

His words sounded oddly desperate. Why was he so concerned about their friendship tonight? What was he afraid of?

"I've had enough change to last me a lifetime." She smiled. "And you know I'll always be here for you."

His eyes deepened or softened or did…something. As if he was surprised. Or moved. Had she done something to make him doubt their friendship? Was it something his grandmother had said? They stood there for a beat before he nodded, stepping away.

"Good."

She turned out the shop lights and headed toward the house with a wave while he walked to his car. As always, he waited until she was inside and had flicked the outside light at him before he drove off.

It seemed important to prove nothing had changed, so she sent a text when she thought he'd be home.

Z: What do a push-up bra and a bag of chips have in common?

It was a few minutes before he responded.

M: I'm terrified to ask.

She giggled.

Z: When you open them, they're both half-empty.

M: Zoey

He followed it with a rolled eyes emoji.

Z: Come on, it's funny!

He didn't answer right away, so she followed up.

Z: Too soon?

She hoped he wasn't still embarrassed about the boob comment. She'd been serious about not wanting any subject to be off-limits…depending on the context. Her phone pinged.

M: What's a boob's favorite swimming style?

Ah, there he was. Her friend was back.

Z: I don't know.

M: The breaststroke <rim shot>

Z: Ugh. Mine was better!

M: As usual. Get some sleep.

Z: I'm glad you stopped by tonight. It's going to be a busy weekend. Surprising Hazel by redecorating the living room.

M: Want any help?

Z: Mary, Piper and Tani are coming over tomorrow. We'll git 'er done!

M: Call if you need me.

Z: I will. G'night.

Call if you need me. It was a normal sentence. Something they'd probably said and texted a hundred times. But it hit her differently tonight.

She hadn't really thought about what would happen to their friendship as they rebuilt their lives after death and divorce. The truth was, those two things had *already* changed it. Redefined it. When they were married, they'd been casual friends who saw each other at picnics, parties or weddings. Their spouses had both been understanding of the bond Mike and Zoey shared. She changed into her pajamas and crawled into bed.

When the marriages were over, their friendship slid back into what it was in school, with all the clowning around and hanging out together. If Mike really *was* at a threshold— ready to find someone new—then no matter what they'd said tonight, their friendship was going to change once more. She lay awake, staring up at the ceiling in the dark. She'd miss what she and Mike had now.

More than she wanted to admit, even to herself.

CHAPTER FIVE

VICKIE GLARED INTO her bathroom mirror and heaved a long, loud sigh. Who *was* this old woman staring back at her? Where had those new lines come from? She'd had *some* last week, but not *this* many. And that vertical crease between her brows had definitely gotten deeper. She was getting older. She was going to have wrinkles. She got that. But new ones every *week*?

She brushed her teeth, then plucked the one black chin hair that kept growing back, no matter what she did. Her eyebrows were acceptable today—no rebellious strands sticking out half an inch like she'd found last week. Aging was so much weirder than she'd anticipated. She'd never expected to have hair *stop* growing in some places, only to grow at hypersonic speeds in *new* places. It hardly seemed fair.

She tugged her old chenille robe more snugly around her waist. She didn't have anything on her calendar until afternoon, when she was meeting Lena at the marina restaurant for a late lunch on the waterfront. She still had plenty of time to figure out what to wear. It was one of those weird May days that could go either way weather-wise. If the sun stayed out, it would warm up substantially from the current chilly temperatures. Maybe even enough to wear the short-sleeved linen shift she'd worn on Easter Sunday. If the clouds rolled in earlier than expected, it would be blazer and trousers weather.

But first…coffee. She slipped her feet into her comfy old fuzzy slippers—the ones she made sure no one ever caught her in—and padded down the staircase to the kitchen. A big, cold, empty house was the downside of being single. The upside was being able to wear whatever the hell she wanted before and after certain hours, when guests were unlikely to come calling.

Her coffee maker was a fancy machine that made espresso, cappuccino and who-knew-what-else-o. It even had its own programmable coffee grinder so she could use fresh beans. It had been ridiculously expensive, but Vickie wasn't one to worry about that once she saw something she wanted. And she'd never regretted splurging on a machine that made coffee good enough to be served at an Italian sidewalk café, right here in the comfort and privacy of her kitchen.

The built-in speakers had synced with her phone and were playing a jazzy Adele tune. Vickie swayed and shimmied to the music, belting out the words like it was karaoke night at the Shamrock. She pushed her hair behind her ears, idly thinking she needed to check when her next appointment was. She'd need highlights soon. Her hips were still swinging as she poured her coffee into her favorite bright blue mug.

It wasn't until she was putting the pot back in place that she heard a sound behind her. Coffee sloshed over the edge of her cup as she plunked it down and spun to face the doors to the lake.

Her contractor was on the deck, staring straight at her through the glass. He was on one knee, with a toolbox at his side and a hammer in his hand. He wore a faded thermal Henley and paint-splattered jeans. And on his face, he wore a wide, amused smile. He pushed up the brim of his ball cap, revealing equally amused gray-blue eyes framed with lines from years in the sun.

In the midst of her rising rage was a quiet *hubba hubba*, but she dismissed it immediately.

"Gordon Lexiter!" She threw open the French doors, channeling a few of the characters she'd played in community theater over the years. It was something she did when caught off guard. Rather than admit embarrassment, she'd grab a character and play them until she found her balance again. Auntie Mame was a personal favorite. She pulled herself as tall as possible. "What the *hell* are you doing out here? How dare you spy on me in my home like some creeper!"

Gordon stayed on one knee. He also stayed amused, which really got under her skin.

"Victoria Mallory Noor Pendergast Rivers Pendergast…" His smile deepened as he accurately rattled off her long list of last names. "You *hired* me to be out here. In fact, you emailed me two days ago and berated me for not being here sooner. And I wasn't *spying*. I was getting ready to go to work when you put on your little show." He rested his arm on his knee. "Gotta admit, I wasn't expecting to start my day with a striptease."

Vickie stiffened. "I was *not* doing a…" She looked down to be sure. *Well, shit.* Her robe had loosened from all of her shimmying and had nearly slipped off one shoulder. She yanked it up and tightened the belt. "It wasn't a show. It was me in what I *thought* was the privacy of my own kitchen at eight o'clock in the morning."

Gordon slowly rose to his feet, reminding Vickie that he'd once been a linebacker on the high school football team way back when. He was tall and broad shouldered, and bicep muscles bunched under that snug shirt. His thick, pewter brows drew together as he frowned.

"I couldn't help seeing you. But I should have let you know you had an audience. Sorry."

She appreciated his apology, but her dignity was rattled. And she still hadn't had any coffee, thanks to him.

"Or you could have turned away and not been an audience at all."

The corner of his mouth twitched. "Yeah…that wasn't a realistic option. You were a sight I couldn't ignore." He managed to control his laughter, shaking his head. "But I am sorry for startling you. Do you want me to come back later?"

She'd only be hurting herself if she made him leave now.

"No, I've been waiting long enough to get this deck fixed. I'll just be more careful about closing the curtains." And she would *not* be coming downstairs in her bathrobe again until he was done with the repairs. She tugged at her robe again and turned away, spotting her coffee cup on the counter. Her first mother-in-law had instilled an entire volume of Emily Post good manners in her, so she couldn't help asking. "Would you like a cup of coffee?"

"No thanks. I picked up a to-go cup from Evie this morning at The Spot." She'd started into the kitchen when he called out to her. "Adele's got nothing on you, Vicks."

Her teeth ground together, but she kept walking, closing the door hard enough to make the glass panes rattle. Not only had he watched. He'd also *listened.* She yanked the heavy damask curtains closed.

She didn't go back downstairs again until she'd showered and dressed in her pantsuit. *Now* she was ready to start her day, no matter who might see her. She looked like the Vickie Pendergast people in Rendezvous Falls expected—

thoughtfully put together from her carefully styled hair to the toes of her Burberry flats. After taking a few bites of a cinnamon bagel, she pulled open the drapes overlooking the deck.

She couldn't hear any hammering. Maybe Gordon had left after all? But no, his toolbox was still sitting there, as well as the travel mug she assumed was holding his coffee. She stepped outside.

"No!" His voice came from beneath her, scaring her half to death. "Don't walk out here, Vicks. It's not safe."

Vicks? Her nose wrinkled in displeasure. At the same time, she had a sudden flashback to sitting under the birch trees in front of the high school at lunchtime, giggling over something with a group of friends. Gordon had joined them with a few other football players, brushing a shock of long dark hair from his forehead. Calling her *Vicks.*

Good Lord, that was almost fifty years ago...

"I'm serious." His voice was firm, if muffled. "Step back inside. Give me a minute to get out of here." She obeyed without a word. He grumbled and shuffled under the deck, which was only a few feet above the ground. The deck was one of her favorite spots to be in the warmer months, with a lovely view of Seneca Lake and the hills on the eastern shore across from her. The deck stretched wide enough to be accessible from the kitchen, formal dining room and the living room, and she used it for entertaining on a regular basis.

Gordon crawled out near the damaged steps, brushing dirt and brown leaves off himself as he stood. He turned to face her, shaking his head grimly.

"Sorry to bark at you, but we have a problem."

"What kind of problem? Did the tree do more damage than you thought?"

"Actually, that downed limb may have done you a favor. No one would have known about what I just saw until it was too late. How old is this deck?" He brushed cobwebs from his salt-and-pepper hair.

Vickie tried to remember when the deck had been added. "I think Malcolm had it built around the time we started dating, so…over twenty years?" Saying that out loud made her realize just how long ago that was. But she'd had the deck sanded and stained every few years, so it had been well maintained. Gordon shook his head again, and she felt like she was being scolded. "Will you stop with the head-shaking" she snapped, "and just tell me what's wrong?"

"For starters, you should have replaced this deck five or ten years ago. They don't last forever, especially on the waterfront. Then add in the fact that this one was *not* constructed properly for its size, and…" He shrugged, as if she was supposed to know what that meant. When her only response was stony silence, he walked up the steps and across the deck in her direction. Apparently it was safe enough for *him*. He pointed down to where the deck met the house. "The ledger board is what anchors a deck to a house. Your ledger board wasn't connected to the house well to start with, and it's rotted over the years to the point where it could pull free at any time. And the joist connectors are cheap tin. They've rusted and grown weak, so if you had a few people all standing in the same area, a joist could easily give way."

That was a visual that hit home. She'd served tea and desserts to Iris, Cecile and Maura just last week out here one sunny afternoon. The idea of *anyone*, but particularly eighty-two-year-old Iris, falling through the deck made her feel ill.

"B-but you're standing on it right now."

"That's the thing—it could last a couple more years without a problem." He looked around. "Or it could go right now." He winked at her, and she had to make an effort not to show any response. A response like...gasping. He had one great wink. "I'm standing here because I understand the risk, and your deck is only three feet off the ground. If you want to come out here, just know that it's dicey. I hate to be the bearer of bad news, but you need a whole new deck."

She sighed. "If it was anyone other than *you* saying that, I'd be skeptical as hell."

"Feel free to get a second opinion." He wasn't offended, just calm and matter-of-fact about it.

"I don't need to do that. Just tell me how much."

He grimaced. "Way more than the original estimate, I'm afraid."

"I'm sure. But my accountant doesn't respond well to requests for *way more.*"

"I'll work up a price for you. It'll be more expensive, but I recommend going with composite decking. It'll last a hell of a lot longer." He grinned. "And you can even choose what color you want, anything from dark blue to rose pink. It's going to take a while to complete." His smile deepened. "Think you can avoid bursting into song that long?"

"Oh, ha ha. Think you can manage to avoid being a Peeping Tom if I can't?"

"No promises, Vicks. You still got it after all these years."

She gave a startled laugh. "Careful about counting years, buster. You were only a year behind me."

He straightened and turned away, but not before she caught his sly grin.

"I remember. That's why you and I would have been such a scandal back then."

She sucked in a breath. He remembered. Well, she *hoped* he remembered, but neither of them had mentioned that night *ever*. Her one and only romp in the back seat of a Buick. In *any* back seat, for that matter.

And now he was going to be in her backyard for weeks. What could possibly go wrong?

"UM…" HAZEL STOOD in the entrance to the living room, which used to be an eighties vision of beige on beige on beige. She blinked a few times, then turned to Zoey. "What did you do? And…how?"

Zoey couldn't hide a proud smile. "*What* I did was paint. And how? With lots of help. Mary, Piper and Taneisha were here almost all day Saturday, and Tani helped me finish up yesterday. She also helped with the shopping."

Hazel stepped into the room. She'd been calling it "the world's most boring tunnel" since they'd moved in. It was long and narrow, stretching across the front of the house. And it *had* been pretty boring, unchanged for decades. But now the wall facing the windows was dark teal, with the other three painted soft silver gray. The wood floors were worn and in need of refinishing someday, but a couple new area rugs with swirls of teal, white and green served as a distraction from that. A dark green sofa and love seat anchored one end of the room around the television. On the other end was a wall of tall white bookcases and a small writing table.

Hazel still hadn't said any more. Zoey had really hoped for a more enthusiastic response, since her daughter followed dozens of "creatives" and "influencers" online. Then again, hoping for enthusiasm from a teenager was usually a mistake. Feeling a need to fill the silence, Zoey walked to the table.

"I borrowed this from Mary's cousin, Kelly. I wasn't sure if we'd want a desk in here, but I think it will be a nice spot for me to take care of household bills and stuff. And you can bring your laptop down and use it for homework if you want." She gestured to the shelves. "Tani got us a great deal on these at the furniture store where she works. They were floor samples. I figure two readers like you and I can fill them up pretty quick."

For now, her dad's history books and reference books on metalworking were scattered on the shelves, along with a few knickknacks.

"You got all new furniture?"

"No, that's Pop-pop's old furniture with slipcovers on. Isn't it great? No more brown and beige plaid. The curtains and rugs came from the Cost-Saver warehouse store in Rochester. Tani and I went up there a few weeks ago. Come on, Hazel. What do you think?"

She didn't answer right away. Instead she turned in the middle of the room, examining every detail as if she was judging that design challenge show she liked so much. A slow smile spread across her face.

"I like it."

That's it? Zoey's shoulders fell. Hazel had complained nearly nonstop about the old house not feeling like home, not feeling like *them*, still feeling like her grandfather's house. Too old-fashioned. Too boring. Tacky. And worse.

And all she could say was *I like it*?

"Is that really all you can say? You *like* it? You showed me that video by the design influencer you liked, and it turns out Tani follows her, too. We all worked really hard on this…"

"Mom, it looks good. I like it." Hazel seemed confused. "Why are you pressed right now?"

She ran through her mental file of current teen terms. *Pressed* meant *irritated.*

"I'm *pressed* because…" Because her daughter didn't react as expected. Which was totally on Zoey. She'd never get used to this whole Teens Are Never Impressed phase. "You know what? I'll take *I like it.* It's definitely better than before, right? At least admit that much?"

Hazel gave her a reluctant smile. "It's better than before." She looked around. "The gray is a miss for me, but I like the accent wall." She walked over and struck an exaggerated pose, with her arms open wide. "It's spectacular, Mother!" Her arms dropped. "Is that better?"

Actually, it was better, but she didn't admit it. "Whatever. I told you we could make this old place meet your very high standards. One room at a time. By the end of the year, it'll be a whole new house. In fact, why don't we do *your* room next?" The kitchen could wait.

That got Hazel's attention. "Yes to doing my room next! But I want to make *all* the decisions."

"We have a budget, young lady—that's why I got slipcovers instead of new furniture. But you will definitely get to make your own choices…within reason." She took Hazel's hands. "Now tell me how the weekend was with your dad."

Just like that, Hazel's smile was gone again. *Uh-oh.*

"Uh…maybe we should sit down, Mom."

"What happened? Did you and Dad argue? Was it Genna-with-a-*G*?"

"Mom." They sat on the sofa and Zoey waited. Her parental radar was sounding all kinds of alarms in her mind. Did she need to be a mama bear for her little girl, or give her a shoulder to cry on?

"Dad and Genna are getting married at the end of June." Hazel said it in a rush, avoiding Zoey's eyes.

"*Next month?* What the fu…" She caught herself, but damn. The divorce hadn't become final until February. He'd already forced her and Hazel out of their house so he could build a new one with what's-her-name. What was the big rush to add one more major event to their daughter's life?

She and Chris had vowed they wouldn't bad-mouth each other to Hazel, no matter how intense things got during and after the divorce. She had to keep her end of the bargain. She'd deal with Chris later. "I mean…that seems…fast. I thought they'd wait longer, but…"

"Genna's pregnant." Hazel's voice was flat, but that didn't soften the cut of those words. Zoey felt like someone had just kicked her in the stomach, to the point where she almost wheezed from the impact.

"I'm sorry, *what*? It's a shotgun wedding?"

"Mom…"

Zoey sucked in her breath and held it, closing her eyes. Chris and she had talked so many times about having another child, but it never happened. The doctor couldn't find a physical reason for either of them, but Chris had still blamed Zoey. He didn't say it out loud, but she'd felt it. There was a blank space between them where more children should have been. And now he was having those children. Without her.

"Mom? Are you okay?" Hazel's hand rested on Zoey's.

"I'm *fine*, honey." She knew her words sounded forced. "It's a surprise, but hey—a baby!" She hoped her smile wasn't shaking as much as she was inside. This conversation wasn't about her. "You're going to be a big sister… How does that make *you* feel?"

Zoey's jaw tightened. This was typical Chris—doing

things for himself with no thought of how they affected the people in his life. Cheating on Zoey. And now surprising Hazel with a new sibling.

"I don't know. I mean…there's going to be almost fourteen years between us, so it's not like we'll hang out or anything." Hazel was trying to be nonchalant, but Zoey sensed her feelings ran deeper than what she was letting on. It would probably take them both some time to process it all.

"Maybe not when the baby's little, but once you're both adults, you could end up being great friends. Tani and her brother are ten years apart, and they're super close now."

"It's a boy."

Zoey bit her lip. Of course it would be the boy Chris had always wanted. Not that he didn't adore Hazel, but he'd always talked about having a son.

"A baby brother. How sweet." She was running out of strength to sound enthusiastic.

Hazel's shoulder rose and fell in a tiny shrug.

"Genna asked me to be the maid of honor in the wedding."

It was a nice gesture. Zoey should be happy her daughter was being included in the plans. It wasn't as if there was any chance she and Chris would *ever* reconcile. That ship had sailed, burned and sunk. But…this made things feel very *final*. Her ex was remarrying. And having a baby with someone else. And what was *she* doing? Well, for one thing, she wasn't indulging *herself* by starting a brand-new family. She was focusing on her daughter. She was doing the right thing, damn it. She cleared her throat.

"Do you *want* to be maid of honor?"

Hazel hesitated, and Zoey realized with a sharp stab to her heart that her daughter was trying to protect her. The kid had enough on her shoulders without thinking she couldn't talk to her mom about certain things. Zoey turned her hand and entwined her fingers with Hazel's.

"It's *okay* to want to be her maid of honor. It's really nice that she asked you. I'm sure you'll have fun. I'm just saying if you don't want to…"

"I told her I would." Hazel's voice was still low and hesitant.

"That's wonderful!" Just freaking fabulous.

"Why are you yelling, Mom? Are you sure you're okay?"

She did her best to smile, for real this time.

"I'm not gonna lie, this is…weird for me. I want your dad to be happy. I don't really know Genna-with-a-*G*…" She stopped, her eyes falling shut. She'd been sabotaging her daughter's relationship with the woman who would soon be her stepmother. It wasn't fair to Hazel. Or to the woman Zoey would be coparenting with. "A-n-d I clearly need to stop saying that. Sorry. I barely know *Genna*, but that will have to change now that she's marrying your father." She'd have to see the perky young blonde as more than just the woman who broke up her marriage. That had always been too simplistic anyway. Genna hadn't lured Chris away—he'd been a willing participant in the affair. She looked into Hazel's eyes. "This is new territory for all of us, and we'll have to find our way through it together."

Hazel studied Zoey's face as if trying to decide how much she should say.

"Genna's not that bad, Mom." Another long pause. "But I'm glad you're…you know…not with anyone. Not dating or…"

Zoey bumped Hazel's shoulder with hers, trying to lighten the moment. "You don't have to worry about that." No way would she bring another person into the mix. At the same time, she felt a pinch of regret, thinking of sleeping in an empty bed night after night. For a really long time. "So what are you wearing to the wedding?"

"Genna's going to take me shopping in Syracuse and let me pick out a dress." Enthusiasm bled into Hazel's voice.

"That sounds dangerous…for Genna, I mean." Zoey ruffed her fingers through Hazel's hair playfully. "Has she seen your Insta account? Does she know how expensive your tastes are?"

"She has, and she does, so *there*." Hazel pushed Zoey's hand away with a grin before growing serious again. "Don't be mad, but she's into fashion and stuff."

It was no secret that Zoey was mystified by whatever people thought "fashion" was from one week to the next. Meanwhile, Hazel kept up with every new trend in clothing, hair and makeup. She not only followed dozens of so-called social media *influencers*, she also had her *own* accounts. Zoey monitored it all carefully to be sure her daughter's posts were age appropriate. Any creepy dudes who tried to follow her were promptly blocked. Even after viewing all those videos and reels and lives and whatever they were called, Zoey didn't get it.

Clothing was a practical necessity in her life, but nothing more. She didn't want to look like a slob or anything, but as long as her clothes were clean and hole-free, she was happy. Her trademark jeans and T-shirts were her own unique fashion statement. Hazel said more than once that sort of trademark only worked with a style that was cutting edge and unique, but Zoey had shrugged her off. From the time she was a teenager, she'd heard other people's opinions—and laughter—about her clothes and hair and house. She was very good at ignoring them.

But now Hazel was going to have a stepmother who loved pop culture and style as much as Hazel did. Zoey felt a flutter of insecurity in her chest. Sure, she'd been good at ignoring opinions…or at least appearing to. But those barbs had still wiggled their way into her self-esteem, both as a young girl and all these years later.

"Mom? It's okay that you're not into it. You know that, right?" Hazel leaned forward. "I just meant Genna likes it like I do. That doesn't reflect on you…"

Zoey couldn't help laughing. "That's what I told you about you being more into glitter and glam than me." She took a deep breath, reminding herself that she was the Mom. "I'm glad Genna likes the things you like. I'm glad you like *her*. I won't lie—it's going to take me some time to get used to her being in the family. But that's my issue, not yours. It's totally normal after—" *having your life up-ended* "—getting a divorce."

"What…being weird?" Hazel's smile was mischievous. Her playful little girl was back.

"Oh, ha ha. And…yes. Weird probably *is* normal for me. Does that work for you?"

Hazel nodded, her eyes twinkling with humor. "I'm used to it."

"Good. Because I'm too old to change. Why don't you go unpack and I'll find something for dinner."

"Um…" Hazel blushed. "There isn't anything to unpack. I left most of what I took at Dad's place. Like you suggested."

Divorce had been the only option when she'd discovered Chris was cheating. So she didn't regret the divorce, despite the pain of a failed marriage. But this journey through the months *after* the divorce was harder than she'd ever anticipated. Like…advising Hazel to make herself more at home at Chris's place, then feeling a stab of pain when Hazel actually *did* it.

"That's *terrific*, honey!" She took a breath and lowered her voice to a more normal level. "Good for you. But I still need to figure out what we'll have for dinner. Gimme half an hour."

She left Hazel to inspect the living room more closely, then went right through the kitchen and out to the back porch. Dinner was lasagna from the freezer. All she had to do was warm it up. Zoey didn't mind cooking, but sometimes she was just too tired. Or, like tonight, too annoyed. She dialed her ex-husband's number. Chris sounded surprised when he answered, but she talked right over his question if Hazel was okay.

"She's fine. And so very full of surprising news." She leaned against the wall of the house, trying to avoid the chilly breeze that was shaking the new leaves on the lilac trees.

"Are you upset about the wedding or the baby?"

"I'm upset that I learned about *both* of those things from our daughter. Our thirteen-year-old daughter. You could have given me a heads-up, Chris. Pick up the phone. Text me, for Christ's sake. This is *not* the coparenting we agreed to. No blindsides, remember? Parent as a *team*?" She tapped her toe angrily. "Ring any bells?"

There was a moment of silence on the line. She was expecting a long string of angry, defensive arguments to deflect the blame, but he surprised her.

"You're right. Sorry."

"Uh…what?"

He gave a small laugh. "I mean it. I'm sorry. We agreed to no blindsides, and I broke that agreement. Genna was excited and she just blurted it out over breakfast this morning. Honestly, I'm feeling a little blindsided myself." He paused. "A baby." He registered Zoey's silence and jumped in to undig that hole. "It's not about us and how we tried…"

"Stop, Chris." Her head fell back and thunked against the house. "You have every right to be happy." After breaking her heart. "But you need to remember this is a lot for Hazel to take in. It's only been a year since we split, and with the move and puberty and now becoming a big sister… I would have liked to have been prepared for the conversation she and I just had."

"She seemed happy when we told her…"

"Of course she acted happy—she knew that's what you expected." An edge had crept into her voice, and she took a calming breath. She'd just scolded Chris about parenting as a team, so she couldn't let her personal feelings take over now. "Hazel's fine with it. A little stunned, but she's okay." Another breath. "She seems to like Genna."

"Genna will never try to take your place, Zoey."

The fact that Chris thought he had to say that stung at first, but then she realized she *needed* to hear it. Her body tension eased.

"I guess I should get to know her, huh?"

"Sure." He didn't sound all that enthusiastic. "I guess we could start with coffee together or something."

"Decaf, of course."

"What? Oh…yeah. Pregnant. No caffeine. Right. It's been a while." He sounded overwhelmed.

"Fourteen years," she answered. There was a long silence, and she actually felt sorry for the guy. "You'll be fine. It's like riding a bike." She smiled softly. "You did good the first time around."

"Thanks. I really am sorry I didn't warn you about the news." He paused. "How are *you* doing? Seeing anyone?"

"Between the business and working on Dad's house, my days are full."

And I didn't have the head start of already seeing some-one while we were married...

She didn't say that. She also didn't tell him Hazel wanted her to stay single. The conversation with Chris stayed with her after the call. It's not like she was grieving his loss or anything. But one of Hazel's homes had to be stable. She couldn't bring some random guy back here. It would be nice to *have* a random guy, though.

She pulled the lasagna out of the oven and called out to Hazel.

Maybe not *random*. But a man in her life. Or at least in her bed.

She blinked.

Yeah, she did miss having someone in her bed.

CHAPTER SIX

"Ooh...speak of the devil!"

Mike saw Cecile Manning waving at him as he walked into The Spot. She looked at her dining partners with a big smile. "Why don't you ask Mike himself what he wants us to do?"

Oh, shit. This couldn't be good.

The booth was occupied by several members of the Rendezvous Falls Book Club. His grandmother was a member, but she wasn't with the gang...er...group today. Iris Taggart was sitting next to Vickie Pendergast, with Cecile and Lena Fox on the opposite side. Iris was the over-eighty owner of the Taggart Inn just off Main Street—the largest and oldest inn in town. Her grandson and his wife were running it now, but Logan and Piper knew better than to make Iris feel that place wasn't her domain in every sense of the word. She was a force of nature, and she knew it. Right now she was fixing a glare on poor Cecile, who was forever the romantic optimist of the group.

"Yeah, I'm sure Mike wants to sit with four old ladies on his lunch hour and be asked his dating preferences. Leave the guy alo—"

Mike pulled a chair over and sat at the end of the booth. They could be a pain, but he liked the old ladies. They meddled, but with good intentions. At least, he hoped so. "Sounds like you're discussing matchmaking instead of books today."

Vickie smiled at him, but not until after she'd scanned him from head to toe. Her mind was as sharp as her appearance.

"You're looking very formal today, counselor," she said. "Court date?"

He glanced down at his dark pinstripe suit and crisp white shirt. It was a fair question, since his usual daily attire was khakis and a button-down shirt.

"Trying to *avoid* a court date," he answered. "I have a mediation meeting up in Geneva this afternoon—trying to keep my client and his siblings from ripping their family apart over their grandfather's will. They're ready to go to war over an estate that's barely in the six figures." He shook his head. "We're getting everyone and their lawyers together in a room with a court-appointed mediator to see if common sense can prevail."

She gave him another once-over with her eyes. "Well, you're dressed for success, my boy."

His cheeks heated. "I'm also having dinner with one of the attorneys after the meeting. She and I went to law school together in Syracuse."

"She?" Cecile blurted out. "I thought you didn't want to date right now?"

Iris grumbled a few curse words under her breath. "Honestly, Cecile—that's none of our business."

Mike didn't point out that their little group had *made* it their business to send him out on dates with various women for the past eighteen months, trying to find him a perfect match. Vickie glared at Iris.

"You have a funny way of showing your disinterest. Wasn't Rachel the librarian your idea?"

Cecile sat up straight, her hand in the air. "No, *I* was the one who suggested Rachel! She was so sweet when I met her at the flower shop." Her smile faded slightly. "But Zoey Hartford said you were off the market for now…?"

He still didn't know why Zoey told them that. "First, tonight is just dinner with a former classmate. It's *not* a date."

"Is she single?" Vickie asked quickly.

"Well…yeah, but…"

"Then it's a date."

It was so *not* a date. Monica preferred dating women.

He shook his head emphatically. "*Not* a date. Just dinner. As for Zoey, I didn't ask her to do that. I'm not ready to get serious with anyone, but I honestly don't mind most of the evenings you set up. As long as you aren't hoping to find me 'the one.'" He raised a brow at Cecile. "And no more cat-lady librarians who live on boats, okay?" Cecile nodded quickly, her blond curls bouncing. Mike leaned to the side to give Evie Hudson room to deliver his burger. She knew he always had the special on Wednesdays. Evie patted him on the shoulder, then hurried back to the counter.

He picked up the sandwich, nodding to the ladies. "Pardon my eating, but I'm on a schedule. And this is the best stuffed burger in New York."

"You know they got that recipe from Mark Hudson, right?" Iris asked.

"Mark and I have been friends since high school, so yes, I know. His burger recipe was his pride and joy, but he gave it up to Evie when he was trying to win her back. He'd have walked barefoot across broken glass if that's what it took."

Vickie chuckled. "If I remember correctly, she came close to making him do just that. She was a tough nut to crack after he broke her heart, but he got through to her."

"And now," Cecile said, "they're married and having babies! Such a sweet couple. We want you to find someone like tha—"

Mike had to finish his bite of the burger before he answered. "If you think a woman and I might have something in common, I don't mind having a nice dinner with her. Platonically. Like my classmate and I are doing tonight. No making babies. Okay?"

"You have our word, Mike." Lena spoke up for the first time, her short dreadlocks held off her face with a colorful scarf. She gave Cecile a firm nudge with her elbow. "If you're giving us permission to find you dinner companionship, we'll keep our eyes and ears open for you." Lena's triple-hoop gold earrings brushed against her neck. An artist with the occasional senior modeling gig, Lena looked every inch the part with her brilliant green top and swaths of gold chains dotted with colorful porcelain beads she'd probably made herself. "And no cat-ladies."

"*You* have three cats, Lena." Iris took a sip of her coffee.

"*I* have no interest in marrying Mike."

He laughed at that. "You ladies are a kick."

"If anyone should understand that you don't want anything serious," Vickie said, "it's the three of us." She gestured at herself, Iris and Lena. "We've been single for years. *Decades* for you, Iris. We don't need wedding bells."

Lena's eyes went soft and wistful. "A dinner companion would be nice once in a while, though."

Vickie nodded in agreement. "True. I've got my routine down to a science after all these years. But I do miss a man's presence across the table in a nice restaurant. Some grown-up conversation over wine. Even a good-natured debate now and then. Someone to walk to the lakeshore and sit on the dock with." She blinked, realizing they were all hanging on her words. Vickie straightened. "But I'm fine *without* it, too."

"I don't know how you do it, girls." Cecile shook her

head, swatting at Vickie's hand when she reached for more fries, then turning her plate so Vickie had easier access. "If I lost Charlie, I don't know how I'd go on. I don't think *companionship* would cut it. He's the love of my life, and he can't be replaced with just any warm body."

Vickie nodded. "After three marriages, I don't think I'd ever get serious with anyone again. But as annoying as men can be, I do miss having one around."

"Agreed." Iris surprised them by jumping into the conversation. Her husband left her fifty years ago. Mike finished his burger, listening to this tell-all lunch conversation.

"Iris, are you saying *you'd* like a dinner date once in a while?" Cecile's disbelief was clear.

The older woman's blue eyes narrowed dangerously. "Yes, Cecile. Even cranky old Iris gets lonely occasionally. And if you think *that's* shocking…" She leaned forward. "Wait until I tell you what I'd like a man to do with my body!"

Mike nearly choked on his soda. "Ladies, please!" He covered his mouth with his napkin to hide his laughter. "Remember you have an impressionable young man at the table."

Iris swatted at his arm. "Impressionable, my ass. But I'll spare you from any more details."

He checked his watch and rose to his feet, sliding the chair back to the table he'd taken it from.

"Gotta run. Thanks for the entertaining company."

As he walked away, the women were listing the things they did and did *not* want a man around for in their lives.

ZOEY HEARD THE laughter before she'd even opened the door to The Spot. Her godmother and some of her book club pals were having a grand time in their booth along the left wall. The counter stretched down the right side of the narrow diner, where Evie Hudson and her mom, Evelyn Rosales, were serving customers and passing each other in the limited space as if they'd done it forever. And they basically had.

Evie's parents had run the diner together, bringing up their daughter in the business. The diner hadn't originally been part of Evie's dream, but after her father died unexpectedly, she'd stepped up to help her mom run the place. It wasn't long before she'd realized this little diner was the virtual heart of Rendezvous Falls, and she needed to keep it going.

"Zoey!" Evie waved from the far end of the counter, where she'd been talking with a good-looking man with perfectly coifed golden hair. "Hey, come meet this guy— he sells appliances!"

"Ohh, yes, Zoey," Vickie said in a low, suggestive voice as Zoey walked by. "Go meet that drop-dead-gorgeous man…"

"Hush, Vickie. You sound like you're pimping me out."

"You just missed Mike," Cecile said, leaning forward and lowering her voice. "He's off to Geneva for a meeting, and he's got a dinner date after that."

"A date? Are you sure?" He hadn't mentioned anything about going on a date. "Is it someone you set him up with?"

"Nope." Cecile shook her head. "This is someone he's known for years."

Years? Who the hell was Mike dating, and why hadn't he told her? Maybe he'd decided to step right over that threshold his grandmother talked about. Well…good for him. Iris glanced over her shoulder then back to Zoey.

"Don't leave that blond Adonis waiting, dear."

Zoey rolled her eyes. "I'm here to fix the dishwasher, not meet a man."

But he *was* handsome, and got even better looking the closer she got. He stood and extended his hand. "Mason Fontino. Evie was just telling me about her friend who repairs commercial dishwashers. That's pretty impressive."

He had denim-blue eyes and a great smile. Zoey didn't feel any bonfire starting inside her chest or anything, but he was a good-looking man who was smiling right at her and telling her she was impressive. She wasn't mad about it.

"Actually…" Evie started, "Zoey can repair just about anything, from commercial products to my grandmother's music box collection. Your boss should put her on retainer."

Zoey groaned. "*Evie.* I'm sure Mr. Fontino's employer has their own service people. What was it you sell again?"

He handed her a card, and her brows rose. He worked for a major international appliance manufacturer. High-end stuff.

"My company uses local repair companies when we can. If you're interested—and qualified, of course—I can get you on the on-call list for warranty work."

"If she can repair that old beast in the kitchen," Evie said, "then trust me—she's qualified."

Mason leaned back and openly appraised Zoey, staring long enough to make her feel uncomfortable. As if he'd sensed that, he sat up and cleared his throat.

"I'll tell you what…if you fix that Model 5389 in there today, without using a manual, I'll take you to dinner, and we'll see how qualified you are." He held up his hand before she could speak. "Okay, that sounded really creepy—sorry. I'm strictly talking about your qualifications to repair commercial appliances. The dinner is separate…"

He coughed, his cheeks turning ruddy. "Let's try this

again. *If* you can fix that dishwasher, we'll talk about your qualifications to be a contractor for the company." His smile deepened. "And *then*, if you're interested, we could also have dinner. Together. *Not* about business."

How about that…he was flirting. While she wore coveralls. Maybe she still had game after all. She fished in her pocket for her business card and handed it to him with a smile.

"I've got your number and now you've got mine. For business. Nice meeting you, Mason." She blinked away from his definitely interested gaze, hoping her cheeks weren't *too* pink. "Evie, is the dishwasher doing that weird knocking thing again?"

Evie nodded. "Except it's even louder—like someone's inside trying to get out. It's getting freaky. Do you think it's on its deathbed?"

"Maybe. Let me take a look…"

"Who's your friend, sweetie?" Her godmother suddenly appeared at Zoey's side, her eyes firmly on Mason Fontino. "I was waiting for you to come back to our table, but then I saw you talking to this handsome man. Did I hear you mention dinner?" She held a manicured hand out to Mason. "I'm Zoey's godmother, Victoria Pendergast. Are you new in town, Mister…?"

Mason's dimples deepened as he tried to contain his amusement. Vickie wasn't known for her subtlety. He stood and took her hand. "Mason Fontino, ma'am. Your goddaughter and I just met. I'm in the area this week for business, then I'm headed back home to Albany."

"Vickie, I told you I was here for a service call…"

"Oh, I know, dear." She patted Zoey's arm. "I know. The girls and I are heading home, but…call me later." She gave

Mason a saucy wink. "I hope you'll follow up on those dinner plans, Mason."

Kill. Me. Now.

"Goodbye, Vickie." Zoey made a shooing motion with her hands. There was a beat of silence after she returned to her friends.

"Interesting lady," Mason said.

"Weirder than ever," Evie sighed.

"Pain in my ass," Zoey muttered.

Vickie and her cohorts waved before leaving, a conspiratorial grin on every face. Zoey headed into the kitchen, shaking her head. "Those old ladies are going to be the death of me, I swear."

CHAPTER SEVEN

MIKE SAT AT the bar at the Purple Shamrock and scowled into his beer. He knew he was scowling because his cousin Bridget had just called him out on it. And she wasn't giving up. Quitting was not the McKinnon way, even if she was an O'Hearn now.

"Hey, Mary!" She called out from behind the bar. "Come over here and tell me what's wrong with your brother."

Mary walked over from where she'd been folding green linen napkins and leaned in to stare at his face. His twin's face was showing an exaggerated amount of interest, but it wasn't all a put-on. He saw the flash of concern in her eyes.

"Oi…he's a sad one today, isn't he?" Mary spoke with a fake Irish brogue. "If I didn't know any better, I'd say the lad was lovesick, but that can't be it. He hasn't been on a date in forever."

Mike straightened. "I took Bonnie Wilkins to dinner just last week! It was right here. You both saw us."

Mary waved him off, dropping her accent. "Puh-leeze. I'm talking about an actual *date*, with furtive glances and hand-holding and a kiss to end the evening. These match-ups the book club has you going on are more like find-a-friend dinners."

"Well, maybe they just haven't found the right friend for me yet."

Bridget scoffed. "They've set you up with every unattached woman in town. You have to actually be *open* to romance before you can find it."

"Maybe I'm really fussy. Or maybe I'm not interested in romance."

Mary rested her chin in her hand. "Then why are you staring into that glass of whiskey in the middle of the afternoon like you were hoping it held all the answers to some great problem?"

"I'm *not!*"

It probably didn't look great. His final appointment for the day had canceled, so he'd come to the bar a few hours ahead of his weekly Friday night bar shift. And that bottle of Irish whiskey had been calling his name.

Mary reached out and pinched his cheek, which she knew he hated. "Twin-sense, remember? I know when you're wallowing, and brother, you are wallowing big-time." She slid onto the barstool next to him. "What's up?"

"I don't know..." He saw her skepticism. "Seriously... I don't know what it is. I tried to explain it to Nana, but I couldn't. I'm feeling restless, but I don't know why. Anxious, but I don't know for *what*." He took a sip from his glass. "It's like...nothing feels satisfying to me anymore. I'm not as sad as I used to be, but I'm not happy, either. I'm in this weird *okay* land. It's not necessarily bad. I'm not hurting. I'm just not feeling...anything."

Mary and Bridget glanced at each other across the bar. They were probably just as surprised as he was by this little speech. He pushed on, needing to just get it out. "Work is okay. I'm paying the bills. Clients are happy." He looked around the pub. It was still early, so it was nearly empty. But after dinner—once the music started—it would be hopping with locals and tourists. "I enjoy working the bar on Fridays. It's something different from the rest of the week.

I know what I'm doing. We have good friends here. But…
it's not like it's my passion or anything. It's a job. I don't
hate it. It's…"

"Okay?" Mary's voice was low and soft. He nodded, sitting back in his seat.

"The dinner dates I go on are nice enough. Some are
better than others, but none of them are exactly exciting.
But that's on *me*, not the women. Most of them are great,
and I like the companionship, but…"

Bridget made a face. "Oh, please tell me you don't mention *companionship* to your dates. If you want companionship, go get a dog."

"I know how to behave like a gentleman, Bridget." He
emptied his glass as a group of diners came in. "Looks like
you'll be needed in the kitchen soon. Don't worry about
me. I'm just having a moody Friday."

Bridget patted his hand before turning for the kitchen.
"Well, I hope you can snap out of it. Baby Moira was fussy
tonight, so Finn is staying with her instead of getting a sitter. It's just you and Timothy on the bar while I handle the
kitchen. Kelly's working the tables."

He grinned. "Being crazy-busy sounds like just the
ticket. I'll be fine. And holler if you need help in the
kitchen—I took a few shifts while you were on maternity
leave and no one died."

He moved to the business side of the bar and took a quick
inventory. As usual, everything was in order. Bridget ran
a tight ship.

Mary continued to stare at him after Bridget left. Finally
he rolled his eyes and turned to his twin.

"What?"

"Nothing." She shrugged, but there was very clearly
something. After a prolonged pause, she got to it. "I met

Zoey for coffee yesterday. She said something about you stopping by her place. A lot."

He frowned. "I wouldn't say a *lot*. Why?"

Her right brow arched. "She said you're there every week. I know you two are close, but how close *are* you?"

Mary didn't often manage to get under his skin, but annoyance shot through his veins right now.

"Jesus Christ, Mary. Why are you making it sound weird? It's *Zoey*."

Her eyes narrowed. "How did I not know you two were spending so much time together? I know you text all the time, but…"

"Mary, stop. Zoey's been our friend since grade school. It's not the way you make it sound. We hang out in the shop while she works on repairs. We drink sometimes. And we talk." He paused, a sinking feeling in his chest. "Wait… did *Zoey* say something?"

Had he been reading things all wrong? Was Zoey uncomfortable with his visits? Nah…she was direct enough that she'd have told him if she didn't want him there. *Wouldn't she?*

Mary studied him again for a moment before shaking her head. "She didn't sound mad about it." He took a drink order from his cousin Kelly, who was waiting tables tonight. Mary watched him pouring three glasses of Guinness, which took a little time to do properly. "You've really never thought about…?"

"Absolutely not." He set the beers on a tray. That wasn't true, of course. The thought had crossed his mind a lot lately. He just refused to let it linger.

Zoey was incredible. And available. But…she wasn't at all like the other women he'd spent time with since Becca. They were casual. Zoey would be anything *but* casual.

She'd be very real, in the same way Becca had been for him. Their connection ran deep. Was his hesitance because he'd loved Becca so much? Was he afraid things might get too real with Zoey? Or even worse, that he might lose her, too? A chill went over him. His heart would never survive that.

His phone chirped in his back pocket. He pulled it out and smiled at the timing. "Speak of the devil, here she is."

He read her text.

Z: You at the Shamrock tonight? I need a wingman.

M: Bartending all night. Why do you need a wingman?

He figured she was coming to the bar with some of her friends. But if she was with her girlfriends, she didn't need him as a wingman. A wingman was for picking up dates, and she wasn't… His phone chirped again.

Z: Guardian angel then. I somehow have a date tonight. Ugh!

What the hell?

M: A date with WHO?

Z: A commercial appliance sales rep—can you believe it?

She followed the text with a laughing-crying emoji. He very definitely could *not* believe it. He stared at the screen, thinking this must be some sort of joke.

Z: Anyway—see you at 7. He seems nice, but if I give you the bat signal, come rescue me. I'm way out of practice.

Mary leaned forward to get his attention. "You haven't noticed two guys trying to order some drinks over there. Is Zoey okay?"

He probably looked as stunned as he felt.

"Zoey's coming here for dinner." He swallowed hard. "She's on a *date*. With some sales guy."

Mary's mouth fell open. "I didn't know she was dating."

"Neither did I."

And he didn't like it. Not one bit. Zoey having dinner with some guy. On a *date*. Right in front of him.

FOR THE HUNDREDTH TIME, Zoey asked herself how she'd gotten herself into this mess. A *date*. With Mason Fontino—a guy she didn't even *know*. She could have said no, of course. But for some reason, she hadn't.

Mason had still been sitting at the counter at The Spot yesterday when she'd walked out of the kitchen and let Evie know that the ancient dishwasher would live to wash dishes for at least another few months. She couldn't make any promises after that—the thing was over twenty years old. Mason had lifted his coffee cup in a toast.

"I guess that means I'm taking you out to dinner this Friday!"

Zoey laughed. "I'm sorry...*what*?"

"That was the deal, right?" His smile was warm and genuine. "You fix that creaky old machine without a manual, we talk about getting you on the list of approved repair techs. And then, totally unrelated, I take you to dinner."

She'd narrowed her eyes at him. "I don't remember actually agreeing to that."

"This isn't a quid pro quo, I promise. But I'm in the area for a couple of days and figured having dinner with an interesting woman would be nice. So... Friday?"

Zoey had started to argue, but the idea of having dinner with a handsome man who found her *interesting* was inviting. She hadn't had a grown-up dinner date since her divorce. Mike was moving on. Maybe she should do the same. And it was just dinner.

"You can pick the place," Mason smiled.

And that's how she came to be walking through the door Mason was holding open for her, into the Purple Shamrock. Yes, it was a pub. But Bridget McKinnon was an excellent chef, and the atmosphere didn't get loud and rowdy until after nine. And Mike would be there. She trusted her friend to keep a watchful eye. Just in case she got some weird vibe from Mason—too pushy, too needy, too boring. Mike would come to the rescue.

She'd insisted on meeting Mason there. She didn't need some stranger knowing where she lived. He'd agreed, and waited outside the entrance for her. Her eyes immediately sought out Mike at the bar when they walked inside.

He was there, staring right at her as if he'd been watching the door. She smiled and waved, but he didn't return either one right away. He looked a little like a lost puppy. She couldn't help looking back over her shoulder at him as she and Mason followed Kelly to a booth by the front windows. Mike hadn't moved. What was his problem? Did he know Mason from somewhere? Was the guy an ax murderer or something? She mouthed *what*? at Mike. He shook his head and mouthed back *have fun*. She couldn't decide from his expression if it was a warning or a genuine wish.

Mason turned out to be charming, and he stood by his promise that this was just a friendly meal. They talked about their work for a while, laughing over their more challenging clients and the differences in repairing appliances from various manufacturers. Most of the time, customers got the extra quality they paid for, but sometimes…all they got was a machine so complicated in design that it was nearly unfixable once it broke.

Over dessert, she talked about her growing business in repairing antiques. Mason was more into contemporary, European design in his appliances and home decor. The more stainless steel, the better, that was his motto. She gave an exaggerated shudder that made him laugh. Stainless steel always made her think of operating rooms.

He showed her a few pictures of his gleaming kitchen on his phone. It lived up to his motto—not only stainless appliances, but also stainless counters and backsplash, against stark white walls. Interestingly, the floor was a mosaic of black, gray and white, providing the only real "punch" in the space. It wasn't her style, but he'd obviously put a lot of thought, time and money into it.

"Wow. It looks like something you'd see in a design magazine."

Mason chuckled. "But not something you'd have in *your* home, right? There is nothing in this town says contemporary. Let me guess—you have a beautiful Victorian home with a refurbished Roper stove in your vintage kitchen."

She started to laugh and saw Mike out of the corner of her eye. The bar was getting crowded as the Friday night crowd assembled. But he was standing still in the midst of the chaos, staring toward the booth she and Mason shared. He was not smiling. When he realized he'd been caught, he gave her a reassuring grin, then raised his brows in curiosity and gave a tentative thumbs-up, asking if all was okay. She nodded quickly, then turned back to Mason.

"I *do* have a Victorian. But it was my dad's house, and it needs some love." She gave him a wink. "When I eventually get to the kitchen remodel, there's a 1951 O'Keefe & Merritt stove in my barn that I hope to have rebuilt by then." She explained her father bought the big double oven, six-burner stove at an auction ten years ago. "Turns out it was missing a fair number of pieces, so he had to collect them over the years. I think all the parts are there now, but it needs to be assembled and painted. And it won't even fit where my stove is, so a kitchen remodel has to happen first."

Mason gave a low whistle. "Of course you have an O'Keefe & Merritt. That's a pure period cooking appliance right there. I'd love to see it once you get it rebuilt."

She arched her brow. "That's presuming quite a lot, Mason."

He held up his hands with a laugh. "I'm hoping we'll be coworkers of sorts when it happens." His smile faded a bit, but his eyes still held some laughter. "I'm getting the sense we won't be more than that?"

Zoey hesitated. "No offense, but I doubt it. I *do* like you, but I'm not feeling anything more than that. And I get the feeling you aren't, either?"

"I think I *could*, but…." He shrugged. "I'm getting a *just friends* vibe for now. Right people, wrong time?"

"Something like that. I'm not *ready* for anything that *is* serious, and I'm not *interested* in anything that's *not* serious. Does that make sense?"

Mason chuckled. "Actually, it does. I got divorced two years ago, and I'm still not sure I'm ready to move on or whatever my friends keep telling me to do. I guess when it's time, we'll know it."

She reached over to cover his hand with hers. "When it *is* time for you, you're going to make some woman very happy. You're a good guy."

"Ditto. Except the *guy* part." They laughed again, and

Mason looked around. "I wonder where our after-dinner drinks went?"

They *had* been waiting awhile for their cognacs, now that he mentioned it. She tried to catch Mike's eye, but he was busy. Or at least he was *acting* busy—when he wasn't making drinks, he was wiping down the counter with a great deal of attention to the task. She flashed a smile at Mason.

"I can get those drinks delivered—I know a guy." She pulled out her phone and texted Mike.

Z: Hey, parched over here!

She added a "hot" emoji with a red face and tongue hanging out. Mike pulled his phone out, and…scowled at it? It was only for an instant, then gone, but that had *definitely* been a scowl. He must be having a bad night. He looked up and smiled, but it felt artificial. She typed again.

Z: You okay?

M: Busy. I'll get it to you.

No jokes. No emojis. Something was definitely not right with her friend tonight.

Z: Want to stop by my place later to talk?

M: Won't that be a little crowded?

It took her a moment to realize what he was saying. She looked up at him and mouthed *Seriously? Her fingers beat out her reply.*

Z: Okay, Tinker Bell.

He looked at her in surprise, his expression telling her he had no clue what she was talking about. So she filled him in.

Z: Short-tempered and jealous?

She meant it to be teasing. It wasn't until after she'd sent the text that she realized she might have nailed the reason for his hot-cold behavior tonight. Except…why would Mike be all pouty and jealous about her having dinner with Mason? Was it because she'd told him she wasn't ready? Well, now she was. Besides, Vickie said *he'd* been on a date in Rochester, so what was the big deal?

"Is there a problem?" Mason's questions made her jump. Her face went hot—how rude of her to ignore him for Mike. She shook her head quickly.

"No, sorry. An old friend's giving me an attitude." She shrugged. "He must be having a bad day."

The sudden *thunk* of glasses hitting the table made them both jump. Mike stood at the end of the booth, a big toothy grin on his face as if he'd just plucked the drinks out of a magician's hat.

"Gee, thanks," she said sarcastically. His weird mood was getting under her skin. "Such prompt and friendly service."

Mike's gaze met hers, and a jolt of electricity shot through her. Her lips parted as she sucked in a gasp of air. She and Mike had argued in the years they'd been friends. A little spat here and there. But it wasn't the annoyance in his eyes that shocked her. It was the…*intensity.* She saw a blend of anger and caring and what looked way too much like longing. From *Mike*. She must be seeing things. She blinked. Sure enough, the look vanished from his eyes and he was Mike McKinnon again. Her friend.

"Sorry." Mike shook his head, chewing on his lip the way he did whenever he felt bad about something. "It really *has* been busy tonight. Tim and I are scrambling behind the bar and... I worked myself into a mood." He extended a hand to Mason. "Mike McKinnon."

Mason introduced himself and they chatted briefly about the pub before Mike stepped back.

"I gotta go before my cousin throttles me." He looked at Zoey for a moment, and she could see he was still struggling with some strange internal battle. There was a vein throbbing on the side of his neck. His smile warmed, no longer a put-on. "Sorry if I was an ass before. Mary called me out on it, too. We'll catch up over the weekend, okay?"

"Sure." Her eyes followed him as he returned to the bar. She couldn't wait to hear what put him in such a mood.

"Well, that explains a lot."

Once again, she'd forgotten about Mason. She blinked at him. "What do you mean?"

"It's pretty clear why you didn't feel sparks with me. There are too many of them tied up between you and the bartender." He chuckled. "And it was very definitely mutual."

She almost choked on the laughter that bubbled up. "Me and *Mike*? No way. We've been pals since grade school, and we've never been more than just friends. *Good* friends, but that's it."

"Okay." He took a sip of his brandy, clearly unconvinced. "He's who you were texting before, right? The dude was giving me dagger-eyes, and his handshake nearly broke my fingers. That's bro-code for *back the hell off*. And when you two had that little stare down?" His mouth slanted into a smile. "That was chemistry, Zoey."

Was that possible? She sipped her drink and thought about it. Mike *had* seemed a little bit jealous. She could have misread him, though. He could have just been concerned for her, with it being her first real dinner date since the divorce. That was probably it. Kelly McKinnon dropped off their receipt, and Mason began to stand.

"Sorry, but you are *way* off base." Zoey started to slide out of the booth, too. "We're very strictly platonic." She tried to sneak a glance back to the bar as they headed to the door. Mike was busy taking a drink order. Mason caught her looking and started to laugh.

"Whatever you say." He walked her to her car and promised she'd be hearing from his employer about being interviewed to be on the approved commercial technician list. They agreed it had been a nice evening, but he suggested next time they met they should stick to coffee or lunch. He'd glanced at the pub. "Just to be safe."

Wow. Was he talking about Mike again?

"Trust me—Mike and I would never spoil our friendship by getting…involved."

Mason made no attempt at a good-night kiss, extending his hand with a smile instead.

"I know what I saw." He turned to go, tossing his final comment over his shoulder. "There's a good chance your platonic friend may be thinking differently about things."

She refused to believe it. Mike would *never.* His mood tonight *mirrored* jealousy, but there's no way it could be that for real.

Could it?

CHAPTER EIGHT

VICKIE PULLED OPEN the drapes and unlocked the doors leading from her kitchen to the currently nonexistent deck out back. That was her signal to Gordon that she was awake and coffee was ready. Ten minutes later, she heard his quick rap on the door before it opened and he walked in, carefully wiping his feet on the new mat she'd placed there just for him.

Over the past couple of weeks, it had become their routine. She'd started by setting out a coffee for him in the mornings. But it felt rude to drink coffee inside while watching him outside. And she was enjoying watching him too much to stop.

The man was freaking hot, and she wasn't ashamed to admit it—at least to herself. The thick hair, the quick smile, the muscular arms and shoulders, the abs she imagined under his shirts, which were often delightfully snug. The way his veins stood out on his neck when he started tearing apart the rotted deck. The smell of his sweat mixed with Old Spice. *Oh, yeah.* She had a solid crush on Gordon Lexiter.

Sharing coffee with him every morning made her ogling easier. It would be unseemly to just stand at the door and drool. After a week, there wasn't any deck left for her to stand on. Handing it out the door to him felt a little too much like he was "the help." Besides, it didn't allow her enough time in his presence. If she was going to fantasize about her contractor, she may as well go all out. So…she'd started inviting him to come inside for coffee.

Fantasizing was all she could do, of course. Her friends habitually teased her about what they called her predatory dating habits. According to them, as soon as she saw someone interesting, she started hearing wedding bells. She couldn't help it if she'd never been a one-night stand sort of woman. Well…not since high school, anyway. No judgment—she had no problem with women who enjoyed that kind of freedom. But Vickie believed in *relationships*, and a relationship should always have the possibility of lasting awhile, if not forever. And anything that might happen between her and Gordon would definitely *not* have a chance at forever.

He was a silver-haired hunk. But he was her *contractor*. Even if it meant living up to her snobbish reputation, she couldn't imagine a future with a guy she'd hired to build her back deck. An architect? Sure. A property developer who *hired* guys like Gordon? Probably. But—God forgive her—she couldn't imagine an actual relationship with him. She could imagine some fun activities, but life was more than that. People had certain expectations of her.

"Are you out of creamer, Vicks?" Gordon was at the refrigerator, looking back at her. He'd made himself right at home in her kitchen over the past few days.

"Check behind the white wine vinegar in the door." Vickie gave herself a mental shake. If she couldn't see a relationship, she should probably stop putting herself in the man's orbit so much. Then he bent lower to search her refrigerator, and his jeans pulled tight across an ass that… *oh, my.* She blinked and turned away, wishing she could fan herself.

A few hours later, she was having lunch with her best

friend, Maura McKinnon, on the outdoor deck of the marina restaurant. She had a weak moment and confessed her
inexplicable attraction to the man they'd both gone to high
school with. Maura's eyes went wide.

"Gordy Lexiter? Wasn't he a linebacker on the football
team? The heartthrob of every girl at Seneca Valley High?
That Gordy Lexiter?"

"Yes." Vickie took a sip of her Prosecco. "*That* Gordon.
He's aged very well, Maura. But good grief, I've known
handsome men all my life and didn't have vapors over
them."

Maura snorted. "You did if you thought they were rich."
She straightened abruptly. "I am *not* a golddigger!"

Maura stole one of Vickie's sweet potato fries from her
plate. "Come on. Back in the day, you were more attracted
to a man's social status or bank account than you were the
man's looks. That's what makes this so interesting." Vickie
flipped her middle finger in the air, which only made Maura
laugh harder. "You know I love you. I'm not saying your
feelings for the men in your life didn't become…real. But
you never once told me you thought any man you were setting your sights on was *hot.* Classy, maybe. Distinguished.
Civilized. And let's not forget *rich.* But hot? Nope, that's
a new one."

Vickie sighed heavily. She wanted to object, but how do
you object to the truth?

"Maybe I've just been off the market too long. I'm getting desperate."

Maura shook her head. "You haven't been off the market that long. You were just dating the college dean last
year, weren't you?"

"Howard Greer and I were more friends than lovers. In

fact—" she drained her wineglass "—we were lovers exactly once, and it was memorable for all the wrong reasons."

"Ooh… I don't think I've heard this story." Maura rested her chin on her hand. "Do tell."

Her face heated. "I've never been a kiss-and-tell sort. Howard is a very nice man."

"And *I'm* not a tell-people-what's-told-me-in-confidence sort. Spill it."

Vickie rolled her eyes. "You know how it is…old person sex can be…complicated."

When she didn't continue, Maura leveled a look at her. "I *don't* know, since my husband's been dead for twenty years. Did Howard have chest pains in the middle of the act or what?"

"No. There wasn't an act at all. By the time he was ready, I wasn't, and it was all just a lot of awkward fumbling. We never discussed it—" she shrugged "—or tried it again."

They'd kept the relationship going, at least in public, for another few months, but they were nothing more than dinner dates for each other. A way to avoid being the odd one out. When Howard found someone else, they'd parted as friends.

"I'm sorry, Vickie. It's got to be difficult to build a relationship without some sort of…physical connection."

"I don't know." She flagged down their server for another glass of Prosecco, since Maura was driving. "I'm probably too old to be feeling horny."

Maura tipped her head back and laughed loudly. "I don't think there's an age limit on horniness. This is the twenty-first century and boomer women are tipping the *little old lady* stereotype on its ear. Look at Cecile and Charlie—if she's to be believed, those two are at it like a pair of rabbits every night. Remember how upset she got when the

book club read that shades book? She complained that the
BDSM scenes were not written accurately enough. I've
often wondered if they have a little 'red room of pain' in
that house somewhere…"

"Ew! God, don't put that image in my mind." Vickie pretended to scrub her eyes. "I don't know if anyone knows Cecile's actual age, but I know Charlie is at least seventy-two."

"I know!" Maura chuckled. "Maybe you should be talking to *her* about this little crush of yours. She might have
more practical advice than me if you decide to welcome
Gordy into some room that's not the kitchen."

Vickie liked Cecile. It was hard *not* to enjoy her quirky,
bubbly personality and the way she always looked on the
bright side of things. But to ask her for sex advice? *No,
thank you.*

Her feelings for Gordon were just a…physical craving.
And she did *not* do one-night stands, damn it. Not since
high school. Not since that back seat romp. With Gordon.

Zoey closed her laptop with a heavy sigh of relief. "Thank
God I don't have to do that every day."

"Mom, it was a twenty-minute video call."

"Yeah, but I spent three *hours* getting ready for it. Turn
off that ring light before I start seeing white circles everywhere." She motioned at the light that Hazel had contributed to her interview with Mason's employer. The appliance
company was based in Germany, but her interviewer had
been located in Baltimore. She'd assumed Mason would
just get her on a list of service people and she'd pick up an
occasional job out of it—there weren't that many commercial appliances in Rendezvous Falls. Instead, he'd recom-
mended her as a possible regional service tech, meaning
she could get jobs from businesses as far away as Rochester

or Syracuse. Either one was only a ninety-minute drive at most, and it opened up the possibility of a *lot* more business.

But first she needed to be interviewed after submitting her résumé. Mike had helped with the résumé—meaning he'd basically done it all. She would have just given them a list of machines she could fix, but Mike had made the document into a work of art, with glowing descriptions of her skill sets. She'd asked him to tone down a couple of lines that just felt over-the-top to her, but he and Hazel had teamed up to convince her to trust the two of them with her future.

She hadn't been sure how Mike would feel about helping, considering the weirdness the previous week with Mason. She didn't agree with Mason's assessment that there were *sparks* between her and her friend, but there had been *something* strange that night at the Shamrock. She and Mike had avoided any discussion of it. How do you discuss *sparks* anyway?

She'd used a riddle to get him to join Team Zoey.

Z: What disappears as soon as you say its name?

M: ????

Z: Silence. This is me, ending ours. I need your help with a job application.

There'd been a long pause, but eventually he'd responded.

M: Where and when?

They'd had a planning meeting at the kitchen table, with

Hazel and Mike both shouting out ideas. Zoey had finally assigned Hazel to help with the video call, and Mike to help with the résumé. Both things were far outside her comfort zone.

"Mom, we have to let Mike know how well this went—you nailed it!" Hazel grabbed her phone and began texting.

"Only because I had such a fabulous personal assistant to manage things. I'd have done the interview in the workshop after a long day and would have looked haggard and pale."

Hazel sat on the corner of the desk. "As if you could ever look haggard…except maybe when you haven't had coffee yet." She reached out and pushed Zoey's hair back over her shoulder. "But this is definitely better than that would have been. And Mike's idea of using Pop-pop's old product manuals on the bookshelves was fire—the guy loved it."

"He did," Zoey agreed. "I never thought of those being collector's items until he asked me to show him that washing machine manual from the 1930s. That belonged to *my* grandfather." It had been the perfect icebreaker on the video call.

It was a teacher's resource day at Hazel's school, so Zoey's little social media whiz was available to set up the lighting as well as take charge of her wardrobe and makeup. Zoey had vetoed a few options right away—no low-cut tops, wild hair or sparkles. She'd had to remind her daughter that it was a job interview and not an online video challenge. And the interview was for a service technician job, so she couldn't look like she was going to a rave.

Hazel had rolled her eyes at that. "No one says *rave* anymore, Mom."

They'd finally settled on a navy blue knit top under a tailored cotton shirt that Zoey had received as a gift from Vickie. The shirt had narrow stripes of blue and white, and the tiniest of eyelet ruffles along the edge of the collar. She'd never worn it before today. Hazel added what she called a *statement necklace*—it was a chunky twist of blue, green and gold beading. Zoey wasn't much for jewelry, but Hazel was so determined and invested in this project that she'd relented. If she lost the job because of a statement necklace, so be it.

But she *hadn't* lost the job. They'd been impressed with her résumé, as well as the way she'd answered their questions on how she'd approach various repairs, how she'd deal with certain customers and how skilled she was at filling out online reports. She'd completely fudged that answer, crossing her fingers in her lap as she assured them how computer-savvy she was.

"Oh, yay!" Hazel exclaimed. "Mike says he's taking us out for ice cream to celebrate!"

"I'll go clean up and change." The makeup felt like cake batter on her face. Hazel had insisted she needed a matte foundation so her face wouldn't shine on camera.

"What? No way, Mom. I worked too hard for this look to not let people see it."

"Not really helping my ego for you to make it sound like such an enormous effort."

"You know I didn't mean it that way. You just look… extra good today."

They met Mike at the Rendezvous Scoops ice cream stand on Route 14. Hazel ran to him the moment she saw him, talking a mile a minute about the interview. Zoey followed more slowly. It warmed her heart to see her daughter and her best friend laughing together. Mike had always been a part of Hazel's life, of course. When she was younger, she'd called him *Uncle Mike*, but a few years ago she'd asked him if *just Mike* was okay, and he'd told her it was fine, but she could drop the *just* because no man wants to be *just* anything. Hazel had giggled then, just like she was giggling now over something he'd said. They had the same irreverent sense of humor, so heaven only knew what it was about.

He'd ordered Zoey's favorite sundae without even having to ask—soft serve chocolate with marshmallow cream and chopped peanuts. When he turned from the window, he let out a wolf whistle.

"Dang, woman! You look like a movie star!"

"Right?" Hazel answered. "She was a queen on that interview. You should have seen her, Mike. I had two ring lights on her, set on soft light, of course. Then the guy noticed the old manuals you put on the shelf, and from that point on, she was *fire*."

Mike looked over Hazel's head to Zoey. "Fire is good? You nailed it?"

"I think so," she answered. They took their seats at one of the picnic tables. "I hope they don't expect me to look like this when I'm crawling behind some restaurant freezer unit, but…it worked for today." She touched her fingers to her cheek. "Let me know if my face starts melting off. I'm not used to this stuff."

He took her hand and pulled it away from her face. But he continued to hold her fingers, giving them a gentle squeeze. "Keep your hands off it if you want it to stay put. You look nice." He turned back to his ice cream—a banana boat sundae. "But you don't need makeup to look nice."

"Aww," she replied. "Look at you being all sweet and stuff. You're a good friend." Her voice was teasing, but she saw immediately that her words hit him somehow. His jaw moved side to side as he stared at his ice cream. When he looked back to her, his eyes were darker than usual. Was he angry? "What did I say?"

His mouth opened, then snapped shut. He shook his head. "Nothing. It's just… I meant it. I wasn't saying it as a friend."

She had no idea what to say to that. Before she could respond, Hazel asked Mike about some history trivia for a school project she was working on. He turned to her and joked that he was not old enough to be the town historian, but of course, he knew the answer. He explained at length that the Hilman House in Rendezvous Falls had two front doors because it was owned by two sisters who'd had a falling out in the early 1900s. They'd inherited the house together, but divided it right down the middle after their feud, keeping everything identical on either side.

When he finished, he told Hazel she'd dropped ice cream on her shirt. When she looked down, he bopped her nose with his finger. He'd been doing that joke for years, and Hazel laughed just like she had every other time he did it. Zoey hoped her daughter would hold on to that childish delight in things, even as she moved into teenhood. And she hoped Hazel would always have *just Mike* in her life to make her laugh so hard she snorted, like she was doing right now. Everyone needed a pal like that.

I wasn't saying it as a friend…

There's a good chance your platonic friend may be thinking differently…

Her plastic spoon fell into her bowl, but Mike and Hazel were too busy stealing each other's ice cream to notice. Had Mason been right about Mike? Was he looking for more than friendship? Her pulse quickened. What would that be like? She studied his profile. It's not as if she'd never noticed how good-looking he was—tall and lean, with that

chestnut hair that never wanted to behave and those chestnut eyes that shone with happiness when he was with her.
That mouth, with the lips that would surely feel strong and
warm on hers… She stabbed at her sundae with her spoon,
banishing that thought.

What about their friendship? She felt a quick surge of
panic. She couldn't afford to lose his friendship. Not now.
Hopefully not ever. And if they did kiss or…anything…
then their friendship would be forever changed. Maybe it
would be worth the risk, but what if it *wasn't*? They'd always laughed that they were living proof that men and
women really could be platonic friends. Why mess with
something that special?

Besides, she was just speculating on his feelings. Even
if he did feel differently toward her, he hadn't acted on
it. Hadn't talked about it. Maybe he'd already decided it
wouldn't be worth the risk to their friendship. Maybe she'd
imagined it all. Just because she was all made up and put
together, that didn't mean Mike McKinnon was going to
suddenly swoon over her. She wouldn't want him to.

She dropped Hazel at her friend Sienna's house so they
could work on their project together for a few hours. Sienna's mom, Monique, was going to bring Hazel home later.
Zoey stopped to pick up the mail from the box at the bottom of the drive and heard the crunch of tires behind her.
She squelched a groan when she saw who it was—Karen
Schiff. Her neighbor. And an annoying thorn in her side.

Karen thankfully didn't get out of her mega-size black
SUV, she just rolled down the window and gave Zoey a
sour look. Or maybe she always looked like she'd just bit-
ten into a lemon. *Neighbor* was a bit of a stretch, since you
couldn't even see the Schiff house in the summer. In the
winter, once the leaves had fallen, you could barely glimpse

the cement and glass monstrosity dug into the hilltop. Zoey's dad had parceled off five four-acre lots along the road from the family's original fifty acres years ago.

"Oh, hi, Karen!" Zoey beamed, silently praying this wasn't another complaint about the farm. "How are you today?"

"I thought you said you were moving those things." Karen's eyes flickered toward Dad's sculptures. She'd been grousing about the so-called *eyesores* since she and her husband moved in three years ago.

Here we go...

"Actually, what I said was that I was planning on relocating the sculptures *eventually*. I have a few other priorities, Karen." She paused, biting her lip to keep from getting too snarky. "My father built them, and he's been dead less than a year, so…"

"Well, you may want to make removing them more of a priority," Karen sniffed. "I'd hate to have to go to the zoning board about you running a business here."

What?

"My father's run a business here for decades."

"That doesn't make it right. I've checked, and this entire stretch is zoned for residential use only." She arched an eyebrow as if she'd hit a slam dunk, but Zoey had no idea what her point was.

"And my daughter and I *reside* here."

Karen sat back, putting her vehicle in Drive. "That argument doesn't help you. This is a residence, and you are operating a business here. Illegally. I'm willing to ignore that if you just tear down all this wreckage in your yard." She gave Zoey a pointed look. *"Immediately."*

"Yeah? Well, I think *you* need to leave…immediately."

Zoey watched her drive away, barely resisting the urge

to throw stones at the SUV. Had Karen just *threatened* her? Was she right about the shop being illegal? That couldn't be true. Dad would have known. But Karen had made her father's life miserable about his eclectic sculptures ever since she bought the place next door. He'd just ignored her, but then again, Karen had never seriously threatened legal action against him.

Zoey drove up to the house, her emotions alternating between fury and worry. It was a good thing she knew a great lawyer, and he'd be in her workshop tonight. Mike would know what to do.

CHAPTER NINE

MIKE LEANED BACK in his office chair and stared up at the ceiling. Zoey Hartford was his best friend. Whatever weird thoughts he was having had nothing to do with her personally. He just needed…sex. Yeah, that was it. He was horny, and for some reason his brain had focused on *Zoey* instead of a more reasonable option. Like that hot little number at the Shamrock this week. Taniesha's friend, Sherry Something. Even better than being hot, she'd been *interested*. She'd slipped him her number on a napkin, and he'd made a big show of tucking it in his front pocket with a wink.

Sherry was young—probably still in her twenties. She'd had a great laugh, and skin the color of a silky night sky. Maybe he should give her a call and see where things led. That might be enough to get his entire being to stop obsessing about Zoey. Who was his *friend.*

It was that night at the Shamrock that amped up his feelings so much. He'd watched her on her date with that Mason guy—tall, dark, handsome Mason. The guy who'd made her laugh. The guy who'd helped her grow her business. Good old Mason. What a great guy.

But not the guy for Zoey. Not when Mike was right there. The more Mike tried to bury his desire for her, the more she haunted his mind. After her *date night played out in front of him*, she'd even begun to show up in his dreams, like the sweetest torture.

The dreams were vivid—Zoey sprawled across a mattress in a tangle of sheets. Cooing his name, gesturing with a curving finger for him to join her on that bed. He'd wake up in a cold sweat every time, just as his dream-self was putting one knee on the edge of the mattress.

It made no sense. They'd never once come close to anything physical. He'd never picked up any hint of desire on her part. He'd never felt anything more than warm affection for her. He was going to single-handedly ruin *everything* if he didn't get his feelings under control. If she ever knew, things between them would change forever. Sure, there was a chance it could be as amazing as his dreams. But what if it wasn't?

He got to his feet so quickly that his chair scuttled backward across the floor and nearly toppled. It was the thought of failure that managed to clear his mind of Dream Zoey. No matter how tempting, *that* Zoey was a figment of his imagination. A logical but meaningless manifestation of his body craving the touch of a woman. Not craving Zoey Hartford specifically. That was just a mind trick, and he needed to ignore it. Because dreams weren't real, damn it.

It was after eight when he got to Zoey's that night, and he was surprised when Hazel came out of the shop as he parked the car. She seemed surprised to see him, too.

"Hi, Mike!"

"Hey, kid. Are you making over Mom's workspace now? I heard you're big on redecorating."

She giggled. "As if. I can't even talk her into repainting the place!" He chuckled, impressed that Hazel had even tried. She held up her phone. "I just needed her permission to babysit for Mary this weekend. But if you're going in there, be careful. She's on a rampage, but it's not my fault.

G'night." She headed to the house without offering any explanation for her mom's mood.

He tapped on the door, then went into the shop. He couldn't see Zoey, but he could hear her. She was off in the corner storage room, tossing things around and cursing a blue streak. He took his usual seat, setting the bottle of chardonnay on the worktable. It sounded as if boxes were being kicked or wrestled with in the storage room, but he did not offer to help. Safer to keep his distance. He managed to keep himself from flinching when she stomped back into the workshop. Her head snapped up when she saw him, then she dropped the armful of small boxes on the table.

"Oh, good—you're here. Open that bottle, will you? I need your legal expertise."

"My *legal* expertise? For what?" The only legal work he'd done for her had been when she and Chris bought—and then sold—their house. And he'd processed her dad's will and got this place into her name. But there weren't any loose ends with anything that he was aware of. He'd very intentionally avoided getting involved in the divorce proceedings, other than referring her to a good divorce attorney in Geneva.

"What do you know about zoning laws?" She pulled a couple of plastic glasses from the cupboard and opened the twist-off cap on the wine bottle.

"Zoning? For what?"

"Is it really illegal for me to have a business here?"

Mike blinked. The question was straight out of left field, and it took him a moment to switch gears.

"I'm lost," he admitted. "Why would you think that? What's happened?"

"It's that miserable, stuck-up *cow* that moved in next door." Zoey glared at him. "Karen Schiff. The one with that butt-ugly modern McMansion. I was getting the mail today when she pulled in the driveway in that gigantic SUV that looks like something the Secret Service would use." Zoey splashed wine into the two glasses and shoved one in his direction. She took a long swig from her glass. "I know she thinks this place is an eyesore, but I always figured that was her tough luck. We were here first. But today..." Zoey's face went stony and her voice hardened. "She told me I needed to *clean up the mess* around here—she was pointing at Dad's sculptures and the house and... God knows what. If I didn't, she'd *report* me for running a business in a residential area."

Mike gave her a reassuring smile. "Zoey, your dad has had this repair shop here for decades. She was just trying to intimidate you."

She searched his face as if trying to gauge his sincerity, which hurt a little. "Are you sure? She said this entire stretch of Hillside Road is zoned for residential use only."

Mike's former law partner, Glen Hilton, had been Rob's attorney when he parceled off the building lots from the original farm. It all happened before Mike had joined the firm. Glen retired five years ago and lived somewhere outside Phoenix these days. But Mike had been the attorney for most of the recent real estate transactions up here, including the Schiff's purchase of the lot nearest Zoe's place.

"The lots your dad sold off were zoned residential." He squinted, visualizing the paperwork from the real estate closings. "And I think this place was, too." That may have been a mistake on Glen's part when he separated the properties—he should have included the business on the original parcel. Unless the town wouldn't let him put that in the deed. "But again, your dad has had his shop here forever, and the Town of Rendezvous Falls has never raised a concern. Have they?"

Zoey hadn't sat down yet. She just stood there, shifting her weight back and forth, almost pacing in place. "I don't know, Mike. Not that I know of." She looked at him, and he could feel her fear from across the table. "Karen sounded so sure of herself. She had this thin, bitchy, mean girl smile like she knew something I didn't."

"What did you say to her after she said that?"

"I told her to get the hell off my property." Her cheeks went pink. "I may have thrown in a few curse words for good measure."

"No law against that." Mike chuckled, but his laughter faded when he saw the distress in her eyes. "Zoey, *relax*. I'll do some digging, but honestly—I think you're fine." He paused. "You said you *know* she thinks this place is an eyesore. How do you know that? Has she hassled you before this?" His protective temper started to rise when Zoey nodded.

"She gave Dad some grief about cleaning up and referred to his sculptures as *junk*." The corner of her mouth lifted. "Let's face it—our front yard is…unique. I was planning on moving most of them, if only to make mowing easier. But I was going to leave the wizard, the dragon and the maiden. They're Hazel's favorites."

He knew which figures she meant. They were his favorites, too. Made of a combination of tin and copper and gears and random parts, they were the closest to the house. Most of the other sculptures were more…modern art… than identifiable figures. The final few, closest to the road, looked like Rob had just welded together whatever pieces of metal he'd found lying around. It did make for an interesting sight. Drivers sometimes pulled over and got out to take selfies with the whimsical artwork.

Zoey wrinkled her nose. "I don't think Karen Schiff has any appreciation for the artwork. In fact, she hates it. She told Dad as much, and he got a few anonymous notes suggesting the *piles of junk* were embarrassing to his neighbors. We always assumed they'd come from her. The very first thing she said to me after Dad died was that she hoped I was going to remove *those monstrosities* from the property. The first thing, Mike. Like…*at the funeral*. Shook my hand, gave me a sad smile for show, then whispered her little threat." Zoey refilled her glass. Good thing she wasn't driving anywhere.

"Why didn't I know any of this?" Mike asked. "Do you still have any of those notes?"

Zoey had finally taken a seat. She swirled her glass in circles, staring at the white wine inside. "I think I do. Dad never threw anything away." She met his gaze. "You didn't know about it because I thought it was a nonissue. Having a busybody neighbor is hardly news. And I *do* plan on cleaning up the front and getting the house painted. But now she's threatening the business, and that's a whole other story. I guess I could rent a storefront somewhere, but that's a big expense. *And* a big hassle. I like being able to just walk out here for parts or to work on projects." She scowled again. "All because someone doesn't like driving past my family home to get to her ugly cinder block on the hill."

Mike walked around the worktable and put his hands on her shoulders, staring right into her wide eyes.

"Take a breath. Stop worrying. She's trying to intimidate you, but I'll check just to be safe. When it comes to zoning, nothing happens fast, and there are always hearings and warnings and a whole process to go through." He gave her a quick wink. "No one from the town zoning office is going to show up and raid the place, I promise. And don't forget, you've got yourself a top-notch lawyer."

It was the first real smile he'd seen from her all evening. "Yes, I do." Her voice was low and soft. They stared at each other for what seemed like long minutes ticking by. Neither of them moved. Neither spoke. He wasn't sure if either of them was breathing by the time he finally blinked. He was still holding her shoulders. And he didn't want to let go.

"Uh… Mike…" Zoey straightened her shoulders, but didn't pull away from his hold. He could kiss her. Holy hell, what a thought. He could *kiss* her. Right now.

And that was enough to make him step back. One wrong move, and he'd ruin everything. He wasn't brave enough to take that chance.

WHAT. WAS. HAPPENING?

Zoey stepped back at the same time Mike did, but distance did nothing to ease the energy pulsing through her. It began the instant his hands touched her shoulders. The moment when his gaze, heated and intense, met hers. Usually, Mike's presence, and his calm, rational advice, made Zoey feel more settled.

But not tonight. Tonight his touch—his close presence— set off a riot of emotions in her that she wasn't prepared for. Was this the chemistry Mason swore he saw?

I'm not saying it as a friend…

Oh, boy. Maybe Mike really *was* thinking of moving them out of the friend zone. Part of her thought it could be a wonderful idea. The other part of her was screaming that it had DISASTER written all over it. He was still staring at her.

"Zoey…" There was a new timbre to his voice, or maybe

she was noticing it for the very first time. A small fire began in her chest. *Whoa.* This was getting a little too real. She blinked, turning back to the table and picking up a screwdriver.

"I don't think I told you about my date with Mason, did I?" Her voice was loud and entirely too enthusiastic to her own ears.

Mike—sweet, smart Mike—shook his head with a bemused smile.

"I was there, remember?"

"Well, yeah. But you weren't at the table. You weren't *everywhere.*" She was just turning the same screw back and forth on the antique mechanical bank in front of her. "Don't you want to hear about it?"

He hesitated, then walked back to his chair on the other side of the table. He was going along with her distraction tactic.

He took a sip of his drink. "So, did you like him?"

It was unusual for either of them—much less *both* of them—to be so careful about what they were saying. There was a very large elephant somewhere in this room, but neither of them was ready to deal with it.

"Yes!" Oh, God, she was almost yelling *Deep breath.* "I mean…he's a nice guy, but it was just dinner. At least I got my first post-divorce date out of the way, right?"

"Sure." His frown was dangerously close to a scowl. "Did you get a kiss out of the deal?"

She snorted. "Uh…no. Just a handshake."

His eyebrows rose at that. "A *handshake*? Is the guy blind?"

"What does *that* mean?"

Mike chewed his lip. "I…uh…nothing. I mean…you seemed to have a nice time. You were both laughing and talking all evening. You're a beautiful woman. I'm just surprised he went with a handshake, that's all. Seems pretty lame on his part."

Zoey straightened, not sure she'd heard right. Had Mike just said she was *beautiful*? And why did that make something go all fluttery inside? It threw her enough that she lost control of her filter for a moment.

"The handshake was *your* fault." She pressed her lips together and closed her eyes. *Damn it.* She had not intended to tell him about Mason's opinions on the two of them.

"*My* fault? How do you figure?" He set his cup down, staring at her.

"It's stupid." She forced a laugh. "When you came over to the table, he thought he saw something between us. You know...*sparks*. Chemistry. I told him he was crazy, but he was sure he picked up some sort of jealousy vibe from you."

He opened his mouth as if to speak, then closed it again. He was staring at the worktable in front of him, and that near-scowl had returned.

"Mike? That *is* crazy, right?"

He blinked. "What? Oh...yeah. Totally." He cleared his throat. "We're just friends. Right?"

They stared at each other, and time seemed to come to a stop once more. His brown eyes were darker than usual. A vein jumped and pulsed in his neck. His jaw was tight, and he chewed on his lip again. She wanted to chew that lip, too. *Focus, Zoey.* They'd never had those feelings for each other before, but if they did...and acted on them...

"It's not like it would be the end of the world," she said, wincing that she'd said it out loud.

"*What* wouldn't be the end of the world? Us together? Zoey, I..."

Something shriveled inside of her. *Oh, God.* She'd misread this whole situation. He didn't want her like that after all. She swallowed hard. That was a good thing. It *was*. At the same time, it also hurt. But…she didn't *want* a relationship with Mike. That could ruin everything they had.

"Forget I said that." She waved both hands in front of her, rejecting the idea completely. "I told you I thought Mason was crazy. Some people can't accept that men and women can be good friends without things turning…icky."

His right brow arched high in amusement. "*Icky?* Is that what you think it would be like to have sex with me?" His mouth twisted. "Oh, shit. Forget I said *that*. I didn't mean to bring sex into this."

"I wasn't thinking the *sex* would be icky. I wasn't thinking about sex at all." But *now* she was! "Look, we're two red-blooded single people who probably haven't had enough—" she couldn't say *sex* out loud again "—of *that* in a while. But having…*that* with each other would be terrible." She rolled her eyes. "I don't mean the *sex* would be terrible. I'm sure we're both competent at that after all these years."

Mike's eyes were almost smoldering now, and her skin went hot when he spoke, his voice rough and low. "I'm more than competent, Zoey. Trust me."

Oh, I bet you are…

She cleared her throat sharply and busied herself putting the cap on the wine bottle and grabbing their glasses. Time to go.

"O-*kay*. This conversation has veered way off course, mister. We should have learned our lesson with that little discussion about boobs we had a few weeks ago. You're my best friend, but you are *not* the friend I'm going to discuss my sex life with. And I sure as hell don't want to hear about your…sexual prowess." Except she suddenly *did* want to know all about that. In detail. Firsthand.

There was a beat of silence before he answered. "I gotta tell you… I think we'd be great together."

She had no doubt of that. Her adrenaline spiked in both anticipation and fear, but reason took hold. "One great night wouldn't be worth the risk, Mike. I value our friendship too much to screw it up by…screwing around."

The heat in his eyes cooled, and she let out a sigh of relief. She wasn't sure how much longer she could remain the practical one while he was doing all that smoldering over there. He nodded.

"As usual, you're absolutely right. I'd never want to ruin us just for some…well, you know." He stood as she came around the table, then followed her to the door. "I'll look into that zoning issue, but don't lose any sleep over it." And just like that, he sounded like her pragmatic friend again.

"Oh…thanks."

Mike held the door open, and she had to brush against him as she walked by. She paused and glanced up, only to see him staring down at her. Damned if he wasn't smoldering again. With his face right there above hers. She could push up onto her toes and kiss those lips. She was clearly losing her mind tonight. This was *Mike*. His mouth quirked up into a suggestive grin for just a heartbeat, then he pulled back and urged her past him. He seemed in a hurry to get to his car and away from her. Zoey waved and headed into the house.

It wouldn't be Karen Schiff who would be making her lose sleep tonight.

CHAPTER TEN

VICKIE SET HER coffee cup down on the table very slowly. She didn't want to overreact, especially since Hazel was only thirteen. But the girl had just dropped an interesting tidbit of information, and Vickie needed to know more. She kept her voice as casual as she could.

"So Mike McKinnon stopped by the other night, eh? Is Zoey repairing something for him?"

Hazel's phone buzzed on the table, and she started to reach for it, then caught Vickie's warning look. Phones were never allowed at the Pendergast table, but they were sitting in the Hartford kitchen right now, so the rules were fuzzier. Vickie had stopped by to drop off some Italian cookies Helen Russo had given her—far too many cookies for Vickie to go through. Hazel sat back in her chair, smart enough to leave the phone where it was.

"I don't think so." Hazel shrugged. "He stops a lot to talk to Mom. They've been friends forever."

She wanted to ask Hazel to define *a lot*, but she didn't. The girl had enough to deal with now that her dad was not only getting married, but also having a baby with Genna.

"Yes, they have. I remember your mom hanging out with Mike and Mary when they were way younger than you are. She was an only child, like you, and the McKinnons gave her a big, noisy family to hang out with."

"I won't be an only child for long," Hazel reminded her.

"You're your *mother's* only child, sweetheart. You're her whole world." Even if Hazel marched to a completely different drummer than her mom.

Hazel's jeans had so many tears in them that Vickie wasn't sure how they managed to stay on her. Her bright pink crop top—which showed way too much skin for Vickie's taste—had white lace sleeves. Her hair was wound into a knot on the side of her head, with strands sticking out in a messy pinwheel that Vickie was sure had been carefully planned and styled. Hazel glanced at the phone again, then got to her feet with a heavy sigh.

"I gotta go study, sorry. I'm not sure when Mom will be back. She had a call over in Penn Yan this afternoon." She slipped the phone into her pocket as subtly as possible. Vickie had a feeling the only *studying* Hazel was going to do would be to check her social media accounts. But she stood and grabbed her bag.

"I need to do my grocery shopping. I'm glad we had a chance to chat. Let your mom know she can freeze some of those cookies if she wants. And tell her to stop by the house sometime. I haven't talked to her in a little while." And she definitely wanted to know more about Mike visiting her shop *a lot.*

She was surprised to see Gordon's truck in the driveway when she got home, next to a large stack of gray-blue wood that matched her porch railing. Or at least, something that looked like wood. This must be the composite deck material he'd told her about. She was gathering grocery bags from the trunk when he came around the corner of the house.

"Hey, Vicks! Look what arrived today!" He gestured at the pile of boards.

She ground her teeth together. "I swear to God, Gordon,

if you don't stop calling me that, I'm going to unplug the coffee machine in the mornings."

He took several bags from her hands and picked up the last few from the trunk, as well as a large package of paper towels. He headed toward the house ahead of her, glancing over his shoulder.

"I'll stop calling you Vicks when you stop calling me Gordon."

"But Gordon is your *name*." They went into the kitchen and she directed him to put the bags on the kitchen island.

"And Victoria is *your* given name, but you get mad if I use that, too." He winked. Good Lord, the man had a sexy wink. "You prefer Vickie. I prefer Gordy."

She started unpacking the groceries. To her surprise, he helped. And even knew where most of it went. He'd been paying attention all those times he'd sat in her kitchen over the past month. Usually just for coffee, but he'd stayed for dinner a few times. Only because she had extra food—cooking for one was a trial.

"Fine." She finally answered him. "Thanks for helping with the groceries, *Gordy*. But just so you know, that name makes you sound like some freckle-faced teenaged comic book character."

"Pretty sure the kids call them graphic novels these days, *Vickie*." He put the flour on the shelf, calling out to her from inside the pantry. "Sorry it took so long for the decking to arrive, but now that it's here, you should be back out there enjoying the view in no time. The framing and footers are all set, so it'll go quick. The color looks nice with the house."

Vickie carried a few cans of diced tomatoes and sauce into the small pantry just as he turned to come out. She couldn't stop fast enough, and nearly dropped the cans.

Gordon… *Gordy*…caught the first one that fell and stepped in close to help her hold on to the rest, his arm wrapping around her waist as he pushed her back against the wall. They both froze. She forgot what a big man he was—inches taller than her, with shoulders that were currently blocking her view of the door.

"Umm…thanks." She stammered the words. Neither of them made any effort to move.

"For what?"

"Uh…*what*?" She'd gotten lost in his blue eyes and couldn't remember what they were talking about.

He chuckled, his breath blowing soft across her cheek. When had he gotten that close? And could he get closer, please?

"What are you thanking me for?" He took the cans she was holding and set them on the shelf. Then he rested his hand on her cheek. "Or should I say…what would you *like* to thank me for?"

Vickie didn't move.

"I'm too old for this, Gordy."

"Too old for what?" His voice dropped even lower.

"For necking in the pantry as if we're hiding from my parents."

"We're not necking. We're…staring. Necking involves at least one kiss." He grinned. "Wanna neck?"

She intended to look offended. Or at least skeptical. Intimidating would work, too. Instead, she laughed.

"Come on, this is silly—" She gasped when he ducked his head and brushed his lips on hers. Her pulse fluttered. *Oh, my.*

"Does that feel silly to you?"

"Gordy…"

"Do you want me to stop?"

"No." She couldn't believe she was thinking this, but…
One little kiss wouldn't hurt anything.

"No, you don't want me to stop?" Gordy asked in a whisper.

"Stop being such a damn gentleman and kiss me!"

She didn't have to ask twice. His hand slid behind her head and his mouth landed on hers, hard with need. She'd kissed men in the past fifteen years. Polite, end of date kisses. She'd once told her friends that it seemed men lost interest in kissing after a certain age. But that all changed in her kitchen pantry late on a sunny June afternoon.

Not only did she want Gordy to kiss her, but the man knew how to kiss. And he was *very* interested in what he was doing. His mouth moved on hers in a way that made her knees go weak. And when he ran his tongue along her lips, she surrendered without a second thought. A soft moan rose in her throat, and he seemed to like that. He pulled her body against his and plunged his tongue deeper. Vicky lifted her hands and ran her fingers through his thick hair, causing him to growl in response. His hands slid down her body. She shivered. And suddenly it was all just…too much.

She couldn't step back, so she put her hands on his chest. She didn't have to push. He sensed her change of mood immediately and released her, stepping away. Vickie closed her eyes and focused on bringing her pulse and breathing back to the normal range.

"Are you okay?" Gordy sounded more amused than concerned.

"I'm fine." She pulled herself straight, trying to muster some dignity.

He chuckled. "Yes, you are most definitely fine."

She smacked his shoulder. "Don't be crass." But she couldn't help smiling at the praise. "I just got overwhelmed."

He laughed softly. "I'll take that as a compliment."

"You should. But I swear to God if you breathe a word about this to anyone…"

Gordy took another step back and raised his hands. "I'm not the type to kiss and tell. But if I was…" He turned to give her room to walk back into the kitchen. The pantry had suddenly become much too close. "…that was a kiss I'd definitely want to brag about. You haven't lost a beat in over forty years, babe. Still the best kisser in Rendezvous Falls."

She couldn't hold back a short laugh as she busied herself folding her grocery bags and setting them near the door to put back in her car. "I'm seventy. I am *not anyone's* 'babe.'" She glanced his way, surprisingly pleased to see how rumpled his hair was from her fingers. "But…that *was* a pretty great kiss. I just don't think it needs to happen again. I don't see a future for us, so what's the point?"

Better to end this now before she got any more invested.

He leaned back against the wall and crossed his arms. "Why don't we have a future?"

"Oh, come on. I'm not on the market. I don't think there even *is* a market for women my age." That didn't mean she wasn't lonely at night, but still. "And you're my contractor. Those sort of romances only work in romance novels—and the characters are *much* younger."

He studied her for a long moment, seeming unmoved by her rationale. "Sure, we've both got some years on us, but hopefully we've got some years *left*, too. You can't stop enjoying life just because of some date on your driver's license." He pushed off the wall and walked over to where she was standing. "We are *not* too old to enjoy a hot kiss. And we are also not too old to enjoy more than kissing, if you're interested." He winked as he headed past her and out the door. "Just to be clear… *I* am very interested."

CHAPTER ELEVEN

ZOEY STARED AT Hazel's tablet screen in something close to horror.

"You want a *black* ceiling in your bedroom?" She'd promised her room would be next, and Hazel had been putting together her wish list.

"A black ceiling with *glitter*." Hazel swiped from one photo to another on the screen. "See? You can buy the special flecks of glitter and add it to the paint. I'll run strings of those soft LED fairy lights around the top of the walls and the whole ceiling will sparkle at night." Hazel was kneeling on her bed, gesturing around the room. "It'll be the perfect background for my videos."

Zoey stared up at the currently normal, boring white ceiling. It was an old house, and the ceilings were tall—probably ten or eleven feet. A dark ceiling might make the room feel cozier. And she *had* promised that Hazel could pick any paint color she wanted. She never thought to exclude the ceiling from the list of options to be painted, but a deal was a deal.

"We'll need to use a *lot* of drop cloths, and we'll definitely want to do that first, before we tackle painting the walls. What color are you looking for there?" Zoey was almost afraid to ask.

Hazel grinned, scrolling on her tablet again. "Look at this deep pink, Mom. Isn't it gorge? And a perfect background color for my videos, right?" She rushed on before Zoey could answer. "If we could find a bed like this one…"

She pulled up an image of a massive upholstered bed, stud-ded with crystals. "It's just like the one Marina Lee has on that fashion video account, remember? It's sick."

Zoey did *not* remember. At this point, all she could see were dollar signs.

"Hazel...honey... I know I gave you free rein on paint..." She was already regretting that. "But there *is* a limit to the budget. I want you to be happy with the room, but we may have to compromise on a few of these items. Deal?"

Hazel's eyes went wide. "You mean I can do the black glitter ceiling?" She gave a wordless squeal and jumped into Zoey's arms.

"AND *THAT'S* WHEN I knew I'd been played." Zoey set her coffee down and sighed.

Vickie chuckled as she refilled their mugs. "By a thir-teen-year-old. I told you that kid was ahead of her years."

Vickie had called Zoey over to her place that afternoon to check the ice dispenser on her refrigerator, but it was only clogged with a few ice cubes. Something Zoey sus-pected Vickie could have taken care of herself.

"She knew if she showed me twenty expensive ideas that I'd reject most of them, but that she'd also *get* some of them. And that black ceiling is obviously something she really wants."

"Black is a trendy color for interiors right now. Lorraine Mansfield...she has that giant dark red Victorian down the road? Well, I was there for a festival committee meeting a month ago and they've done the entire entry hall with matte black walls. Not my taste, but they framed a few large paintings in heavy gilt frames and I have to admit it looked like something straight out of a home design magazine."

"We both know how trendy my daughter is, and how

expensive her taste is. That upholstered bed she wanted was eight thousand dollars. I'm not paying thousands for a sparkly bed in a room that'll be empty when she heads to college in five years."

Vicky looked thoughtful. "I might be able to help you with that. Come with me."

Zoey followed her upstairs and into one of Vickie's guest rooms. There was a towering upholstered bed against the wall. Vickie gestured toward it. "I've always thought that bed was too ornate for a guest room. It was a gift from my second mother-in-law, but I'd like something simpler in here. Hazel can have it if you think it meets her standards."

Vickie ran her hand over the tufted gold brocade on the headboard. "It looks dated now, but if we glue some big crystals over the buttons in the tufting, and run some sparkly trim around the edging on the top, I bet it'll be glitzy enough even for Hazel."

It definitely had potential. "Vickie, I can't let you just *give* us a bed. Put a price on it and I'll buy it."

Her suggestion clearly offended Vickie. "I *can* give my goddaughter's daughter an old, outdated bed if I want to. Either you take it or I'll donate it to the charity shop at St. Vincent's."

She knew Vickie would do it, too, if only out of spite. But still…

"What if Hazel does something to the fabric? Spills nail polish or grape juice or…"

"Is Hazel in the habit of splashing nail polish around?"

"No."

"Does she drink grape juice in bed?"

"Not that I know of, but—"

Vickie held up her hand. "Then stop worrying. All we need to do is get it from here to your house."

Zoey knew when she was defeated. "Wow…thank you,

Vickie. I won't be ready for furniture until after the painting is done, though."

"Good. That'll give me time to glitz it up before Hazel sees it."

They went back down to the kitchen, and Zoey took the coffee mugs to put them in the sink. Except…there were *already* two coffee mugs in the sink. And two sandwich plates in the dish rack. And two forks. "Looks like you've had company today…besides me, that is."

She thought nothing of it, assuming it was Maura or Cecile or one of the other book club ladies. But Vickie's long silence made her turn in curiosity. She'd known Vickie all her life, and she didn't think she'd ever seen her blush. Until right this minute. Well, this was interesting.

"If I didn't know better, Victoria Pendergast, I'd say you've had a gentleman caller." Vickie's blush deepened. "Oh, my *God*, you *did* have a man here. For coffee and…" She glanced at the plates. "Something. Who was it?"

Vickie straightened, her chin rising. "It wasn't a date or anything." She ran her hands down her tailored linen trousers. "If you *must* know, it was just Gordy Lexiter. We were discussing the work he's doing on the deck. And I served him coffee, because that's the kind of hostess I am."

Vickie *was* a great hostess. But there was more to this story than etiquette.

"And you didn't want to tell me because…?"

Vickie's eyes narrowed. "Because I knew you'd make a thing out of it, just like you're doing right now."

Zoey looked out the window at the dreary rain that had been falling all day long. "He wasn't working on the deck today, was he?"

"Not physically, but he still checked in."

I'll bet he did…

"And did he check in with you physically?"

"I'm not getting physical with anyone." Vickie's voice sharpened. "I just turned seventy, for God's sake. And I wouldn't be so tacky or desperate as to hit on my contractor." She sat and gave Zoey a quizzical look. "But you, on the other hand…"

Zoey shook her head with a snort. "You think *I'd* hit on your contractor?"

"No. But are you hitting on your attorney?"

The question left Zoe staring, her mouth open. All she could think about was the near miss she and Mike had the other night. He'd wanted to kiss her—she was sure of it. But that was just a moment. It didn't mean anything. She definitely didn't want people gossiping about it, so she rushed to deflect Vickie's curiosity.

"Have you hit your head recently? Are you smoking weed?" Zoey was protesting too strongly, and Vickie knew it.

"A simple *no* would have sufficed. Why does my simple question have you so worked up?"

They stared at each other for a moment before Zoey smiled. "Maybe for the same reason you got worked up about Gordy. Seems like both of us are in denial or…something. Do you *like* Gordy?"

"I've known him since high school."

"Do you *like* him?"

Vickie stared at the counter. "Yes, I think I do. And do you like Mike?"

"Mike and I are best friends. You know that."

"Hazel mentioned that he stops by your place quite a bit in the evenings."

Zoey felt a chill. "Was she upset about it? It really *is* innocent—we talk while I work on repairs. That's it."

Until he almost kissed me…

"Relax," Vickie said. "Hazel didn't seem concerned. I was just surprised when she said he's there *a lot*." She tipped her head to the side. "How often is *a lot*?"

"I don't know…a couple times a week."

Vickie arched a manicured eyebrow. "He's been coming over a couple times a week for *years* and nothing's happened? Not once?"

"Neither of us would risk our friendship for some…fling. Sex changes everything."

"I was thinking more like *dating*, but it's interesting that you jumped right to mentioning *sex*."

Zoey didn't have an answer for that. Her thoughts about Mike were getting more *interesting* all the time.

Vickie studied her, and a slow smile grew on her face. "So you *have* thought about it?"

Not until recently…

"Have you thought about sex with Gordy?" Vickie's mouth opened, but she didn't answer. Zoey chuckled. "I'll take that as a yes. So we've both got sex on the brain."

Vickie's mouth twitched. "I still say I'm too old. But you're not."

Zoey shook her head adamantly. "Even if Mike wasn't… well, my very best friend in the world, I wouldn't get into a relationship with him or anyone else. This is *Hazel's* year, not mine. She's been through enough upheaval. And she's told me more than once that she's glad I'm not dating."

She had to protect her daughter. Even if it meant resisting the delicious temptation of Mike McKinnon.

"HEY, DO YOU guys know anything about Karen and Edward Schiff? Up on the hill near Zoey's place?"

Mike was sitting in a booth at The Spot with Luke Rutledge, Logan Taggart and Mark Hudson. He'd originally planned on meeting Mark for lunch, but when they spotted Logan and Luke coming in, they'd shared their booth. It was tourist season and the place was busy.

Luke made a face. "Aren't they the ones who built that stupid cement house that looks more like a bunker than a home?"

Logan nodded. "I've seen that place—it's cut right into the side of the hill. Are they survivalists or something?"

"Believe it or not, Ed's an architect and author," Mark answered. "I've met him a few times at the college—he teaches some classes there." Mark taught classes at Brady College as well, being a well-known mural artist. "He's writing a book about the guy who designed all the Victorian houses in town He's quiet, but seems okay. Why?"

"His wife is hassling Zoey about her dad's place…well, it's *her* place now." Mike frowned into his coffee mug. "She hasn't had a chance to move those so-called sculptures of Rob's from the lawn, and Mrs. Schiff threatened her about having a business in a residentially zoned area."

Evie Hudson walked up to the table with a fresh pot of coffee and rested her hand on her husband Mark's shoulder. "Are you talking about *Karen* Schiff? Ugh. She's a stuck-up bee-yotcha. Nothing's ever good enough for her. The few times she shows up here, she spends the whole time loudly whining about Rendezvous Falls being so 'backward' and 'provincial.' They moved here from Long Island, and we're clearly not up to her exquisite standards."

She refilled their coffees and left the pot as she cleared the table. Mark smiled as she walked away with an armful of dishes. "Motherhood has not softened my wife's opinions in the least."

"Zoey has the same basic opinion of the woman," Mike

answered. He didn't like the idea of anyone causing Zoey any more stress than she already had in her life right now.

"She can't really cause trouble for Zoey, can she?" Luke asked.

"I don't think so. I'm working on it." Mike wished he could be more sure, but there were some odd little glitches in the zoning rules and how properties could be considered grandfathered so that newer rules didn't apply to them. He was still researching the history of Zoey's house, which had been in her father's family for multiple generations.

Logan frowned. "How can this guy be writing about Victorian houses when he built that eyesore?"

Mark sat back and spread his hands. "Art is subjective, guys. Ed told me once that his focus is on how every generation had a 'cutting-edge style' that was a modern sensation in its day. Like the over-the-top Victorian houses around here. In their time, they were the newest fad. They were considered contemporary then, just like his place is considered contemporary now."

"I get what you're saying about art," Logan said, "but personally, I'm hoping cement bunkers don't become a fad."

Even Mark agreed on that. They chatted about their respective businesses and families a bit longer, then headed out. Mike cautioned them to keep the conversation about Zoey to themselves, knowing they'd probably all tell their wives anyway.

He stopped at Zoey's that night and filled her in on what he'd found so far. He didn't mention the possible gray area about whether the place qualified for a grandfather clause. He didn't want her worrying about something that might never become an issue. Karen Schiff was probably bluffing anyway.

"I'm going to move some of Dad's sculptures," Zoey

said, her attention on the old sewing machine in front of her. She scowled down into the workings of the machine. "That seems to be her biggest beef, so she might back off."

"What are you going to do with them?"

"I haven't decided. For now, I'll put them behind the barn and out of sight."

That didn't feel right to Mike. She shouldn't have to hide her dad's artwork, no matter how quirky it was. He wasn't giving up on this battle with this Schiff woman.

Zoey took a can of air and sprayed it inside the sewing machine now that she had the top off, blowing out little bits of dust. Next came a small bottle of oil with a long, narrow tip on it, and she started putting drops of oil in the sewing machine. First on the camshaft in the front, then near the back, where a little arm moved the needle up and down, and finally in the bobbin area under that. She set the bottle down and blotted the excess. He enjoyed watching her puzzle out how to fix things.

"I don't think the sculptures are going anywhere this week, though," she sighed. "The weather's supposed to be really lousy."

"Yeah, I heard that, too. A couple of storm systems coming one after the other. Mary said we could get over five inches of rain by the time it's over." He made a mental note to get his Mustang securely in the garage.

She nodded. "Sounds like a good weekend for painting. Hazel will be with her dad, so I'm going to tackle the sparkly black ceiling she wants in her bedroom." She took a sip of the wine he'd brought. "We moved most of her furniture out this week, and I don't want her living in chaos for too long."

"So she just asks for a black ceiling and…gets it?" He couldn't help thinking it would be easier to just say *no*.

"Oh, you sweet, sweet innocent, you." Zoey rolled her eyes. "It's so obvious you don't have kids." There was a short silence before she rushed to apologize. "Oh, shit, that was insensitive as hell. I'm sorry, Mike."

He absorbed the hit and hid the sting. "It's okay. I get it. Not a parent. But can't you just refuse to use black paint?"

She tucked a folded piece of scrap fabric in the sewing machine and ran it, seeming pleased with the fact that it no longer made that clunking sound like it had before. As she screwed the top back on, she glanced over at him through long lashes.

"Have you heard the term *pick your battles*?" He nodded and she continued. "Half of a parent's life is spent doing just that. Deciding what's worth the argument and what's not. What decisions a child needs to make for herself, and which might be too risky to allow. Hazel's at that fun age where she *feels* grown-up, but she's really not." Zoey sat back and ran the sewing machine again, giving a nod of satisfaction as she slid it to the side. "So I try to give her some leeway to start being responsible for her own decisions. And I made a minor miscalculation that isn't her fault."

"What was that?"

"I told her she could pick the paint colors in her bedroom. It never occurred to me that she'd go with a black ceiling, but I made her a promise. And who cares what color the ceiling is, anyway? It's not like I'm worried about resale value—pretty sure I'll be living here for a long time to come."

"And if she hates it when it's done?" That seemed pretty likely—it was a *black* ceiling—but then again, he wasn't a thirteen-year-old girl.

"If she does, then she'll learn an important lesson about having the ability to make decisions. Sometimes we make *bad* ones, and there are consequences. In this case, the consequence would be living with it, or earning the money to repaint it."

Was it any wonder Mike never thought he'd make a great parent? Zoey seemed to be such a natural, but he had the feeling he'd do everything wrong.

"How do you know which battles to choose?"

"Well, that's where *I* have to deal with the consequences of decision-making." Her mouth twisted. "It's not a perfect science. Rule number one for me is Keep Her Safe. After that, it's a crapshoot. I figure if I *fight everything* she wants, she'll resent me and ignore any life lessons I try to teach. If I *give* her everything she wants, I'll create an entitled brat who'll have a hard time succeeding in life as an adult. And that's my job—to create a good adult." She shrugged. "I'm doing it all without a lot of guidance, since I didn't *have* a mom growing up. A lot of times I'm winging it— just doing the best I can."

"Such a huge responsibility..." He spoke the words more to himself than to her.

"And a huge privilege," she answered. "Occasionally, it's rewarding and...dare I say it...fun." Her head tilted. "Kids were a hot topic for you and Becca, right?"

He chewed his lip, staring at the table. "She wanted to start a family, but I kept saying I wasn't ready. She realized I might *never* be ready, and...yeah, it was a problem for us."

He hated thinking of the tears Becca shed because of him. He'd kept putting off the decision to start a family, figuring they had time. And then she was gone.

"But you *like* children, right?" The surprise in Zoey's voice made him feel worse.

"I'm not an ogre, okay? I *love* my nieces and nephews and all the new little cousins. I just never knew if I was parent material. There are people who would crawl across hot coals to have kids, and I've…" He swallowed hard. "I've never felt that way. So I kept putting it off until…"

Zoey surprised him by coming around the table and catching him up in a fierce hug. He was still sitting, and she pulled him tight so that his head was on her shoulder. He stiffened at first, then relaxed into her embrace. Her voice went soft and low.

"I never said you were an ogre. I've seen how great you are with children. But it's okay to *not* have kids, Mike. Lots of people make that choice."

It was odd how comforted he felt with his head resting on her. When was the last time he'd been held like this? He couldn't remember.

"Looking back, I think Becca hoped I'd change my mind eventually. We'd argued about it the weekend she died."

That last argument had been one of their worst. Hurtful things were said very loudly. The next day she was gone, leaving a gaping hole in him that would forever be filled with guilt. Zoey gave him a gentle squeeze and stepped back, breaking their contact. It took all his strength not to pull her back to him.

"It's sad that you argued about it before the accident, but your argument didn't cause what happened. And she knew how much you loved her. My God, everyone called you the biggest lovebirds ever. The two of you lit up a room. You would have figured it out if you'd had the chance."

Mike rubbed the back of his neck. "Maybe. She would have been a great mom."

"Becca? Oh, my God, yes."

"She never got the chance…" Because of him.

There was a beat of silence before Zoey cleared her

throat. "Did I tell you Chris is having a baby? I mean... *Genna's* having a baby, with Chris."

He stared, trying to gauge her feelings. "And what do you think about that?"

"I'm happy for them, I guess. But also annoyed. We tried for more children and it just didn't happen. And now...surprise! As soon as he leaves me, he's having a baby." Her gaze met his. "My point in telling you is that parenthood and having children or not having children...it's all really fucking complicated, okay? All you can do is your best, and then cross your fingers that your best is good enough."

"Do *you* want another child?"

She laughed, and his mood lightened immediately at the sound. "Oh, *hell* no! Hazel's thirteen—no way do I want to go back to changing diapers again. No, thank you." Her laughter faded. "There was a time when she was younger that I would have liked to have another, but that moment has passed." She tipped her head to the side. "And *this* is a conversation I never expected us to have. We've talked about everything else in the world, but wanting babies is...whew."

"Yeah." It was a dumb response, but it was all he had right now. Zoey was still showing up in his dreams at night—more so since that little *moment* they had last week when they got lost in each other's eyes. Something had shifted in their relationship without either of them doing anything to create that shift. It was just...there. *She* was just there. In his thoughts. In his dreams. All this baby talk and the hug and the deep sharing was not helping. Hopefully, this odd little phase they were in would pass before either one of them did something stupid.

CHAPTER TWELVE

"THERE YOU GO, IRIS. Your old vacuum cleaner should run good as new now."

Zoey set the twenty-year-old upright vacuum inside the door to Iris's apartment at the Taggart Inn. She didn't always offer pick up and return service, but when her client was over eighty, she made an exception.

"Thanks so much." Iris looked at the vacuum with approval. "Logan offered to buy me a new one, but I've never been a fan of this trend where everything is disposable. This one is light enough for me to use easily, and as long as it keeps sucking up dirt, I'll keep using it."

Zoey reached in her pocket. "That reminds me…the vacuum picked up more than dirt this time." She handed Iris a small cat toy shaped like a bird. "This was stuck in the intake tube, and that's why it lost suction."

"Well, hell." Iris scowled at the toy. "That darned Mr. Whiskers must have batted it under the bed or something. I'll be more careful. What do I owe you?"

"Nothing." Zoey talked over Iris's protests. "I charged you for a tune-up just last month, and all I did was spend sixty seconds pulling out the cat toy."

Iris, petite and silver haired, stared hard, then stepped back. "At least come in and have some tea with me." Zoey knew Iris was a big Anglophile. The woman loved her British porcelain tea sets and delicate Victorian furniture. And she always had a tin of Scottish shortbread on hand. It was tempting, but she shook her head.

"I'd better not. The wind's already picking up outside, and I want to get home before that cold front hits."

Iris looked at the large windows behind her. "Oh, it is getting dark out there, isn't it? You go on, then, and batten down the hatches for you and Hazel before the storm."

"It's just me this weekend. Hazel's with her dad and Genna. They're working on the new nursery." Maybe the more she said it out loud, the better she'd feel about it. But that hadn't worked yet.

Iris's blue eyes narrowed in concern. "And how do you and Hazel feel about a new baby? And a wedding, too, right?"

Zoey blew out a sigh. Iris had been a part of her life for as long as Vickie had been. And Iris was even *less* likely to accept a bullshit answer.

"It is what it is. I'm trying to stay upbeat for Hazel's sake, and…" She lifted a shoulder. "It's not like I don't want Chris to be happy. He and I are *over*-over. Genna's been nice to Hazel. And a baby is, well…it's a *baby*. I can't resent them for having a baby."

"Sure you can," Iris scoffed. "You can feel any way you want to. But don't you think it would be easier to handle if you were building a fresh start of your own with someone? Are you sure that nice sales guy, Mason, didn't raise any sparks?"

"Not a single one," she answered. Although he'd noticed the sparks between her and Mike. "Besides, I've got my hands full with the house and Hazel. A man in my life is the last thing I need right now. And it's the *very* last thing Hazel needs. She has enough new people entering her life." She gave Iris a reassuring smile. "When the time's right,

I'll put myself out there again. When Hazel's ready." She reached up to brush her hair behind her ear and winced, forgetting about the wrist she'd strained last night.

Iris, who never missed anything, reached out and took Zoey's forearm. "Your wrist is swollen. What happened?"

"It's nothing. I'm painting the ceiling in Hazel's room and I missed the last rung on the stepladder last night." The moment when she'd stepped back into nothing but air had been scary. But she was only a foot above the floor, so the fall wasn't bad. She'd tried to break her tumble with her hand and her wrist had paid the price. She saw the worry in Iris's eyes. "I'm *fine*. I'll put ice on it later."

She headed out to the truck and spotted Iris's grandson, Logan, and his wife, Piper, bringing in the tables and chairs from the inn's wide, wraparound porch. They ran the Taggart Inn now. Zoey maintained their commercial kitchen appliances and they'd become friends. Piper's son, Ethan, was in high school. Her daughter, Lily, was seven, and she was…*helping* her mom and stepdad with the furniture storage right now. But mostly, she was getting in the way, which Logan pointed out several times. Lily spotted Zoey and ran out to greet her in the parking lot.

Logan, for all of his grumbling about Lily being more hindrance than help, immediately noticed her absence and looked for her.

"Hey, Zoey!" He put down the stack of chairs he was carrying and came down off the porch. "Gran told me her old vacuum was acting up. Is it time for a new one?"

"Nope." Zoey had lifted Lily for a hug, and the little blonde was wrapped around her like Velcro. She remembered when Hazel used to be this small…and this affectionate. "Oof… Lily, you're gonna be too big for hugs before long. At least hugs where I have to pick you up!" Logan plucked Lily from Zoey's arms and propped her on his hip. Well over six feet tall and built like a mountain, he had no problem holding the girl. Zoey laughed. "Well, *you'll* be able to carry her around for quite a while longer. Your grandmother vacuumed up one of the cat's toys and clogged it, that's all."

"Silly Mr. Whiskers!" Lily giggled. "I wonder if it was the catnip toy I gave him last week?" She squirmed and Logan set her down so she could go help her mom on the porch. Piper gave a wave to Zoey and a pointed look to Logan, tapping her watch. Logan nodded, then turned back to Zoey.

"Every weather report I hear makes this storm sound worse. I can't decide if they're overreacting or if it really is going to be that wild. They're talking about hurricane-strength straight-line winds tonight." He nodded toward the stacks of tables and chairs on the porch. "We figured better safe than sorry."

Zoey thought about the lawn chairs and grill out on the back patio at the house. "I'll let you get back to it. I need to bring in a few things myself."

"You need help?"

Zoey opened the truck door. "Nope. I'm fine." The answer was automatic. As her friends liked to point out, she wasn't great at accepting help. "Just a few things to put in the barn, then close it up tight and hunker down in the house. I'm painting Hazel's bedroom this weekend while she's at her dad's. I hope to get a second coat on the ceiling today. It's one of those projects that's easier to do alone. You know how it is."

"Yup," Logan answered. "Kinda like moving porch furniture *without* the help of a seven-year-old. Still…don't hesitate to call if you need anything."

The northern sky grew steadily darker as she drove home. Her phone lit up with alerts from the weather app, but the worst of it wasn't supposed to hit until the overnight hours. The rain racing in now was supposed to be brief, leading the system in advance of the primary storm front. She carried the lighter chairs into the barn and slid the heavy Adirondack chairs close to the side of the house. She stared at the grill, trying to decide what would be safest. Next to the house seemed like a bad idea, so she wheeled it across the driveway and inside the barn.

By the time she had everything secured and was headed into the house, there was thunder rumbling in the distance. She warmed up a frozen dinner in the microwave. Cooking for one was often more effort than it was worth. Once she'd eaten, she headed upstairs to attack Hazel's ceiling.

It was very definitely black after two coats. But it was not sparkly yet. She read the instructions on the packages of glitter paint additive. She'd watched half a dozen online videos on how to use the stuff successfully, but she was still nervous. She stirred two packages of silver glitter into a gallon of black paint. Hazel said she wanted it *really sparkly*. Zoey added two *more* packages, then stirred until the glitter seemed to vanish into the paint. All the instructions said it would reappear as it was applied, and would sparkle once the paint was dry.

It took two hours to finish the ceiling. The extra-thick paint and glitter mixture made the roller heavier than usual, and her wrist was beginning to throb. She was just finishing up the last corner when her phone buzzed and made a weird alarm sound. It was the weather app. That couldn't be good.

The predicted storms were now turning into some sort of mega system that was creating both tornadoes and derecho winds—straight-line winds up to 100 mph in spots. Power was out for tens of thousands in Buffalo and now Rochester. And it was due to sweep through the Finger Lakes in the next half hour.

She ran through a mental checklist as she washed up the paintbrushes and roller in the basement utility sink. Patio furniture? In the barn. Grill? In the barn. Hanging flower baskets on the front porch? She'd taken them down and grouped them together next to the house. Her car and work truck? In the barn. Dad's sculptures were on their own, but most were bolted on cement bases. Other than that, she just had to worry about the house and barn themselves, and there wasn't much she could do about that but pray.

Both structures were well over a hundred years old. Her dad hadn't been much for paint and frills, but he was a fixer, and he'd been proud of the sturdy old family homestead. He'd replaced the roof on the house not that long before he died, so that should hold. Unless they got a literal tornado... But this was Upstate New York, not Kansas. That seemed unlikely.

There were two large maple trees in front of the house, and a tall, ailing ash tree near the driveway. There was nothing she could do about them, either. She decided against cowering down here in the dark, low-ceilinged basement for the next two hours. If a serious warning came across her phone, it would only take her a minute to dash down the stairs to safety from the kitchen.

Thunder was rumbling when she got upstairs, and it sounded more ominous than usual. It was just boomboom-boomboom without stopping. She'd never been afraid of storms, but this sounded bad. She was glad Hazel was with Chris and his new house with a built-in generator. They'd all be fine.

Dad taught her to appreciate the power of nature, so she

stepped outside the back door to watch the light show in the northwest sky. She could easily dash inside when it got too close. The crunch of tires behind her made her spin in surprise. *Mike?* He hadn't texted that he was coming over. Had he not heard the forecast?

He tucked his SUV right next to the barn. She would have opened the barn doors for him, but there wasn't any room left inside. He got out and looked up at the eerily flickering sky, then around the backyard. If he was worried about trees, he was safe. The giant oak that had once shaded the parking area had come down in a storm ten years ago. Other than that, the largest "trees" back here were lilacs and rose of Sharons.

"Mike, what are you doing here?"

"Checking on you."

CHAPTER THIRTEEN

THOSE THREE SIMPLE words did something very complicated to Zoey's heart. She could be offended that he thought she *needed* checking on. Instead, she felt flattered and…cared for. *Could* she take care of herself? Of course. But it was nice to know someone else cared enough to show up. The fact that it was Mike McKinnon added a layer of warmth to her complicated feelings, softening the edges and making her skin tingle. The man who'd been showing up in her dreams lately—and *not* as just a pal—had come through for her without being asked.

The first giant drop of rain that splatted on her cheek felt like someone had thrown a tiny water balloon at her face. And another. And *another*.

Mike walked by her, sliding his arm around her waist and pulling her with him toward the house. "Inside seems like a really good idea right now."

She went along without saying a word until they were safe and dry in the kitchen.

"Mike, you should get home before it gets bad—"

A huge crash of thunder overhead made the pictures on the kitchen wall rattle. The lights flickered briefly.

"Too late for that. I ran into Logan at the grocery store—the place was nuts with people grabbing milk and bread—and Iris told him you'd hurt your wrist. I wanted to make sure you were able to batten down the hatches here." A flash of lightning lit up the windows in blue light, followed by thunder that sounded like dynamite being set off outside the walls. Her shoulders tensed, and Mike moved closer. "But I guess I'm too late for that, too. You were able to get everything put away?"

She nodded. "I would have opened the barn door for you to park inside, but it's full of patio furniture and vehicles."

"My car will be fine where it—"

The wind slammed into the western corner of the house so hard the timbers groaned from it. It wasn't just a single gust—it stayed at the same intensity, whistling at a high pitch as it roared past the windows and doors and wrapped around the house.

"Jesus," Mike muttered. "Can't believe I'm saying this, but…basement?"

"Good idea." Zoey opened the door and headed down ahead of him. They were near the bottom of the wooden stairs when the power went out abruptly, throwing them into pitch darkness. Mike pulled out his phone and had the flashlight on within seconds, lighting the way. She reached up on a nearby shelf and found an LED lantern. There were half a dozen of the things scattered around the house for emergencies. She didn't mind storms, but she hated being stuck in the dark.

She turned it on and held it high. "I guess they weren't kidding about this storm being bad, huh?"

The wind was still pushing hard against the house. She was confident the place was solid enough to take it, but for how long? Even with the lantern on, dark shadows made the old basement look scarier than usual. She was glad she wasn't hiding down here alone. "Thanks for coming, Mike."

His eyebrows lowered, sending angled shadows across his cheeks. "That's what friends do."

She couldn't help thinking that she had plenty of friends, but Mike was the only one who'd shown up in the face of hurricane-strength winds.

"You're hiding in my basement with me, which kinda goes above and beyond the call of friend duty."

Mike was looking up, listening to the groans of the old house in the wind. "Well, maybe we're beyond being just friends."

He went still, as if realizing what he'd said. Their eyes met, and Zoey cleared her throat. "Umm…maybe you're right. You're already the best friend I have, so… I mean, we're more than casual friends…" She was babbling.

"We're definitely more than casual," Mike agreed. "And yeah, I guess you could say we're *besties*. I can talk to you about anything. You make me laugh like no one else can. And we…"

"We show up for each other?" She took a step forward and rested her hand on his arm. Was it the shadows from the lantern light, or did his eyes just go dark with intensity?

"We show up for each other." He rested his hand over hers, still on his forearm. "And lately, it feels like something else might be happening, but Zoey…"

"It scares you?" She rushed on. "I know, it scares me, too."

There was a long pause where the only sound was that of the wind whistling past the basement windows.

"What if…" Mike hesitated again. "What if we're making this more than it is? You know what they say—people always want what they can't have. Maybe this…obsession we have is just that. One of those things that feels bigger the more we try to ignore it."

"So…" she started. "If we gave in to temptation, the feeling might just…go away?" She seriously doubted it, but temptation was just that—tempting. Powerful. Hard to ignore.

He started to answer, but was interrupted by a brand-new sound from outside. A horrible ripping sound, then a loud, solid *thump* that made the house shudder. Mike slid his arm around her waist. "Pretty sure that was a tree coming down. Or at least part of one."

"Damn it. I love my trees." It came from the front of the house, so it had to be one of the beautiful maples or the big ash.

"The good news is I don't think it hit the house. I didn't hear anything breaking up there."

They both listened, carefully avoiding going any further with that tiptoeing-toward-temptation conversation before the crash.

What if...?

Mike stepped back. "It sounds like it might be letting up." He opened his phone screen and pulled up his weather map, showing it to Zoey. The dark red line along the front, filled with warning cones, was moving south and east of Rendezvous Falls now.

They headed up the stairs, led by the light of the lantern Zoey was holding. She took another from the kitchen cabinet and set it on the table, then handed a long black flashlight to Mike.

"This was Dad's, and he swore by it. It's got eight batteries in it, so it weighs a ton, but that thing is bright."

Mike held it up with a grin. "This could double as a weapon. Let's go see the damage out there."

His SUV was safe—covered with leaves and twigs, but no damage. In the darkness and soft rain, it seemed the entire yard and driveway were carpeted in leaves stripped from the trees. A few larger branches were down, with one big limb leaning against the end of the barn. They walked over to look, but it didn't seem to have hurt anything. Zoey let out a gasp when they turned to look down the driveway.

The ash tree was down. It lay across the driveway at an angle, with the top of the tall tree brushing against the front porch. Tears sprang to Zoey's eyes. It was like looking at the remains of a giant old friend. While she mourned, Mike was more practical. He walked down to inspect the tree, the driveway, and finally back up to look at the porch. She caught up with him there. He shook his head in her direction.

"You lost a piece of railing and a section of the rain gutter, but nothing that can't be fixed. It fell at just the right angle to miss the house and most of your dad's sculptures. I can't tell if it missed them all, but this is the top of the tree, so it may not have hurt them too much."

"Losing Dad's artwork would really make Karen Schiff's day, wouldn't it?" She glared into the darkness in the direction of the cement house. Looked like power was out over there, too, because everything was pitch-black. In fact… She looked down into the valley. "Wow—the whole town lost power." Where Rendezvous Falls usually glowed with streetlights and houselights, there was nothing but darkness. The only light around the lake was the flickering lightning from the quickly receding storm.

Mike pointed. "You can tell who has generators." Here and there, tiny points of light were appearing in a scattered pattern. "I don't suppose you…?"

She shook her head. "No such luck. Dad never saw the need. The power doesn't usually go out for long up here. We have a gas stove for cooking, a fireplace for heat and windows to open in the summer to stay cool."

"Sounds like Rob's logic." He shone the flashlight along

the tree trunk. "I hope you can cook breakfast on that stove, 'cuz I'm not going anywhere until that tree is moved, and that's not happening until daylight."

It took her a moment to realize what he was saying. The driveway was impassable, with no way to get around the tree, at least not in a vehicle. Mike was going to be spending the night. All night. With her. Well...not *with* her, but under the same roof. All. Night. Long.

She took a deep breath. "Uh...sure. No problem. You can use Dad's old room." Her mind was doing its best to avoid considering the opportunities this would present. *Take your mind off Mike. Think about anything else. Like...*

"Hazel." She reached for her phone. "Oh, my God. I need to check on her. And Vickie. And..."

Mike took her arm and led her toward the back door. "I need to check on my family, too. Let's get inside." He held the door open. "I may have to charge my phone in the car later."

"I always keep a couple of solar phone chargers in the kitchen window. They should take care of it if you want to keep your phone handy."

Mike chuckled. "Why am I not surprised?"

"What does that mean?"

"Nothing. It's just..." He turned off the flashlight and grabbed the spare lantern from the table. "You're the type to be prepared for things. The lanterns. The flashlight. The chargers. Other than a generator, you're ready for anything." He headed out of the kitchen. "I'll make my calls in the living room so we're not talking over each other. Got any whiskey in the house?"

She rolled her eyes. "Of course. Ready for anything, remember?"

He laughed as he headed down the hallway.

The only thing she *wasn't* ready for was Mike McKinnon spending the night in her house.

MIKE PINCHED THE bridge of his nose and closed his eyes. He should have just texted his twin sister instead of calling. She was having entirely too much fun on his behalf.

"So you're saying you're *stuck* at Zoey's all night? How...convenient."

"Mary, I doubt Zoey finds anything *convenient* about a giant tree across her driveway. She can't get out, either, remember?"

"You said Hazel's okay, right?"

"Yes, she's with Chris." Zoey had popped her head into the living room a few minutes ago to announce Hazel and her dad were okay, other than no power. That seemed to be the case throughout most of Rendezvous Falls. "Sis, I gotta call a few other people yet, and I only have so much battery left. You're sure Nana's okay? And the pub?"

"Yes. Timothy brought Nana to his place for the night because he has a generator. Finn said the pub is still standing, but there was a roof leak in the dining room." She paused, saying something about ice cream to someone near her before coming back to the call. "I promised the kids we'd 'rescue' the ice cream in the freezer before it melts. Tim said the roads are a mess—trees down, power lines down. Utility vehicles showing up everywhere. But he drove by your house and said it looks okay. I don't know about your office, but I heard that downtown wasn't too bad."

"That's what Logan said." He walked over and looked out the window before remembering there was nothing to see out there but darkness. "A big limb did some damage to the garage behind the inn, but he walked over to Main Street and said the storefronts all look okay."

He made one more call after talking to Mary. Owen Cooper had recently opened a landscaping business in town. His new bride, Lucy, ran the flower shop on Main Street. Owen answered after the third ring, sounding out of breath.

"Owen, is everything okay at your place?" he asked.

"Mike? Yeah. We're good." He blew out another heavy breath. "We just got back inside from inspecting things, and I tripped over a damn limb that came down. Knocked the wind right out of me, and amused my wife to no end. How about you?"

Mike explained the situation at Zoey's, with a tree that needed removing before he'd be able to leave. Obviously it would have to wait for daylight. There was a long pause.

"You know I'm a landscaper and not a lumberjack, right?"

"Yeah, but you still deal with trees," Mike replied.

Owen laughed. "Dude, I plant saplings." He paused. "Let me make some calls. I know Zayne Rutledge has a chainsaw and has done some tree work. We should be able to at least get it off the driveway, but not until morning."

He could hear Zoey's laughter in the kitchen as he ended the call. The sound was irresistible. He followed it to find her sitting at the kitchen table with her knees under her chin and her feet on the chair seat. For a tall woman, she was pretty flexible. He quickly banished all thoughts of her flexibility from his mind.

She was in jeans and a flannel shirt worn open over a T-shirt, with the sleeves rolled up to her elbows. He sometimes teased her about the *Zoey Uniform*, but it suited her. She looked up at him with a wide smile, holding the phone to her ear.

"I promise we're fine, Whitney. I'm glad the winery is okay. You guys stay warm and safe tonight." She listened to Whitney's reply and rolled her eyes. "Oh, come on. Mike and I are friends, and I have a spare room. This is not an only-one-bed situation." Another pause. "I'm hanging up now." She half sang the words, then put the phone on the table and shook her head. "Now that our friends are all getting married, they've turned into mushy romantics."

He grabbed a bottle of whiskey from the counter and two glasses from the cupboard. Then he joined her at the table and splashed whiskey in both glasses. He held his glass up with a grin.

"I'm not sure I know how to drink with you using actual glasses instead of red plastic cups." He drained his glass, closing his eyes as it warmed him from the inside. Zoey returned his toast and took a sip.

"Ooh, that feels so good..." The words came out as a coo, soft and sensual.

Damn. He'd done so well *not* thinking about Zoey sleeping in a bed just one room from his tonight. Now it was the *only* thing he could think about. Would she wear a nightgown? Pajamas? Did she sleep in the nude? What would *that* look like? He refilled his glass.

Zoey let out a long sigh. Her cheeks had just a touch of pink by the lantern light. Was that from the whiskey, or was she thinking the same thing he was?

She took a bigger gulp of her drink, then coughed a little as it went down. Before he could say anything, she dropped her feet to the floor and stood, looking determined.

"Speaking of sleeping, we may as well head up and get some." Her cheeks darkened. "Some *sleep*, I mean. The power's not coming on anytime soon, so there's not much else to do."

He could think of several things to do, but she was right. It was early for him to go to bed, but the sooner they got themselves into separate rooms, the better. He stood and handed her one of the lanterns, then followed her up the stairs. Zoey's very fine backside swayed back and forth in front of him, and, well—he *was* a man, after all. He forced his body to stand down, but it wasn't easy.

She pointed to her dad's old room. Mike hadn't been upstairs in this house in years, but he knew the way. Rob had taken the smaller room so that Zoey could have the master suite as her own as a teen. She'd told Mike she'd moved right back into it after she and Hazel took up residence, because Hazel wanted the long, narrow bedroom with the view of the wooded hill behind the house.

He started toward his room, then stopped, turning to ask Zoey where the sheets and towels were. To his surprise, she was right behind him. So close she almost walked right into his chest when he turned. Her eyes went wide.

"Whoa." She cleared her throat, but didn't step back. "I was just going to tell you to be careful in the bathroom. It takes a while for the hot water to get up here from the basement. And it's brimming with teenage girl stuff. It's basically Hazel's bathroom, so...sorry."

"I think I can handle it. Where will I find sheets and towels?" He didn't step back, either, so they were face-to-face in the hallway. Almost touching. Staring at each other.

Shadows from their lanterns moved across the walls like ripples of water. He felt the moment when the mood changed, almost as if someone had flipped a switch. His adrenaline spiked. Oddly enough, he had a fleeting thought of Becca. How he'd been afraid to begin a family. Afraid to commit. Afraid, period. And here he was, with Zoey standing so close. And he was afraid again.

Zoey's pupils dilated, and her nostrils flared just a little. She'd felt it, too.

She cleared her throat. "Right. Uh…the bed is made. Towels are in the linen closet."

She pointed, and the motion brushed her arm against his. She froze.

"Zoey…"

She didn't answer, just stared at the linen closet behind him. *"Zoey."*

Her gaze snapped up to meet his. He wanted her. He wanted his lips on hers. He wanted his arms around her. But he couldn't ignore those *Danger* signs flashing in his brain. She ran the tip of her tongue along her lower lip, and he let out a low groan. He was tired of being afraid.

"You're killing me here, girl." He rested his hands on her hips. "What are we doing?"

"I think…" Her voice was raspy. "Whether we should or not. I think we're going to kiss each other."

Kissing her would put thirty years of friendship on the line. He didn't know if it was worth the risk. He only knew it was going to happen. Right now.

CHAPTER FOURTEEN

OH, GOD. OH, GOD. Oh, God.

Zoey's heart began to flail around in her chest.

Mike McKinnon's going to kiss me.

A shudder ran from her toes to her scalp. He must have felt it passing under his fingers where he gripped her hips, because he smiled. This wasn't Mike's joking smile, or his friendly smile, or even his whiskey smile. This was a smile she wasn't familiar with. This smile was pure sexual attraction. Confident. Predatory. From anyone else, that would be a turnoff, but coming from Mike? *Yes, please.*

"Zoey…" He kept doing that—repeating her name, as if it was all he could think to say. She was having the same problem, so she waited for him to continue. Or just say her name again, with that sexy growl in his voice. He closed his eyes, and that seemed to help him come up with more words. "Is that what you want? For me to kiss you?"

All she could manage was a nod. But that was all Mike needed. Just the briefest of touches was enough to make her forget everything but the sensation of his mouth brushing against hers. Back and forth. Back and forth. Each pass brought him closer, until his mouth held hers. They both froze. This was it. The line had been crossed.

His hand slid up her back, pulling her against his solid body. Her own hands had been just hanging there at her sides until now. She wrapped her arms around his neck, and suddenly the kiss shifted from tentative to urgent. She wasn't sure which of them instigated it, but their mouths crashed hard against each other now. Their heads turned to allow more access, and his tongue pressed its way into her mouth.

He turned and held her against the wall, his hand now working around to her front. Under her T-shirt. Hot against her skin. Brushing the bottom of her breasts. That was the touch that made her flinch. The passion rising in her was too much. The sensation. The emotion. The desire to have their bodies entwined together without any cumbersome clothing in the way.

But damn it, this was Mike McKinnon.

Mike felt her turmoil, and let out only the smallest groan as he pulled away from the kiss. She was mortified when she felt herself rising up on her toes to maintain contact, but he stopped her with his hands, now back on her hips, holding her steady. He was staring at her, his eyes dark and conflicted. She knew just how he felt.

"Definitely worth it."

She barely heard his words as they brushed past against her cheek. It took her a moment to make sense of them, and a chill ran across her skin when she did. He was telling himself the kiss was worth the risk to their friendship. That gave her a brief burst of pride, which evaporated as soon as she thought about what they'd just done. She shook her head slowly, feeling a wave of sadness.

"We'll never be the same again."

The words hurt him. She saw it in the way the skin around his eyes tightened. The way his hands released her. She reached up to touch his cheek.

She tried to smile, but her lips trembled. "I'm not saying that as a bad or good thing. It's just the truth. We can't possibly be the same after kissing like that. It was an amazing kiss, but…" She had to ask the question that kept poking at her. "What have we done?"

His forehead furrowed deeply. He jammed his fingers through his hair and took another step back. "That's a damn good question, isn't it? I don't want to ruin what we have…"

"But you said it was worth it."

"Well, yeah." A mix of humor and heat flared in his eyes. "And *you* called it *amazing*."

"It was."

The LED lanterns lay on the floor, on their sides, casting a gray light up the walls. She hadn't even noticed that they'd both dropped them during the kiss. They'd been so eager to be as close to each other as possible. For better or worse, she *still* felt that way. But Mike's gaze cooled and he glanced away. The moment was broken.

"I think—" he pressed his mouth into a thin, straight line "—the question is not *what have we done*, but *what do we do now*?" He looked down the hall toward her father's room. "And this doesn't feel like the best place or time to figure that out. We should both get some sleep. Behind closed doors." The corner of his mouth twitched. "Away from temptation."

She could always rely on Mike for a calm, reasonable examination of any situation. She, on the other hand, was a tangle of emotions wrestling each other right under the surface of her skin. She could use a little alone time to sort them out. She reached down for her lantern and held it high, as if it was an old-fashioned candle, and did her best to smile.

"You're right. We'll think more clearly by daylight than by LED light." She reached for her door, but Mike stopped her.

"Before we retreat to our separate corners, let's agree on one thing."

"What's that?"

"Neither one of us *ever* considers that kiss to be some kind of mistake. It was…perfect." He swallowed hard. "If it only happens once, so be it. But Zoey…let's not ever regret it."

Her heart swelled with affection. "I can agree to that. It was…um…quite a kiss. Well done, you."

He chuckled. "Well done, *us*. Good night, Zoey."

He picked up his lantern and headed to his room. He didn't look back, which was good. If he'd so much as hesitated, looked her way, asked her to follow him—she'd have done it without a second thought.

The lantern gave enough light for her to find a short nightgown and pull it on. Zoey stared at herself in the mirror. She pulled her hair up on her head and inspected herself in the lace-trimmed, but simple, cotton nightie. Did she look like a woman who was capable of a *perfect* kiss? She lifted her chin.

She pursed her lips and turned her hips a little, then dropped her hair and laughed at herself. She had no idea how to be a seductress. But Mike had made her feel desired. *Mike.* She sat on the edge of the bed, still looking at the mirror, trying to figure out who she was looking at. Mike's friend? Mike's…lover? No. He'd backed away from that. He said they should think about things. She dropped her head in her hands.

What did she *want*? That was easy—she wanted to climb Mike McKinnon like a tree and make love to him all night long. The admission shocked her, but…there it was. The truth. Her dreams were *nothing* compared to the reality of his hands brushing her skin. Touching her breasts. Kissing her. She lay back on the bed and stared at the ceiling, cursing her brain for not giving her a moment's rest.

She didn't want to lose her friend. But right now, she *wanted* him in a whole different way. Could she have both? Her friend *and* the man? She reached for her phone.

Z: You awake?

M: Go to sleep, Zoey

Z: I can't stop thinking about that kiss

M: GO TO SLEEP ZOEY

Z: If we kiss that well, imagine what it would be like if we...

There was a long pause. Floating bubbles appeared, then disappeared. She started pacing by her bed. She imagined him doing the same in his room. Finally her phone buzzed.

M: It would be spectacular. But it could also be a colossal mistake

Z: Focus on spectacular

M: GO. TO. SLEEP.

She opened her door quietly, looking down the hall. She wasn't good at flirting. Never had been. She and Chris had met at the Shamrock, hit it off, got married. No flirtation required. Maybe that had been part of their problem. Neither of them made the effort. She gave herself a mental shake to get her ex out of her head. This was about *Mike*.

Then she heard it—the squeak of that one floorboard in Dad's room. The one by the dresser. She heard it again. Mike was pacing the floor right now. As agitated, and possibly as downright horny, as she was. She started tapping on her phone.

Z: Pretend we're sitting in the shop. I tell you I met a nice guy and I want to have sex with him. As my friend, what would you advise?

M: I'd tell you to be careful

More bubbles floated and she knew he was adding something.

M: And to trust your gut

Something fluttered in her chest.

Z: My gut says we can do this. I want you, Mike.

There was another very long pause.

M: It's a good thing we're in separate rooms behind closed doors right now.

Her mouth twitched.

Z: My door's wide open.

Total silence. No more squeaky floorboard. His door slowly opened, showing him in silhouette against the lantern light behind him. He'd taken his shirt off, and his solid chest had a shadow of dark hair across it. His jeans were unbuttoned and hung low on his hips. He looked like some Hot Men calendar model. Or a movie star. His hair was a tousled mess—he'd clearly been running his fingers through it the way he did. His eyes were dark and smoldering, fixed firmly on her.

She was sure she did *not* look like a movie star, despite her pose against the doorframe and the short nightgown. But she did her best, lifting her chin in mock confidence. Waiting for him to make the next move.

Each step Mike took seemed to take an eternity. She wanted his hands on her, but she forced herself to wait. He stopped in front of her and let his gaze move lazily down her body. She felt its path as surely as if he'd touched her. His eyes met hers, and his mouth slid into the sexiest smile she'd ever seen on a man.

He cupped her cheek with his hand, brushing his thumb against her skin.

"So we're doing this?" he asked.

She caught just enough air in her lungs to let out a soft laugh. "If we *don't* do this, I swear I'll never speak to you again."

"Well we can't have that, can we?" His smile faltered. "This is one night out of a lifetime of knowing each other. One night doesn't get to ruin that."

She nodded, chewing her lower lip. "We're two people agreeing to spend the night together with no expectations of…more. We have chemistry. We're going to enjoy that chemistry. And we're going to remain friends."

"With benefits." He winked, and she finally relaxed. This was her friend. And they were about to *benefit*. Younger people did it all the time, so why shouldn't they?

"Friends with benefits. I like it."

He leaned in and kissed her lips softly, holding there for a moment before speaking against her mouth.

"I like *you*."

MIKE COULDN'T BELIEVE this was happening. Zoey, in nothing but her cute little nightie, was pressing against him, returning his kiss with a great deal of enthusiasm. He was instantly and impossibly hard against the zipper of his jeans.

He slid his arms around her, his fingers moving against the soft cotton that barely covered her. He cupped her buttocks and held her firmly against him, wanting her to know how turned on he was. She let out a soft moan into his mouth. His fingers moved, scrunching up her nightgown until he found skin. Soft, warm skin, silkier than anything he could remember touching. His fingers kept exploring, cupping her butt cheeks and reaching below to find a wet, warm target between her legs.

Zoey gave a soft gasp and trembled as he moved against her, using his fingers from behind as well as rubbing his still-enclosed erection against her stomach. Her head fell back, giving him easy access to trail kisses down her jaw and then her neck. He flicked his tongue against the spot at her throat where her pulse raced. The move made her legs wobble, but he had a firm grip.

He moved her to the bed and lowered her. She lay there, staring up at him with unfocused eyes before she blinked and reached for his jeans. He didn't move as she lowered the zipper, pushed down his briefs and freed him. She sat up and ran her fingers up and down his length, and he thought he might burst right there. He squeezed his eyes closed and brought himself under control as much as he could—which wasn't much.

"Damn it, woman." He pushed her back onto the bed and kicked off his jeans. "You're going to finish me before I even get started…" He stopped, struck with a horrifying thought. "Shit! I don't have any condoms. Um…do you?"

She looked panicked for a moment, then sighed in relief. "Yes! Vickie gave me a box as a gag gift when the divorce was finalized. Now, where did I…?" Her forehead furrowed, then she gave him a bright smile. "Tall dresser! Top drawer! Way in the back…"

He was already on the move, reaching into the drawer, which he suddenly realized was full of brightly colored lacy lingerie. Was *this* what Zoey wore under her flannel shirts? Good thing he'd never known that before now. His fingers found the small box. *Eureka!* He laughed when he read the package.

"Multicolored? Really?"

Zoey laughed, too. "I told you it was a gag gift! But they're still real condoms, right?"

He read the box again. "Thank Christ, yes." She was still splayed out on the bed, nightgown bunched at her waist, casually revealing herself. He wiggled his eyebrows at her. "Orange or blue?"

She squirmed on the bed. "Whichever is on top."

"In a hurry, eh? Blue it is." To match his balls if he didn't get inside her as soon as possible. He tossed the packet on the bed, then followed it, crawling over her and sliding her nightgown up as he did. Zoey shrugged it over her head and tossed it on the floor.

"I know it wasn't very sexy, but it's the fanciest one I own."

Mike settled over her, tracing kisses from her ear down her neck.

"It was the sexiest damn thing I've ever seen, because

it was on *you*." He kissed her skin again, then nipped her lightly, smiling when she gasped. "We need to talk about that underwear drawer later. Have you been hiding a lace undie fetish from me all these years?"

She ran her fingers up his spine, tapping as if playing a keyboard. "Just because I wear jeans doesn't mean I don't like feeling…" She paused. "I don't know—girlie?—un-derneath."

"Like I said about the nightie, you make anything sexy just by wearing it."

"Oh, please." She sounded annoyed, and he lifted his head in surprise. "We don't need to do that silly banter stuff. This is *me*, remember? We can be honest."

Mike shifted, staring straight into her eyes to avoid any doubts about his sincerity. "This isn't me asking you what your sign is, Zoey. I'm not trying to butter you up. I have *always* been honest with you, and that doesn't change just because we're naked in your bed…" He chuckled. "Never thought I'd be saying *those* words. But seriously—when I tell you you're sexy, I mean it. Your brains are sexy. Your strength is sexy. Even your sassy mouth is sexy." He ran his hand down her side to her hip, watching its progress before looking back into her eyes. "And this body? This body is on-fire sexy. I want to take my time and cover every single fraction of it with touches and kisses, but I also want to be inside you so much it literally hurts."

She relaxed under him, her eyes softening. "Maybe this is the trouble with the whole friends with benefits concept. Friends talk too much."

He kissed her softly. "So maybe we should both zip it, huh?"

Her smile deepened. "Exactly. Less talk. More action."

"Yes, ma'am."

He had all night to *slowly* explore the wonder of Zoey, but right now he just wanted her. Urgently. He cupped her breasts in his hands and massaged them, pinching the peaks until she was writhing beneath him. He took one rosy tip into his mouth, his heart pounding as she groaned out his name in the sexiest damn voice he'd ever heard.

He didn't release her, but kept caressing and kissing and nipping until she was trembling in his arms. His free hand found that sweet spot between her legs again, and he worked her harder and faster. She arched her back and gave the tiniest of gasps. It was a gasp of surprise. Of pleasure. She'd just come from nothing more than his fingers and his mouth.

Hottest. Thing. Ever.

"I need to be in you," he said hoarsely, reaching for the condom.

"Hurry."

She was as desperate as he was, reaching to help open the wrapper. Neither of them cared what color the condom was—they just wanted it *on*.

He sank into her, closing his eyes tightly to let the pleasure roll over him. But Zoey wasn't waiting. She moved her hips, nearly undoing his control. His eyes snapped open. No way was she taking over. Maybe later, but not now. Not when he was finally where he'd dreamed of being. He rocked against her, kissing her mouth hard as they melded together.

It didn't last as long as he wanted, but good Lord, it was so good. Their speed increased until they were panting in each other's ear, faster and faster. They cried out in unison and exploded. Her fingernails dug into his shoulders so hard he hissed at the pain. His grip on her buttocks was probably going to leave bruises. Neither of them cared. They just held on as wave after wave of sensation washed over them. For a moment he wondered if it would ever end, but he finally collapsed on her as her arms fell to her side. Neither of them spoke right away, lost in their own thoughts.

He'd just made love to Zoey Hartford.

It wasn't a dream.

It was better.

He kissed the soft skin below her ear. "That was…incredible." No mere word could possibly capture what he felt.

She reached up and patted his shoulder absently, eyes still closed.

"Agreed." She was almost whispering. "Wow. I guess chemistry doesn't lie."

He huffed out a laugh of agreement before moving off her to dispose of the blue condom, then returned to pull her into his arms. She snuggled against his chest, and a brand-new sensation ran through him. It was an odd mix of possessiveness and tenderness and something else he couldn't—*wouldn't*—explore right now. Instead, he planted a kiss on the top of her head and gave her a squeeze.

"Funny, but I was never a fan of chemistry in high school. Now, though…"

Zoey's laughter reminded him who she was. His friend. She raised her head to rest her chin on his chest, staring at him.

"Remember when we flooded Mr. Green's lab our junior year?"

He grinned at the memory. "Flooding it was better than burning it down, which is what would have happened if the sprinklers hadn't come on. I can't help it if my lab partner didn't tell me the Bunsen burner was on."

"Excuse me? The whole point of the experiment was to use the burner. How did I know *my* partner was going to spill methylated spirits on the table? And then try to put out the fire with his jacket, which promptly burst into flames?"

"Yeah, that was my favorite jacket, too." They smiled at each other, his affection for her reflected back at him. "I think we proved again tonight that chemistry can be exciting."

She looked up at the ceiling. "Pretty sure if I had sprinklers in here, they'd have gone off from the heat."

"You know what's fun about science?" he asked. "It's important to be able to reproduce the results, which means you have to do it again. And again." He pulled her in, and she crawled on top of him, propping herself on her arms. Her dark hair fell forward, brushing his chest.

"Is that what you're suggesting, Professor McKinnon?"

"I think it's worth studying. For the sake of science. But I'll need an assistant."

Zoey put her finger on her chin, playfully pretending to be in deep thought.

"Well, I guess we could." She winked. "You know—for *science*."

Mike rolled her onto her back in one smooth motion, staring down into her sparkling eyes.

"We're going to take it nice and slow this time around. *Real* slow. I want to catalog every single sensitive spot on your body, for future reference." He felt her tremble. "And after that, Professor Hartford, we'll switch places and you can do the same to me." He kissed her lips. "For science."

CHAPTER FIFTEEN

ZOEY WATCHED THE sky outside her window gradually brighten in shades of pink and gold. She'd stop it if she could. She'd gladly leave the world in darkness forever if it meant this night with Mike would never end.

He was sprawled crossways on her bed, sound asleep. She smiled and stroked the top of his head, which was heavy on her chest. She had a feeling an *actual* science lab explosion wouldn't wake him right now. She was exhausted, too, but she couldn't sleep. Her body was humming with energy, as if she'd had half a dozen energy drinks at once.

Mike McKinnon was naked in her bed. They'd used up all four condoms—the green one was the funniest—and then they'd explored a few ways to find pleasure without needing a condom. There was a delicious ache between her legs, telling her that it had been way too long since she'd had sex. And also reminding her that she had *never* had sex like that before.

Zoey had always considered herself a practical, non-experimental lover. Sex was fun, but her married sex life usually consisted of Chris rubbing her shoulders and saying "wanna do it?" He hadn't been a selfish lover, but he hadn't been very creative, either.

But Mike was a whole new ballgame. He knew things. And *did* things. And those things were very, very intense. Her fingertips gently circled against his scalp. The fact that she trusted him completely made it easier to let herself go and enjoy the ride. She smiled to herself. *So to speak.* The last year of her marriage hadn't exactly been intimate. So *any* touch was likely to get her turned on.

No, it was Mike's touch. Her friend. And now...her lover.

Last night, she'd told him nothing would ever be the same. Was it possible that it would be *better*? Tonight could be a bubble that would burst at any moment. But the bubble was oh, so sweet. It was something she'd want to tell her best friend about. The best friend who was currently naked in her bed.

"That feels amazing," his low voice rumbled against her skin. "But don't forget we're out of condoms."

She hesitated, then began moving her fingers in circles again. "I didn't mean to wake you."

"I don't think you did. I just...woke up and felt your fingers moving. Oh, shit..." He shifted a little, looking at the window. "Is that...?"

"Morning? I'm afraid so."

"What time is it?"

"Almost six thirty." She let out a long sigh. "We need to get up. The power's still out, but the real world will be at the doorstep by eight. Isn't that what time Owen and Zayne said they'd stop by?"

Mike nodded, stretched, then met her gaze. She could easily get lost in his eyes and ignore the real world. But that world wouldn't ignore them, and she couldn't allow anyone to find them like this. A chill went across her skin. She couldn't allow anyone to know about last night—especially her daughter.

"Hey..." Mike's eyebrows lowered in concern. "What's wrong?"

"What happened last night can't—"

He put his finger against her lips to silence her.

"We agreed that we wouldn't call this a mistake."

She shook her head. "I wasn't going to call it a mistake. It's just...whatever it was needs to stay between us. Whatever comes next, it can't be some public boyfriend-girlfriend thing."

"On one hand, you're saying there's a *next* for us, and I'd really like to do this again." He swooped in for a quick kiss. He was really good at that. "On the other hand, you're saying we have to be a big secret. Why?"

"I have a daughter, Mike."

"I'm aware of that." He frowned. "Oh. You don't want Hazel to know. That makes sense." His expression didn't match his words. He did not look happy.

"You know how this town is. If *anyone* knows, *everyone* knows. At least for now... Hazel can't know I'm with you. With anyone. She thinks I'm totally single, and she wants me to stay that way."

"Is that realistic?"

"It has to be. At least for now." She gave a slight shrug. "She needs at least one home that's stable, and *this* is that home."

They stared at each other. Mike sat up, and she felt their moment coming to an end. She moved to get out of bed, but he took her arm.

"I get it. That doesn't mean I like it." He sighed. "But I can handle being your dirty little secret." He gave her a reassuring smile. "We're getting ahead of ourselves anyway. Last night was...impulsive. Let's figure out what's real, where we are and where we're headed before we worry about going public." He gave her another sneak-attack kiss. "I promise to behave outside this room. In here, all bets are off."

She normally loved his pragmatic approach to things. But this wasn't quite that simple.

"Hazel's room is right across the hall." She felt the same disappointment she saw in his eyes, but his expression brightened again.

"I have a house, too, remember?"

"I can't leave a thirteen-year-old home alone all night."

"I'm just saying that *if* we decide to play chemistry class again…" He winked and she couldn't help but giggle. "I'm betting we can be creative. Keeping this on the down low might even be fun."

"Fun? But…" Her voice trailed off.

She was a forty-year-old single mom of a teenager. She was a struggling business owner. She was trying to bring this big old house into the twenty-first century. She was constantly exhausted and borderline broke.

And yet—bad idea or not—the thought of sneaking around to have secret sex with Mike McKinnon sounded like the best idea *ever*.

VICKIE DID HER best to focus on the conversations swirling around her on the porch of the Taggart Inn. Iris Taggart served afternoon tea there in the warmer months, and it had become a gathering place for locals as well as guests. The main topic of conversation today was the big storm over the past weekend. The town had lost a few of its beautiful trees, and many people had been without power for a day or two, but things were getting back to normal.

The marina had suffered some minor damage to boats and docks. Some of the area wineries had been hit hard, but not as badly as those on the opposite side of Seneca Lake. Her friends at the table—Maura, Cecile and Rick—had fared well, as had Vickie. She'd spent the storm with the

Nelsons, but other than some branches down and her dock being pushed sideways, her property was fine.

Her thoughts, just as they had for the past few weeks, kept wandering back to kissing Gordy in her kitchen pantry. Other than knowing glances and a mischievous grin, he hadn't said a word about the kiss. She suspected he was playing a game with her—waiting for *her* to be the first to mention it. But she was strong enough to win that game. She hoped...

"Vickie!" Rick Thomas snapped his fingers in her face. "What the hell is going on with you today?"

She slapped his hand away with a scowl. Rick, a professor at Brady College, was one of her best friends. The two of them were equally cynical and sarcastic. They both loved watching—and gossiping about—people. Neither of them was easily intimidated.

"If you put that hand in my face again, you might just lose it," she warned.

"Well, you didn't answer Maura *or* me, so I thought maybe you'd retreated into some sort of catatonic state." Tall and lanky, with dark but graying hair, he leaned back in his chair at the small metal table and arched an eyebrow high. "Where were you?"

In the kitchen pantry...

"I was just going through my mental to-do list for the SummerFest in August. I'm in charge of the Saturday night gala, remember?"

She hadn't *really* been thinking about that, but she *should* have been. Selecting and celebrating the Local Business of the Year was a big responsibility. Not that she couldn't handle it. Through the years she'd held just about every role in every one of the local festivals Rendezvous Falls was so famous for.

"Bullshit," Rick snorted. "You could wait until the night before and *still* have a successful event. You're the Hostess with the Mostest. It's your superpower. What were you *really* thinking about?"

Luckily, Cecile came to the rescue with a distraction. She leaned forward and lowered her voice dramatically.

"Did you hear about Connie? She has a *man*!"

Rick fixed his attention straight on Cecile, who, as usual, was dressed in cotton candy pink, her too-blond-to-be-natural curls swinging around her face.

"Seriously?" Rick asked. "*I* can't find a man to save my life, but the grumpiest florist in town found one?"

"I keep telling you you're trying too hard, Rick." Cecile shrugged. "Connie just said 'good morning' to some guy at church, and *bam*, they're dating!"

"At *church*?" Maura leaned in. "Who?"

"Stan Perelli," Cecile answered. "I guess he's been wanting to ask for a while, but couldn't get past her prickliness. When she wished him a good morning, he figured that was as close as he was going to get."

Vickie scoffed. "He'd be waiting a long time if he expected any more than that from Connie."

Connie Phelps's husband left her years ago, and it had taken a *long* time for her to get over it. But if she was dating, things were definitely turning around for her.

"Stan's a decent guy," Vickie said, earning a surprised look from Rick. "What? You think I don't know every ma… I mean, *person* in this town? Stan owned a little variety shop on Main Street for years—souvenirs and stuff. He was active on the festival committee, and supported St. Vincent's children's drive with a truckful of new toys every year."

"Well, now he's boinking Connie Phelps." Rick sipped his ice tea and winked at Vickie.

"Oh, please. They're both in their seventies. I think they're a little too old for boinking, don't you?"

"Victoria Pendergast." Cecile set her glass down, her eyes wide. "You're seventy yourself! Are you suggesting *you're* too old for sex?"

If nothing else, she was old enough to *worry* about being too old for sex. The porch was oddly silent. Vickie looked around and found several other patrons staring at their table. Her eyes narrowed on Cecile.

"Gee, why don't you shout that a little louder? I don't think the people in the next town heard you."

Rick laughed, pushing his chair back from the table. "I'm not quite as ancient as you ladies, but I can tell you I'm not planning on slowing down my sex life…" He stood. "Although finding a good man is taking longer than I'd like. I have to run. I'm meeting with a contractor about remodeling the kitchen."

As the other diners resumed their conversations, Cecile put her hand on Vickie's arm, her voice dropping to a whisper.

"Sweetie, I know it's been…a while…since you've had a relationship, but trust me, you don't have to age out of enjoying sex. It just gets…different." Cecile sat back. "Wait… why *are* you worried about this? Are you seeing someone?"

Her thoughts strayed to Gordy just long enough to pique her friends' interest. Now it was Maura who was on the edge of her seat.

"Ooh… Cecile, I think you're onto something. That's definitely Vickie's *I've got a secret* face. What have you been up to, and why haven't you told me about it? I'm your bestie, remember?" Vickie kicked herself, because Maura's voice was teasing, but there was a flash of hurt in her eyes. They'd been best friends since their school days.

"I'm *not* seeing anyone." Her eyes closed. Why was she talking about this? "You both know that Gordy Lexiter is building a new deck at my place, right?"

Maura's and Cecile's expressions were identical— mouths open, eyes round. Before they could say anything, Iris Taggart walked over and took a seat at the table. She was in what Vickie called her *sweet old lady* garb, complete with ruffled apron. She'd smiled at all the other tables, greeting them as the charming elderly innkeeper, chitchatting about the big storm and suggesting places for her guests to visit. But once Iris sat, she took in the scene and started laughing.

"Spill it, girls. What's going on? What has Vickie done now?"

Maura's mouth finally closed and slid into a smirk. "The question is *who* Vickie's doing."

"Oh, hot damn," Iris rested her chin in her hand. "Do tell."

"I'm not doing *anyone*," Vickie hissed, looking around to make sure no one was listening. "We just kissed, for God's sake."

The three women sucked in deep gasps at once.

"You *kissed* him?" Maura clamped her hand over her mouth, realizing how loud she'd just spoken. Her voice dropped. "You *kissed* Gordy? Didn't you two have a little thing in high school?"

"What?" Cecile shook her head, as if she hadn't heard right. "You and Gordy back in high school? Are we talking first base or home run?"

Iris's eyes widened. "Well, good for you!"

"How was it?" Maura's voice turned tender.

"The kiss? Amazing." She couldn't help smiling a little. "He said he wants more, but…" She glanced at Iris and lifted her shoulder. "He really *isn't* my type. And it's been a long time since I was with anyone…that way."

The three women stared at each other, then looked back to Vickie. Maura spoke first.

"I agree with Iris—good for you. I know you care about your image or whatever, but we all know the real Vickie." Maura reached out and took Vickie's hand. "The one who didn't exactly grow up in a waterfront mansion."

That was true enough. Her mom raised her in a humble bungalow on the edge of town—it wasn't a Victorian, and it definitely never made it onto any historic home tours.

"I don't live in a mansion…"

"You have one of the grandest homes in Rendezvous Falls," Iris pointed out, "and you live there alone. It's okay to let another man into your life, especially a decent one like Gordy. And he's a hot silver fox, too."

"But… I'm not a kid anymore. Men just seem to keep on going with their sex lives, but what if I can't…satisfy him? I'd be mortified."

The thought sent a chill through her. Vickie hated feeling vulnerable, and the idea of literally being naked and… *failing*? She didn't know if she'd survive the humiliation.

Iris huffed out a snort. "Men get the benefit of millions of dollars in science research to take care of *their* aging issues. Old guys can't get it up? Here's a blue pill! Women dry up? Oh, well, there's always younger women. It sucks."

Cecile, usually so bubbly and upbeat, fixed a stern look on Iris, and then Vickie. "Bullshit. I mean…yes, science favors the men, just like everything else does, but that doesn't mean we're helpless. There are products out there to help… keep things moving. Everything takes more time, but if you use that time creatively, sex at our age can be better than ever."

Vickie and Cecile didn't have a lot in common, other than the book club. But she felt a new surge of affection for the woman. Cecile and Charlie, from all accounts, had always had a spicy, adventurous sex life. And Cecile often hinted that it was still very much that way. So if *she* could do it, then so could Vickie. Maybe.

Cecile started to chuckle. "Just make sure you wear your glasses when you're shopping for lubricants. I picked up a bottle of something that had the word *fire* on the label. I thought it was a normal warming oil, but they were referring to an additive that made my *hoohah* feel like I'd just literally set it on fire." She laughed out loud now. "We had to stop everything and go clean up with cool washcloths. We laughed so hard we cried!"

Vickie and her friends laughed at Cecile's story. Then she sat up abruptly, realizing she'd just broken a promise she'd forced on Gordy.

"You can't tell *anyone*, girls. Seriously—I made Gordy promise not to kiss and tell, and now I've gone and done it. If I hear any rumors going around town, I'll know where they came from." She pointed at each of them threateningly, but they didn't seem at all intimidated. "I don't want people laughing at me."

"I don't tend to go around telling people about my friends' sex lives," Iris huffed. "But I do want to live vicariously through your suddenly interesting love life."

"*Suddenly* interesting?"

"Let's face it," Iris replied. "You've been hanging out with some real snoozers the past few years. The trivia-playing college dean. That wine competition judge from California…"

"Oh!" Cecile added. "Don't forget that obnoxious attorney from Rochester who was on the hospital board with you. He barely spoke to anyone when he was in town."

"Speaking of attorneys…" Maura brushed her short hair behind her ears. "What's happening with my grandson and our matchmaking efforts? Zoey told us he wasn't interested, but Mike never said that."

Cecile perked up. "Hey! Why don't we set them up on a date with each other and see—"

"I tried that," Vickie said. "But Zoey said there's nothing there but friendship."

Maura sighed. "It's too bad. Zoey's always felt like part of the family. But I've never picked up on anything between them."

Cecile grabbed her bag and stood. "Well, I think they'd be adorable together."

Mike and Zoey *were* spending a lot of time together. And Zoey said she'd *thought* about it. Vickie would have to keep a closer eye on those two.

CHAPTER SIXTEEN

MIKE DIDN'T USUALLY need help coming up with riddles and dad jokes—that was kind of his specialty. But coming up with a joke while reaching out to the best friend he'd *slept* with two days ago was new territory for him. Zoey had been so adamant that they keep everything quiet from their friends and families, so that Hazel wouldn't find out. Friends with benefits, that's all they were.

Really good friends. With some spectacular benefits.

That night of the storm, he and Zoey had nothing short of life-altering sex. And it was all *her* idea, which somehow made it even hotter. When he'd opened his door to see her standing there in the doorway to her room in the skimpy little nightie… His body responded so fast that it was a miracle he'd been able to walk down the hall to her.

The hottest dreams he'd had were nothing compared to the actual feel of her in his arms. The fires her fingertips created everywhere they traveled. The soft, needy whimpers that rocketed through him like lightning bolts. And being inside her, feeling her warmth and…

Mike got up from his desk and started pacing his office. He had a real estate closing in half an hour and he couldn't walk in there with a teepee in his pants. It had only been two days, but it felt like an eternity since he'd touched her. He needed to see her tonight, even if only to talk. Like old times.

We'll never be the same again…

He raked his fingers through his hair, then curled his hands and tugged on it in frustration. He hadn't liked hearing those words from Zoey, but she wasn't wrong. He had a hard time imagining that anything would ever be *like old times* between them. But they'd promised to try to keep the friendship intact. He needed to keep things light. He started tapping on his phone.

M: What do bird couples call each other?

There was a long pause, and he wondered if she was on a service call somewhere. Or had he made a mistake using the word *couple*? A floating bubble finally appeared.

Z: No idea

He grinned, crossing his fingers that he wasn't crossing a line. Where *were* the lines? Did they *have* lines now?

M: Tweetheart

Z: Well, one thing hasn't changed. Your jokes are still awful.

M: Thank you. Wine tonight?

Another long pause. There clearly *were* lines, and they were both terrified of them.

Z: Sure. In the shop. 8?

M: C U there

She'd never specified the shop before. It was always a

given. But now that he'd been in her bedroom, she must think she had to clarify. He'd love to visit her bedroom again, but Zoey had Hazel on school nights. He frowned to himself as he sorted through the folders on his desk.

Mike understood why Zoey wanted to keep their, um— *benefits*…from Hazel. But it complicated things. Anything they did, no matter how casual they insisted it was, would impact Hazel. And if it became more than casual? Hazel was a great kid—funny, kind, creative. But thirteen was a complicated age, and her life was already complicated on top of that.

Would Hazel *ever* be ready to accept Mike—or any man—into Zoey's life? Would she welcome him showing up at her breakfast table just because she knew him? Or would she do everything in her power to end things? He headed to the small conference room in his office to get ready for the appointment.

He'd never considered the ramifications of dating a single mom. The word *dating* was a stretch after just one night, but if it ever reached that point… He hadn't thought he was ready to become a father with Becca, so what made him think he could be a stepfather? *Aw, hell.* He was getting way ahead of himself—something he'd always counseled his clients not to do. Be prepared, but don't respond to things that hadn't actually happened yet. He needed to heed his own advice. One step at a time.

MIKE WAS SO distracted when he arrived at Zoey's that night that he almost didn't notice the big elm tree had been cut up and wood stacked near the driveway. The morning after the storm, Owen and Zayne were so busy with tree work around the area that they'd simply cut enough of the tree to be able to drag it off the driveway and away from the house, promising to return later. He was glad to see they'd kept that promise.

He parked his SUV by the barn and, instead of texting a joke, just walked right into the shop. Zoey was at the workbench along the back wall, and spun with her hand on her chest.

"Holy hell, Mike!" She shook her finger at him. "You scared the daylights out of me. Since when do you just burst in without at least knocking?"

"I'm sorry." He raised his hands in front of him. "I was thinking about something else, and honestly—" he grinned "—I was kind of in a hurry to see you."

He'd been aching to see her all day. Touch her. Kiss her. But the information he'd learned a few hours ago was also rattling around his head and distracting him.

After the closing that afternoon, which had thankfully been a friendly, straightforward transaction, Mike had waited for the money transfer to go through. He drove to the town clerk's office to record the paperwork. While he was there, he'd quietly checked on a few property records for Zoey's place, just in case Karen Schiff decided to carry through with her threats. He wasn't happy with what he'd found. If Schiff was just blowing smoke, it wouldn't matter. Even if she wasn't, Mike still might be able to make a few legal maneuvers.

"You're forgiven," Zoey said, turning back to the workbench and providing him a fine view of her behind, all curvy and taut in snug jeans.

Admiring his best friend's ass was something new and different, but Mike couldn't make himself feel bad about it. He set down the bottle of wine, walked over and slid his arms around her waist, but instead of melting against him, she tensed, looking back at the door.

"Hazel's home tonight."

"She's not out here."

"And what if she comes out for something? What if she flies through the door like you did? What if—"

"Slow down the what-ifs, girl." Despite her worries, she hadn't moved away from his easy embrace, so he tightened his hold. "The door can be locked if it'll make you feel better."

Her head dropped, and her dark hair fell around her face to cover it.

"Locking the door will just raise suspicions. Besides, there are windows, remember? The shop can't be our getaway, Mike. It's too risky…"

Everything felt risky these days. He'd gone from being a small-town lawyer with a nice, low-key life to sneaking around and hiding from a thirteen-year-old, just so he could kiss his best friend. And maybe get her naked.

He gave in to the temptation of the now-exposed skin on the back of her neck, brushing his lips against it before pressing a kiss there. She sighed, rolling her head to the side to give him better access. He was no fool—he took advantage of the opening and started trailing kisses up her neck toward that silky spot behind her ear.

As soon as his tongue reached out to taste her there, she rested her hands on the workbench and gently shrugged away from him. He released her immediately and stepped back, cursing himself for pushing her after she'd just said she was worried about being caught.

"I'm sorry, Zoey." He rubbed the back of his neck, taking another step backward. She turned, staring at him with dark, troubled eyes.

"Don't be sorry. I just don't want to lose control, and you had me awfully close just now. We should…uh…talk this out before we do anything."

He tried to focus on her concerns, and not the quick shot of joy at the idea that she'd almost lost control at his touch. But first—talk.

"I'll just retreat back to my side of the worktable." He walked to his usual seat, putting the table securely between them. They were friends first. She needed *normal*. And he probably did, too. He tapped his fingers on the table with a grin. "Where's my cup? And a corkscrew?"

Zoey's shoulders eased. "Coming right up." She slid the corkscrew across the table and turned to get the cups from the cupboard. "So how was your day?"

This was their shop night comfort zone. This felt like… home. This was what they had to preserve, no matter what.

"Well, *tweetheart*, it was fine." He poured the wine. "I actually had a real estate closing that did *not* include tears or yelling. I always consider that a win."

Lord knew he'd had his share of stressful closings. Large money transactions did not always bring out the best in people. And some considered themselves a lot better at negotiating than they actually were. He remembered his stop at the town offices.

"Hey, you haven't heard any more from the Schiff woman about the zoning thing, have you?"

"No. Why?"

"I figured she was just yapping without intending to do anything." He drank some wine, mentally crossing his fingers. "She was all talk."

"Let's hope so. I don't need the hassle. You don't think she has any chance of actually causing trouble, do you?" He didn't answer right away, and Zoey picked up on it. "Mike?"

He sighed. "I haven't done a deep dive, but your dad fought the town about zoning—and won—thirty years ago."

"That's good, right?" Zoey studied his face. "If he won?"

"What he won was an argument that this was *not* commercial property. He didn't want to pay commercial property taxes or deal with commercial zoning requirements." He paused, then saw her crestfallen expression. "But that doesn't necessarily prevent a private enterprise or workshop from being on the property. Rob argued that he didn't have a storefront here, which is true. Just because someone's self-employed doesn't make their home a commercial property." He frowned. "But the fact that he fought being called a business could…complicate things if we try to claim it's grandfathered as a business. That's only *if* your neighbor gets serious about her threat, which she probably never will. So please don't lose any sleep over it, okay?"

She studied his face, then plunked herself down on her work stool with a heavy sigh. "Right now I have a pretty long list of other things causing me to lose sleep. Starting with you."

He put his hand on his chest, eyes wide. "Who, me? I hope you mean that some pretty awesome memories are keeping you awake at night."

The corner of her mouth quirked upward. "That's part of it. I'm wondering if we should—"

"Do it again? Absolutely."

"Mike, I'm serious. Don't act like my boyfriend when I need my *friend*-friend."

"*Am* I your boyfriend?" He winced, knowing they hadn't defined *what* they were. "I'm sorry. This is…it's going to take some getting used to. Figuring out how to separate the *friends* from the *with benefits*."

She nodded, biting her upper lip. "That's what I'm worried about. I mean… I'm worried about a lot of things. And when I'm worried about things, *you're* the one I want to talk to. But when what I'm worried about *is you*…" He hated the sadness and confusion he saw in her eyes when she looked up. "Mike, I don't know what to do."

What he *wanted* to do was rush to her side and hold her. Comfort her. Kiss her. But she was right—they'd blurred a lot of lines when they'd slept together. And they needed to deal with that first.

"The last thing I want is for you to be worrying about anything to do with me. Let's agree to operate from the position of being *friend*-friends first and foremost. No more hugs or kisses or…stuff…unless we both know and agree to be in boyfriend…" Damn, the word made him feel far better than it should. "Or *girlfriend* zone." Yeah, that one felt pretty good, too. "We default to *friend*-friends unless otherwise noted. Agreed?"

She gave a quick nod, but she wouldn't meet his gaze. "That sounds reasonable." Then she looked up with a small smile that warmed his heart. "I'm not sure *reasonable* applies when it comes to the other…*stuff.* But we can definitely try to compartmentalize our two different relationships."

He returned her smile, settling into his familiar role as her logical attorney friend. "The key is communication. We've always been brutally honest as friends. There's no reason we can't be the same way about…*stuff.* We're not teenagers getting away with something. We are two very mature adults, and we're capable of…how did you put it? Compartmentalizing."

She huffed out a short laugh. "Easy on the *very* mature labels, pal. I don't mind being called *mature*, but let's not get carried away."

"Fair enough. Now tell me exactly what has you so worried, point by point, and we'll figure out how to deal with it."

And then they could get back to kissing…and stuff.

CHAPTER SEVENTEEN

ZOEY DIDN'T KNOW where to begin. Since the night of the storm she'd discovered so many things to worry about. It had been a wonderful night. She wanted it to happen again. She *ached* for it to happen again. But she wondered if it ever should.

"So what are we going to do?" she asked. "Have a code word for when we switch gears to being more than friends?"

Mike chuckled. She remembered the feel of that laughter against her skin, but she shoved that memory away. This wasn't the time. He straightened in his seat.

"That's not a bad idea. It should be something that sounds…innocent. Just in case we slip up and say it where someone can overhear." His smile deepened. "You know, like *nooky* or *booty call*."

She laughed. "I think both of those are definitely out. Even *benefits* is too suggestive—our friends and family aren't idiots."

He snapped his fingers, eyes bright with humor. "I've got it! Tonight you and I have both referred to, uh…physical relations, as *stuff*. If we say we have *stuff* to do later, no one would think twice, whether it's Hazel or Mary or my blessed grandmother."

She couldn't think of an objection, so she nodded. "Fine."

"Fine?" Mike grinned. "That's not exactly a ringing endorsement, but I'll take it." His smile faded. "What's wrong?"

"You *do* realize that was the easiest worry on my list to solve, right?"

"Hit me with the next one. We've got this, Zoey."

For over an hour, she ticked off her concerns and they talked it out.

Hazel could not know about their casual sexual relationship.

This one was nonnegotiable, and Mike agreed.

Their friends and family did not need to know about their casual sexual relationship.

The more people who knew, the more chance Hazel would find out. Mike agreed, but only after pointing out he wasn't crazy about the word *casual*. As long as they were doing whatever it was they were doing, they would be exclusive. She was in total agreement.

They were friends first and forever. Lovers on occasion.

They both valued their friendship too much to put it at any more risk than they already had. He agreed.

"And who knows?" Zoey finally asked. "Maybe it was just a onetime, stormy-night thing. And if that's the case, fine."

Mike's eyes narrowed on her, his mouth sliding into a crooked, deadly sexy grin that made her pulse quicken. "You don't believe it was a onetime thing any more than I do. That was way too good to be some fluke. Right now, after all this talk, talk, talk—I'm *still* thinking about how much I want to walk over there and kiss you."

Her lips parted, and heat pooled low in her belly. She wanted him to do that. Kiss her. Right now. She swallowed hard.

"Okay."

He straightened. "Okay *what*?"

"*Okay*, come over and kiss me." She stood, and he did,

too—so quickly his stool skidded backward across the floor. "But humor me and lock the door first."

She tried to stay focused on what she wanted to say, but the sight of Mike slowly walking toward her made that difficult. She had to blink away for a moment to gather her thoughts. "Just to clarify, you're not a *dirty* secret. But we do have to be a secret for now. If that's a dealbreaker…" She stepped back as he stopped right in front of her, determined to finish her point. What *was* her point?

"It's not a dealbreaker, Zoey," he said softly. "I get it. But…"

That little burst of heat she'd felt cooled immediately as soon as he said *but*.

"My daughter will always come first. If you aren't ready for that, we should stop right now."

"I *get* that, Zoey. It's just…we might have something really great happening here, but not if we suffocate it under a rock."

She shrugged. "I'm a mom first."

"I *know*!" He took a breath, his voice softening. "I swear I get it. It's one of the things I admire most about you. And I love Hazel—she's terrific. This is *not* a dealbreaker. I'm just saying give me a chance to wrap my head around it."

She nodded in agreement. "This is so new. We should at least wait to see if we want to continue…"

His smile turned devilish, his hand sliding under the hem of her T-shirt. Mike's other hand cupped her chin gently and tipped her head up until she had no choice but to look at him. Their bodies were pressed together now and, even though they were fully dressed, she felt his erection twitch against her stomach.

His voice was rough and low. "Oh, I definitely want to continue." He lowered his head and brushed his lips across hers, making her moan with need. The hand on her back was splayed out now, pulling her even closer. God, she wanted this man so much. But there wasn't a bed in sight.

"Where?" she asked against his mouth. The word parted her lips just enough for him to push his way inside as he kissed her. The kiss was hard and frantic...for both of them. She reached up to grip his hair with her fingers.

"There has to be somewhere..." He ground out the words. "Wait...isn't your dad's old worktable back in—"

"Dad's office? Yes!"

Her father's so-called office was really just a small alcove behind the pegboard wall with all the parts on it. Dad had done most of his paperwork on the kitchen table in the house, but he liked the idea of having an official office. He'd moved his own grandfather's ancient worktable back there. It made for a very large, sturdy desk. Almost...bed-sized. He'd added an office chair and a few tall metal file cabinets.

Mike was already pushing her backward in that direction, still kissing her, when she put her hands on his shoulders.

"Wait."

He froze. "You want to stop?" His eyes were warm with concern. And more than a little disappointment.

"Oh, no—not stopping." She gave a soft laugh. "I was just going to say there's a pile of old blankets and pads in that plastic bin in the corner. Dad used them to protect things he brought back here for repair, especially the antique stuff. They'll be a lot softer under my butt than solid wood."

Mike chuckled. "I'm more than willing to be the one with his butt on the desktop, but that sounds like a great idea. For the record..." He winked as he turned for the bin. "I'm really glad you weren't telling me you wanted to stop."

"Did you bring protection?" She cut in front of him so she could move a few papers—and wipe a good layer of dust—from the table. It was already pushed into the corner of the office space. That would reduce the chances of them rolling onto the floor if they got carried away. She couldn't stop marveling at what they were doing.

"Yes," Mike answered, "But they're not as colorful as last time."

Zoey shook out the blankets and made a nest with them on top of the desk, tossing some pillows in the corner. "Despite all your grumbling, you're pretty good at this *dirty little secret* thing."

"Oh, honey," he answered, stepping behind her and wrapping one arm around her waist. With the other, he tossed the condoms onto the blankets. "I'm good at a lot of things."

He kissed the back of her neck while his fingers found the zipper on the front of her shorts. He unfastened them and pushed them below her hips before turning her to face him.

"And one of the things I'm good at is imagining you sitting on the edge of this desk while I sit in that chair and devour you."

The image was so flat out sexy that it seemed to stun both of them. They stared at each other, wide-eyed, as if to say *are we really doing this?* Then Zoey came to her senses and kicked off her shorts and panties before hopping onto the desk. She swept her hair back over her shoulder and arched one eyebrow high.

"Well, what are you waiting for?"

MIKE WASN'T ONE to leave a lady waiting, so he pulled the desk chair over, took a seat and gave his best friend *two* screaming orgasms. Then he joined her on the desk after shedding his clothes. The packing blankets didn't exactly make the desk feel like a mattress, but they helped make kneeling over her easier.

Once he'd teased her into another little pop of pleasure with his fingers, he grabbed a condom and settled into her with a happy groan. The desk wasn't great for catching traction for pushing, but they worked themselves around so that his feet were against the file cabinet and her head was against a cushion propped against the wall. There was laughter involved, which didn't diminish the sexiness of the moment one bit.

He rocked into her again and again until his vision went white and he came with a barely contained cry of wordless sound. Making love to this woman in silence just didn't seem possible.

And now she was asleep in his arms, her leg wrapped over his thigh, her breasts soft and warm against his chest. Her head was on his arm, which had itself fallen asleep half an hour ago, but he didn't care. It was a warm night, so they were able to lie there without a covering. They hadn't turned any lights on in the office, but there was plenty of shop light coming over the wall and through all the holes in the pegboard.

Desktop sex was a first for him. All in all, the big old table worked well. With a few more pillows added, he'd be very happy to do it here again. Hell, even without pillows, he'd make love to her right now...if she was awake. She snorted a soft snore and stirred before cuddling back against him with a sigh. He ran his fingers through her long, dark hair, clearing a few knots formed from their vigorous lovemaking. He traced his knuckles lightly across her cheek.

This office would get chilly in the wintertime, but for the next couple months, they could make this work. He smiled. Because there was no way in hell this...uh...*casual sex*...

wasn't going to keep happening. He wasn't giving her up, and he had a feeling she wanted it as much as he did.

She shifted again next to him, and he gripped her tightly. Her eyes swept open.

"Relax. I'm not going to fall off the desk."

He eased his grip a bit. "Just making sure." He shifted his own weight to ease pressure on his hip. "A real bed would be safer and more comfortable, though. Maybe come to my place next time?"

"You're presuming there'll be a next time." She kissed his neck, taking the sting away from the words. "Kidding— of course I want a next time. But how am I supposed to sneak into your house without the whole damn neighborhood talking about it?"

She had a point. His house was in an older neighborhood where people loved to watch the goings-on. "I could have a bed delivered out here some weekend when Hazel's with her dad."

Zoey snorted. "And if she sees a freakin' *bed* out here, how am I supposed to explain it?"

"Does she ever come out here?" He realized how clueless that sounded as soon as he said it. "I mean, of course she does—I've seen her. It's where you work."

She rolled onto her back with a sigh. "She never comes out here because she's interested in my work. I don't think she's destined for a career in appliance repair. But it's her Pop-pop's barn, and she's had some fun adventures out here through the years. She's not a tomboy like I was, but she still likes to explore up in the hayloft when she wants alone time."

He leaned over and brushed a kiss against her forehead, smiling at an old memory. "We used to hang out up there as kids. Is that big old rope we used to swing on still hanging from the rafters? We used it to jump on the sawdust pile in the aisleway."

Zoey's body shook with laughter. "I remember. We went up there one January day and you swung off the rope to discover that sawdust freezes solid in a cold barn in the wintertime. God, the way you screamed… Mary and I thought you broke your leg."

He'd been around fourteen then, showing off for his sister and Zoey. Rob had a huge pile of sawdust there as bedding for the few beef cows he had at the time. But Mike was no farmer—he had no idea the moisture in the sawdust froze when the pile sat undisturbed in below-zero weather. Mike hit that pile of rock-hard sawdust from ten feet up, expecting a pillow-soft landing and not getting one. He chuckled.

"Your dad was so pissed. He'd told us a hundred times not to swing from the loft onto the pile because we'd get hurt, but we were so much smarter than grown-ups. I'm lucky it was only a sprained ankle." He grinned. "And if we thought *your* dad was mad, man, mine nearly killed me. And then Nana got in line." He thought about the memories they'd had in this place. "And now you and I are naked on your dad's desk. I don't think any of us saw this coming."

It took a minute before he realized Zoey had gone still. *Shit.* Her dad had been gone less than a year. And they'd just had sex on his desk.

"I keep putting my foot in my mouth, don't I?"

She pursed her lips. "It's okay. You're not wrong. I'm sure my dad *never* imagined us here. But…"

"Are you starting to worry again? Old worries, or something new?" He traced a random pattern on her stomach with his fingers and smiled when he felt her shiver. "Look, neither one of us wants this to end anytime soon. We're gonna stay friends. We'll keep it quiet. We can do this. We're both having fun, right?" His fingers moved lower, and her back arched when he found his target. "Are you having fun, Zoey?"

"I'm having fun." She took in a shaky breath. "I just don't know if I *should* be."

His fingers continued to move. "This isn't some random hookup. This is *me*. You know I'll never hurt you." His fingers were still moving, and she let out a moan that sent electricity racing through his veins. He kissed her, soft and slow, then smiled against her mouth. "I can't keep my hands off you. I don't *want* to keep my hands off you."

She huffed out a soft laugh. "Then don't."

He reached for another condom. All he had to do was keep telling himself this was nothing more than *casual, dirty little fun* between friends. He already knew that was a lie—it was much, much more than that—but he'd try his damnedest to believe it. For Zoey's sake.

CHAPTER EIGHTEEN

"YOU WERE WORKING late last night." Hazel spoke around the spoonful of cereal she'd just put in her mouth. "Big project or something?"

Zoey was glad her back was to her daughter, because she was sure her face had just drained of color. She cleared her throat, her eyes firmly on the coffee maker in front of her.

"Why? Did you come out to the shop?" Had Hazel discovered the locked door? Mike *had* locked it, hadn't he?

"Duh," Hazel answered. "You'd have seen me if I'd come out there. I heard you come upstairs, and it was late."

Zoey blew out a silent sigh of relief and finally turned around, her coffee cup in hand. "Let me guess—you were in bed, but not asleep. Maybe video-chatting with Sienna?"

The sparkle of guilty humor in Hazel's eyes told Zoey all she needed to know. She'd successfully moved the conversation away from *her* sneaking up the stairs—apparently badly—close to midnight. Between her brief desktop nap and Mike tempting her into a second round of lovemaking, and then more napping… Well, she was lucky Mike had nudged her awake when he did.

"Sienna's so pissed at her mom right now." Hazel stood, looking around with a frown. "Ugh—I left my backpack upstairs. BRB."

"I've told you before that those hipster abbreviations don't work in polite conversation." She knew it meant *be right back*, but she didn't want Hazel reducing her vocabulary to groups of letters being announced out loud.

"OMG, Mom. Using *hipster* is so cringe." And she was gone, the sound of her feet thudding on the steps. Zoey would have to get inside earlier from now on. Which was a shame because her time with Mike had been incredible.

They'd talked things out and, as usual, Mike had made her feel better. And then he'd made her *feel* better—from head to toe. It was shocking what his touch did to her. Maybe it was the secrecy and excitement of something new. Maybe it was that she hadn't been active since Chris, so she had some pent-up sexual needs. Maybe it was Mike. Maybe they had a chemistry thing going on that neither of them saw coming. What was it Mike had called it?

Casual, dirty little fun...

She could believe every single one of those words except one. What they were doing didn't feel *casual* at all. She finished her coffee and called out to Hazel before heading out to the car—no service calls this morning, so she could run some errands after dropping Hazel at school. This was the last week of classes, but Hazel was going to start working part-time for Mary McKinnon for the summer. Mary was rebooting her website design business from home, but she couldn't do it without someone to help manage her three youngsters. Having a toddler burst into an important video conference naked and screaming at the top of his lungs was only funny in viral videos, not in real life.

The arrangement was a win for everyone—it would keep Hazel busy while giving her money to spend on her fashion accessories. It was helping Mary build her client list. And it was giving Zoey some free time during the summer to get more updates done at home. The kitchen was next on her list, and that would be a major project. And maybe she'd make time to meet Mike somewhere for…stuff. She tapped the horn to remind Hazel she was waiting.

That might be awkward. *Hey, Mike—my daughter is at your sister's place, so let's have a little afternoon delight.* Ugh. This whole thing was awkward. But she wasn't willing to give it up yet. To give *him* up yet.

Hazel burst out of the house and into the car, giving Zoey a breathless grin.

"Sorry. Sienna wanted to FaceTime."

"Aren't you going to see her in school in like…five minutes?" Zoey drove down the driveway and headed toward town.

"Well yeah, but it's not the same. We can't really talk until lunchtime."

"Which is three hours from now. You'll both live. What's she so wound up about, anyway?"

"Her mom is *dating.*" She emphasized the word with a horrified tone that made it sound like Monique Johnson was a serial killer. Zoey swallowed hard. She didn't know Monique that well, but she knew Sienna's parents had divorced just before Chris and Zoey broke up. It was one of the things that had helped the girls bond so closely when they'd met last year in middle school. She concentrated on keeping her voice light.

"And that's a bad thing? Her mom dating?"

"Ugh. It's *so* gross. She's using a dating app, and she shows Sienna the guys she likes before she swipes them." Hazel gave a fake shudder. "*Cringe!* As if Sienna wants to be involved in her hookups. Promise me you'll never do that."

Zoey's mouth went dry. "*Date?* Not ever?"

Hazel hesitated. "Do you *want* to date? I thought you said you were happy with just you and me? *Thelma and Louise.*"

Yes, and look what happened to them...

"I *am* happy with just you and me." *And Mike on a desk in the barn...* She turned into the school lot. "But there's nothing wrong with Monique wanting to find a man to have in her life. She might be over involving Sienna in that decision, but it could be her way of seeking Sienna's approval of the men she likes." She took a deep breath. "It's not easy to be an adult and to feel alone in some ways. I mean...your dad is getting *married.*"

Hazel stared at the dashboard, making no move to leave the car now that Zoey had pulled to the curb. Her eyebrows lowered.

"Would it be awful if I said that was different?"

"Um...*yeah*, it would." She would keep her promise not to bastardize Chris to their daughter, but she wasn't about to allow some sort of double standard.

"But Dad was seeing Genna right from the start, as soon as you guys broke up. He's not out there." Hazel looked over at Zoey. "He's not playing the field."

No, he'd done that during their marriage. That's how he'd met Genna. Hazel had either conveniently ignored the possibility that her father and Genna had been together before the divorce, or genuinely hadn't figured it out yet. But Zoey got Hazel's point. Sort of.

"So it's not a dads-can-date, moms-can't thing. You're saying the issue is that Sienna's mom is dating multiple men instead of having one steady relationship?"

"I... I guess. It's just weird." She paused. "Mom, you said it's hard to be an adult and feel alone. Are *you* lonely, even with me at the house?"

They'd always been honest with each other. But the whisper of disappointment and worry in Hazel's voice was enough for her to push past the honest answer—yes—and reassure the thirteen-year-old looking at her with wide, solemn eyes.

"Of course not. You're my whole world, kiddo. I told you this year was all about you and me." She reached out to tousle Hazel's carefully straightened hair, but the girl was too quick. She had the car door open in a flash and slid out. When she bent over to say goodbye, Zoey finished her thought. "I'm positive that Sienna is Monique's whole world, too. As moms, as *parents*...we're all just doing the best we can."

"Okay." Hazel's friends called her name. "Gotta go. Just..." She met Zoey's eyes. "Dad getting married and having a baby is...a lot. I'm already slip-sliding to third or fourth place in his house. Promise me you'll stay single for a while, Mom. Like...*convent* single. Okay?"

This wasn't the time or place, but they were going to have to discuss that comment about where Hazel ranked with her dad. She'd talk to Chris about it, too. They couldn't let Hazel feel she was being pushed aside. Her friends called out again.

Zoey flashed her a game smile. "I'll talk to Father Joe about where I can find the nearest convent." *Right after I sleep with Mike McKinnon.*

"Sister Zoey Hartford has a nice ring to it. Later!" With a quick wave, Hazel was lost in the throng of teens moving toward the school entrance. The excitement of summer break was palpable in their animated voices and quick steps.

Zoey needed to talk to someone. Anyone. Well...anyone except her best friend, Mike. Or her other best friend, Mary. Mike's twin sister. *Nope.* Vickie? Nah, she'd push Zoey into Mike's arms no matter what. She felt too close to tears to visit Evie at the diner. It was too early to catch

Bridget at the Purple Shamrock. Besides…she was Mike's *cousin.* Damn this small town.

Instead, she drove to Taneisha Warren's house, not far from the Taggart Inn. This was one of the oldest sections of town, where some of the first fanciful Victorian homes were built shortly after the Civil War. The town's famous architect, Willard Wilkins, came home from the war disillusioned, but determined to bring happiness back to Rendezvous Falls. Wilkins embraced the "new" Victorian style and kicked it up a notch with lacy gingerbread trim and bright color combinations.

Tani's house was a perfect example. A small round tower anchored one corner, and a wide porch graced the front of the house and wrapped right around the tower and down the side of the home toward the detached garage—originally a carriage house—in back. The home had been painted a dark blue when Tani bought it. But she and her husband Terry discovered the home was originally painted a bright lavender with turquoise, navy, mint and ivory trim, and she'd restored every one of those colors. Rendezvous Falls had many colorful homes, but Tani's was definitely in the running for most festive.

Zoey texted her friend before getting out of the car.

Z: I need coffee. And a good listener. And maybe tissues.

T: Where R U?

Z: In your driveway. Got time?

T: Wut? Come in, silly!

Tani and Zoey had become friends while working on the

annual elementary school talent show. Tani's son, Tyson, was the same age as Hazel. The two moms had bonded over their distinct dislike of the ladies on the committee who'd claimed they wanted help from some of the younger moms. Then they sabotaged every idea Tani implemented as new chairperson because it wasn't the way they'd done it in the past. At one of the meetings, Tani stood up, swept her long, narrow, purple-tipped braids over her shoulder and pointed at the previous chairwoman.

"*You're* the one who recruited me, Maryellen. You said the committee needed new ideas. I'm starting to wonder if all you needed was some *diversity* on the team to rubber-stamp your stale-ass *old* ideas." Tani had grabbed up her bag and turned to go. "Find another token."

At that point Zoey had stood as well, collecting a lot of wide-eyed stares from the other moms. "She's right. You're stonewalling her ideas, which hurts our fundraising, which will hurt our kids. And if Tani goes, *I* go. And so does my dad."

Rob Hartford had built all the stage sets and props for the school pageants and fairs since *Zoey* was a student, and they were stored in his barn. Maryellen begrudgingly backed down. Tani promptly named Zoey her vice-chair. There was still a *precious* group of women who tried interfering with their plans, but Tani and Zoey outwitted them at every turn, and raised more money than Maryellen's pals ever had.

Just as Zoey reached the top step, the front door opened. Tani was just as colorful as her house was, wearing an orange and blue tribal-print caftan duster over black leggings and camisole. Her headscarf matched the duster—which she'd undoubtedly made herself—and was knotted above her forehead. Her lipstick was dark orange, matching her nails. The woman was a walking fashion magazine spread, even on a weekday morning.

"What a wonderful surprise!" Tani cried. "Come on in and I'll start a fresh pot of coffee. I hope you were kidding about the tissues, but I put a box on the table just in case. I take it this isn't about decorating advice?" She stepped aside as Zoey came in.

"No need for that—Hazel's designing her own room. Black ceiling and all." They were going to paint the walls that weekend, then Vickie would deliver the glammed-up bed as a surprise. She followed Tani into her modern white kitchen overlooking a backyard in full bloom. "I need parenting advice. Or dating advice. Or dating while a parent advice."

Tani's eyebrows rose. "I haven't dated in a long, *long* time." She and her husband, Terry, had been married over twenty years, fresh out of high school.

"I know." Zoey sat on a stool at the marble-topped kitchen island. "But I need to talk this out with someone I trust to keep it between us and who isn't going to have her own agenda."

"Hang on," Tani answered, pressing the button on the coffee maker to grind fresh coffee beans for the brew. When the noise subsided, she pulled two mugs from the cupboard and turned. "The more you talk, the more questions I have. Who has an agenda? What parenting advice could you possibly need? And most importantly, who the hell are you dating? The last I knew, you said you weren't ready to even think about it."

"Maybe I should have stayed with that thought," she replied. "And I'm not really *dating*, we're just—"

"Flirting?"

"More than flirting…"

"Kissing?"

"More than that."

"Oh, shit—you've already gone to bed with the guy, haven't you?" Tani's eyes were round. "You skipped over the preliminaries and just hopped right in the sack. Damn, girl. Are you having regrets or aching to jump his bones again?"

Zoey closed her eyes with a sigh.

"Both."

"Ahh…and that's the problem, isn't it?" The coffee maker beeped, and Tani filled the two mugs and sat next to Zoey. "Tell me everything."

She did, although it took a while for her friend to get past the news that the man involved was Mike McKinnon.

"*Mike?* The guy you've known since you were little? Mary's brother?" She paused. "Well, that explains why you can't talk to Mary about it. Or the half-dozen McKinnon cousins who live in town. Hell, it's hard to think of *anyone* in Rendezvous Falls who doesn't know Mike… and like him." Her eyes narrowed. "Wait, didn't you tell Piper Taggart and me a couple months ago that you would *never* feel that way about Mike because you were besties and you didn't want to ruin that? Oh…" Tani put her hand on Zoey's arm. "You ruined that, didn't you?"

There was a very good chance she had. "Are you going to let me tell you the story, or would you rather play twenty questions?"

Tani raised her hands in innocence, then made a gesture as if to lock her lips and throw away the key. Zoey told her everything, from that night in the shop a month ago when she and Mike had that weird conversation about her boobs to last night's adventures on Dad's desk—although she didn't provide as many details as Tani would have liked.

And then Hazel's painfully timed comments that morning about wanting Zoey to remain virginal.

Tani snorted. "Ship's already sailed on that one. Or should I say the *desk* has already sailed? Damn." She paused, staring into her mug, then standing as she realized both their mugs were empty. She refilled them, then sat again, still deep in thought. "I know Monique Johnson pretty well. Just because she's using a dating app doesn't mean she's out there going wild with a new man every night or anything."

"I'm not judging Monique at all. She's a grown woman and can do what she wants. She deserves to be happy."

"The same could be said about you," Tani pointed out.

"Maybe. But when my daughter literally asks me to be a nun when it comes to dating—twelve hours after I had sex with my best friend on my late father's desk—I don't know how to wrap my head around that."

There was a long beat of silence in the spotless kitchen. Tani reminded Zoey a lot of Vickie—stylish, with never a hair, or dish, out of place. But Tani was more laid-back than Vickie—it seemed to come more naturally to her. The style. The wisdom. That's why Zoey valued her feedback. She knew it would be honest and direct, even if it wasn't what she wanted to hear. But the longer it took for Tani to answer, the more anxious Zoey felt. Finally, Tani straightened in her seat.

"You're trying too hard."

"At what? Screwing up my life? My friendships? My daughter?"

"See—that's what I mean. You're not just thinking one step ahead. You're trying to see *fifty* steps ahead of every single move you make." Tani gripped Zoey's hand and squeezed it. "You can't control everything. And you shouldn't try. Let's start with the basics. You're a great mom. You have a moderately successful business. Your house is paid for. You're a smart, attractive woman who, regardless of the opinions of a thirteen-year-old child, *deserves* to have a man in her life if she wants one."

Tani dipped her head lower so she could look up at Zoey's face. "Mike makes you happy? The sex is good? You're still friends?"

Zoey didn't hesitate. "Yes. But…"

"No buts. You are two mature, compassionate people who are not doing anything wrong. You've talked it out, right? You're both going in with the same expectations? Friendly and on the down-low?"

Zoey nodded.

"As far as Hazel goes," Tani continued. "I understand you want to shield her from any more stress. But the reality is, her parents are divorced. You moved her into a new house. Chris is marrying Genna, who's having a baby. It's a lot, but Hazel has navigated all of that really well." Zoey started to argue, but Tani talked over her. "Was she upset when you and Chris told her about the divorce?"

"Very." There had been weeks of tears and bargaining and pleading.

"Is she okay with it now?"

"Relatively. She'll never be thrilled, but she accepts it."

"And Chris and Genna? Isn't she about to be in their wedding party?"

"Well, yes, but it doesn't mean it was easy for her to reach that point," Zoey answered, thinking of her comment about coming in third or fourth in her dad's life. She needed to feel number one to Zoey. And Hazel didn't hate Genna. They were bonding over dress shopping. *Hooray…*

"Exactly," Tani said with a nod. "Hazel has handled everything life has thrown at her so far. If your relationship with Mike goes anywhere, she'll deal with that, too. It's not like she *really* wants you to move to a convent. Kids tend to just say ridiculous stuff like that." She chuckled. "When Tyson was ten, he told me that if I *really* loved him I'd quit my job so I'd always be home when he needed me. But I told him he wouldn't have been very happy without all the toys and amusement park trips my income gave us."

Zoey drained her coffee cup and walked over to the sink to rinse it. Then she stopped, turning to face her friend with narrowed eyes.

"Three years ago? Isn't that when you went from full-time to part-time at the furniture store? So you'd be home more?"

Tani laughed. "Yes, okay. I *did* adjust my life for him. My point is that I didn't upend it completely, or deny myself a job I love because of something my little boy said when he was upset. My job makes me happy. And that makes me a better person. Which makes me a better mom."

"Are you saying having a wild love affair with Mike McKinnon will make me a better person?"

"You've already said he makes you happy, so…yeah." Tani stood and joined Zoey at the sink. "Of course, that's assuming one of you doesn't break the other's heart."

CHAPTER NINETEEN

"VICKIE, WE NEED to talk." Gordon… *Gordy*…set his coffee mug on her counter.

"Oh, God." She rolled her eyes. "Is this about the deck? Did you find something *else* that needs to be rebuilt?"

"It's not about the deck. It's about you and me. And your kitchen pantry. And a certain kiss from a couple weeks ago that you haven't mentioned since."

"You haven't mentioned it, either." Vickie straightened, arching her eyebrow to emphasize her winning point.

He folded his arms, not looking defeated in the least. "Kinda hard to mention something to someone who won't stay in the same air space as me for more than three seconds."

That was fair. She *had* been avoiding him. Half because she didn't want them to get carried away again. And half because she was hoping they would. And that would be… A disaster? Wonderful? She hadn't decided yet.

"Well, I'm standing here now," she said. "What do you want to say?"

His square jaw, covered with salt-and-pepper stubble, moved back and forth as he studied her. "Look, if you don't want to kiss me again, just say so, Vickie. I can handle it." He took a step in her direction. "But I get the funny feeling you're avoiding me because you *want* to kiss me, and you're scared. The thing is, the Vickie Mallory I used to know wasn't scared of anything. So… I'm confused." He scrubbed his hand over his face, making that stubble sound like sandpaper. "I don't like this silent treatment you've been giving me. Tell me what's going on in that pretty head of yours."

Vickie pressed her tongue against her top lip and stared at the floor, struggling to hold in her thoughts. And failing. Still looking down, she let the words tumble out.

"I'm a vain woman, Gordon Lexiter. Always have been. You know that. If we kiss again, I'm going to want…more. And I haven't *done* more in a long time. I'm not the high school senior you shagged in the back seat of your mom's Buick. My body has changed. *I've* changed…"

Memories of that long ago night had been keeping her awake ever since they'd kissed in the pantry. Homecoming dance. A warm fall night. A short drive to a dark country road in the hills above Rendezvous Falls.

She'd argued with her *actual* date for the dance—Jerry Rogers. They weren't an official couple or anything, but he'd asked and she'd accepted. He'd tucked a flask into his jacket and sampled it liberally all night. He'd gotten more and more handsy with her as the night went on. She knew why—she'd made the mistake the year before of sleeping with another football player. It hadn't exactly been a stellar first-time experience, made worse by the fact that he bragged to his pals about their sweaty, uncomfortable fumbling around in the guy's basement. She'd finally convinced herself it didn't matter if kids were whispering about her. She'd held her chin high and looked down at everyone as if *they* were the ones in the wrong, not her. They couldn't hurt her if she didn't let them.

But she didn't want to miss her senior year homecoming dance, so she'd accepted Jerry's invitation. He seemed like a good kid, and it wasn't like they had to pretend to be in some lovey-dovey relationship. She'd found a navy blue bridesmaid dress at the secondhand shop and her grandmother had shortened it and made a few alterations so that it fit like a glove. Grandma told her she looked like Audrey Hepburn.

When Jerry first saw her, he'd looked as if he'd just won first prize in some contest. He wouldn't leave her alone. Pinching her ass, groping her chest, leaving a trail of wet sloppy kisses on her shoulder. When he'd tried pulling her behind the bushes near the steps to the gymnasium, she'd swung her purse at him. It was a glittery cocktail bag on a narrow chain. It had a hard plastic case, and it impacted Jerry's nose with a loud whack. When he realized he was bleeding, he'd taken a threatening step toward her. That's when Gordy had stepped between them.

She didn't know what he'd said to his football teammate, but it was enough to send Jerry stumbling away, muttering curse words. Gordy asked if she was okay, and the kindness of his words had broken through her icy shields. She'd started to cry, and he'd led her to his car. They drove around for a while, then parked and talked for hours.

And somehow, her head had ended up on his shoulder, with his arm around her. They'd kissed. And sweetly, tenderly, slowly…they'd made love right there in his mom's car. It wasn't sweaty or awkward at all.

"The girl I remember from that night…" Gordy was now at her side, his hand touching her arm, pulling her closer. "Was vulnerable and real. She dropped all those protective walls and let me in, if only for that one, perfect time."

Vickie slid into Gordy's arms as easily as she might shrug on a warm winter coat. Once again, fifty-some years after the first time, her head rested on his shoulder and her eyes closed. She inhaled and held on, reveling in the scent of him—man and spice.

She'd been afraid back then, too. Not of Gordy, but of what people might say, what dating him for real might do to her plans to conquer the world with her class and her wit.

She'd wanted to be like Grandma's idols—Bacall, Kelly, Hepburn—and the classy socialites they portrayed on the screen. A rough-edged linebacker wasn't part of the plan. She'd explained it to him then, and that memory made her cringe. She must have sounded like such a bitch. But he'd just given her that laid-back, slanted smile and told her he understood.

She sighed softly. "It really was pretty perfect, wasn't it? And then I tossed you aside. How could you possibly forgive me for being such a snob?"

Gordy rested his cheek against her hair. "That snob routine was your armor. It wasn't *you.* And you were right—I didn't fit into the neat little life of your dreams. You were *Breakfast at Tiffany's* and I was *On the Waterfront.*" His arms wrapped around her and she snuggled even closer. "You weren't the only one with big dreams back then. I got that football scholarship to Syracuse and thought I'd go straight into the pros from there." His chest rumbled with low laughter.

"Reality smacked me in the face when I busted up my knee two years later. The pros were out for me, and I was a slacker in the classroom. So I came home to Rendezvous Falls to work for my dad, and found you married to Stanley Noor and living in that big stone mansion near the college. You were barely twenty-three and already on the fanciest charity committees in town, hostessing your little white glove tea parties just the way you'd dreamed of doing."

Vickie heard the edge in his voice. She pulled back and

looked up into his gray-blue eyes. "So you *were* angry with me."

"Nah." He grinned. "Well, maybe a little. More *envious* than angry. You'd chased after your dream and caught it, just like that. And me? I'd chased and failed." He kissed her temple, leaving his lips against her skin. "But I got over it. I built a good life. Had a good marriage. Raised good sons. And I watched you shine like the star you are." He kissed her temple again. "And now I'm holding you in my arms again, so one of my goals *did* come true."

She put her head back on his shoulder and they stood there in silence. Outside, a soft breeze was coming in off Seneca Lake, making her wind chimes play a sweet, tinkling melody. Birds were singing, someone's dog was barking in the distance. A Jet Ski sped by on the water, sounding like an angry hornet.

She'd been afraid so many times in her life, fretting about what people would think. But right now she was standing in her kitchen, held close by a man who'd made it very clear he wanted her—just the way she was. And suddenly she wasn't afraid anymore. Not of him. Not of what he wanted. She kissed the base of his neck, feeling the pulse in his throat as it picked up speed.

"I think we should…uh…you know…" She kissed his neck again, but he pulled away and tipped her chin up with his fingers so they were staring into each other's eyes.

"You gotta say it. Tell me what you want. Do you want me to take you to dinner first? Share a little candlelight and champagne tonight before we—"

"No. I want you *now*. Before I change my mind."

His eyebrows rose. "*Now?* Victoria Pendergast, are you seducing your contractor on a work morning?"

"It might just be now or never, Gordy. What's it going to be?"

He cupped her face in his hands. "Hey, I didn't mean to make it sound like I was pushing you. I just wanted us to talk about it. We don't have to—"

"Is that a no then?" She pulled her shoulders back and pushed his hands away, her pride stung. "Guess you should get back to wo—"

His mouth fell on hers, swallowing the rest of her snark. And taking all the air from her lungs. She grabbed at him as if he were a life raft, pressing her fingers into his shoulders. She returned the kiss and their mouths did an intoxicating dance. His fingers slid down to grip her bottom and hold her hard against him.

"I could never say no to you, woman." He spoke the words against her lips, then tipped his head back, staring up at the ceiling with a wide grin. "I'm just *damn* glad I stopped at the pharmacy on the way over."

"For what? Condoms?" Lord knew, *she* didn't have any around.

"I always have one or two of those handy—a habit since high school." He caught her up in a short, intense kiss. "But I stopped to pick up a refill on my pills, so…if you'll let me run out to the truck…we can definitely do this."

It took a moment before she figured out what he was saying.

"Are you talking about little blue pills?"

His shoulder lifted. "Neither one of us is the same as we were in Mom's Buick, babe. I may need a little help, but trust me, in an hour I'll be good to go. And in the meantime…" His eyes darkened with desire. "I promise you won't be bored."

Vickie sucked in a sharp breath as his hand cupped her

breast. The heat that blossomed low in her belly felt achingly familiar. She hadn't forgotten how to be sexy after all. She just hadn't met a man in years who made her feel this kind of desire.

She rose on her toes and kissed him, throwing her cares away as she ran her tongue along his lips, forcing them apart. His hand continued to knead her breast as she pressed into his mouth. They were taking each other, right there in her kitchen.

No, not in the kitchen. She pulled away, her breath ragged.

"When you get back from your truck, you'll find me upstairs."

His eyes went warm and tender.

"Yes, ma'am. I believe I will."

"SON OF A BI—" Mike glanced at his seven-year-old niece, Katie, and grimaced. "I mean son of a *bee*, that hurt!" She giggled, and he pretended to be offended. "What's so funny about your uncle Mike hurting himself?"

"Uncle Mike, you were going to swear!" Katie pointed at him, her other hand on her hip. Mary's daughter was a carbon copy of her, with the same self-righteous attitude. "Momma says we swear a lot 'cuz we're Irish. Do you think we swear 'cuz we're Irish?"

"Total blasphemy!" Finn O'Hearn stepped out onto the patio, where Mike was attempting—and failing—to repair a loose railing. Owen Cooper was right behind him. Finn, who was actually born in Ireland, gave Katie an exaggerated look of seriousness. "Ireland is the land of poets." He winked. "And even when we curse, we elevate it to artistry." Finn then frowned at Mike. "Oi, you're bleedin', lad."

Mike glanced at the cut on his palm, where the screwdriver had grazed him when it slid off the screw head. It burned, but it wasn't deep enough for concern.

"I'm fine. Damn wood on this deck is tough as steel. I told Mary I'd secure the railing, but I don't want to leave the screw sticking out where one of the kids can bump it and I can't get the fu—" Katie was still watching with interest. "...*freakin'* thing to set all the way."

Owen stepped forward, his hand out. "Give me the screwdriver." He knelt on the step and leaned into the effort, getting all three screws in and flush with the wood. He stood, handing the screwdriver back to Mike with a grin.

"Don't feel bad, boys. The world needs lawyers and professors, even if you can't build anything."

Finn scoffed. "Says the lad who plants flowers for a livin'."

"I like flowers!" Katie announced proudly.

Owen tapped her nose with his finger. "As you should, young lady. That's why the world needs landscapers and flower shops." He pointed to Mike and Finn. "But we'll still keep these fancy boys around, just because we like them, okay?"

The girl's auburn curls bounced as she nodded in agreement before running back inside. Finn handed Mike one of the beers he was holding, giving another to Owen. They sat at the patio table and tapped the bottles together lightly in a toast before drinking.

There weren't many things better than a cold beer on a hot June afternoon. It was Father's Day, and Mary had insisted on having a house party, even though her husband Sam was practically immobilized by the contraption he was strapped into after having shoulder surgery a few days ago.

She wasn't handling the work of entertaining alone— their grandmother, Maura, was in the kitchen with Finn's wife, Bridget. Owen's wife, Lucy, was sitting with the book club seniors at the dining room table, sharing some funny bridezilla stories from the flower shop. Mary was making Sam, a state legislator, comfortable in the recliner while Hazel did her best to keep up with their three kids. And Hazel's mom was walking toward the open sliding doors to the deck.

Zoey's hair was loose, with one side pinned back from her face with a plain barrette. She was wearing a dress— something rare enough that everyone made note of it. He could tell it annoyed her from the way the corners of her mouth tightened, even as she smiled at their comments. The pale yellow dress had tiny daisies scattered on it. It was loose, although he could definitely see her curves beneath the soft fabric as she walked. She wore white sandals, so flat and strappy that she may as well have been barefoot.

"Is this a meeting of the men's club out here?" she asked, smiling, but carefully avoiding making direct eye contact with Mike. They'd discussed this cookout in great detail last night, and she'd given him a long list of dos and don'ts. Mary was her friend and his sister, so it would be awkward if they didn't attend. But Zoey made it clear that they could not arrive together and could not even be seen together, unless in a group. They could not touch under any circumstances, and definitely could not sneak upstairs for a hot kiss, as Mike had suggested.

They'd successfully kept their relationship under wraps for three weeks now. They still texted jokes to each other, although the humor had turned a bit more risqué. They still had their friendly chats in the shop, and, depending on where Hazel was sleeping that night, they'd eventually find their way to Zoey's bedroom or back to her dad's old desk, now well fortified with blankets, cushions and pillows.

She'd even come to his place a couple of times, but she was so worried about the neighbors seeing her car that she'd parked on Main Street and *walked* the four blocks to his house. Which meant, as a gentleman, he had to get dressed and walk her back to her car. Where he wasn't allowed to kiss her, because it was Main Street and someone might see them. It was annoying, but worth it.

Because the sex was spectacular. It had nothing to do with what they did physically. It was the way sex with Zoey made him *feel*. The way she gave herself to him so completely, yet never lost herself in the process. She was a partner—giving and taking and being direct about what she liked or didn't like or wanted him to do again right away. It made the experience unlike any other he'd had with a woman. Making love with Zoey was just that good.

It wasn't until this very moment, as she breezed onto the sunny deck wearing that dress and that smile, that he realized how challenging today would be. Keeping his feelings for her to himself—especially in front of friends and family—was going to be hellishly difficult. As Owen and Finn greeted her and made room for her to join them, Mike found himself standing and stepping away.

"Where're you goin'?" Finn asked. "You can't leave when a pretty woman arrives at the table."

A wave of panic rose in his chest, making his lungs burn. This particular pretty woman was his best friend. His lover. The one who insisted they keep things *fun* and *light* and *casual*. And *secret*. She was staring up at him now with wide eyes and a blush of pink on each cheek. He couldn't possibly stay anywhere near Zoey and pretend he wasn't falling in love with her.

Oh, damn. He was falling in love with Zoey. The thought

made him go both hot and cold all at once. Thrilled and terrified. He realized they were all still staring at him.

"Uh… I promised Mary I'd help with…things." He stammered out the words and bolted into the house. He blinked a few times to acclimate his eyes after sitting in the sunshine. Mary stopped plumping pillows for Sam and looked over in surprise.

"Did you get stung by a bee or something?"

"No. Why?"

"Oh, I don't know—maybe because you ran in here like your ass was on fire?" She patted Sam's good shoulder and walked over to Mike. "Everything okay?"

"I just wanted to get out of the sun. I didn't put sunscreen on this morning." It was a feeble excuse.

"You poor fragile flower." She headed toward the kitchen, talking over her shoulder. "There's plenty of sunscreen in the upstairs medicine cabinet. Help yourself."

Instead of going upstairs, he sat in the living room with his brother-in-law, who was still pretty woozy from pain meds. Mike wondered if this party was really such a great idea, considering the man of honor was ready to nod off. But Sam brightened when his youngest, Gavin, toddled into the room, Hazel not far behind him.

She looked frazzled, searching the room with her eyes.

"Have you seen Nathan? I swear that kid can run right through walls and disappear on me." Nathan was the terror of the three kids. The four-year-old had been on the run from the time he was born, always looking to turn things upside down and dance on the wreckage.

Sam rolled his eyes. "Leave Gavin here with Uncle Mike and go find him before he builds a castle in the dining room out of the dining chairs." He looked at Mike. "He did that last week, then climbed the chairs with the intention of swinging on the chandelier like he'd seen some dude do in a cartoon. I can't decide if he's going to be president some-day or run a crime syndicate."

Mike took the two-year-old from Hazel and couldn't help returning the child's bright, drooling grin. Gavin was the mellowest of the three. He seemed genuinely happy wherever he was and with whomever happened to be there. Maybe it was because he was born on St. Patrick's Day.

"Well," Mike said, "at least you've got a lawyer in the family if he decides to go the criminal route, but I think he's too smart for that. That kid's brain is always spinning."

Mike bounced his knee and Gavin giggled. He didn't know why he'd been so hesitant to have kids with Becca. Why he'd kept her from having the family she'd wanted when she wanted it—never imagining they'd run out of time. Fear had been part of it—doubt about his ability to be a good father.

Now here he was, at forty, falling for a single mom. He made a funny face at Gavin. Becca would have loved the thought of him finally being a father figure to someone. She'd never doubted his ability to love a child. She'd be-lieved in him, even when he couldn't believe in himself.

But did *Zoey* believe he could do it? Was that one of the reasons she was determined to keep them a big, dark se-cret? Call him sensitive, but her insistence on keeping him apart from her life with Hazel was like a small burr under a saddle. It wore on him. Poked at him.

His grandmother appeared at his side, blowing kisses at Gavin while patting Mike's shoulder. "Food will be ready in twenty minutes, so someone better start grilling some meat. I think Finn fired up the grills already, but right now he's guzzling beer at the table with Zoey and Owen.

Bridget is putting Moira down for a nap. Can you take charge out there?"

"Sure, Nana." He didn't want to, but he couldn't tell her that without saying *why*. Because the *why* was drinking wine at the outside table, right next to the grill. "But I've got this little guy…"

He knew that excuse wouldn't fly. Nana lifted the boy with an exaggerated groan. "My God, child! You're grow-ing like a weed."

Mike stood, giving himself a mental pep talk. He could do this. He could be Zoey's buddy for the afternoon. Just pals. And maybe later they could pay a visit to the repair shop…and that sturdy old office desk.

The problem was, he was beginning to want *more* than stolen moments. *More* than being friends with benefits. He wanted *all* of Zoey. And she'd made it clear that wasn't going to happen anytime soon.

CHAPTER TWENTY

ZOEY WAS ON EDGE. And that sucked, because Mary's house was usually one of her favorite places to be. Her friend had an effortless style—which Mary insisted should be called *exhaustion*—when it came to entertaining. She treated everyone like family, and she figured family should be very forgiving of toys on the floor and a little dust on the shelves. And if they *couldn't* deal with that, they were welcome to leave. McKinnons were like that. Love me or go. Your choice.

Like the way Mike had left as soon as she'd stepped outside. As well as she knew him, she hadn't been able to read the emotions skipping across his face when their eyes met. A quick smile. A frown. A wrinkled forehead. Then up on his feet and gone.

Yes, she'd been extra firm about them not doing anything obvious to give their new relationship away with so many people around. But she never meant they should treat each other like strangers. She smoothed her hands down the yellow dress. Was it the dress that had thrown him off?

She didn't wear them often, but it wasn't like it had never happened before. Her legs were currently twisted around the legs of the patio chair like she was sitting on a barstool in jeans and boots, and she moved to cross them in a more ladylike manner. Vickie had always taught her to cross at the ankles, not the knees, and even better, do the royal "princess slant" with legs together but not crossed, knees leaning to one side.

Her godmother, sitting inside right now, would be thrilled to know Zoey remembered those etiquette lessons. She didn't know why she'd opted for a dress today. Maybe she was getting bored with jeans and T-shirts. Or she might be trying to show Mike she could have some style when she wanted to. Zoey had no intention of breaking their secret anytime soon, but *someday*, when Hazel was older and life had settled a bit, she hoped she and Mike could be an actual, normal, *public* couple.

Mike was a respected attorney from a prominent local family. His parents were involved in some powerful political circles in Albany. His first wife had been beautiful and sophisticated. Becca hadn't been a snob or anything— she was kind and generous with everyone she met. She'd worked in real estate, and, like Vickie, had always worn the latest styles. She'd set the bar very, *very* high for whoever came after her in Mike's life.

Zoey didn't know when their *someday* would be, and she knew the wait was chafing at Mike. It was becoming more and more difficult for her, too. Because she was very sure she was falling in love with him.

She'd never intended for it to happen, but she had moved w-a-y beyond the friend zone with Mike in her heart. She couldn't imagine ever going back to being just friends. She didn't even want to try.

Finn was telling a story about the baby Moira's knack for waking up hungry every time he and Bridget were trying to have some fun in the sheets. Zoey drained her wineglass in one gulp, wishing it was whiskey. Maybe it really *was* this dress making her feel so weird today. It wasn't like her to worry about what Mike thought of her appearance.

He'd told her multiple times he thought she was beautiful, but she couldn't help thinking that eventually he'd want a woman more like Becca to settle down with after having some fun with his good pal Zoey.

She blinked a few times, shocked to realize her eyes were watery. She stood, mumbling something about finding her sunglasses, before heading inside. She met Mike in the doorway, carrying a platter stacked with hot dogs.

His steady brown eyes calmed her instantly—how did he do that? She started to reach for his hand before remembering where they were. He caught her fingertips, giving them a quick squeeze before releasing her.

"Nana put me on grill duty," he said. He studied her face. "You look upset. What happened?"

"Nothing. I'm fine."

"Don't bullshit me, Zoey." His voice was barely a whisper, then he gave her a soft smile. "Go grab the platter of burgers from the kitchen and join me at the grill." He dipped his head to meet her eyes with a playful grin. "No one will think twice about you and I arguing over how to cook hot dogs."

She got the burgers from Maura and met Mike outside, where two grills were blazing. He'd put the hot dogs on one, and she put the burgers on the other. Mary stepped outside and laughed when she saw them together.

"I hope everyone wants their hot dogs burned to a blackened crisp," she announced loudly, "because that's how Zoey likes them. My brother, on the other hand, wants his burgers so rare they're still mooing when they go in the bun." She pointed at the two of them. "I love you guys, but try to meet in the middle on cooking times, okay?"

Everyone laughed and went back to their own conversations, giving Mike and Zoey a semblance of privacy at the grills.

"I've never seen you grill in a dress before—be careful." His voice was low and slightly amused.

She rolled her eyes. "I know how to wear a dress and still function, thank you very much."

One of his eyebrows rose. "I know that. You look nice, by the way. Really nice." He leaned his head closer. "I look forward to peeling that off you later."

She licked her lips, then shook her head sharply. "None of that talk here. We agreed to be *friend*-friends today, remember?"

"That was before you sashayed in here looking like sunshine, babe."

She stepped back, shaking her spatula at him and fighting a smile. "Knock it off. Everyone's watching."

His gaze flickered up to the house and back to her. "No one is watching. They just want their dinner." He made no effort to hide *his* smile. "And I just want you."

"Seriously, Mike. We can*not* do this here. My daughter is in the house."

The light in his eyes cooled so quickly that she wondered if she'd been worried about the wrong obstacle to a future with Mike. Maybe living up to Becca's example wouldn't be enough. He said he'd told Becca he wasn't ready to have children. How would he feel about helping to raise someone else's child? If he wasn't ready to be a stepparent, then what was the point of bringing him into Hazel's life at all?

"Do you really not want children?" The question came out before she could stop it.

"Holy shit." Mike stepped back, his eyes wide. "I'm not allowed to even flirt with you here, but *you're* okay dropping that bombshell of a question on me right now?"

"I'm sorry. I didn't mean..." Today was a bad idea. She sighed. "Maybe I should fake a headache or something and just leave."

"Hey..." Mike's fingers entwined with hers for just a moment. "Don't do that. But let's put a pin in the do-I-want-children discussion until we're alone, okay?" The corner of his mouth tipped upward. "You're burning my burgers."

She jumped, then started flipping them. "They're not burned. They're *cooked*. I know that's a novel concept for you."

And just like that, they were back on steady ground again. This was an argument they'd had all their adult lives. She wanted her hot dogs and bacon crispy and blackened. He wanted his steaks and burgers barely warmed. She always told him he was going to die of salmonella, and he always said she was destroying perfectly good food by incinerating it.

She forced him to leave the burgers alone and he insisted on pulling the hot dogs before they were completely charred. They were laughing together while they cooked. As they plated the food, she pointed out the one burger she'd pulled off early—and pink—for him. And he'd left two hot dogs—her favorites—on the grill until they were black and crispy.

When they both turned around with their platters of food, they found Mary standing right behind them, eyes narrowed.

"Is something going on with you two?"

"Besides our usual cooking debate?" Mike asked. "No, why?"

Her expression hadn't changed. "I don't know. I can't put my finger on it."

Mike answered again, steady as always.

"Good. Because I don't want your finger on me *or* my food. If you'll get out of the way, I'd like to take this inside so people can eat." He brushed by her, but Mary stopped Zoey, stepping directly in her path.

"Are you and Mike…?"

Zoey channeled some of Mike's snark.

"Best friends? Yes, we are. Excuse me…" She maneuvered around Mary, but as she walked away, she heard her muttering behind her.

"Best friends, my ass."

MIKE WAS IN a better mood after everyone ate. He was sure it had something to do with the laughter he'd shared with Zoey as they cooked. Having fun with her just made the world seem right. He wasn't sure what had piqued his sister's attention, but he wasn't as bothered by it as Zoey was.

Zoey made sure she and he didn't sit together. She'd taken a seat next to Vickie Pendergast—the only empty seat left at the dining table inside. She winked at him when he spotted her, as if she'd just won a battle. Vickie was staring at him intently. What had they done that caught so many people's attention? Nana was staring at Zoey. And that Rick guy from the book club was watching Vickie watch Mike. *Great.* He decided to eat outside.

He had a nice meal with Owen, Lucy, Finn and Bridget. Owen's landscaping business was running hot and heavy now that summer weather had arrived. He was still doing a few cleanup jobs from the storm, but mostly he was planting and doing some hardscaping projects, installing stone patios and retaining walls. Lucy was working more hours than ever at the flower shop, now that the original owner—and now partner—Connie was dating Stan Perelli. Connie was edging closer and closer to retirement.

Finn and Bridget had one topic of conversation—life with baby Moira. The lack of sleep. The silly sounds the baby made. The lack of sleep. How adorable she was. The lack of sleep. Mike nodded and laughed when appropriate, but the conversation brought him back to Zoey's question about whether he wanted children. They'd talked about that before, and she'd been clear that she didn't want another baby now that Hazel was thirteen.

Had she changed her mind? Was she feeling him out for the possibility of having a child together? His fork fell from his hand. Was Zoey *pregnant*?

"Dude, you okay over there?" Owen asked.

Mike blinked and looked around the table. He had no idea what they'd all been talking about. His skin went clammy. He had to know why Zoey had asked, and he had to know *now*. Because if she was pregnant… He stood, doing his best to smile at his tablemates as his stomach churned.

"Fine. Sorry. I'm fine. Just remembered something I forgot to do at the office, so I'll uh…have to go in early tomorrow. But it's fine." He glanced inside the house and saw Zoey heading into the kitchen with a stack of dirty paper plates. With any luck, he could catch her alone in the kitchen and get some answers. He gathered up his plate and utensils. "I'm going to check out the desserts…"

Bridget winked at everyone else at the table. "I'm sure they're *fine*."

He didn't know why there were snickers around the table at that. He shrugged it off and headed to the kitchen. Zoey was there alone, putting the paper plates in the trash.

"We need to talk." He barked out the words like an order.

She looked up in surprise. "Now?"

"Right now." Once the thought of pregnancy was in his head, it wouldn't go away.

"O-kay." She glanced over his shoulder and he realized his grandmother had joined them. Hopefully she hadn't heard him demanding Zoey's attention like that. Nana smiled, not showing any indication she'd heard a thing.

"Thank goodness for disposable plates and dinner-ware—cleanup is easy!" Nana put more used plates in the trash bag. "And you even have a helper. You make a good team."

"We're not a team." He winced at how that sounded. There was just something in the way his grandmother was examining them that made him defensive. "I mean… I just happened to come in the kitchen while she was here."

"Well, as long as you're in here, you two could clean the pots we used for the corn on the cob, and that big pan we baked the beans in." Nana looked up as Mary started to enter the kitchen and waved her off. "You go take care of your husband, Mary. Mike and Zoey are in charge of the kitchen. Too many people in here will make it impossible to work."

"I see," Mary replied, giving Mike a strange twin-vibe look that he couldn't interpret. "Let's leave the two of them alone, then."

Zoey's forehead furrowed as the women left.

"I feel like we're being set up."

"I'm just glad we're alone for a few minutes." He put his hand on her arm and steered her toward the sink, which was loaded with pans.

"So what's this urgent matter we need to discuss?" Zoey sprayed dish soap in a pan and started filling it with hot water.

"It's about that question you asked earlier." He took the

pot from her and started scrubbing while she filled the next one. Zoey's eyes closed and her cheeks went pink.

"Oh, that. I saw you with Gavin earlier and remembered what you said about you and Becca not having children and…"

"Are you pregnant?"

The pot dropped from her hands, banging against the sink and making them both jump.

Mary appeared in the doorway. Mike couldn't help thinking she arrived freakishly fast. "Everything okay in here?"

"Yes—sorry!" Zoey waved, the pink gone from her cheeks. There wasn't much color left in her face at all.

Mary sent Mike what looked like a watch-your-step look, but she was gone again before he could question what her problem was. He looked to Zoey and quickly backed away from her glare. He wasn't fast enough, because she reached out and pinched his forearm. And twisted, just like she used to do when they were kids.

He didn't want to bring Mary back by yelling, so he pulled away and whisper-yelled instead. "Shit, Zoey! What was *that* for?"

"Seriously?" She was using his same low whisper, but hers cracked with fury. "You ask me that question in a house full of people? In a house where my *daughter* could have heard you?" She paused and took a steadying breath, confusion replacing some of her anger. "And for the record, the answer is no."

CHAPTER TWENTY-ONE

MIKE'S EXPRESSION WAS such a quick flash of sadness then relief that Zoey suspected *he* didn't know himself how he felt about her answer. Her hand instinctively went to her stomach, and she had to admit she felt a little stab of sadness herself. Having Mike's baby would be... *Wait just a damn minute.* They were forty years old. She did *not* want to have a baby. Not even with Mike. But what if he'd decided *he* wanted one?

"Oh, God. Did you *want* me to be pregnant?"

"Shhh!"

He glanced at the entrance to the kitchen and she realized she'd forgotten to whisper the question. But there was a steady flow of conversation and laughter coming from the rest of the house, and Mary hadn't popped up in the doorway again. They were safe.

"Of course I don't want—" he looked to the door "—*that.* I mean...if you were, it would be okay. But I'm glad you're not, because...wow. That would be a lot." His face was ashen.

"That's an understatement." They both turned back to the sink. "Whatever gave you the idea I might be?"

"I don't know. You asked me about kids and it seemed important to you. Once my brain went there, I couldn't stop wondering."

She handed him a dish towel for the pans and started

working on the glass casserole the baked beans had cooked in. This one was going to take more effort to clean. She tried to shrug her hair away from her face, and Mike reached out to sweep it back over her shoulder. His touch, even just his fingertips, settled her somehow.

"First, if I *was* preg…" Now it was her turn to glance at the door. "If I was that, I'd *tell* you. In private. I wouldn't beat around the bush about it at some cookout, because… well, it wouldn't matter if you didn't want children at that point. And second? Yeah, it *would* be a lot. For *me*." She paused her scrubbing long enough to meet his bemused gaze. "Why are you laughing?"

He chuckled, gently flicking the end of his dish towel at her butt. "You're right. You would tell me straight out about it. That's what I lo— um…like about you and I." He took the baking dish from her hand. "I admit I did a panic spiral, okay? I'm sorry. But what made *you* ask that question about kids?"

It was time to be honest.

"I picked up a weird vibe when I mentioned being careful because Hazel was here. You cooled off so fast that I wondered if you resented her being a factor between us."

He set the pan on the drying rack before turning and taking her hands in his. "I never meant to suggest that she's between us like that. It's hard for me to keep this a big, dark secret. That's not my style. But I can be frustrated and still understand completely why you need it to be this way."

She stared at him for a moment, and he lightly ran his hands up and down her arms, somehow knowing she needed his soothing touch. She hadn't really considered how much their secret was weighing on him.

"I'd love for us to *not* have to sneak around and tell all these little white lies to the people we care about. But I

need to do the right thing as a mom. That's who I am first."
She rested her hands on his chest. "It's hard, turning those
switches on and off—friend, lover, mom. I want it all, but
having it all is…impossible right now."

Before he could respond, they heard Vickie calling out
loudly from the dining room. "Oh, *Hazel* honey, if you're
going into the kitchen, could you take these dessert plates
with you?"

Zoey and Mike jumped away from each other and scur-
ried to get busy. He started drying the pans all over again,
while she wiped down the sink with the sponge. A minute later Hazel came in, Gavin propped on one hip and her
other hand holding a tilting pile of small paper plates and
napkins. Zoey hurried to take the plates, tossing them out.

"Thanks, Mom." Hazel laughed. "Vickie was bound and
determined that I had to stop and collect every plate on the
table before I came in here. All I wanted was to get a glass
of juice for this little guy and say goodbye."

Zoey nodded, ignoring the catch in her throat. The
worst part of divorce by far was the bargaining over their
daughter's time. But it *was* Father's Day, so of course Hazel
should spend time with Chris.

"Your dad's picking you up here, right?"

"He's picking me up in five. You sure it's okay for me
to stay there for a couple of days?"

"Of course it's okay." Zoey filled a sippy cup with juice
and handed it to Gavin, who grabbed at it with a big grin.
"You should be with your dad on Father's Day. And school's
out, so staying until Wednesday morning is fine—just don't
forget you're working for Mary for four hours on Tuesday.
What are you planning to do with your father?"

"Genna made reservations at the marina restaurant for
dinner tonight—that's why I couldn't eat here. She's put-

ting the final wedding plans together this week, and she wants my help. We're going to get my dress fitted." Hazel's *never-impressed-with-anything* attitude dropped for a moment, replaced by little girl excitement. "It's going to be my first custom-fit dress, just like a model!" Hazel reached out and tugged at Zoey's dress. "Speaking of dresses, this is dope. You should wear more yellow."

Hazel gave Zoey a quick peck on the cheek, then turned and left the kitchen, giving Mike a quick wave.

"Is *dope* a good thing?" Mike asked Zoey.

"I think so. With social media, the *in* phrases seem to change weekly."

"So your daughter could be totally shading you without you knowing it?" He laughed. "I don't know how you do it."

"A lot of parenting is just dumb luck," she admitted. "I spend a lot of time crossing my fingers that I'm not totally screwing her up for life."

"Hey." His arm slid around her waist. "You're a natural at being a mom. I'd be lost."

"I'm lost all the time, Mike. I don't really remember my mom, so I have no example to follow. I'm operating blind here." She leaned her head against his chest before remembering where they were and stepping out of his embrace.

"Well," he said, "I think you're amazing. The parenting thing has always been intimidating to me. It's not the kids, but being *responsible* for them. I don't know if I have that skill set."

She patted his shoulder. "There's a lot of on-the-job training, that's for sure. But you have a good heart and a great sense of fairness. You'd do fine."

Mike would be a wonderful father. A wonderful stepfather. She just had to figure out how to bring him into Hazel's life. She had a funny feeling that he was right—

waiting wasn't going to make that any easier. She swallowed hard, looking around the kitchen. "I think we're done in here."

When they walked out of the kitchen, the house fell instantly silent. So did the table out on the deck, beyond the open doors. Everyone was staring at them. Her heart sank.

"What happened?"

Mary was standing near Sam's recliner. She folded her arms and arched one eyebrow high.

"I think it's time for you two to tell *us* what's happening."

Zoey's mouth opened, but she couldn't construct words. Mike seemed to be suffering from the same problem. Vickie's prim voice filled the silence.

"When I think of me asking you—more than once, I believe—if there was anything between you and Mike and you flat out *lied* to my face." There was more amusement in her voice than offense. "My own goddaughter!"

"I'm thinking the same thing, Vickie." Mary added. "I quizzed my brother and he denied it every time."

Zoey tried to jump-start her words. "There's nothing…" *Oh, what was the point?* "Okay, there is *something*, but…" She looked around the rooms, and Mary quickly reassured her.

"Hazel left a few minutes ago and busybody Katie is out on the swings. You can speak freely. And *honestly*, if you try real hard."

"Okay, *fine*. Mike and I might be more than friends these days. We've added…benefits now. Satisfied?"

Mike straightened, finally regaining his voice. "No offense to my family and friends, but this is nobody's business but ours. If we decide to sleep together, that's *our* problem… I mean, that's our decision."

Did he think sleeping with her was a *problem*? She looked over at him, and he quickly mouthed *sorry* before continuing. "Look, it's only been a few weeks, and…" He looked to her for help.

"And," she added, "we didn't *lie*, we just didn't share because, like Mike said, it's really new." She gave Mary and Vickie a stern look. "And we do *not* want Hazel hearing about it from *anyone*. With Chris getting married and the new baby, I'm the only stability Hazel has right now."

Mike slid his arm around her waist. They could finally relax a little in front of their friends. He gave a quick squeeze. "What gave us away?"

A roar of laughter filled the house. *Yikes.*

Mary wiped her eyes. "Let's just say if you don't want Hazel to know, you need to avoid being in the same room around her. If I hadn't kept her so busy with the kids today, even *she'd* have no doubt what you two are up to."

Zoey and Mike looked at each other in confusion. Where had they gone wrong?

"Yup," Owen laughed. "From the moon eyes you kept making at each other to the little finger brushes you did every time you passed each other. It's like you two were magnets." He made a gesture with his hand toward his wife, Lucy, and she obliged by pretending to be pulled toward him against her will.

"Okay, okay." Mike chuckled. "It wasn't *that* bad."

"Pal, you had your arm around her at the grill!"

Zoey and Mike stared at each other before she protested. "We did *not*!"

A chorus of voices answered. "Yes, you did!"

Bridget coughed, trying to hold in her laughter. "I almost tripped over my own feet when I walked outside and saw you two down at the grill, snuggled close together and giggling. And then Mike's arm went around your waist for just a second, and your head hit his shoulder, and…well…it was pretty clear it wasn't the first time it happened."

"I don't giggle," Mike grumbled.

"Oh, brother of mine," Mary piped up. "You were giggling. And cooing. And melting."

Zoey and Mike *had* been laughing and reminiscing at the grill, and if he'd touched her waist, there's no doubt she could have leaned into it, forgetting where they were.

The seniors at the dining table had been listening with a great deal of amusement. Mike's grandmother, Maura, nodded toward him.

"And let's not forget the way you marched into the kitchen and announced you *needed to talk*. What was that urgent conversation about, I wonder?" She turned to Mary. "You were guarding the door—what did you hear?"

MIKE FROZE. If Mary *had* been listening, she knew he'd asked Zoey if she was pregnant. Her eyes met his, and this time he clearly read the twinspeak. *Relax. I've got your back.* She smiled at their grandmother.

"Just a lot of lovey-dovey stuff, Nana. New love is so adorable."

His relief at her little fib evaporated with her last sentence. He and Zoey spoke in unison.

"We're not in love!"

"Okay," Finn said with a laugh, holding up his hands to quiet everyone. "Let's not pick on them too much, friends. We all remember those early days of our relationships." He pulled Bridget close and kissed her forehead. "They're probably putting themselves through enough self-inflicted torture without us adding to it."

"I'd say so, yes." Mary gave Mike a pointed look. So she *had* heard the conversation about babies.

"Honestly, everyone, this…" Zoey gestured between Mike and herself. "This truly is brand-new."

"And burning hot, from the looks of it." Owen raised his beer bottle in a toast, and Lucy jabbed him with her elbow. "What?" He put his arm around her. "It reminds me of *us* when we met at Atlantic Beach way back when. We burned hot, too, remember?"

Mary walked over and gave Mike and Zoey quick hugs. "It's hard to think of you two as new when you've known each other for decades."

Zoey groaned. "Thanks for making me sound ancient."

"Duh—I'm the same age as you." Her voice dropped. "For the record, I approve of this. Very much." She turned around to face her guests. "We've had our fun, but let's remember that Zoey has a very good reason for wanting to keep this quiet, so mum's the word." She pointed at the book club group. "That includes you old troublemakers. Leave them alone and *no gossip*."

"Watch who you're calling old," Rick Thomas answered, winking as he did. "I'm still a working member of society, young lady."

Smaller conversations began to pop up, and people seemed to lose interest in pushing Mike and Zoey any further. Mike let out a long, slow breath and closed his eyes. They were still a secret—just a more fragile one now. Anyone could screw this up, not just him.

"I suppose that could have been worse." Zoey's voice was rich with humor. "Although I can't imagine how."

"Oh, I can think of a few ways, like if Mary had spilled the beans on what she heard us talking about."

Zoey's mouth dropped open. "You think she *heard*?"

"I know she did. She's probably saving it to hold over my head at some future date."

"Or *my* head. She's going to be pissed at both of us for not telling her."

Mike thought about that for a moment. Mary would support them both, no matter what. After all, the three of them had been a team since third grade.

"She'll be fine with it." He watched Mary take a slice of Nana's peach cobbler to her husband. "She's probably planning our wedding as we speak."

"God, I hope not," Zoey muttered. Then she looked up, her face pale. "I mean… We're nowhere near that point. Just because our friends and families know about us, we're still not…public. Hazel…" She winced again. "I must sound like a broken record, like I'm using her as an excuse, but…"

"I understand." He didn't, completely. But he was trying. "At least we can relax around *some* people." He gave her a quick smile, because she looked like she needed one. "I promised Mary that I'd help with cleaning up and making sure Sam has everything he needs. Meet you at your place later?" He leaned over and kissed her softly—their first semipublic kiss—ignoring the catcalls they were getting from their friends.

She nodded, also ignoring the teasing. "Vickie has someone delivering a bed she's donated for Hazel's room around six." She grinned. "Now that she knows about us, you don't have to worry about playacting around her."

He pulled her into an embrace, just because he could. Owen was right.

They were burning hot.

And he couldn't get enough.

CHAPTER TWENTY-TWO

VICKIE FROZE WHEN Gordy playfully tapped her on the behind as he walked around his truck to tie down the upholstered headboard.

"Don't you *dare* do that at Zoey's place!"

"Why?" He was laughing. "Is sleeping with me something taboo, like having an affair with your pool boy?" He tied a knot in the rope. "Or is it because I'm so precious to you that you want me all to yourself?"

She blinked. It was a little of both, but she wasn't about to tell him that.

"I don't have a pool boy. I have a robot thingy that keeps it clean."

Gordy walked up to her, resting his hands on her waist. It wasn't fair how good he looked in his dark T-shirt and cargo shorts. He smelled good, too. And that thick hair was constantly begging to have her fingers in it. And then he smiled, quickly melting her heart.

"I don't have to worry about you having a fling with that robot thingy, do I?"

She laughed. Vickie never thought of herself as the melting type, but she was definitely melting right now. Into him. *For* him.

"I've got a contractor who's keeping me pretty busy these days." She shrugged playfully. "Let's get this thing over to Zoey's. It's been a long day."

He opened the passenger door to his truck, then helped her get up into the four-wheel drive vehicle with at least some of her dignity intact. She'd changed into embroidered denim capris and a blue knit top after getting home from Mary's. She wasn't sure if it was appropriate *furniture-moving in a pickup truck* attire, but it was the closest she could come up with.

Gordy hopped into the driver's seat. "The sooner we get this delivered, the sooner we can come back and, uh…rest."

Vickie just snorted in response. What he had in mind had nothing to do with *resting*. And that was just fine with her.

The past few weeks had been unlike anything Vickie ever expected to have happen at this stage of her life. Gordy was staying at her place nearly every night now—sometimes after working there all day. He'd bring a change of clothes, then shower before dinner. And after dinner, they'd sit by the water and watch the sun set, usually with him drinking beer and her sipping wine.

They'd talk. About his two sons and five grandchildren. The closest son lived in Buffalo, while the other was in Vermont. The Buffalo son had driven down with his family to take Gordy to brunch earlier for Father's Day. They talked about his late wife, Kathy. Vickie remembered her from school as a sweet girl, who'd apparently been a wonderful, supportive wife. She'd died of cancer when the boys were in college. And they talked about Vickie's marriages.

She'd loved her first two husbands in different ways. Stanley Noor had given her a taste of wealth and security she'd never had before. He'd lavished her with gifts, but as much as they loved each other, they were never *in* love with each other. Even in the divorce after five years of trying to make it work, Stanley had been generous as always. Her second husband, Malcolm Pendergast, had been her true love. A county district attorney, he bought her the lakefront home as a wedding gift. They'd tried for a family, but it wasn't meant to be. After twelve years of happy marriage, a sudden heart attack took him from her. She and Malcolm had shared a deep, true love and appreciation for each other. That's why she went back to *his* last name when her third husband, Conway Rivers, turned out to be a gold-digging fraud. She'd kicked him to the curb, *without* any of her money, after a regrettable seven months.

She'd never realized how lonely she'd been lately for the company of a man. Sure, she had her friends to talk to, and she rarely held anything back from them. Despite their sarcasm and teasing, they supported her 100 percent at all times. But…it wasn't the same as talking to someone who'd known her intimately. There was a wall that fell once you'd slept with someone. What was the use of hiding anything when they'd seen everything? Especially at her age.

Her first time with Gordy a few weeks ago had been an adventure in vulnerability. He'd needed a pill. She'd needed lubrication. She was awkward and uncharacteristically shy. Gordy was calm and extremely patient. They'd talked their way through every step, until it reached the point of being funny. And once they'd started laughing, things got so much easier. And sexier.

His touch had made her body blush and react in ways she thought were long gone. Who knew old ladies could still have fun at this? What an idiot she'd been to wait this long. But then again…waiting for a man like Gordy Lexiter may have been the perfect plan. Maybe it had taken *him* to reawaken her desire.

They didn't make love every time he stayed over. Sometimes they just cuddled and watched some show on a streaming service, falling asleep in each other's arms.

Gordy was firmly hooked on British crime shows, and Vickie was starting to enjoy them, too.

"Whatcha' thinkin' over there, Vicks?" Gordy reached out and took her hand. She was beginning to adjust to the nickname he continued to use. He always said it with so much warmth and intimacy that it was hard to argue about it. "We're almost there and you haven't said a word."

She blinked, surprised to see they were up the hill and turning onto Zoey's road already.

"I guess I just zoned out. Like I said, it's been a long day."

"How was your cookout with your friends?"

It had been a very revealing cookout, but they'd promised not to share the news about Mike and Zoey.

"It was nice. Most of my book club friends were there, so we chatted and let the younger people do their thing."

"What does your book club actually *do*?" He glanced at her. "I don't think I've seen you pick up a book since we started—"

"Started our torrid affair?" She squeezed his fingers. "I've been a little busy. We try to read a book a month, but our meetings tend to wander *way* off topic."

"Uh-huh." He grinned. "I'm working on a landscaping project with Owen Cooper on the other side of town, and he said you guys love to play matchmaker. I never thought of you as a romantic."

She felt stung. "I'm plenty romantic! I've been married three times, haven't I?"

"I just meant…" He tapped his fingers on the steering wheel. "You're Miss Practicality. You're the no-nonsense Lady in Charge. The idea of you trying to set up young lovebirds is…" He rolled his eyes. "You know what? Never mind. There's no way for me to say it without it sounding bad, and I don't mean it that way. I was teasing." He turned the truck into Zoey's driveway. "Jesus—Rob sure had a thing for his so-called *art*, didn't he?"

She looked at the dozen or so metal figures scattered around the deep lawn. Some were recognizable as people, dragons or various animals. Some were just a jumble of wires, springs and pipes.

"Zoey wants to move most of them out of the yard so it doesn't look so...overwhelming. Some of the neighbors are giving her grief about it being an eyesore."

"That's dumb." Gordy gestured at the yard. "I think it looks cool—like a sculpture park or something."

Vickie thought about that. Was there a place in town where they could *create* a sculpture park? Would anyone want one? It might be worth bringing up at the next festival committee meeting. Rendezvous Falls was known as much for its monthly festivals as it was for their Victorian homes. Maybe they could tie a local sculpture park idea into the art show that happened alongside the Summerfest in August.

"Oh, good, we've got able-bodied help," Gordy said.

Mike was standing on the front porch. He didn't need to hide his presence at Zoey's place any longer—at least not when Hazel was at her dad's. Vickie needed to talk to Zoey about that. Secrets were rarely a good idea.

She glanced over at Gordy as he backed the truck up to the front porch. It wasn't fair to think that about Zoey, since Vickie was keeping her own relationship private. This trip to deliver a bed was the closest they'd been to going anywhere publicly as a couple. He'd invited her out to dinner, but she always came up with an excuse not to go.

Zoey came out the front door as Mike guided Gordy to back the truck up to the steps. This way they could go straight in and up the stairs to Hazel's room. As the two men got to work untying the ropes and moving the bed, the woman sat on the porch to watch.

"It was nice of Gordy to volunteer his time and truck on Father's Day," Zoey said, watching Mike climb up into the bed of the truck.

"I told him I needed a hand with this and he offered." Gordy slid the headboard toward Mike. "He had brunch with his son's family earlier today, so he was free. He'll see the Vermont son on the Fourth of July—he was at some art show in Maine this weekend but they had a video chat this morning."

Zoey gave her a funny look. "That's a lot of personal information for you to have on your contractor."

Vickie bristled, annoyed with herself that she'd let all those details slip out. "He's at my house constantly. We talk. Don't make a big deal out of it." Before Zoey could answer, Vickie nodded toward the guys. "You'd better get the door for them and tell them where to put the bed."

They all got upstairs with the headboard and footboard intact, but it wasn't easy. The headboard was over seven feet tall, and even though the old house had high ceilings, the stairway was steep and had a turn at the landing halfway up. Zoey and Gordy had the lower portion, while Mike led the way, holding the top. Vickie followed, offering suggestions at first, but stopping after the third flat look she got from Gordy. *Fine*. She had no idea how to move furniture. There was no harm in admitting it.

Hazel's room looked amazing. The dramatic black ceiling sparkled in the light from the small chandelier hanging in the center. The pink walls softened the drama of all that black.

Gordy and Zoey put the bed together. They were the handy ones, and Mike and Vickie were smart enough to stay out of their way. Mike nudged Vickie's arm, his voice low.

"Gordy's a good guy. Are you two…?"

"No… I mean…well…" She made a face, dropping to a near whisper. "We're…friends. How did you put it earlier? With benefits?"

Mike gaped for a moment, then recovered and smiled softly in Zoey's direction as she swore at a bolt that refused to tighten properly. He looked back to Vickie, and she was surprised at the troubled look in his eyes.

"Be careful about labels, Vickie. They can be traps, especially if one of you decides they want more than just casual *benefits*. That they don't want to sneak around anymore. If you're in a relationship, own it. Don't hide it."

She touched his arm. "You want more from Zoey?"

He hesitated again, then nodded.

"And she doesn't?" That surprised Vickie. Zoey wasn't the casual sort when it came to relationships, friendship or otherwise. She was an all-in type.

"I don't know. I don't think so. She always brings up Hazel, and that stops the conversation cold."

"For who? You or Zoey?"

He chewed his lip for a moment. "I think *she* uses it to stop the talking, and I don't push past it. So…both?"

"Hey, Mike?" Gordy called. "I think we have this thing assembled. Can you help me get the box springs and mattress onto the frame?"

He excused himself from Vickie and went to help finish the bed. Zoey directed them where to place it, and the four of them stood together, admiring the finished product.

Vickie had tacked glittery trim along the edges of the headboard and footboard, and glued big rhinestones over the buttons anchoring the quilted upholstery. It didn't look like a "little girl" bed. It was more of a sparkly grown-up one.

Zoey embraced Vickie tightly. "Thank you so much. Hazel will love it."

Vickie looked at Gordy, who'd been careful not to act affectionate since they'd arrived. He was being a perfect gentleman, following her request to keep their relationship quiet. Then she looked to Mike, who slid his arm around Zoey's waist, but still had a shadow behind his eyes. Vickie had told Rick earlier that she was going to warn Mike not to break Zoey's heart. But the heartbreak might be heading in the other direction.

"Gordy and I are together," she announced. It felt good to say it out loud and make it real, even if the words earned her three stunned expressions.

"Okay, then." Gordy laughed, his eyes warm. "I guess we're official."

"Uh…" Mike hesitated, giving Vickie a quizzical look before nodding in approval. "Congratulations."

"Definitely congratulations in my direction," Gordy answered, his gaze still on Vickie. "I got lucky, and then some."

Zoey folded her arms. "After the guilt trip you sent me on a few hours ago when you found out about Mike and I? You even played the *godmother* card on me. And this whole time, you and Gordy have been…" Her brows lowered. "What exactly *have* you been doing?"

"We've been screwing, Zoey. Old people still do that, you know."

Gordy started coughing. "So we've gone from keeping things quiet to discussing our sex life." He leaned toward Mike, putting one hand to the side of his mouth like he was telling a secret. "Which is pretty damn good, if you're wondering."

"I'm not." Mike shook his head, holding his hands up in front of him with a laugh. "I'm *really* not."

Gordy's eyes widened. "Wait... Zoey, you said something about you and Mike... Are you two...?"

Mike nodded, sliding his arm around Zoey again. "Must be something in the water. Looks like everyone in Rendezvous Falls is doin' it like rabbits these days."

Zoey was still staring at Vickie. Her mouth slowly slid into a smile. "Well, look at you, Victoria Pendergast. Gettin' it on with the contractor. Good for you—both of you. Is it serious?"

Vickie rolled her eyes. "No, I always hop in the sack with random people employed at my home."

Gordy pretended to whistle, looking around the room as if he no longer wanted to be part of this conversation. Vickie took his hand before continuing. "You told everyone earlier that you and Mike are brand-new. Well, so are we. I'm not sure where this train is headed, but I'm happy I took the ride. And I don't want to hide it anymore." It occurred to her that she hadn't asked Gordy before sharing their news. She swallowed, turning to him. "Unless you want to? I don't mind—"

He silenced her with a kiss, firm and steadying. Then he looked straight into her eyes. "I told you before that you were worth bragging about, and I meant it. I'd be proud to have you on my arm anywhere you want to go. I'm also happy just hanging out at your place. Quiet. Loud. Public. Private. The only thing that matters is being with you. The rest is just noise."

Her knees trembled, and she forced them to stay steady. But when her heart trembled, skipping a beat or two, she had no control over that. She was falling in love with Gordy.

Oh, hell—who was she kidding? She'd already fallen.

The question was...had *he*?

CHAPTER TWENTY-THREE

ZOEY WATCHED HAZEL and held her breath. Would she like the bed from Vickie's, even though it wasn't exactly what she'd had on her wish list? The paint was what she wanted, so that had to mean something. And she'd picked out the chandelier herself at Tani's furniture store. They'd been able to use Tani's employee discount, so it had fit in Zoey's budget—especially since she didn't have to buy a bed.

"Mom…" Hazel turned in the center of the room. "This is… Wow. It's perfect!" She ran over and wrapped Zoey in a tight embrace. "I love it! But you said we were on a budget…where did you get that amazing bed? Tani?"

"No, the bed is a gift from Vickie."

"She bought me a bed?"

"No, sweetie. She had the bed and didn't want it anymore. It was close enough to your dream bed that she thought it might work." Zoey nodded toward the headboard. "She added the jewels herself."

"OMG! This is going to look so sick on my videos."

Zoey grimaced. "Just don't forget the rules, okay? No videos that show *any* skin or anything risqué, right? Safety first."

"Yes, Mom." Hazel's voice drawled out like a verbal eye roll. "I *know.* You tell me every other day. You know I only do fashion and stuff, right?"

"And you know it's my job to keep you safe and happy,

right?" Zoey didn't want to start an argument right now. "Does the room make you happy?"

Hazel's smile returned, brighter than ever. "*So* happy, Mom. It's amazing. Can I have Sienna stay over this week? She'll scream when she sees this."

"Sure, honey. How's Sienna doing?"

"Better. She and her mom talked, and her mom's gonna lay off the dating app for a while."

Zoey hid her dismay at the answer. "Really? Doesn't that make her mom sad?"

Hazel raised an eyebrow. Damn, where did she learn to do that like such a grown-up? Her daughter folded her arms, Zoey-style. Oh…*that's* where.

"Didn't you just say it was a mother's job to keep her children safe and happy?"

"Well, yeah, but…moms like to be happy, too."

She knew Mike was frustrated with waiting to tell Hazel. But it was bad enough that Zoey had allowed her marriage to fail. That she'd lost Hazel's childhood home. That her daughter was dealing with so much upheaval in her life. She couldn't, in good conscience, bring more stress into this house by saying *hey, I'm dating Mike McKinnon and we've been shagging in Pop-pop's old office! Cool, right?*

They'd have to wait just a little longer. Hazel lost interest in the conversation—she was too busy checking out her new bejeweled bed. At least the bedroom was a win.

Zoey told him her decision that evening, out in the repair shop. "So you see, Mike, I can't add *more* into her life right now." She'd just finished what felt like a lame explanation, and she couldn't see his face to see how he was feeling about it. She was wrapped up in his arms in their desktop nest in the shop. Her back to his chest as he leaned on the cushions in the corner. His legs were wrapped up and over hers, entrapping her completely. It was usually her favorite place to be, but this conversation had her on edge.

"I'm not sure what you're saying, Zoey. Are we…done?"

"No! I don't *want* to be done." *Please, no.* "Unless *you* want to be? We just have to keep it quiet awhile longer… maybe a long while. I think we can do that, don't you?"

"Oh, we definitely *can* do it." He kissed her hair. She smiled—he wasn't angry if he could still crack jokes. "But I gotta be honest, I'm not thrilled about the Hazel situation."

She stiffened. "This isn't a *Hazel* situation, Mike. She's a thirteen-year-old kid and she hasn't done anything wrong."

"I didn't mean it that way. It's just…when do you think she might be ready for you to be dating?" He shifted his weight, holding her securely against him. "And how's she going to feel if she finds out on her own? Or finds out you've already *been* dating for a while without telling her?"

"We're not dating." The denial came automatically. *Dating* was something public and official. They weren't doing that. But now it was Mike's body that went very still behind her.

"As much as I love the feel of you naked against me, I want to have you *dressed* and against me—*with* me—too. I want to be a part of your whole life, Zoey. And that includes Hazel. You know I think she's great. And she seems to think I'm a relatively acceptable adult. Can't we at least try…?"

She didn't answer right away. She wanted to be with him outside of the bedroom, or this old office, too. But that was what she wanted as a *woman*. The *mom* in her made a promise that had to be kept. She turned her head and looked up into Mike's eyes.

"Look, I don't know how to do this. She's already worried she's becoming less important in her father's world because of Genna and the baby."

"I thought she liked Genna?"

She reached up to touch his cheek. "You can like some-one and still be afraid they're taking your place."

He frowned. "But she won't think I'm doing that. I'm a guy. I'm…"

"You're yet another person invading the threesome that used to be her family—Chris, me and Hazel." She sighed, her heart heavy. "Thirteen is an awful age, and she's going through an awful time right in the middle of it."

"So you're sacrificing your happiness…"

"Mike, my happiness will always come second to hers." She shifted to look straight into his eyes. "I'm falling for you. I can't afford to lose you as my friend, and I don't want to lose you as my lover. Please be patient a little longer."

He put his own hand over hers on his cheek. "You're falling for me, eh?"

Despite the tension between them, she couldn't help laughing. "Are those the only words you heard?"

"Those words matter the most to me." His eyes dark-ened with emotion. "I'm falling for you, too. I'll be patient, but babe, you can't segregate yourself into two different people—Zoey the woman and Zoey the mom. Hazel de-serves *all* of you, and frankly, so do I."

She turned again, leaning back against him as he held her tight. "Let me at least get Hazel past Chris's wedding this weekend before we talk about bringing you into the picture, okay?"

"That's fair. How's she doing with all that?"

"Surprisingly well. I've got to say, Genna has been great about including her in all the plans. The four of us had breakfast together last week at The Spot, and it was…fine. Weird, but okay. I had to set aside the fact that Chris left me for this woman. That they were sleeping together for months before he asked for a divorce." She paused, swallowing back the stinging pain. "And there I was, drinking coffee right across from her. For Hazel's sake."

"That must have been rough," Mike said, resting his cheek on her head. "I hope Hazel appreciates how hard that had to be."

"I don't want her looking at it that way. Like it's some big sacrifice for me to be near her father." She tugged at the light blanket that had fallen to their waists. The night air was getting cool. "Chris and I made a vow not to badmouth each other to her, but I wasn't always kind about Genna. Not until I learned they were expecting a child and getting married."

"Why did that change things?" Mike asked. "I mean, I know it's a big change for Hazel, but Genna is still the woman who broke up your marriage."

Good old logical Mike. If only logic worked on thirteen-year-olds.

"Genna is also the woman who's going to give Hazel a baby brother. It would be horrible for me to put some wedge between them out of my own personal spite." She heard the critical edge in her voice, and so did he.

"I'm not suggesting you do anything out of spite. I just think you should—"

"Hazel needs to know that she can rely on the adults in her life *behaving* like adults. If you had children, you'd…" Her voice trailed off when she saw those words land hard on him.

"I'd…what?" His voice was brittle. "I'd automatically be gifted with the ability to make all the right decisions?"

She shook her head sharply. "I've told you before, no parent has all the answers. We're *never* ready for the feeling of watching our own heart walking around outside of our body in the form of this little person who starts developing her own opinions and attitudes and takes risks and gives us a new reason to have nightmares every damn day about what might go wrong." She paused. "And I've *already* screwed up. Chris has screwed up. Genna has screwed up. It's our job to make it all okay for Hazel."

"And you don't think I can help with that? Do you think I'd be some bad influence in her life?" The hurt in his voice tugged at her.

"God, no. She'd be lucky to have you. But she *has* a father. And a mother. And a stepmom. And a brother on the way. Adding one more layer to her life right now would be overwhelming, and it would be *my* screwup to fix if it doesn't go well." She leaned forward and kissed him softly. "Let me figure out how to introduce the idea of her mom dating. I told you what happened when her best friend's mom tried it. Hazel literally told me to be nunlike." She kissed him again. "Let me figure out how to do this."

He stared into her eyes before returning the kiss, his arms sliding around her waist. "Do what? Be virginal? I've got bad news for you—it's too late." He held her tight and turned her so that she was beneath him, his legs straddling hers. "We'll figure it out together."

They made love, both knowing they were distracting themselves from the heavy conversation without resolving anything. But as long as they were moving in perfect rhythm with each other, sweat running together wherever their bodies met, with physical need overwhelming logic—well, all seemed right with the world.

Their problems could wait.

"UH-OH, FINN," BRIDGET SAID, leaning over to look up into Mike's eyes. "Lover boy is looking blue today."

Finn was behind the bar at the Shamrock with Mike. It was Friday night, and it looked to be a busy one. They had a DJ coming in later, and the dancing crowd was already coming in to grab their tables. And their drinks.

Mike tried to shrug away the unwanted attention, but Bridget's husband took one look at Mike and gave an exaggerated frown. "Is he looking blue or is he just not getting enough sleep? I remember our early days, love, and we were very energetic back then."

Mike scowled. There were times when being part of a big, nosy Irish family was a pain in the ass.

Bridget snapped a bar towel at her husband. "You make it sound like it was fifty years ago. It's not like we've stopped being *energetic*. Maybe not quite as often, but with the baby—"

Finn grabbed her and planted a long, fervent kiss on her mouth. "T'wasn't lookin' to sound sulky, babe. Our love life is perfect as it is. I'm just saying in those first few months, we were *very* busy with each other."

"I can't argue that," she chuckled, cupping his face with her hands and kissing him back. "I gotta get back to the kitchen." She gestured at Mike. "Fix him, okay? He's bringing down the vibe in here tonight."

Finn turned to Mike, but he shook his head. "Don't, okay? I'm fine. I've got a lot on my mind, but I'll put on my smile for the customers." To prove it, he turned to greet a couple of young women and take their order, giving them his best smile and exchanging easy banter as he prepared their drinks. He'd been bartending here on and off since he was in college. He understood the assignment.

"Good work," Finn said. "But I'd still like to know what's on your mind." Finn's gaze went to the other side of the bar. "Oh, hey Logan, Father Joe."

Mike breathed a quiet prayer of thanks for the distraction. His agitation was pulsing right under his skin today, and he didn't think talking it out was going to make it any better.

Finn had already begun to pour two Guinnesses for Logan Taggart and Father Joseph Gough, pastor of St. Vincent's Church in Rendezvous Falls. The priest knew almost everyone in town and loved sharing his wisdom with anyone who'd listen. And the town adored the man who, like Finn, was from Ireland. Joe's brogue was a bit softer than Finn's, as he'd been in the US much longer.

"It's a fine evening, lads." Joe nodded in thanks as Finn slid his beer toward him. He lifted the glass in a toast. "May the good Lord bless you, and may you all be in Heaven half an hour before the devil knows yer dead."

Mike lifted the splash of whiskey he'd poured in a shot glass for himself. He didn't normally drink while working, but he needed something warm to soothe his restlessness. He'd agreed to be patient with Zoey, but the waiting was grinding on his nerves. He'd tried to discuss it with her. Tried to convince her the secret would continue to become heavier—worse than the truth. But no matter what he said, he was wrong because he wasn't a parent.

Zoey never said exactly that, of course. But she didn't want her two worlds colliding, and the strain was wearing on them both.

"That is one very long face for a Friday night, Michael." Father Joe looked over the rim of his beer glass. "Why so glum?"

"Oi, he's got *love* problems, Father," Finn said. He immediately stopped, mouth open and eyes wide. "And I'm a complete eedgit for saying that. Blame the lack of sleep that comes with fatherhood. Sorry, Mike."

Mike wasn't sure which was more annoying—that Finn had spilled the beans about him having a relationship, or that he'd brought up parenthood. Some days it felt like everyone he knew was a parent except him. *Wait.* He looked at Logan.

"You don't have kids, do you?"

"Excuse me?" Logan's broad shoulders straightened, his voice hard. "Did you really just ask me that? You know damn well I have *two* children. Ethan and Lily." Logan leaned forward, squinting at Mike, his anger fading. "Did you hit your head or something?"

"I know you have Ethan and Lily, but—"

"Stop right there," Logan warned, the cold edge returning to his voice. "I may not be their biological father, but those two are my children and I love them as much as I love Piper."

Finn took a drink order from a group of young people who had just walked in. He nudged Mike. "Why don't you take a break, yeah? You're all wound up in your head tonight. Timmie is here, and he and I can handle the bar for a bit."

He wanted to object, but he *was* wound up. Father Joe patted a barstool between him and Logan. "Come on out here, Michael, and tell us what's got you so…confused. Is it true you've found love again?"

As Mike was lifting the bar gate to join them, Logan answered the priest, his voice quiet.

"It's not public knowledge, but Mike and Zoey Hartford have been, uh…getting acquainted."

Mike stared at Logan. Everyone at the cookout had been sworn to secrecy, and Logan hadn't even *been* there. Then again, this *was* Rendezvous Falls. "If it's not public knowledge, how the fu—" he glanced at Father Joe and reworded his question to Logan. "How do *you* know about it?"

Logan's shoulder rose and fell. "It's not like I *try* to keep up with the latest gossip, but my grandmother is a master at it, and someone in the book club brigade squealed. Gran told Piper and I." He leaned forward. "Don't worry. I'm better at keeping secrets than sleep-deprived Finn is."

Mike gave him a pointed look. "*You're* the one who just told Father Joe."

"Well, yeah. But… I said it quietly." Logan's expression changed as if he'd had a sudden revelation. "Oh, shit— sorry, Father—*that's* why you're asking about kids. You're dating a single mom. And trying to connect with her kid."

"More like trying to get Zoey to *allow* me to connect. Hazel's the reason we're a big, dark secret, and Zoey won't even consider telling her daughter that she—a grown woman—has decided to be with me—her best damn friend. Sorry, Father."

Father Joe raised one hand. "You'll never get this conversation anywhere if you two apologize to me every other minute. I've heard more curse words than you two probably *know*, so as long as you leave the Big Man's name out of it. I preabsolve you both."

Logan sipped his beer, then shook his head. "A woman is always going to put her kids first."

"Of course she will," Mike answered. "I want Zoey to do what's best for Hazel, but—"

Logan laughed, but there was little humor in it. "There are no *buts*, man. A good mom is *always* going to be willing to sacrifice her own happiness for her kids' sake. Even when she doesn't need to."

That's what Mike was afraid of. "You and Piper had an issue with that?"

Logan rolled his eyes and nodded. "It almost ended us."

Mike looked down the bar to see if he was needed back there. Tim caught him looking and gave Mike a thumbs-up, mouthing *stay there.*

He turned back to Logan. "How did you and Piper work through it?"

Logan grimaced. "My situation was different from you and Zoey. Piper's husband died a literal war hero. His parents were super involved with Piper and the kids before I showed up. In their eyes, I was an interloper." His eyes grew distant. "So I had to win *them* over as well as the kids. I had to help Piper move past her guilt, and I had to win over Ethan and the grandparents. Little Lily just wanted everyone to be happy."

"I've known Hazel all her life, and we get along great. But she only knows me as her mom's friend…not her mom's *friend.* But Hazel's really mature for her age."

Father Joe, who'd been drinking his beer in silence, looked up.

"Zoey seems like a kindhearted girl, but tread carefully with children who seem mature for their age. It's not uncommon for only children like Hazel to be seen that way, but sometimes it's a bit of an act to hide their fears." He shrugged. "They're mimicking what they see, and what they see most in their world is adults. So they *act* like adults without *being* an adult."

Mike did his best to tamp down the panic rising inside him. How could he possibly relate to a teenage girl when he had no idea if she was pretending to be mature beyond her years? Mary had said more than once that Hazel had always been a miniature version of Zoey. Was she mimicking her mother, or did she really have Zoey's strength of spirit? Maybe Zoey's worries were justified—Hazel could be more fragile than he'd thought. He looked between Joe and Logan.

"Where do I even begin?"

Logan scrubbed the back of his neck. "I can't help you much when it comes to girls. Lily was four when Piper and I met, and she fell for me before her mom did. She called me her giant." That made total sense—Logan was well over six foot and built like a mountain. "Ethan was around Hazel's age, but…he was a boy. It was like dealing with a younger version of me—a sullen, moody teenager who was mad at the world. I understood him, and I respected his need to be the man of the house." He paused. "If it helps, what worked for me and Ethan was honesty—I laid it all out on the line, man-to-man, and reassured him that I wasn't taking over, and that his mom could love me and still love him and Lily just the same as always. It was touch and go for a while, but he finally let me in."

"Honesty is always a good place to start," Joe said. "But you can't work on winning Hazel's approval until Zoey is ready to share your relationship with her daughter. It's not your place to go against a mother's wishes."

"I know, Father Joe. I think the sooner we tell her, the better, but every time I bring it up, I get reminded that…" He formed air quotes with his fingers. "… I'm not a parent."

"Ouch," Logan said. "That's why you asked me if I was a *real* dad?"

"Yeah. Sorry. I keep getting tripped up by all the parenting talk. I end up saying the wrong thing, which reinforces Zoey's doubts." Finn splashed more whiskey into Mike's glass as he walked by, and Mike drained it in one swallow. "I try to tell Zoey I think she's a great mom, and I swear it comes out sounding like I'm saying kids are a pain in the ass. She keeps asking me to be patient…"

Joe lifted one eyebrow. "And you don't love her enough to do that for her?"

"Of course I do!" He realized what he'd just admitted. "I *do* love her, Joe. I want to be part of her life, and not just as a friend. Her whole life—including Hazel. I want us to be *together*."

He'd never in his wildest imagination expected to love another woman after Becca. Despite their disagreements about when to start a family, she'd held his whole heart. A heart that had *not* felt whole since her death. But now… he could feel a part of him, long dormant, coming to life again. And somehow, inexplicably, he knew that Becca would approve. She wouldn't want him to be alone forever.

Father Joe sat back, his forehead deeply furrowed.

"That's all well and good to say what *you* want. But what if she needs you to be her friend awhile longer?"

Mike no longer felt that restlessness he'd been battling for months. His life had a purpose. And that purpose was to love Zoey Hartford. Which meant doing whatever it took to make her happy, regardless of what that may do to him.

"If that's what she needs, Joe, that's what she'll get. For as long as it takes." He looked between the two men and smiled. "If it's at all possible, considering where we live, I'd appreciate keeping this conversation between us. I haven't told Zoey those three little words yet."

Logan extended his hand. "You got it, man. The road may get bumpy, but I'm living proof that you can love your way through it. I'll be rooting for you."

Mike accepted the handshake, then shook Joe's hand as well. He felt light as air now that he'd admitted his love out loud. They were going to figure this out. He wouldn't—*couldn't*—give up. He refused to think about losing Zoey.

He'd never let that happen.

CHAPTER TWENTY-FOUR

ZOEY'S PHONE PINGED with yet another picture from her daughter. Hazel was the maid of honor at Zoey's ex-husband's wedding that sunny Saturday afternoon. Her daughter seemed to be having a great time, sending a new photo every few minutes now that the reception had begun. The cake. The happy couple. The rest of the bridal party. The venue at a lakeside vineyard in Geneva. She was happy for Hazel. And she supposed she was happy for Chris, too.

That feeling was a little tougher to hang on to. Not being happy for him felt petty. That didn't make it any easier to see all the photos of his blissful wedding day.

But she answered every single text from Hazel with heart-eyes emojis and once in a while an *OMG!* All that mattered was that Hazel was happy.

"You don't *have* to read every text as it comes in, you know." Mary put her hand over Zoey's phone on the table. "I feel like I'm watching you die a little death with each one."

Tani was on the opposite side of the booth at The Spot, nodding in agreement. "What I don't get is why you care so much. It's not like you'd ever want Chris back, right? So let the bastard go get married to his cute young thing. You've got your own—" she caught herself "—uh…life, now."

Zoey sighed. "Mary knows about Mike and I."

Tani's eyebrows rose. "And does Mary approve of her brother's nighttime activities with his bestie?"

Mary took a sip of her soda. "Mary very much approves. Mary thinks they waited too long in the first place, and Mary would like to see them come out of the shadows and make it official."

Zoey couldn't help laughing. "Mary seems to have a lot of opinions."

This was why she'd asked her friends to have lunch with her today—to distract her from the wedding updates.

"I love you both," Mary answered, now serious. "I don't want to see either of you hurt, and I have a feeling that all this slinking around is going to lead to just that—someone getting hurt. The deeper you get into making it feel like you're doing something wrong, the worse it will be if it blows up."

She was right. Things had moved way beyond *casual*. They'd admitted they were "falling" for each other, but—at least in Zoey's case—it was more than that. She was in love with Mike McKinnon. She was *supposed* to be focusing on making sure Hazel had some stability in her life, but love had other plans.

"It feels like I'm being…" she started, "I don't know—selfish?—to fall in lo…" She tried to stop, but it was too late. Mary moved her hand from the phone to Zoey's arm.

"You're in love with Mike?" Her voice was tender and hopeful.

All Zoey could do was nod in response.

"Girl—" Tani gave a soft laugh "—I knew it. I see it in your eyes every time you say his name. Good for you." She paused. "As far as thinking it's selfish to fall in love? I say *bullshit* to that nonsense. You deserve to be happy. Grab on to that man and hang on to him."

"Exactly," Mary agreed. "You two fit together so perfectly. You *both* deserve happiness. But honey, why do you keep hitting the brakes?"

"You know why—I have a daughter to consider."

Mary pulled her hand away, bristling just a little. "And you don't think Mike can be a good stepdad?"

"Don't be silly. Of course he'd be great. But Hazel has specifically and repeatedly told me she does not want me *dating*, much less getting in a relationship."

Tani nodded thoughtfully. "I get that. But Hazel is a thirteen-year-old. She's half child and half woman. It's the child in her that doesn't want to share you with anyone. Children *never* like sharing. But she's smart and she's adaptable, and she'd want you to be happy." Tani nibbled on one of the french fries from her plate, even though it had to be cold by now. "It's time to bring her in the loop and deal with it."

"I agree with Tani…" Mary reached over and stole one of Tani's cold fries. "Just because Hazel may be upset at first doesn't make you a bad mom. Hell, my kids are mad at me over something every damn day."

"I hear that," Tani said, lifting her soda glass in a toast. "Doing what's best for your children does *not* mean making them perpetually happy. Hazel's a good kid—she'll deal."

Zoey went home from lunch to an empty house. Mike had gone to an auto race in Watkins Glen with some friends, and wouldn't be back until late. With Chris and Genna headed off to their honeymoon in Vegas, Hazel would be with Zoey all week. Maybe this was the week she should tell her daughter about Mike. Or…maybe not. She'd often said that growing up without a mother left her feeling like she had no road map, and that was something she could really use right now. She was going to miss her mother even more over the coming years as Hazel navigated her way to adulthood.

Two days later, Zoey was sitting on the front porch, still

trying to solve the puzzle of raising Hazel, when Mary dropped Hazel off at the bottom of the driveway. She'd been babysitting Mary's children while Mary worked. When Zoey wasn't worrying about Hazel, she was worrying about what to do with Dad's sculptures. She hadn't heard anything from her neighbor in a few weeks, but she had a feeling the other shoe was going to drop eventually. Karen Schiff didn't seem the type to give up easily. But Zoey didn't like the idea of just stacking them in a pile.

Hazel jogged up the steps and accepted the cold can of soda Zoey held out. "Slow day in Repair-ville, Mom?"

"For once, yes."

The past few weeks had put Zoey on the road more than she was used to, but the increased commercial work had helped put the business solidly in the black. She was much happier heading into business settings than going into strangers' homes.

She was picking up more vintage repairs, too. The local antiques dealer, Clive Markham, had shared her name with other antiques dealers, and she had a shop full of clocks and mechanical toys. Collectors paid good money for her work, and she enjoyed it.

"To be honest," she said, finishing her drink. "I'm working now. I'm waiting for a delivery. A guy up in Penn Yan wants me to rebuild his vintage jukebox. It sounds like it will be quite a project, but I've got a month to finish it. He wants it working in time for his sixtieth birthday party."

"Better than scrambling under some old man's kitchen sink, huh?" Hazel had heard some of the house call horror stories, but she had no clue about the worst ones.

"Definitely. How were Mary's little ones today?"

"Wired!" Hazel laughed. "Katie's birthday is coming up, and she was determined to find where her presents have been hidden, so I had to really keep an eye on her so she didn't destroy anything in her search."

"Did she find them?"

"Not a chance. Mary put them all at Mike's place." Hazel leaned forward, her eyes bright. "He said even if Katie comes to his house, she'll never find the stuff up in his attic!"

Zoey caught her breath. "Was Mike at Mary's place today?"

"Today? Yeah. He stops by quite a bit, just like he does here." Hazel gave her a sad look. "Mary says he doesn't like to be at his place alone, so he finds excuses to go hang out with people. Is that why he comes here? Because he's lonely?"

"Well…" Zoey licked her suddenly dry lips. "Mary's right about him being lonely since he lost his wife. He knows he can hang out here anytime he wants. Does that bother you?"

"Why would it? Mike's chill." Hazel was pulling her phone from her pocket. "This is Sienna…she wants me to stay over at her place tonight. Is that okay?"

"Sure, as long as it's okay with her mom. Don't forget you're working for Mary again tomorrow, though. I'll pick you up there when you're done." Sienna lived just down the street from Mary and Sam, so Hazel could walk to Mary's in the morning. "But most important is checking with Monique first to get her permission."

Hazel's eyes rolled dramatically. "She'll probably be on another hot date."

"I thought she stopped dating?"

"She said she would, but she's just being sneaky about it." Hazel typed a quick answer to her girlfriend. "As if Sienna can't track her with her phone app. She's been going to the Purple Shamrock when she says she's going shopping or to visit a sick friend." She stood and headed for the door, then turned. "Sienna didn't like her mom yapping to her about all her dates, but it's so much *worse* now that she's *lying* about it. Sienna doesn't trust her anymore." Hazel was in the house and up the stairs before Zoey could respond.

Her heart dropped. Everyone else had been right—hiding the fact that she and Mike were together was a mistake. She was going to sit her daughter down this week and get it out in the open. Tomorrow—right after they got home from Mary's. Hopefully it wasn't too late. She didn't ever want Hazel thinking she couldn't trust her mom.

A red pickup truck came up the driveway with a beautiful old jukebox strapped in the back. This project was going to be interesting. And profitable.

She had the jukebox in pieces in the shop that evening when her phone pinged with a text from Mike.

M: What do farmers give on Valentines Day?

Z: A load of manure?

M: LOL no. Hogs and kisses! Just like the ones I want to give you right now.

She looked up to see him at the door, a warm smile on his face. She'd texted him after she'd dropped Zoey at Sienna's, letting him know she'd be unexpectedly free tonight. She waved him in, meeting him on that side of the worktable to accept that promised hug and kiss. He bent her over in a low dip, as if they were dancing, and she grabbed his shoulders with a gasp.

"Easy there, Fred Astaire!"

"Don't worry—I've got you, Ginger." He pulled her upright and grinned. He'd been more relaxed the past few days. Lighter, somehow. And he'd stopped pressuring her about sneaking around. He held up a bottle. "The liquor distributor gave Bridget a bargain on some bottles of this new liqueur, so I snagged some for us. It's an apple spice brandy." He set the bottle on the table, keeping one arm around her waist. "He's trying to get us to order a case or two before fall. I told him this area is more focused on grapes than apples in September, but we do have orchards up north, so it could work."

He finally noticed the jukebox. "Whoa. That thing is awesome. Are you rebuilding it?"

"Yes. The customer found it in the corner of an old barn, and it was sitting there for a very long time. Long enough for mice to make multiple nests inside."

Mike opened the bottle of brandy while Zoey brought down the cups. The stuff had a real kick to it, but it was delicious. She cleaned out more of the jukebox parts, jotting an inventory and taking lots of photos with her phone so she'd know how to reassemble it later. Mike kept splashing more brandy in their cups. He told her about the auto race that past weekend and how much fun he'd had with his old college pals.

She waited for him to say something about how much he wanted her to meet them, like he usually did, but he never mentioned it. Maybe he really *had* accepted her request to lie low for now. Or maybe the glow of their little affair was wearing off and he was getting ready to let her go. She looked over at him, suddenly fearful.

"What?" he asked, spreading his hands wide. "Why do you suddenly look like you want to skewer me?"

She couldn't ask him why he was doing exactly what she'd asked him to do—stop pressuring her. She held up the plastic cup. She was a little surprised the sides hadn't melted from the strength of the brandy.

"I'm mad at you because you brought this alcohol here on a night when I thought I'd get some actual work done." She blinked after taking another swallow. "This stuff is wicked strong, but I can't stop drinking it."

Mike drank from his cup, blowing out a breath after he swallowed. "It *is* strong. But damn, that apple kick is fun, isn't it?" He splashed more in both their cups, then squinted at the label. "Holy shit—this stuff's almost 120 proof. No wonder we're feelin' it." He grinned. "But I don't have to drive anywhere tonight, do I?"

She took a sip of brandy, then shook her head. Things went fuzzy for a few seconds. "Hazel's at her friend's house, and she'll go right from there to Mary's in the morning. So there's no need for you to leave until after breakfast. Or even lunch." She wiggled her eyebrows up and down. "And we get to use my bedroom instead of the office. No mosquitoes to worry about."

Mike stood, grabbing the bottle and tamping the cork into the top with his fist.

"In light of this wonderful news," he announced with a grand gesture, "I propose we move into the house forth-with, along with the bottle of brandy, which I'm sure has rendered you incapable of doing repairs safely." He pointed to the door. "Safety first, right?"

Zoey giggled, then covered her mouth in surprise. She wasn't normally a giggly sort of girl, but now she couldn't stop. "I accept your proposal, sir. Let's go find a bed. And real glasses that won't dissolve at the touch of this…" She gestured at the bottle he was holding. "This…this…apple-flavored rubbing alcohol you brought with you."

When she was close enough, he put his arm around her

and pulled her tight to his chest, planting an apple brandy–
flavored kiss on her mouth. "I've got news for you," he
whispered. "I've got another bottle in the car!"

"Oh, no!" she laughed. "Let's go rescue it immediately!"

The rest of the evening was a blur. A fun, sexy blur,
but still…a blur. They gained a bit of clarity after Zoey
warmed up some lobster mac and cheese she had in the
fridge. Vickie had brought it over yesterday for her. It was
leftover from a dinner party Vickie had at her place to introduce Gordy to some of her book club pals.

Zoey would have loved to have been a fly on the wall for
that party. Gordy didn't seem very bookish, but she had a feeling he could hold his own against the sharp-tongued seniors.

"Someday soon, we'll be having a party like that," she said.

"With the book club?" Mike sounded confused.

She winked at him. "With anyone you'd like. Of course,
we pretty much have the same circle of friends, so it won't
really be an introduction." He was looking at her as if she
was speaking in another language. She smiled. "I'm going
to tell Hazel this week. I don't know how she'll take it, but
it's time to face the music."

When Mike realized she was saying they were going to
go public, he'd grabbed her by the waist at the news, lifting
her up and swinging her around the kitchen before nearly
dropping her. Turned out apple brandy didn't mix well with
spinning in circles. They'd laughed, tossed the dishes in the
sink and headed upstairs with the second bottle.

Was drunk sex different than sober sex? They were
about to find out. The problem was, it was hard to remember all the details to make a fair comparison, but it was definitely a fun time. The alcohol loosened their few remaining
inhibitions, and they spent hours laughing and attempting
adventurous new positions. At one point, Zoey had hit her

head on the headboard, but she couldn't remember what they'd been trying to do. It was a good thing her neighbors weren't close, because she'd screamed his name out loud when she'd come, her legs locked around his hips, sweat running between her breasts.

They weren't robots...they needed sleep. But neither had been willing to spend too much time with their eyes closed. It was that kind of night—wild, unbridled passion.

And now the sun was coming up. Mike was sound asleep, with his head on her stomach and her fingers weaving circles through his damp hair. She was lying crossways on the bed, so she could see out the east-facing window, where the sky was turning pink and orange. The blankets were on the floor somewhere. Along with most of the pillows. She closed her eyes. Had last night been real? When she opened her eyes again, the first thing she saw was an empty bottle of apple brandy on her nightstand. *Oh, yeah. It had been real, alright.*

The alcohol had contributed to the wildness of their activity all night, but she was sober now. More than apple brandy had happened between them. Something had shifted. Something had *lifted*. Mike's joy in the kitchen when she told him she was going to talk to Hazel was the start of it. The secrets had to end. *All* of them. Today she'd tell him she loved him. Then she'd talk to Hazel. They were going to be able to go out on actual dates to real restaurants and be with people and hold hands and kiss and…

"Your heart is picking up pace and it's hurting my head." Mike's voice was a gravelly rumble against her skin. She moved her hands through his hair again.

"Sorry," she whispered. "Bit of a hangover?"

"That would be putting it mildly." He turned his head to look up at her, his chin resting on her ribs. "Don't you?"

"I don't think so. I must have sweat it all out of me." She smiled into his dark eyes. The eyes of the man she loved. She almost said it out loud, but held back. Blurting out her love for him when he'd just admitted to a blaring hangover seemed like really bad timing.

"Would breakfast help?"

He nodded. "Maybe. But you know what they say about hangover cures…hair of the dog and all that."

"You want more brandy?" She couldn't even *think* about that stuff without her stomach protesting.

Mike's gaze fell to her breasts, now directly in front of his face. One corner of his mouth slid upward.

"I never said my hangover came from the booze."

She huffed out a quiet laugh. "Are you saying you're suffering from a *sex* hangover?"

"I don't know if it's possible to overindulge in sex with you, but my body is telling me we came damn close." He winked. "I coulda' died. I still might."

"And the cure for too much sex is…more sex?"

He lifted one shoulder before slowly sliding up and over her. "The body wants what it wants."

She wrapped her arms around him. This was the perfect way to start a day—with a man who couldn't get enough of her. As he sank into her, she whispered the words she'd tell him out loud later.

"I love you, Mike McKinnon."

THE SUN WAS up in the sky the next time Mike opened his eyes. It took him half a minute to remember where he was—in Zoey's bed. And once again using Zoey as the best pillow ever. Her fingers were in his hair again, but they weren't moving. Her breaths came slow and deep in slumber.

Man, what a night.

Who knew 120 proof brandy was that much of an aphrodisiac? He didn't think it was humanly possible to do all they did last night. They were probably both going to have some aches and bruises today. *Totally worth it.* He kissed her stomach and rolled over. He didn't think he had any morning appointments, but he had to at least show up at work. What time was it? He scrubbed his eyes and pushed himself to his feet. His knees felt like water, but they held.

He forgot about the time when his gaze fell to the bed. Zoey was sprawled out, starfish-style, across the sheet. There was hardly any bedding left on the bed. Just her beautiful naked body. Tangled dark hair covered her face and shoulders. He spotted a few little nibble marks he'd left on her rosy skin. Would he *ever* have enough of her? If last night was any proof, the answer was a definite *no*. He was going to love this woman for the rest of his life, and even that wouldn't be enough. He wanted and needed her that much.

The sunlight streamed through the window, reminding him that he could *not* crawl back in bed with her. But he *could* make them some breakfast before he left. And tell her how much he loved her.

He found his cargo shorts on the floor—which was a mess of clothes and bedding—and pulled out his phone. Wow. Almost nine thirty. Breakfast would have to be quick. Zoey's foot was hanging over the side of the bed, and he ran his fingers up and down the arch until she twitched and kicked at him.

"What?" she mumbled, reaching up to brush her hair off her face, then squinting at the window. "Damn. What time is it?"

"Nine thirty. I'm going to take a quick shower, then I'll scramble some eggs for us, okay?"

Her head fell back on the bed. "Okay." She stretched out

like a cat, her arms and legs extending gracefully. "I guess the real world's coming, whether we want it to or not." She opened one eye and looked at him holding his shorts.

"What are you doing, putting on a show there in the middle of the room? Get in the shower, mister." She sat up, kneeling on the bed, still looking half-asleep and sexy as hell. She was completely comfortable being naked in front of him. And he felt the same way. To prove it, he playfully swung the shorts around on his fingertips, swaying his hips back and forth like a dancer.

"Do you *want* me to put on a show for you? 'Cuz you know I will." He swung his hips again, and Zoey burst out laughing.

"Oh, my God, I love you!"

Two things happened at that exact moment.

Mike remembered that she'd whispered those words to him as they'd made love earlier. *I love you, Mike McKinnon.*

And the bedroom door swung open behind him. He started to turn, but Zoey's horrified cry was enough to freeze him in place as she scrambled for anything to cover herself with. She finally pulled up the sheet from the mattress.

"Hazel! *No!*"

Mike hurriedly tried to cover his backside with the shorts, making sure she couldn't see his front.

"Mom?" Hazel's voice was confused at first, then rose an octave. "Oh. My. God. *Mike?* What are you…? You're *naked*!" Hazel let out a scream. He couldn't move, not even when he heard another set of footsteps hurrying up the stairs.

"Hazel? What's wrong?" It was Mary's voice. As if this couldn't get more embarrassing. "Oh! Oh, shit! Uh…come here, honey, let's give your mom and her *friend* some time to get *dressed.* It's okay…don't cry…go on downstairs…"

The door slammed shut behind him, then flew open again. It was just Mary this time, her voice hissing like a serpent.

"Are you fucking kidding me in here? It's the middle of the morning! Get your asses dressed *now*. And you'd better come up with a damn good story for that girl." Mike looked over his shoulder and Mary closed her eyes. But not before he'd seen the corners of her mouth twitching with laughter. "Jesus Christ, *Magic Mike*. Get some pants on and get out of here."

"Get out where?" He started looking around, as if a new exit would appear.

Mary stomped to the bed and tossed a robe at Zoey, who was white as a ghost. His sister gave him a withering look as he made a feeble attempt to cover his privates now that she was in front of him.

"I don't care if you slide down the waterspout and get yourself a buttload of well-deserved splinters. Get dressed and get out."

"I can help explain to Hazel…"

"No!" This time it was Zoey who'd spoken. "She's right. You need to leave. You won't be able to help with anything right now." She looked at him, her face a picture of devastation. He wanted to help her. But he didn't know how. He felt useless. He yanked on his shorts without bothering to look for his briefs. He scooped up his polo shirt and pulled it over his head. He had no idea where his shoes were. Probably downstairs.

Mary picked up the empty brandy bottle and waved it at him like she wanted to throw it at him.

"Seriously? What are you, seventeen?"

Zoey was moving, but she looked like she'd collapse into a puddle at the slightest provocation.

"Why are you here, Mary?" She sounded shattered. "Why is *Hazel* here?"

Mary's expression fell. "I'm *so* sorry. She forgot to pack

a shirt for today, and she'd spilled something on the one she wore last night. I didn't think twice about letting her run inside to get a clean one…at *nine thirty* in the morning. I never saw your car…" She looked at Mike. "Where is it, anyway?"

"Back by the barn."

She nodded sadly. "We came in the front door. I had no idea that you two would be…where you were. Doing whatever you were doing." She held her hand up. "And I do *not* want to know what that was. The scene is already burned into my eyeballs for eternity without knowing details."

Downstairs, they could hear Hazel banging around in the kitchen, slamming cupboard doors and crying. Zoey looked at Mike, her eyes filled with unshed tears. She pulled on a pair of shorts and took a T-shirt from the dresser. "This is my worst nightmare times ten. Both of you go out the front door. I'll go talk to her." She looked to Mary. "I don't think she'll be babysitting today."

"After this, I don't think I'll be working today anyway. I'll take the kids to the park or something." She pulled Zoey in for a tight hug. "I really am sorry. If I can help…"

"It's not your fault. We were careless."

"But we *weren't* careless," Mike insisted. "We had no reason to think she'd—"

"We were *careless*." Zoey's eyes were hard, still shimmering with tears. "And my daughter has been hurt because of it. She saw you *naked*. In my *bedroom*."

"Technically, she only saw me from behind. For a split second. I'm sure she's seen bare butts before, probably on a cartoon. Or some video game or TV show."

Yes, this was bad. But it wasn't the catastrophe she was making it out to be. *Was it?*

"Are you trying to make a joke out of this?" Zoey stopped next to him in disbelief. "Is this *funny* to you?"

His sister was behind Zoey, making frantic slicing moves with her hand at her throat in the universal hand signal to *shut up*.

"It's not funny, babe. I'm just saying…" What was he saying? Mary was still slicing at her neck, but he had to finish the sentence. "I'm just saying it could have been worse, right?"

Mary covered her face with her hands behind Zoey, who was staring at him, color rising in her cheeks. "You were dancing. Naked. In front of me. While I was naked. The fact that she didn't get a full frontal is *not* a comfort to me, Michael."

He didn't think he'd ever heard her call him by his full name, except in jest. She was definitely not jesting right now. Her shoulders dropped sharply.

"Just go. Please. Leave me alone."

That sounded way too permanent for his liking.

"I love you, too, Zoey."

Behind her, Mary threw her arms up in the air and clutched her hair. Yeah, the timing wasn't ideal. But he had to say it. He cleared his throat.

"You told me you love me. You need to know I love you, too. We can figure this out."

Zoey shook her head, waving her hand weakly at him.

"I can't do this right now. My daughter needs me."

She hurried past him, wiping moisture from her cheeks and pulling herself tall. She was going into warrior mode to protect her family.

He wanted to cry out *I need you, too!* But that would be an asshole move. He wasn't the teenager here. He took a deep breath, reminding himself of what he'd told Logan and Father Joe. It wasn't about *his* needs. If he really loved her, he'd give her what *she* needed.

And right now, she needed him gone.

CHAPTER TWENTY-FIVE

"I'M GOING TO go live with Dad. Forever."

Hazel's voice was hard as diamonds. At least the sobbing had stopped. When Zoey first walked into the kitchen an hour ago, her daughter was purple faced with fury and soaked in tears. She'd railed at the top of her lungs against her mother, and Mike, and anyone else she could think of. Now she was settling into a quiet, cold rage. Zoey wasn't sure which was worse.

She'd poured herself a mug of coffee, resisting the temptation to drink it straight from the pot. She let Hazel get everything off her chest, nodding and making small sounds of sympathy and regret. Talking would have been pointless while Hazel was raging. Besides, Zoey was still in shock from the whiplash of laughing with Mike one moment, proclaiming her love for him…and then seeing Hazel's face when she opened the door. Mike had been swinging his shorts over his head like a cowboy swinging a lasso, stark naked in the middle of the morning. While *she* cheered him on, naked in bed. She dropped her head into her hands, muttering her words through her fingers.

"Your dad is on his honeymoon this week, so you're stuck with me."

She didn't even want to think about *that* conversation. Chris would be angry, which is understandable. She shuddered…would he use it to try to change the custody arrangement? He'd never been that kind of guy, but with Hazel so determined to live with him, he could take advantage. Hopefully things would cool down by the time he got back.

"I'll go to Sienna's then." Hazel's voice was firm. "I am not staying here."

Zoey raised her head, taking in Hazel's defiant stance, her arms folded tightly, chin high, eyes puffy and red. Hazel was trying to assert some control into the situation. Zoey understood, but she had to be the mom. Maybe a bad one, but she was still the mom.

"You *are* staying here. This is your home."

"Won't I be in the way of all your naked games with Mike? No wonder you defended Sienna's mom so much—you were doing the same exact thing, sneaking around without telling me. You probably have more fun when I'm not around anyway, so why—"

"Stop it!" Zoey stood, waving her forefinger. "Don't you *ever* think I don't want you here. I *love* you. You're angry. I deserve it. I screwed up. But what happened with Mike and me has *nothing* to do with my love for you, and does not change the fact that this is your home. I promise you that."

"Yeah, right. Just like this is *my* year. You promised me that, too, remember?" Her voice was mocking. "And the whole time, you and Mike McKinnon were slinking around and humping each other..." Her face screwed up in disgust. "*So* gross. Why should I ever believe you again?"

Zoey closed her eyes, her chest pressing on her heart like a vise. This was everything she'd feared and then some. She'd broken her daughter's trust.

"I've already explained why I didn't tell you. I had no idea if Mike and I were going anywhere as an actual couple. I didn't want to upset you if it turned out not to be serious." They'd become *very* serious. In *love* serious. But that was all on hold now.

She walked over to Hazel, brushing her hair away from her face and staring straight into her eyes. Hazel's body was as taut as an overstretched guitar string, ready to snap at any moment. But she held her ground.

"Sometimes," Zoey said softly, "we can think we're doing the right thing and be completely wrong. I wanted to protect you, and I ended up hurting you. I know it probably won't happen today, but I hope you'll forgive me."

Hazel's mouth was a thin, tight line. She shook her head, dropping her gaze to the floor.

"I don't even know who you *are*, Mom. All that talk about honesty when you were…" She took a ragged breath. "You're no better than Sienna's mom." She held up her hand between them. "I can't look at you right now. I'm going to my room."

Hazel started to turn away, then stopped, giving Zoey a hard look.

"As soon as Dad and Genna are back, I *am* going to move in with them."

"We'll talk about that later," Zoey replied. There was no way it was going to happen, but Hazel was in no mood to hear it. She left Zoey standing in the kitchen, feeling like a complete failure in every way possible.

She sat at the table, turning her empty coffee mug back and forth. She couldn't imagine how to bring Mike into Hazel's life now. It made her heart heavy with sorrow… for everyone. She knew it would hurt him terribly. But her daughter came first. He'd always known that. Her phone jumped and buzzed on the table, making her flinch. She checked the caller ID. Vickie. She thought about ignoring it, but that wouldn't solve anything. Her godmother would just show up at the door if she didn't take the call.

"Hi, Vickie. Not a great time—"

"So it's true? Hazel saw you and Mike…?"

Zoey glanced at the wall clock. It had been less than two hours since Mike and Mary left.

"How the hell do you know that already?"

"Mike went to Maura's. She just called me." Vickie's voice was soft. Worried. "What happened?"

Zoey gave her the highlights of the story, sparing a few of the details. She told Vickie about Hazel's reaction, from the hysterics to the icy anger.

"It had to be quite a shock for her," Vickie said, stating the obvious. "She's a hormonal thirteen-year-old who just watched her dad marry another woman. She's going to have a baby brother. Now she sees her mom… Of *course* she acted out." Vickie paused. "Don't take her words to heart—hell hath no fury like a teenager who just discovered life isn't always going to go their way."

"It was my job to help her navigate that lesson *without* her finding me naked with a man in my room." She was still turning the coffee mug with her free hand, back and forth. Back and forth. Stuck in the same pattern, over and over.

"Yes, it was," Vickie replied. "But life is like that—we often end up learning our lessons the hard way. She's a smart kid. She'll come around to see things more clearly once she stops having her temper tantrum."

"She walked in on us *naked*. And…we were…clowning around. Laughing. Mike was dancing…" The image made her cringe. "Thank God he had his shorts in his hand, so he could cover up a bit. You can't imagine how bad it was."

"I don't think I want to." Vickie chuckled softly. "But I'm assuming he didn't have you tied to the bed or anything?"

"Of course not." Although he had playfully threatened to do that someday.

"And he wasn't spanking you? No cat-o'-nine-tails in his hand?"

"A *whip*? No! We were just laughing. While naked."

Vickie was silent for a moment. "Naked laughter is some of the best laughter." Vickie coughed softly, and Zoey wondered if her godmother and her new beau, Gordy Lexiter, had shared naked laughter together.

"She walked in on us, Vickie."

"She walked in on two adults having fun. I know you didn't want your daughter seeing you like that, but you weren't *doing* anything wrong. You could even think of yourself as role modeling a healthy relationship."

For the first time in hours, Zoey smiled. "I know you're trying to make me feel better, and I appreciate it, but...no. It's such a mess. I miss my mom." Those last words surprised her, coming straight from her brain to her lips. Tears pooled in her eyes. "I miss *having* a mom, Vickie. I got cheated out of that, and now I'm just flailing around with no clue what I'm doing. And I miss Dad, too." It made her even more sad to realize that hole would always be there. Both her parents were gone. She took a breath and tried to stop the crying jag she felt coming on. "Did Maura say how Mike was?" She'd basically thrown him out of the house.

There was a pause. "She said he opened a bottle of her favorite whiskey, drank one shot, then put it away again. He's worried about you and Hazel."

Zoey stared out the window at the bright and sunny day, such a contrast to the atmosphere inside the house. She was worried about her and Hazel, too. And she was missing her best friend.

Hazel cranked up the volume on the music in her room

upstairs. It was now at window-rattling levels. She was probably trying to bait Zoey into coming up there and telling her to turn it down, just to spark another argument. But she was out of luck, because Zoey didn't have any fight left in her.

"Zoey? Did you hear me? Do you want me to come over? What's all that noise in the background? Are you watching a movie?"

"No, don't come over. I'm wrung out, and Hazel and I need to hash this out on our own. When she's ready." She stretched, then stood and took the coffee mug to the sink. "Thanks for calling, Vickie, but I have to go."

She was good at fixing things, but repairing *this* particular mess could require skills she wasn't sure she had.

"Sitting at the bar on a Tuesday?" Finn O'Hearn slid onto the barstool next to Mike. "I'm surprised you came out of your house, now that you're famous and all."

"Famous?" He looked up from his dark beer to see his friend grinning. Mike groaned. He knew the story of what happened last week had made the rounds of their friends. They all knew Hazel had walked in on him and Zoey, and that Zoey had ghosted him ever since. But none of them had dared tease him about it yet. "I'm nowhere near ready to laugh about this, Finn."

"Okay, but you gotta hand it to Hazel. She knows how to make a moment go viral." Finn nodded at Kelly behind the bar, and she began pouring him a pint of Guinness. When it was done, she slid it across the bar.

"How's our little Moira doing today?" she asked Finn.

Finn's smile returned, wider than ever. "She's brilliant, thanks. Still doesn't want to sleep all night, or even half the night, but brilliant other than that." He took a sip of his beer. "I sure hope she never gets mad enough to burn me and Bridget the way Hazel burned this guy."

"I know, right? Hazel's account has gone wild since she posted that." Kelly wiped down the counter.

"Okay." Mike sighed heavily. "You two are clearly looking for a reaction from me, but I have no freakin' clue what you're talking about."

Kelly pulled out her phone like she was taking down a bad guy in a gunfight. She tapped the screen and turned it so Mike could see. It was Hazel in her room—he recognized the pink paint and black ceiling. She was doing some sort of dance, pointing at the words scrolling on the screen. The audio that was playing was going "Oh, no..." over and over.

Mike snatched the phone from Kelly's hand so he could read the captions:

That moment when you catch your mom. Playing naked games with her attorney boytoy. In her bedroom.

In the video, Hazel put her hands to her face and said "oh, no" in time with the music.

Jesus H. Christ. Mike closed his eyes, wondering how much worse this situation could get.

"Did you say this is going viral? Does Zoey know?"

Kelly shrugged. "I think it's safe to say the whole town knows by now, but I honestly don't know about Zoey. And I wouldn't exactly call it *viral,* but she's gotten a lot of action on it."

Finn gave an exaggerated sigh. "I've always wanted to be someone's *boytoy.*"

"Shut up, man. This isn't funny. Her dad's on his honeymoon. What if he sees it before Zoey talks to him?"

Finn's smile faded. "Chris and Genna got back on Saturday. Bridget said Zoey's already talked to him. Didn't she tell you?"

Hard for her to tell him anything when she refused to take his calls. She told him he needed to give her *space*, whatever the hell that meant. He only knew he didn't like it.

Kelly patted his hand. "Hazel's a teenager. This is her way of dealing with what happened. And if she's making jokes about it, maybe that's a good thing?" Mike tried to see it from that angle, but couldn't. Kelly explained. "She's actually getting a lot of positive feedback, in between the trolls, of course. Most of the people are being really supportive, saying it was bad timing but that her mom must be cool—or whatever kids say these days—to be having an affair with a guy who makes her laugh." Kelly looked up at him. "Did you know that's why she opened the door? Because she heard her mom laughing like she hadn't heard in ages? She told someone that in the comments." Kelly winked. "More than one suggested that if her mom had locked the damn door, they could have avoided all this drama."

He scrolled through the comments, ignoring the obviousness of that suggestion. "But why did she have to say I was an *attorney*? People in town will know this is about me."

Finn chuckled. "You're upset about the word *attorney*, but *boytoy* doesn't bother you?"

Mike didn't answer. He was reading an exchange between Hazel and a young girl who was telling her that she wished a man would come along that could make *her* mom laugh again after her divorce. Hazel had responded with a heart emoji and the letters *IKR?* It stood for *I know, right?* Hazel wasn't acting as traumatized as Zoey had described the last time they spoke, which was the same day Hazel had walked in on them. That's when Zoey officially put them on Pause.

"My focus has to be Hazel," she'd said on the phone. "I can't do us right now. I *want* my friend, but we've gone way past that point, and I don't think we can go back."

He'd pleaded with her to let him come over to the shop, as a *friend*-friend, with a bottle of wine and a supply of bad jokes. But she'd told him no.

"I told Hazel we were cooling things," Zoey said. "I need her to trust me again. It's killing me that she doesn't." Her voice had cracked. "We knew what we were risking. And now we'll have to pay the price. You have to stay away, Mike. At least for now."

He'd asked how long she wanted them to avoid each other, and she hadn't answered. But he had a feeling that in her mind, this was more than a temporary break. She was ending things. Ending the *best* thing he'd ever had.

That's why Mike had been at the Shamrock most evenings, sitting on his usual barstool, nursing a Guinness for an hour or so before downing a shot of whiskey and going home. He missed both Zoey's sharp wit and her silky skin. He'd had *two* of his favorite people torn away—his best friend *and* the woman he loved. Losing Becca had nearly broken him. Losing Zoey on top of that would be unbearable.

Kelly took her phone back, then looked over Mike's shoulder and went pale. "Oh, shit. Speaking of viral moments, here comes the ex-husband to confront the boytoy."

Mike ground his teeth together, then stood and turned to face Chris Bennett. He'd known Chris ever since the guy started dating Zoey. They'd gotten along well through the years, talking football and drinking beer together. Chris had always been decent enough. Until he cheated on Zoey and left her. Mike hadn't had anything to say to the guy since then.

Chris stopped right in front of Mike. Tall and sandy haired, Chris was usually the life of a party, but not today. His eyes were narrow and hard, and a muscle ticked in his cheek. *Oh, great.*

"We need to talk," Chris said. His voice was flat.

"Sure." Mike stood, gesturing to the booths lining the wall by the windows. "Drink? On me."

"Beer sounds good."

Kelly gestured that she'd take care of the order and the two men walked to the booth and sat. They stared at each other in silence until she delivered the drinks and left, looking worriedly between them but not saying a word.

As an attorney, Mike knew how to keep his emotions at bay in a conversation. He kept his body relaxed and his expression neutral. Despite his personal feelings about Chris, the man was Hazel's father. He deserved to have his say after what happened.

Chris took a sip of his beer, then met Mike's gaze. "So I came back from my honeymoon to discover that not only was my ex having some guy sleeping over at her house, but that my teenage daughter *caught* them together. Tell me why I shouldn't take you out back and beat the shit outta you."

Mike's first reaction was *you and whose army?* He was agitated enough to want a good scuffle, but that wouldn't help anyone, least of all Hazel.

"Well, for one thing, what your ex-wife does or doesn't do is no longer your problem. You left her for another woman, remember? The one you just married?" Mike's voice was sharper than he wanted, but damn, the guy had just threatened him with violence.

"What the mother of my *daughter* does is very much my problem." Chris glared some more, then sat back with a sigh. "Damn it, man—my daughter *saw* you buck naked with her mother. What am I supposed to do with that?"

"I covered myself. It was just a few seconds…" There was no good way to spin what had happened, especially to Hazel's father. "I'm really sorry. We had no idea she'd be in the house that morning."

"I know. Zoey made that clear. And so did Hazel."

"How are they doing? Zoey and Hazel?"

Chris looked at him, his eyebrows rising in surprise. "You haven't talked to her?"

"We're on pause or something." Mike took a sip of his beer. And then another. He had no idea what Chris knew or how much he could trust him. Chris drank his beer, too, and the booth filled with awkward silence.

"I know you and Zoey have been friends since you were kids." Chris wiped his mouth. "But I did *not* see this coming. Were you two together while we were…?"

"Married? Absolutely not."

"Was it serious?"

"It was for me. I'm pretty sure it was for Zoey, too." He hoped that was still true. "You need to know that Hazel was always her top priority. She didn't tell her because she was trying to protect her from more stress in her life." It occurred to him that Chris might use this to make a change in custody arrangements. "She's always put Hazel first."

"I know," Chris said. "Zoey was waiting for Genna and me when we got home from the airport. I was ticked off when she first told me what happened." Chris shifted in his seat, looking out the window. "Hazel was with her, and announced she was moving in with us."

That must have destroyed Zoey. His heart ached for her.

"You can't take her daughter away from her."

Chris's jaw tightened as he looked back to Mike. "She's *my* daughter, too." He took a breath. "But she's not going anywhere. She stayed with us a couple of nights, just so the two of them could get a time-out from each other. But she's back with Zoey now." Chris leaned forward. "If you're serious about Zoey, then you need to be serious about building a relationship with Hazel."

"Hazel's a great kid, Chris. I want to do right by her. But Zoey's basically kept us apart since she and I got serious."

Chris nodded. "That's her usual fallback position—any threat to the family makes her put Hazel in a fortress to keep her safe. But that kid is tough and smart, and she can handle more than Zoey thinks."

"Maybe Zoey just thinks Hazel has *handled* more than she should have at thirteen." Mike's voice was steady, but Chris got the point.

"I know what *I've* done to hurt Hazel. I've never blamed Zoey for anything that happened in our marriage, not to Zoey and definitely not to Hazel." Chris looked straight across the table at Mike. "And I've told Hazel that her mom deserves to have someone in her life. Is that what you want? To be in Zoey's—and Hazel's—life for the long run? Because I think Hazel might accept that now that a little time has passed."

"There's nothing I want more."

"Then what are you waiting for?"

"Zoey won't even talk to me." Mike threw his hands up in frustration. "She won't answer my calls. She doesn't want me around Hazel. And now Hazel's put out that video thing…"

Chris winced. "I told her to take that freakin' video down, but you know the internet—once something's out there…"

"…it's out there forever," Mike finished. "I know."

The two men went back to drinking their beer in brooding silence. When Mike drained his glass, he set it down firmly and folded his arms on his chest.

"Why are you here, Chris? If you really wanted to take me out back and beat me up, you'd have done it by now— or at least tried. Are you mad at Zoey? Me? What?"

Chris shook his head. "I'm not mad at anyone. I *was*, at first. Zoey and I made a promise to keep each other in the loop about anything that might affect Hazel's life, and she broke that promise by not telling me about you." He shrugged. "But I've broken it a few times, too. Good intentions and all that." He shrugged again. "As far as why I'm here? It seemed like the responsible dad thing to do—to at least talk about what happened. And…" His eyes filled with regret before he glanced away. "Everyone knows Zoey didn't deserve what I did to her. I should have told her I was unhappy instead of…well…"

"Sleeping around?" Mike offered helpfully.

"I didn't sleep around. It was only Genna." Mike didn't point out the hypocrisy of that statement. "Zoey deserves to be happy." His eyes narrowed on Mike. "I don't want to see her hurt again."

"I don't, either," Mike answered. If she ever let him back in, he'd make sure of it.

"And about that video…" Chris scrubbed a hand over his face. "Hazel's teen years are going to test me at every turn. I told her she needs to apologize to you."

"She doesn't need to—"

"She *does.* Look, if you and Zoey make a go of it, we're all gonna be joined at the hip for every life event in Hazel's life—graduation, marriage, kids." He shook his head as if the thought overwhelmed him. "Zoey's a package deal, and the package is more than just Hazel. It's every side of Hazel's now-extended family. Genna finally grasped that. You're gonna have to step up, too."

He wasn't taking on a woman. He was taking on a ready-made family. He just had to love Zoey enough to wait her out.

And for once, the idea no longer terrified him.

CHAPTER TWENTY-SIX

"No, NOT THERE. I want the patio table in the other corner. Where's the umbrella for it?" Vickie looked around the new deck behind her house as if the brightly striped umbrella might be hiding in plain sight.

"It's still in the storage shed," Gordy replied, sliding the glass-top table to where Vickie was pointing. "I'll get it. Relax, woman. This isn't an international summit. It's a kid apologizing to a grown man."

She'd been surprised to get the text from Hazel yesterday. Vickie wasn't much of a texter, so she'd called Hazel back, earning herself a lecture on modern communication from a thirteen-year-old. Eventually Hazel got to the point—she wanted to apologize to Mike for that ridiculous video, but she wanted to do it somewhere without her parents, or anyone else, looking on. Somewhere like Vickie's new deck.

Vickie had grilled Hazel—did her mom know about this? Did her dad know? Did *Mike* know? The girl waffled a bit on the Mike issue, but she'd assured Vickie that both parents were aware. In fact, it was her father who'd insisted on it. *Good for Chris.* This could be the first step toward reconciliations all the way around. Vickie hoped so, because Zoey had been moping around for over a week now. She tried to keep a happy face on for Hazel, of course, but Vickie knew better. The woman was hurting.

She stood back, examining the table location, then let out a squeal when Gordy swept her into his arms without warning, kissing her senseless before setting her back on her feet with a cocky grin.

"What was *that* for?" She touched her fingers to her lips. Damn, the man could kiss.

"I needed to break up your panic cycle." He grinned. "Everything will be fine. When are your matchmaking masterminds showing up?"

"They're not coming until four." She glanced at her watch. Electronic computer watches were all the craze now, but she still loved the sleek look of her classic Movado. "Mike and Hazel are doing their thing at two. I should finish getting the appetizers ready. You're staying for book club, right?"

Gordy's face twisted, and he made a face at her. "Do I have to?"

His pleading made her laugh. She'd never thought of herself as a complete sourpuss, but Gordy had a way to get her to laugh at things far more easily and often, including laughing at *herself.*

"Yes," she said, swatting at him when he walked past her. "You promised. Besides, they like you."

"I'm just the new curiosity. They like making swoony eyes at you and I, like we're in a freak show. You're not going to make me actually join this little club of yours, are you?"

"You don't want to join my book club?" They were a couple. They should want to do everything...

"Just because we're official now," Gordy said, as if reading her mind, "that doesn't mean we have to be joined at the hip. Do *you* want to come to my poker night at the golf club?"

"Hardly," she said with a sniff.

Gordy spread his hands wide. "Exactly. Chuck Manning's wife doesn't make *him* come."

It took her a second to realize he was talking about Cecile's Charlie.

"Fair enough." She wagged her finger at him with a smile. "You're off the hook *after* today. I already told them you'd join us, and they all want to talk to you."

"Interrogate me is more like it," Gordy grumbled. His expression lifted. "But if you promise me a trip upstairs after everyone is gone, I'll consider it." He was facing her now, arms crossed.

"You are a dirty old man."

"And you are a dirty old broad. Is that a yes?"

She slid one of the patio chairs closer to the table. "Of course it is. Did you bring a change of clothes for church tomorrow?"

"I wasn't planning on *going* to church tomorrow."

"Well, change your plans, mister. We can stop at your place in the morning. But…" She walked to him and he slid his arm around her waist. "Do you think it might be time to start keeping more things here?"

"Why, Victoria Pendergast, are you asking me to move in with you?"

Her eyes went wide. Was she?

"Well…what would you think about that?"

"I won't be a kept man, Vickie." His eyes sparkled with laughter, but then he grew serious. "I know your place is bigger than mine. And fancier. And on the water. But my house is where my kids grew up. I don't know if I want to part with it. I guess we could rent it." He looked around the deck. "Or rent this…"

"Are you suggesting we move into *your* house?" He was a contractor, so of course he had a beautiful home. Smaller and simpler than the home Malcolm bought for Vickie all those years ago. Located in town, not far from the Taggart Inn. It would be a big change for her, but moving would be a big step for Gordy, too. She finally went on her tiptoes to give him a soft kiss.

"Sounds like we have some decisions to make, but they don't need to be made today. We have all the time in the world, right?"

He pretended to think about that. "Well, you *are* seventy, so maybe not *all* the time in the world…"

"Thanks, smart-ass. Go get the table umbrella, funny guy." She smacked his shoulder, then headed into the house. She was shocked to realize she was actually considering leaving this place. Her heart belonged wherever *he* was. In the end, this was just a building. And Gordy was the man she loved.

ZOEY STOOD ON the front porch as Mike's Mustang came rumbling up the driveway with Hazel in the passenger seat. It was a sight she hadn't prepared herself for—her two hearts together. Hazel had tried to explain why she had to meet Mike at Vickie's place to apologize. She'd said she didn't want anyone listening in, and she especially didn't want to do it in front of Zoey or Chris. Hazel said that would make her nervous. But Zoey was glad Mike was here because she really needed to talk to him, and it had nothing to do with their relationship. A relationship she still had on hard Pause. A relationship she missed desperately, but was terrified to start again.

Hazel's eyes were bright and shining, her hair wild around her face when Mike stopped the souped-up car. She saw Zoey and jumped out of the car.

"Mom!" she shouted. "Have you ever ridden in this? It's

amazing. Mike took me all the way up to the top of the hill by the waterfalls, and then we came down the hill so fast..."

Mike leaned forward, still sitting at the wheel. "Not *that* fast..."

But Hazel was still going. "We went by Falls Legend Winery so fast it was a *blur*!"

Mike was still in the car, shaking his head. "Not a blur."

"It was a *blur*!" Hazel insisted. She ran up the steps and gave Zoey a quick hug. "It was fun."

"I'm glad. How did your talk go?"

Hazel paused, as if the car ride had erased her memory of the apology meeting that should have happened before it.

"Oh, that. It was good."

When Zoey just kept staring at her, waiting for more, Hazel rolled her eyes and heaved a tortured sigh. "It was *fine*. I apologized. He apologized. I cried a little, but he dealt."

Zoey looked at Mike. He couldn't possibly hear them over the rumbling car engine, and he tipped his head as if wondering what she was thinking. He had probably *not* dealt that well with Hazel's tears. He'd told Zoey years ago that he had an auto-response to tears and wanted to cry with the person, which he considered to be horrifyingly humiliating. He didn't seem to be near tears now, though. He was smiling, even though she could see concern in his eyes. She turned back to her daughter.

"Why did you cry?"

Hazel shrugged. "I felt bad. And *he* felt bad, which made *me* feel bad, and then we talked about the video and I *really* felt bad."

"He shouldn't have made you feel bad about that."

That video had nearly given Zoey a heart attack when she first saw it. And she didn't see it until Tani called her

and said all the kids were watching it. Her first reaction had
been white-hot rage, but she'd quickly cooled off. Hazel was
thirteen. She'd needed to express her feelings about what
happened, and that silly video seemed to have done that for
her. She'd been more settled since she'd done it. But anyone
local who saw it knew exactly who she was talking about.
Everyone now knew that Hazel's mom, Zoey, and her *attorney boytoy*, Mike McKinnon, had been naked together.
That couldn't have been great for Mike.

"He didn't *make* me feel bad, Mom. I just *do* feel bad.
But I told him I came up with a way to fix it." Hazel had a
suspiciously gleeful look in her eyes.

"What do you mean, *fix it*?"

"Never mind. Just an idea I had."

Mike turned off the car and got out, but he stayed on the
far side of the Mustang. "Can we talk, Zoey?"

She remembered why she'd come out there to greet them
in the first place.

"Yes, we need to."

"Mom, I'm *starving*." Hazel reached for the front door.
"Vickie only had these gross tuna things she called sandwiches, but they were more like *doll* sandwiches, and they
had *cucumbers* in them." She made a face. "I'm gonna
make myself some real food." And she was gone.

A week ago, Hazel wasn't speaking to Zoey or Mike,
demanding to move out, sure her life was ruined. Now she
was raiding the kitchen after joyriding with Mike. If this
was any example of the roller coaster ride her high school
years would be like, they were all going to have gray hair
at her graduation.

Mike came up the steps slowly, making Zoey feel like
she was some dangerous animal he was trying to approach.

"I'm not going to bite you, for God's sake. Come up and sit. I need your help."

"You got it." He came up and sat in the Adirondack chair next to hers. "I'll do whatever you need. I just want to…"

"This is about zoning." She stopped him cold. If she let herself think that this was *Mike* sitting next to her— the Mike she hadn't touched, had barely spoken to—she wouldn't be able to focus on… What was she saying again?

"The Schiff lady?" Realization dawned on his face. "What did she do now?"

Zoey fished the certified letter out of her pocket and handed it to him. "I got this in the mail today. The town is reviewing whether or not this property is being improperly used as a commercial business in a residential zone." She blinked, wondering how much stress one human heart could take in a week. "Karen Schiff is behind this. With the storm and everything, I haven't gotten around to moving Dad's sculptures, and now…" She shook her head. "Mike, I'm just starting to turn a decent profit with the repair business, but I can't afford to rent another building somewhere. What am I going to do?"

His hand settled over hers. It was probably meant to be calming. But his touch immediately amped up her heart rate. He stared right into her eyes. "The first thing you're going to do is take a deep breath. I know this letter sounds very formal and even a little threatening, but this is boilerplate language for zoning disputes. The town has to cover their butt legally, so they create word salads like this." He held up the letter.

When she'd opened it an hour ago, a wave of panic had washed over her. It was bad enough that her relationship with Hazel was so shaky. That her relationship with Mike— *both* relationships, friend and lover—might be ruined. And now her business was on the line. Commercial property wasn't easy to come by in Rendezvous Falls, and it wasn't cheap.

"Zoey, it's gonna be okay." Mike's voice brought her out of her spiral. "You've got a great lawyer on your side, and we'll take care of this."

"You promise?"

"I promise we'll find a way through it. Together." He squeezed her fingers. "Have I ever let you down?"

He held her gaze. She'd missed her friend so damn much. "You've never let me down."

He grinned. "I'll take care of this. The zoning meeting is a week from now, and we'll be ready." He reached for her, but she leaned away.

"Hazel's inside."

She didn't intend to sound so quick and cold, but fear did funny things to a person. It had taken every bit of her strength to talk things over—and *over*—with her daughter. To convince her *not* to move in with her dad full-time. To convince her that this old house was their *home*. Just them—two women together against the world. No boys allowed. At least not anytime soon.

Mike sighed heavily. "Babe, you keep insisting that loving me and loving your daughter are two separate things. As if doing both at the same time will lead to something horrific, like that chemical fire I set off in the high school science lab." His mouth twitched, almost smiling at the memory.

She stared at him in disbelief. "Loving you *did* lead to disaster, or have you forgotten that we traumatized my thirteen-year-old daughter last week?"

"What happened last week was…not great," he conceded. "But it was an accident—a combination of circumstances no one could have predicted. And it *was* a shock for Hazel. Not because she caught us clowning around… while we happened to be undressed." He leaned forward, taking her hand back and holding on, waiting until she met his gaze before continuing. "It was a shock because we hadn't told her anything about our relationship. I know I let you take the lead on that decision, but Zoey…it was a mistake not to tell her."

"I was just trying to be a good mom."

"You *are* a good mom." Mike raised her hand and kissed her knuckles. "And I don't need to be an actual parent to see that. You're the best person I've ever known, so you can't possibly be a bad mother. I just spent over an hour with that kid of yours, and you have raised one awesome young human. She's the spitting image of you."

Now it was Zoey's turn to try to keep from smiling. She failed. "Sometimes it's like looking in a mirror."

"I'll bet." The lines around his eyes eased a bit. "So I'll have *two* of you to deal with."

Zoey pulled back again. "Not so fast. We still need to wait before we…go any further together."

"Okay." His quick agreement surprised her. "As long as we're *waiting* and not *over*. I love you, Zoey Hartford. And since she's your carbon copy, I'll love Hazel, too. When you're ready to let me."

He stood, pulling her up with him. But he didn't pull her into an embrace. He was waiting, which was what she *said* she wanted. So why did she feel disappointed?

"I am so confused, Mike." She shook her head. "I can see a future for us, but I can't make myself move toward it. I never thought of myself as a coward, but… I'm terrified of making another mistake." She didn't have any confidence in her decision-making.

"I'll be brave enough for both of us," he whispered, leaning forward to brush a kiss against her hair. "But you have to take that next step on your own."

She dropped her forehead onto his shoulder and sighed. She was overthinking this. But Mike was willing to wait for her to think straight, instead of in circles. She raised her head and smiled.

"Just a little more time. Let me talk to Hazel. And let's deal with this zoning nightmare. That sounds like I'm putting you off, but…"

"One battle at a time. I get it. I'm not going anywhere." He shrugged. "Well, I'm going somewhere right now. I'm going to the town clerk's office to do some more research." He tapped her nose lightly with his finger. "We've got this."

CHAPTER TWENTY-SEVEN

"I TOLD HER *we got this*." Mike tossed a sheaf of papers across his grandmother's dining room table. "But I'm not sure we do."

His grandmother and her book club pals sat around the table in silence, watching him rant.

"The way the zoning laws were rewritten back in the seventies is making this like putting together a jigsaw puzzle upside down, so you can't see the picture. I need an angle to argue, but I can't find one."

"That's a shame," Iris Taggart said, "but I still don't know what you think we can do. *You're* the attorney."

"I think you meant to say *attorney boytoy*," Rick added helpfully.

Mike ignored him. He'd gotten used to hearing his new nickname, thanks to Hazel. "You've all been around longer than me. You have knowledge, and maybe some influence, that I don't." He hesitated. "And… I'm desperate."

His grandmother smiled softly. "You think you have to win this thing to get Zoey back?"

"No." He frowned. "Maybe. I *promised* her, but I haven't found anything yet that's a slam dunk for the town board meeting tomorrow."

Cecile reached out and grabbed the scattered documents. She started sorting them and handing them around the table. "Okay, everyone take a few pages and let's see what we can find. It'll be like those lawyer shows on TV, where the paralegal finds the detail that turns the case around!"

Everyone took a few pages as ordered, including Mike. He'd been over this stuff a dozen times. Technically, the repair shop *could* be considered commercial property. And technically, thanks to Zoey's father, the land *was* zoned residential. And technically, the zoning laws narrowed the definitions of residential and commercial, limiting what could be grandfathered in.

So technically... Mike might be screwed.

He and Zoey had talked only once since she'd handed him the certified letter, and it was about the case, not their relationship. Mike made sure of that. He didn't want her feeling pressured, because he knew it could make her withdraw even further. Like Logan had said, a good mom is *always* going to be willing to sacrifice her own happiness for her kids' sake. Even when she doesn't need to.

Iris, her glasses low on her nose, looked over the rim at Mike. "You saying we have knowledge you don't was a lawyerly way of saying we're old. But it's true that some of us have had our run-ins with the town board and annoying neighbors through our many years on the planet." She nodded toward the file. "A historic declaration can shut down a lot of arguments."

"You mean having her place declared a historic landmark?" Mike asked. "That might help, but...on what grounds? It's an old Victorian, but so are three-quarters of the houses in town."

"I remember Zoey's grandfather—not her dad, but *his* dad..."

Vickie made a face. "That's generally how grandfathers work, Iris."

"I'm just making a point, Victoria." Iris scowled, then

continued. "The point is Rob's dad started the appliance repair business, but *his* dad—Rob's grandfather—was a blacksmith. And he worked out of that shop. And I'm pretty sure the earlier Hartford generations did the same."

Mike remembered seeing a giant anvil in the back corner of the barn. "So you're thinking if the barn was always used as a business…for generations…that might sway the zoning board." He jotted some notes on his tablet. "That might work. Let's see if we can find any mention of that in these papers."

Rick Thomas pulled out his phone. "Papers-schmapers. Let's look online. What's the address up there again? If I search that against blacksmiths and Hartfords, I might find something."

While Rick scrolled, the rest of them read line after line of census information, deeds and property tax records on the farm. They may not have enough proof to declare the property had always been a business, but they might have enough to earn a zoning exemption. The zoning board had the ability to exempt certain properties from zoning rules, but they had to have a good reason.

Nana reached over and patted his arm. "There's nothing this town likes more than its own stories, Michael. We'll appeal to their history-loving little hearts, don't you worry."

Helen Russo nodded. "She's right. And if we pack the room with supporters for Zoey, that can't hurt. Those old cronies on the board don't like conflict, so if the crowd wants Zoey to get an exemption, they'll listen."

"But what if that awful Schiff woman wants to pack the room with *her* supporters?" Cecile asked. There was a beat of silence.

"First," Vickie started. "I don't think Karen Schiff *has* a roomful of friends. She's the only one who's complained, and I've yet to meet anyone who knows her well, much less agrees with her."

"Hmmph," Iris sniffed. "I heard she's such a snob that she doesn't *want* to know any of the locals. So good luck filling a room with her supporters."

"And second," Vickie continued. "I have an idea how we can make Karen Schiff back down *and* make Zoey happy, too. And it'll be just in time for Summerfest weekend."

Summerfest was a combination art and music festival held every August in Rendezvous Falls. The college campus hosted it, and local businesses sponsored the awards and the bands. Mike looked across the table at Vickie, and she gave him a bright smile.

"What? She's my goddaughter, remember? I'll be damned if some outsider is going to make her get rid of her father's legacy. I'll also be damned if I'll let her best friend let her down." She winked at him. "So *you* put together the legal argument for the board, and *I'll* tell you all how we're going to handle Karen Schiff."

By the time Vickie finished unveiling her plan, which—being Vickie—she'd presented with a little more drama than necessary, there was applause around the table. Mike only wished he'd come up with it.

"Zoey is going to love that idea!" his grandmother exclaimed.

Iris nodded in agreement. "I hate to inflate your swelled head any further, but damn, Vickie—that is a great idea. Not just for Zoey, but for Rendezvous Falls."

"And Summerfest is the perfect place to announce it," Cecile added. She turned to Rick at her side. "I'm guessing you helped with this?"

He shrugged. "I may have dropped a few words in the

dean's ear, but don't forget Vickie *dated* the guy, so she probably had more influence over Howard Greer than I did."

Mike sat back in his chair with a smile. The tide had turned. If they could make this work, and he had no doubt this group of senior troublemakers could bend the entire universe to their will, then Zoey might finally see how much the people in town believed in her. And maybe that would give her the courage to take that step toward loving him.

His phone pinged with a message from… Hazel?

H: Boytoy Redemption plan is on. Click link. Learn steps. Meet me @ Mary's 9am.

Oh, damn. He'd forgotten about the promise he'd made at their apology meeting. Or more accurately, he was hoping *she'd* forget about it. Hazel had insisted she wanted to make up for the video she'd made, and that her plan would be *fire*. He had a feeling this was more about *Boytoy humiliation than redemption. B*ut Hazel was Zoey's daughter through and through. Once she declared a plan, it was going to happen. He read it again and grimaced. What *steps* was he supposed to learn? He was afraid to click the link.

"Trouble?" Nana asked, nodding toward the phone.

Mike ran his fingers through his hair.

"More than you can imagine, but I guess I'd better get used to it."

Hazel had declared a semitruce at their apology chat. She liked Mike, but she was still undecided about him being with her mother. She'd agreed to give him a chance, though, and he'd agreed to be completely open and honest with her…and to *always* lock the door from now on. He was sliding the phone back into his pocket when Helen held up a piece of paper excitedly. "Hold on! This might be what we're looking for!"

Mike's hope grew brighter. He might be able to keep that promise to Zoey after all.

IF ZOEY THOUGHT she'd been shocked at the number of cars in the parking lot at the town hall, she was even more shocked at the dramatic turn of events at the zoning meeting right now. Mike was standing in front of the standing-room-only crowd, explaining why "Hartford Farm" should be declared a historic landmark property.

The town board itself couldn't do that, of course, but he told them he'd already submitted paperwork to the county and the state in an attempt to make that happen. By doing so, he argued that they shouldn't make any changes to the zoning status until they heard back from both.

Zoey looked down to her lap, trying to hide her smile. Decisions like that could take months, sometimes years, to churn through committees. It was a clever ploy on Mike's part. Unfortunately, it would delay the problem rather than solving it. Because Karen Schiff was sitting right there in the front row with her husband, on the opposite side of the center aisle from Zoey.

Edward Schiff looked like he'd rather be on the surface of the sun than in that meeting. Zoey leaned to the side to get a better look at Karen. The woman, with her cropped blond hair looking like a helmet, was glancing around the room with a hint of uncertainty in her eyes. She was probably as surprised by the turnout as Zoey was. And the crowd was clearly there for Zoey—the room burst into applause every time Mike made a point.

The only thing missing was a cape attached to his shoulders as he paced the floor in front of the board, pleading her case. He was her hero right now. He caught her eye just then and gave a quick wink. He was enjoying this. And she was enjoying watching.

"Ladies and gentlemen, I believe we'll find that the Hartford Farm will qualify for historic designation. The original owner, Horace Hartford, was the blacksmith who created some of our town's original and most ornate iron fences, including the intricate gate at the entrance of Brady College."

Hazel was sitting next to Zoey, and they stared at each other in surprise. She'd never heard that story before. Mike explained how records proved that her great-great-grandfather had helped create the iconic look of the town that was world-famous for its Victorian style. Since the town itself had been recognized as a *national* historic landmark, with many individual homes also sporting signs from New York State describing their significance, then surely, Mike insisted, the home of Horace Hartford would also qualify. It was fascinating, but Zoey couldn't help thinking that it might not keep Karen Schiff from getting her way. Rules were rules.

"In addition, if you'll take a look at Exhibit E in your packets," Mike was saying. He gestured to the glossy, bound booklets of material he'd handed out to the board members and everyone who walked in the door until they'd run out. Zoey was flipping through hers to find the list of old census copies. She saw Horace Hartford's name on several of them, and then her great-grandfather, her grandfather and her dad.

"If you look at the occupation entered by every generation of Hartford men until Robert Hartford," Mike said, "you'll see it listed as blacksmith or ironworker. Since these gentlemen all appeared to use the barn and the attached workshop as their smithy, I think we can agree that the property has continually been home to a business since the 1800s. Which means it should qualify for a grandfather clause, allowing a business to continue there now."

Marty Watson, a longtime town employee and current head of the zoning board, pushed back his ball cap and scratched his head. "Look, Mike, just because there was a smithy there a hundred years ago doesn't mean there should be one there now. Besides—" the old man gestured in Zoey's direction "—Zoey ain't no blacksmith. She fixes vacuum cleaners. That's hardly historically significant."

Karen Schiff raised her hands to start clapping at what seemed a point for her side, but her husband's withering stare stopped her. Her hands fell back to her lap.

"Well," Mike replied, "if you look at Exhibit—"

Marty slapped his book closed. "I don't need to read some damn *novel* to make a zoning decision." Zoey's fears returned. Maybe this wouldn't work, after all. "I've known you since you were running around your grandpa's bar in diapers, Mike McKinnon. You don't need to come in here and razzle-dazzle us with all your legal wizardry."

Marty pointed to the Schiffs. "The reason we're here to-night is because we've had a nuisance complaint, and that needs to be resolved." A rumble of discontent rolled through the audience, and Karen Schiff visibly shrank in her chair. She had to know she was outnumbered here.

Lou Smith spoke up from the far end of the table the board was sitting at. "Marty's right. This is compelling, Mike." Lou chuckled as he held up the fancy booklet. "Even if it *is* a bit of overkill. I'd like to see if we can come up with something that will make everyone happy." He shook his head with a wry smile. "Or at least equally *un*happy."

Lou looked at the Schiff couple. "Mrs. Schiff, what will it take to satisfy your complaint that your neighbor, Miss

Hartford, is—" he slid on a pair of readers and squinted at the paper in front of him "—uh…'destroying the residential nature of your surroundings.' Can you describe exactly how that's happening?"

Zoey steeled herself for insults and mockery from her neighbor when Karen stood.

"Thank you, Mr. Smith." Karen looked around the room, color rising in her face. "I only want to protect my property value, and the appearance of Miss Hartford's place, with all that—" she waved her hand in a circle "—that *stuff* in the front lawn, and the business operating right there, it's…detrimental."

Hazel bristled, standing before Zoey could catch her. "Detrimental to *what*? You can't even see our house from your place, and my grandfather's sculptures are *art*, and your house is just ugly cement—"

Zoey yanked her daughter down to her seat as the audience applauded Hazel's outburst. *Not helping.* "I apologize, Mr. and Mrs. Schiff. I don't want this to get personal."

"But this *is* personal," Mike said, rising from the seat he'd taken when Marty and Lou had started to question him. He faced Karen Schiff and her husband. "I understand the artwork in front of Zoey's home isn't your taste…" Karen huffed as if to say *obviously* as he continued. "So what if the sculptures are removed, with the exception of a few near the house. Would that help ease the…uh…detriment of the property?"

Hazel started muttering. She loved her Pop-pop's sculptures. Even for Zoey, the thought of stacking them in a heap felt fundamentally wrong, especially less than a year after losing Dad. She expected another outburst from Hazel, but her daughter was surprisingly relaxed and quiet again. There was even a trace of a smile on her face.

"I suppose it would," Karen Schiff conceded, with her husband nodding in agreement.

"And if Miss Hartford promises not to open a storefront or anything that would attract extra traffic to the area, would that be satisfactory?" Mike asked. He glanced quickly in Zoey's direction, the corner of his mouth barely twitching, signaling he felt a win coming on.

"Yes." Karen's response was so soft that hardly anyone heard it except the front row. And the zoning board.

"Okay!" Marty tapped his gavel on the table. "I make a motion to the board that we grant the property at Twelve Valley View Road an exemption for a small repair business to be operated without a storefront or business hours posted, and with the condition that the…uh…artwork is removed. All in favor?"

Seven hands went up at the table in agreement, with none in opposition. Zoey let out a long sigh of relief as the crowded room cheered. Her love life might be upside down, but at least her business was still intact. Thanks to Mike. She stood just as he reached her chair, and he lifted her into his arms.

"I told you we had this," he whispered in her ear.

"Mike!" Hazel threw her arms around Zoey and Mike's waists. "You did it! That was like watching a true crime show or something. You are the OG in this town, for sure!" He looked at Zoey for a translation. She laughed.

"It's kind of like being the top banana."

His arm went around Hazel's shoulders so he was embracing them both. Like a family. Both her worlds. Both her hearts. In one tight little circle. Hazel tugged on Mike's sleeve.

"Wanna see it before I post, or should I let it rip?"

"I trust you, kid. Let 'er rip." He closed his eyes tightly. "It's only my hard-earned reputation on the line."

Zoey frowned. "What are you two talking about?"

The room was still abuzz with people congratulating her and patting each other's backs in celebration. Hazel gave her a playful shrug. "Nothing major. Just fixing your boytoy's image."

"Or destroying it," Mike added.

"He's not my...wait, *what*?"

Marty's gavel came down sharply on the table three times before he called out.

"Okay, okay, have a seat, people! We have more business to conduct tonight."

She glanced at Mike. "I guess we can go, right?" She didn't really care about any other zoning decisions right now. To her surprise, though, all of her supporters—friends, neighbors, the book club crew, Mike's family—all sat down, seeming eager for the next order of business.

Hazel tugged her hand. "Sit, Mom. You'll want to hear this." Hazel turned and gave a thumbs-up gesture toward Vickie behind them. Mike sat on Zoey's other side, so she was between him and Hazel. The two of them kept leaning forward to look at each other with conspiratorial grins. Zoey felt like she was the only one in the room who didn't know what was about to happen.

"We have a motion," Marty said, "to allow a one-acre parcel of land formerly owned by Brady College, located at the corner of Main Street and College Street, to be declared a public town park." He held up a paper and read from it. "More specifically, the park will be designated as a sculpture garden, to be maintained year-round by the town in partnership with the festival committee. The town board has approved the acquisition with the stipulation that the zoning be approved. It's my understanding that the land will be landscaped by Cooper Landscaping at no charge to the town, with environmentally safe lighting paid for by the Taggart Inn. The pedestals for both permanent and temporary sculptures on display are being donated by Mc-Kinnon Law Firm. Maintenance will be paid for by a grant set up by Victoria Pendergast for that specific purpose." Marty cleared his throat. "With all of that taken into consideration, can we have a vote?"

The room again erupted into applause when the vote was unanimous. Zoey thought it was a nice idea, but she didn't understand exactly why her friends and her godmother were so invested in a sculpture park.

Wait a minute…

"Mike?" She grabbed his arm. "What have you done?"

At the front of the room, Marty was trying to formally adjourn the meeting, but no one was listening.

Mike slid his arms around her again. "This one is all your godmother's work, along with her matchmaking cronies."

"Mom!" Hazel was practically bouncing. "Vickie says Pop-pop's sculptures will be on display in the garden, right in town. And guest artists will display *their* sculptures, too. And the whole thing will be named after him."

Zoey looked at Mike, who nodded. "The Robert Hartford Memorial Sculpture Garden. It will be right near the festival grounds."

Dad would never believe it. His artwork on permanent display in an actual park named after him. She ended up in another circle hug with Mike and Hazel. She met his gaze over her daughter's head. He nodded at the top of Hazel's head, his smile wide, but his voice low enough not to be heard by the crowd.

"Look—she's between us again."

Zoey laughed, but Hazel was solemn.

"Duh… I'm not *between* you. I'm *with* you."

And just like that, Zoey felt…healed. Whole. And happy. She didn't have two worlds anymore—no more two Zoey's, mom vs woman. She had *one* world. And it was right here in this circle of love. Mike's eyes were glowing with affection…and a touch of heat.

"She said she's going to give us a chance, so what do you say—time to take that step forward?"

She went up on her toes to reach over Hazel to kiss him. "It's long past time, I think. I love you both so much it hurts."

"Okay," Hazel protested, squished between them. "You're making this a gross Hazel sandwich."

Mike loosened his grip on the two of them, but just enough to give Hazel some breathing room. He tipped his head down to look right at her. "Are you okay with this, kid?"

Hazel rolled her eyes. "Are you going to keep your end of the deal?"

He laughed again, the sound ringing through Zoey's heart like Christmas bells. "Keep the doors locked? I promise."

Mary ran up to them just then, holding her phone up. Zoey noticed others in the room were looking at their phones, then laughing and pointing toward her and Mike and Hazel. Mary threw her arms around the threesome quickly for a hug.

"Congratulations, you guys. That was quite a win, *and* the sculpture garden will be incredible. I'm donating a website for that, by the way." Mary ran her hand through Hazel's hair, tousling it and making Hazel squeal. "And *you*,

you little rascal! How the *hell*... I mean...*heck*...did you get my brother to dance like that?"

Bridget and Finn walked over, and Finn couldn't stop laughing. "Well, I guess instead of *boytoy* we'll have to call you *twinkletoes*, eh?"

"What is everyone laughing about?" Zoey grabbed at Mary's phone. Oh, God. Hazel had a new video up. Zoey gave her a warning look before opening it.

It was Hazel, and it looked like she was in Vickie's back-yard. The lake was bright blue behind her. She was dressed in a costume of some sort, in a green leotard and a tall striped hat. Was it anime? A cartoon? Some TikTok trend? She'd never been able to keep up with them all. She clicked the Play button, and Hazel was dancing to some song with a catchy, funny beat to it. And then Mike appeared behind Hazel, crossing over in the opposite direction as her, but doing the same skipping steps. And he was *also wearing* a giant green top hat, although he'd been spared the leo-tard—instead he wore green sweatpants and a green T-shirt.

Zoey's hand went over her mouth. She couldn't believe what she was seeing. Her daughter and her—she glanced up at his blushing face—her *boyfriend* were doing a dance challenge together. And it was hysterically funny.

"What...what am I watching?" she asked, to no one in particular. She couldn't stop laughing at the silliness of it. Mike moved behind her, sliding his arms around her waist. She glanced up to find Hazel watching them. Her daughter was smiling. Zoey relaxed back against Mike's solid chest, hope and joy dancing circles around her heart.

"Read the caption," he said, his breath moving the hair by her ear. His chin rested on her shoulder.

She'd been so busy laughing at her two beloved clowns dancing that she'd missed the small scrolling caption, similar to the one on that first embarrassing video Hazel had done. She held the phone closer and read it out loud.

When your mom's attorney boytoy. Turns out to be what the olds call cool. I'm dead that he did this! OG all the way.

It was followed by a string of laughing crying emojis. She looked at Hazel, who now was laughing with everyone else.

"So," Zoey wiped her eyes. "This is teenspeak for 'my mom's boyfriend is now acceptable to me because he allowed me to humiliate him in a dance challenge'?"

Hazel rolled her eyes. "He'd have been acceptable before that if you'd *told* me about him." Zoey winced, knowing she'd screwed up. But then Hazel looked at Mike and broke out in another torrent of giggles. "But humiliating him *was* pretty fun."

Mike reached around Zoey in a playful attempt to catch Hazel, who jumped back with a squeal of laughter. He looked at Zoey. "Your daughter is a menace." He kissed Zoey's cheek. "Just like her mom. Here, I've been saving this one up for today. What did the sculptor say to his girlfriend?"

Vickie and Maura had finally made it through the crowd around them. Vickie heard Mike's riddle and sighed to Maura. "Oh, no, here we go with the jokes…"

Zoey turned in his embrace, sliding her arms around his neck. "I don't know—what *did* the sculptor say to his girlfriend?"

"I love you with all of my art."

Everyone groaned except Zoey. She knew he meant it. He loved her. She gave him a quick kiss on the lips, then drew back. They were in public, after all. She settled against his arms and grinned.

"I've got one for you, too. Why did the notebook marry

the pencil?" she asked. There were more groans around them. Mary called out, asking if they'd always be this disgustingly mushy.

Mike ignored them all, his gaze fixed on her face.

"I don't know. Why?"

"Because she finally found Mr. Write."

He didn't laugh, and neither did she. There was no one in the room but them. No sound but their two hearts beating in perfect rhythm. Together again. Forever.

"Yes," Mike finally said. "She did. Think I can convince *you* to marry *me* someday?"

Zoey nodded, rising on her toes to kiss him again before whispering…

"I do."

* * * * *

ACKNOWLEDGMENTS

THIS BOOK WAS put on hold for a bit after we lost my mom, and it was a relief to have such a funny, touching, best-friends-to-lovers romance to come back to. It's a bit odd to say that this book was inspired by my own friendships with guys through the years that *never* included anything more than friendship, from high school to today. I say it's odd since, naturally, in the book Mike and Zoey *do* move out of the friend zone because, you know, it's a romance novel! But as a woman who was a bit of a tomboy growing up, whose father taught her how to change a spark plug by the time she was ten, who repaired Himself's toilet after we'd been dating for all of two weeks and who has always felt more comfortable with "guy talk" than "girl talk"... Well, I wanted to honor women like me, and thank the strong, secure men who are our friends. From Glenn to Kevin and more, those friendships have lasted and have added to my life in many funny and meaningful ways.

I thank my editor at HQN, Michele Bidelspach, for her wise guidance. And a huge thank-you to a constant and invaluable member of my writing team: my agent, Veronica Park, who always tells it like it is and has my back no matter what.

And most of all, thanks and so much love to my very own best friend *and* hero—my husband of twenty-six years, John.

Can't get enough of Rendezvous Falls?

*Please turn the page to read Jo McNally's Lost in Love,
a Rendezvous Falls novella.*

LOST IN LOVE

CHAPTER ONE

"WE HAVE A PROBLEM."

"No, we don't." Andrea Wentworth looked over the rim of her coffee cup at her friend. "I've already told you—there *are* no problems, only opportunities."

Taneisha Warren folded her arms, leaning against the opening to Andrea's cubicle in Brady College's administrative offices. "Yeah? Well, let me rephrase. We have the *opportunity* to not have a corn maze for the festival."

Andrea pushed back from her desk, ignoring the thread of panic those words caused.

"Impossible. The corn maze has been on Cliff Thompson's farm for over twenty years. We were there when this year's maze was planted back in May, remember?"

"Yeah, I remember." Tani sat on the corner of Andrea's desk. They were the only people in the office that early August Saturday. "And do *you* remember that Cliff seemed a little out of it that day? He didn't even remember that we were coming with the television crew from Rochester."

Andrea bit her lip. She *did* remember that. "Cliff's in his seventies, right? I just figured it was an age thing."

"Sweetie, Cliff is eighty-five. And—" Tani paused, clearly not wanting to say what came next "—he doesn't own the farm anymore."

"I'm sorry...*what*?"

Okay. This wasn't a problem. It *couldn't* be, because she'd declared that this year's Blessing of the Grapes Festival would be problem-free. It was her first year as chair-person of one of the festivals that made Rendezvous Falls famous. At the youthful age of thirty-seven, she was the youngest chairperson ever. This was a town that took its festivals *very* seriously, and where the elder matriarchs tended to run things until they dropped. She needed a suc-cessful festival—an *impeccable* festival.

Andrea was eyeing the newly vacant job of director of academic advising at Brady College. Pete Greenfeld had left for a larger university in Boston. Andrea was one of the advisers on staff, and she wanted Pete's job. Unfortu-nately, so did Steve Menkes. And even though she'd been working here longer and had outworked Steve at every turn, the dean kept mumbling about *leadership experience*. How was she supposed to get experience if they never let her lead anything? That was why she'd scrambled this spring to take the chair position on the festival when Marion Hall had to step down to have hip surgery. There could *not* be a problem with this festival.

Tani put her hand over Andrea's. "I guess Cliff's mem-ory issues got pretty serious, bless him. His family moved him into an assisted living place near them in Pittsburgh."

"How did we not *know* this? Wouldn't we have heard when the farm went on the market?"

"They sold it directly to a friend of Cliff's. No broker."

Andrea scowled at her desk. "Wait a minute!" She snapped her fingers. "We had a contract with Cliff, right? It's like if there's a renter with a lease when a property is sold. The lease generally carries over." *Problem solved.* "So this *is* an opportunity. We can build a relationship with the farm's new owner!"

"I don't think you underst—"

"Tani, it's fine." *It had to be fine.* "Do you know who

bought it? They're probably wondering why we haven't reached out before now. I'll drive up there, introduce myself and get this all sorted."

Her friend didn't look convinced. "I couldn't find any contracts in the festival file boxes, so I asked Iris Taggart, and she thinks Cliff was what she called one of their *handshake partners*. She said in the early days of the festivals, a lot of things were done that way—friend-to-friend agreements."

Andrea's mouth fell open. "No contract?" She blinked. How could that happen in the twenty-first century? "But we've already paid for the maze. It's *planted*."

"That's the thing…"

"Tani, we watched it being planted." She had a horrifying thought. "Oh, God, have they plowed it under or something? Tell me they haven't plowed it under."

"More like the *or something*. It hasn't been plowed under, but Mike and Zoey drove by there this week and said it's looking…overgrown."

"Well, overgrown isn't a big deal. It's supposed to be tall so people can't see their way out."

"It's also supposed to have trails for them to follow."

"Of course. Cliff always…" He kept the pathways mowed short and neat all year. It was a point of pride for the old guy. But mowing could happen anytime. *Right?*

"Who bought Cliff's farm? Was it someone local?"

Please let it be someone I know…

"Y-yes. He's local." Tani's gaze went around the cubicle—anywhere but in Andrea's direction. "It's Zayne Rutledge."

"Zayne?" Andrea almost laughed, which was her first clue she was on the edge of genuine panic. "You're telling me Zayne Rutledge, the bad boy of a *family* of bad

boys, came up with the cash to buy Cliff Thompson's farm? Wasn't he living in a trailer somewhere?"

"Careful, Andrea. You're sounding like your mother."

Well, that wouldn't do. She had a lot to prove—one of those things was that she was *not* her mother. She cleared her throat.

"Sorry. It's just… *Zayne? Really?"

"Zayne's got his own business now—he does custom woodwork for old homes. He made all the gingerbread trim on the Three Sisters houses." The Three Sisters were three nearly identical smaller, but very fancy, Victorian homes near the Taggart Inn. Tani slid off the desk and onto her feet. "He's still a bit of an introvert, but who can blame him after the rough start he had in life?"

Andrea cringed inside. She may have played a small part in that rough start he'd had. Correction—she'd *definitely* played a part in their senior year. She and Zayne had been friends until…they weren't. Her mind spun, looking for ways to approach this new development.

"The good news," she started, *really* looking for good news, "is Zayne is local. He knows about the festivals—" even if she'd never seen him at one "—and he won't want to ruin one of the town's biggest events."

Tani started to respond, then hesitated. "Like I said, Zayne's still…um…not the most social guy in the world."

"Meaning he's still a wild-haired hermit with no-tres-passing signs all over his property?" She remembered going up to the Rutledge family home with Tani and Tani's aunt, Lena Fox, ten years ago to deliver one of the annual community Christmas baskets. Zayne had been the only one living there at the time, and the place had been an over-grown, run-down mess. If he was living like that on Cliff's old farm, the maze might actually be doomed.

Tani laughed. "Not quite that bad. He's still got a mountain-man vibe, but not in a scary way. It kinda works on him, to be honest."

Andrea chewed her lip again. This was…not ideal. But since she didn't believe in problems anymore, it had to be an opportunity.

She couldn't help thinking it might just be an opportunity to fail.

CHAPTER TWO

ZAYNE RUTLEDGE TRIED to shake off his irritation as he walked out of the house and down to the woodworking shop. He knew when he bought Cliff Thompson's place that it would need upkeep—the Victorian house and barn were nearly a hundred and fifty years old. What he hadn't known was that Cliff had been cobbling half-assed repairs together on the property with bubble gum and baling twine for years. He'd agreed to the direct sale from Cliff to him with no real estate agent to save money for everyone. Part of the deal was no home inspection.

He needed a place where he'd be able to keep up with the ever-increasing volume of work he was getting, and Cliff had a great workshop next to the barn. It was originally the milk house, back in the old days when this was a dairy farm. The long cinder-block building was perfect for Zayne's growing woodworking business.

He just didn't expect to be spending so much time tracking down where the house roof was leaking and why the kitchen sink didn't have hot water and why the window in the upstairs bathroom refused to open. Meanwhile, woodworking orders were pouring in on his website, and everyone wanted everything *now*. He was unlocking the door to the shop when he heard tires on the gravel driveway.

Shit. He didn't have any client appointments today and he definitely did *not* have time to handle a walk-in client. He turned as the dark blue compact parked near the shop. The driver's door opened and a petite redhead got out, looking at him across the roof of the car. She rested her arm there and pushed her large sunglasses up onto her head.

Oh, double shit. Andrea Wentworth. What the hell was *she* doing here?

She flashed him a wide smile, as if they were dear old friends instead of sworn enemies. At least, that was what they'd been their senior year—enemies, pure and simple. After being the best of friends growing up.

"Zayne Rutledge!" she cried. "Look at you! And look at this place! It's wonderful!"

Her voice was all singsong-y and sugar sweet. Yup, this was the Andrea he remembered—as if a smile from her should be received with gratitude that she'd deigned to notice your very existence.

He tried to keep his voice level, thinking of his business and not what he wanted to tell her personally. High school was a long time ago and… *Ah, screw it.* He didn't need to impress her. He turned his back, opening the door to the shop.

"It's Sunday. If you need work done, set up an appointment on my website. I don't do walk-ins and I'm busy."

"Oh! Um…" He thought he detected a bit of hurt in her voice, but that was impossible. You needed a heart to feel pain, and he knew she didn't have one. Seeing her put him right back in the crowded high school hallways, avoiding the other kids' taunting. Andrea coughed, and her voice cracked a little. "I understand you're busy, but I really need to speak with you."

He stood in the doorway, refusing to look back at her. He didn't want to remember those days or the finger-pointing.

The times Andrea stood there in icy silence as he was called *another Rutledge loser* and worse. His shoulders felt tight.

"I'm not bumping anyone ahead of the line, even if their name *is* Wentworth. Go to the website, Andrea. Or better yet…go away."

"Mature as ever, I see." There was a familiar whip-sharp edge to each word. *There she was.* This was the Andrea he knew. "I don't need carpentry work. I need to talk about the agreement we had with Cliff Thompson about the corn maze."

He turned slowly now, his interest piqued against his better judgment.

"Any so-called agreement you had with Cliff left the farm when he did. So…*bye*."

Her heart-shaped face went pale, her brown eyes wide with alarm. Zayne frowned. He didn't mind pissing her off, but he didn't like whatever this was. It looked too much like fear. Then he remembered who he was talking to. Andrea Wentworth had never shown fear in her life, as far as he knew.

Her looks had hardly changed at all. Long, straight red hair falling just past her shoulders. Trim and pretty, with nothing out of place. He'd always thought she'd looked like a porcelain doll, and she still did. Then he remembered dolls didn't have souls.

"I'm *busy*, Andrea."

"Zayne…*please*." Her need sounded genuine. Not his problem.

"Go away."

"Are you still mad about high school?" Anger sharpened her words again. "My *God*, aren't we both supposed to be grown-ups by now?" She moved around the car and stalked toward him, her blood clearly boiling. Color was rising on her cheeks. "The least you could do is listen."

The passenger door opened behind her. A small child hopped out of the back seat. The boy was making a bee-line for the big red barn, yelling about seeing the *doggy*.

"Wait… Hudson! No!"

Oh, triple shit.

He ran after the kid and heard Andrea give a small cry of alarm before she followed.

Duke, the bullmastiff, was snoozing in the shade near the barn doors, unaware of the three humans rushing his way. Duke didn't like surprises. And Zayne had no idea what the giant dog thought of children. He was fine with his nephew, Anthony, but Luke and Whitney's child was a baby. Zayne called out for the boy to stop, but it was too late. Duke looked up, blinked and jumped to his feet faster than any hundred-and-seventy-pound dog should be able to move. The boy slid to a halt when he realized he was basically eye to eye with a dog that outweighed him three times over.

"Duke, *sit*!" Zayne shouted the sharp command.

The dog's butt hit the ground, but his eyes were on the child in front of him. His massive head moved forward, and Duke took one big slobbering lick up the side of his face with enough force to set the boy back on his heels. The kid started laughing.

"Good dog," Zayne gasped as he reached them. It hadn't been a long run, but it had been a fast one—uphill—and his left leg was already telling him it had been a bad idea. He patted the dog's head and couldn't help smiling at the goofy look he got in return. "Thank you for not eating the tiny human."

"Is that supposed to be *funny*?" Andrea grabbed the boy

by the shoulders and pulled him back against her, eyeing Duke through narrowed eyes. "Why isn't that monster on a chain or something?"

Zayne and Duke both turned their heads toward Andrea.

"This *monster* is on his own property and knows how to behave."

"Then why did you run as if you thought Hudson was in danger?"

"Uh…" He realized he'd probably scared her half to death. "Look, your kid should know better than to run up to *any* dog like that. As far as Duke goes, when this dog barks in your face, it's enough to scare an adult, much less a baby."

"I'm not a baby!" the child yelled angrily, yanking his shoulders free from Andrea's grip. "I'm *four*. I'm a young man!"

Zayne's eyebrows rose, and he looked at Andrea. "Let me guess—he's yours."

She grabbed the boy's collar and gently pulled him back toward her. She wasn't wearing a wedding ring. "Yes." She blew out a long breath. "Hudson, I think you should apologize to Mr. Rutledge for scaring his dog."

Zayne began to cough violently. Andrea was trying to teach her son a life lesson, so he didn't want to point out the large brindle-colored dog had already lay back down and was almost asleep again now that there was no actual threat.

"Sorry, Mr. Rudd-idge." Hudson stared wistfully at Duke. "Your dog was just so…special."

Zayne dropped to one knee to look Hudson in the eye. "He *is* special. And he's a very good dog." As if knowing what was being said, Duke opened one eye and looked up at him. "But not *all* dogs are good, especially when someone runs up to them. That's why you should never do that."

Hudson was staring at him with solemn eyes. "In fact, you should always ask for an adult's permission before touching any animal, okay?"

"Okay." A mischievous gleam appeared in Hudson's eyes. "Can I touch your dog again?"

"No," Andrea answered quickly. "Hudson, I told you that you had to behave today. What you just did was *not* behaving. Now, Momma needs to talk to Mr. Rutledge." Andrea turned to Zayne. "I'm sorry about bringing him along, but my babysitter bailed at the last minute. Once he settles in with his tablet and a few games, you won't even know he's around."

Hudson shrugged away from her grip, skipping back down the hill toward the car. Zayne gave Andrea a pointed look.

"I won't know he's around if he *isn't* around. Take him home, Andrea. Please."

"Give me ten minutes. *Ten.* That's all."

"Oh my God, woman. What do you *want*?"

"It's the corn maze." She gestured down the hill, where a jumbled mix of corn and hay was growing. He figured it was another one of Cliff's weird ideas. He just hadn't had time to plow it under yet.

"That's a corn maze?"

"It's supposed to be." She grimaced. "The Blessing of the Grapes Festival is next month. I'm the chairperson."

"And?"

They followed Hudson down the hill toward the shop. Zayne had always done his best to steer clear of the Rendezvous Falls festivals. That wasn't easy, since they seemed to be constant in this town, clogging the roads with traffic and tourists. He knew they kept local businesses going, but it was torture for someone like him, who hated crowds.

Andrea had to hurry to keep up with his longer stride, but he didn't slow for her. He had work to do.

"Look," she said breathlessly, "that's our corn maze. We *paid* for it. It has to be cleaned up and ready."

Her son was running his hands through the tiger lilies growing by the entrance to the shop as if he was playing a colorful harp. Zayne stopped by Andrea's car, hoping she'd take the hint.

"Ready for what?"

"For the *festival*!" Andrea threw her hands in the air as if he'd just asked the stupidest question. "We bus people to the farm from the festival and they go through the maze. Kids love it. Families love it. *Everyone* loves it. And it's the biggest fundraiser we have."

"Fundraiser for *who*?"

"For the committee, of course. We have to pay for insurance, advertising and prizes, then we need seed money for *next* year's festival, and the remaining money goes into a fund to support the local vineyards." Andrea looked up at him. "Did I mention Cliff has hosted the maze for over twenty years?"

None of this was making any sense—probably since he didn't care about any of those things. Except maybe the local vineyards, since his brother Luke ran one of them.

"Cliff doesn't own the farm anymore. And I am *not* letting buses full of tourists come up here. Your ten minutes are up—" Her face fell, but there was no way he was allowing crowds of people on this farm. Then he thought of something she'd said. "What did you mean before when you said you *paid* for it?"

She brightened, probably thinking she still had a chance. She didn't. He was just curious.

"The committee hired maze designers about ten years

ago. That's how we get the digital designs and…" Her voice trailed off. "You have no idea what I'm talking about, do you?" He shook his head and she rushed to tell him. "It's all digitally designed these days. The companies sketch it out, then they come and *plant* the maze using GPS to guide the tractors and deposit the seed as densely as possible. We paid to have that field planted this May."

"Well, they did a piss-poor job of it. That field's a mess."

"It's only a mess because it hasn't been maintained!" Her voice rose and she paused to take a breath. "You're supposed to mow the trails all summer, and the corn is not in rows on purpose, and…" She rolled her eyes, waving her hand. "There's nothing wrong with the maze, damn it. Just mow the trails! In case you've forgotten, we paid good money to have that thing designed and planted."

"And in case *you've* forgotten, that's *your* problem." He headed for the shop. "Find someone else's cornfield to screw up."

CHAPTER THREE

ANDREA COULDN'T BELIEVE Zayne Rutledge had the nerve to turn his back on her as if her future wasn't resting on the success of this festival. He walked into the shop, the door closing slowly behind him. She dashed forward and grabbed the handle just before it latched. She grabbed Hudson's little hand and tugged him along as she marched inside.

The woodworking shop was larger than she expected. There were machines scattered around the floor. The drills and saws were slightly menacing. The walls were lined with racks of lumber. A massive worktable was directly in front of her, and there was a partially assembled fretwork there. It looked like beaded rays of the sun extending from a curved piece of molding. She'd seen similar frets inside the many Victorian houses in town.

"*This* is the woodworking you do?" She walked over and traced her fingers down one delicate spindle. Hudson put his fingers on the edge of the table and stood on tiptoe to see.

"It looks like lace, Momma!"

Zayne was glaring at her. "I didn't invite you in."

"You didn't ban me from entering, either."

"I told you to go away. I think the banning was implied."

"Well…" Andrea looked around the tidy shop. "You know what they say about assuming…"

He didn't answer. Instead, he went to work, laying out spindles and comparing them to a printed pattern nearby.

He was trying to freeze her out, but that wouldn't work. She stayed right where she was, waiting.

He wasn't the awkward, angry boy she remembered. Well, maybe the angry part was still there. But there was nothing at all boyish about him. Tall and broad-shouldered, he had more of a brooding presence than he'd had as an angsty teenager. But then again, their high school days were almost twenty years ago. A weight settled on her shoulders. Twenty years. And what did she have to show for it, other than a son, a small apartment and a pile of college debt? Meanwhile, Zayne was building wooden lace for a living.

He looked up and caught her staring. He propped his hip against the bench and folded his arms on his chest. "If you think you can just annoy me into changing my mind, you can forget it. You may be used to getting your way all the time, but that won't happen with me."

Tani was right—the brooding presence thing was really working for Zayne. An energy radiated from him that made the hair on the back of her neck stand up. It was like being outside as an electrical storm approached, when the air crackled with electricity. His face had the same sharp angles as always, but with a few scars mixed in, and a shadow of dark stubble along his jaw. His bright blue eyes had always been a contrast with his black hair and heavy brows. As a boy, those eyes had often danced with laughter. She didn't see laughter there now. And he had a serious limp. She had seen him rubbing his left thigh earlier, and he moved with a slight limp. That had to be from the car accident she'd heard about. The one that left another man dead.

He'd gone back to working on the fretwork in front of him. She felt a touch of wonder that the ultimate bad boy was now an artist. An artist with a stubborn set to his jaw as he tried again to ignore her. But she was Andrea Wentworth, and she wasn't going down without a fight.

"There has to be *some* way we can come to an agreement on this issue. The committee paid for the maze, and we're going to have to recoup that money from you if…"

"Are you threatening me?" He straightened, looking more amused than offended. "Of all the tactics you could have tried, trust me, that's the worst. Your agreement was with Cliff. If you want to go after an eighty-five-year-old man in a nursing home for your money, have at it, but it won't make you or your precious committee look very good."

Andrea heard several things in those few sentences. He was right about going after Cliff. That was a losing proposition in every way. But more importantly, he'd made it sound like there might be a tactic that *could* work. She was just going to have to figure out what it was.

Hudson was sitting in an office chair in the corner, spinning himself around in circles. The chair was near a small table…or was that supposed to be a desk? Hard to tell, since it was buried in papers. There was a flat screen and—she looked underneath the desk—yup, it was a computer. Dusty and ancient, at least in computer years. At the corner of the desk, there was a chunk of carved wood that looked like a broken piece of gingerbread trim from some house. There was a giant nail or spike sticking straight up and impaled on that nail were pages of paper. She looked closer—orders? Invoices? Some had folded corners. A few had notes written on them in bold, but illegible, handwriting. She reached out to hold the corner of the one on top to read it better.

"Leave that alone! I have a system." Zayne barked so sharply she jumped. She turned, leaving her hand right on that piece of paper in defiance. Her eyebrow rose.

"You call this a *system*?"

He gestured toward the antique spike holding at least twenty papers. "The orders are on there in order, oldest on top, so I can take one look and see how much work I have on tap. If a corner is folded up, that means I've started it. If a corner is folded down, I don't have a deposit yet, which means it moves farther down the pile. It's a system."

This was just the opening Andrea needed. She did *not* need to take on extra work right now, but if she could barter services for the corn maze...

"Does your computer not work?"

"It works." He sounded defensive. "I have a website. People send me orders." Zayne's feet shuffled uncomfortably. "I print them. That's all I need it for."

"But how do you keep track of your income and expenses?"

Without making eye contact, he nodded in the general direction of a rusted file cabinet. She pulled open a drawer, which immediately twisted and groaned under the weight of papers stacked inside. Not in folders. Not organized in any apparent way. Just...stacked. Her mouth fell open, but at least she'd discovered what he needed.

"I can fix this," she declared.

"The drawer?"

"What's *inside* the drawer." She pulled out a pile of wrinkled papers with holes stabbed through the middle of them. "I can organize all of this into an actual accounting system for you."

"So now you think I'm going to *hire* you?" Zayne rested his hands on the workbench, making the muscles in his biceps bunch under his T-shirt. Andrea swallowed hard. He was definitely not a boy anymore.

"I'll do it for free." His eyes widened at that. She had his interest, so she rushed on. "In *exchange* for you cleaning up the corn maze and allowing us to use it." He started to shake his head, but she couldn't give up now. She was too close to victory—she could sense it. "Just for this year! We'll find another farm, but it's too late now." His mouth opened, but she didn't give him a chance to speak. "I know you don't care about the festival, or me, but think of the business owners and vineyards that would be impacted. Isn't your brother a winemaker?"

She knew he was—Luke Rutledge ran the Falls Legend Winery. He'd married the owner's niece, Whitney, and they were now raising their family on the award-winning vineyard. She had no idea how close the brothers were, though.

The whole Rutledge family was a lesson in dysfunction, thanks to their parents. Their father had died in prison and their mother had died from alcoholism years ago. The four children had been dirt-poor and teased for it in school. Her face heated. No one had any idea back then that she and Zayne had been friends. He and she would meet at the old willow tree halfway between their homes and talk for hours. But in their senior year, she'd been one of the kids laughing—or at least standing by and watching. It was clear that he hadn't forgotten.

"Zayne, I know how much I hurt you back in our senior year. Let me make it up to you."

He chuckled, but there wasn't much humor in it. "The past can't be changed. Don't make this about that. You just want your damn maze."

"Okay. I'll make up for my bad behavior some other way. This *is* about the maze." She tossed her hair over her shoulder, sensing victory. "I'll barter the new bookkeeping system for the use of the maze."

He didn't turn her down, but he didn't look excited, either.

"Spreadsheets and fancy software programs are just gibberish to me." His voice hardened. "And I'm not ready to promise anything yet. I'll *consider* the maze."

"I'm not an idiot, Zayne. I'm not going to do all this work without some kind of agreement on the maze."

"I'm not an idiot, either. How do I know you have the

skills to even do all the stuff you've promised? You're desperate enough to tell me anything, and the Andrea Wentworth I knew couldn't be trust—" He glanced at Hudson, who was now following the conversation with interest. Zayne coughed. "Well, you know what I'm saying."

She nodded slowly. "I do. How about this—give me ten days to make a dent in this…this…*system* of yours. If you like what I put together, the corn maze is *on* for the festival." She smiled. "By the way, I have a bachelor's degree in business, and I minored in accounting. I have the skills."

They stared hard at each other for several long, silent minutes. The ball was in his court. She wouldn't get much sleep if he agreed, but she'd save the festival—and her reputation—from disaster.

Zayne finally let out a loud sigh and held up his index finger for emphasis. "I'm only doing this to get you out of my hair. Ten days. And all I'm promising is to *consider* the maze. But you're really going to have to impress me, because I don't want people traipsing all over my land." He pointed to the door. "*Now* will you go away?"

She'd won. She tried to hold back a gloating smile.

"Can I take some of the older files with me to work on at home? And…" She looked at the messy stacks of papers. "I'll have to stop by here a few evenings this week after work, too."

He picked up a chisel in one hand and a wooden mallet in the other, no longer focused on her. "I'm usually around."

Once outside, she couldn't help doing a little skip and hop on her way to the car, swinging Hudson in the air with a victorious laugh. Zayne Rutledge was no longer a problem. He was an opportunity.

A good-looking, grumpy, talented opportunity.

CHAPTER FOUR

"IT'S FRIDAY NIGHT," Zayne said. "Don't you have some-place better to be?"

Andrea looked up from her perch on his office chair. She never really *sat* anywhere. She was always at the edge of the seat, as if ready to leap up and tackle someone.

"I only have a few days left to finish this up. No rest for the weary." She straightened. "Oh, are you saying *you* have someplace to be? I don't mind working here alone."

"Yeah, you're definitely interfering with my busy social life, Andrea." He shook his head and went back to work on the custom gingerbread trim he was designing for a client. Mrs. Shellar's house was really more farmhouse-style than Victorian, but she wanted it to fit in with the historic Victorians the area was famous for. She was adding new trim to the peaks and porch posts, but she wanted them to look like they'd always been there.

The problem was that he was more focused on Andrea's presence most evenings than on woodworking. And using a large band saw was not something you wanted to do without being fully focused—that was a good way to lose a finger.

It was warm in the shop, and a soft sheen of sweat made Andrea's freckled skin shimmer like satin. Her hair was pulled up into a clip, with a few long red strands breaking free and clinging to her neck. She was in shorts today, her legs just as freckled as her arms. Her yellow knit top was clinging to every mature but familiar curve. She'd seemed an untouchable goddess when they were in school—a girl he could laugh and dream with when no one was looking, but never one to be touched.

He'd become accustomed to her work patterns this week. She'd scatter papers across the desk, sorting them into piles by some unknown logic of hers. Every once in a while she'd stop and just stare at them with a scowl. Then she'd come to a decision and pounce, quickly re-sorting the piles to solve her puzzle. Most evenings she'd had Hudson with her, but not tonight. Zayne was surprised to realize he missed the kid's constant questions.

What'cha makin'?

What's that for?

Is that danjah-rus?

Can I try, Mr. Zayne?

They'd settled on *Mr. Zayne* because Hudson just couldn't figure out how to say *Rutledge*. The shop was quiet without him.

"Is Hudson with his dad tonight?"

Andrea looked up in surprise, then shook her head. "Zoey Hartford's daughter, Hazel, is babysitting him for a few hours. You must be loving the quiet without him."

"Is his dad around here?" Zayne knew it was none of his business, but the question just came out.

She sat back in the chair. "Why are you asking?"

He lowered his head, staring at the half-carved chunk of wood in his hand. "I have no idea. Sorry."

After a moment, she gave a sigh. "His father isn't in his life. It was a mutual decision."

He thought about that, then shrugged. "Fathers aren't always the best influence for a kid."

His dad had gone from petty crimes to far more serious ones, including selling drugs and committing armed robbery to get *more* drugs. His last robbery had left a man dead. Dad hadn't pulled the trigger, but he'd ended up facing life in prison.

"That's true," she agreed. "But it's also hard to be two parents in one."

"You're doing okay. He's a cute kid."

Some pink appeared beneath the freckles on her cheeks. "Thanks. I think I'll keep him."

They both chuckled, and she turned back to her work. But he couldn't stop looking at her. He normally hated small talk, but he couldn't resist trying to keep the conversation going.

"So, my brother says this festival is a pretty big deal."

He'd stopped by Falls Legend Winery yesterday and had a chat with Luke. They'd had their tough years as brothers, but now that Luke was married and a father, and Zayne was building a business and life of his own, they'd started rebuilding their brotherly bonds.

"It's a *very* big deal," Andrea answered. "The Blessing of the Grapes is one of the biggest festivals in town, and probably the most important because of the work the foundation does."

Luke had told him about that, too. The festival hosted a prestigious wine competition, plus the fun stuff—at least, fun for people who liked that sort of thing—like parades, vendor booths and the corn maze. The profits went into a foundation that offered grants to winemakers who might be struggling.

Luke had pointed to the rows of grapevines marching up the hill at Falls Legend. "We're successful enough these days to be able to survive a tough weather year, but some of the smaller places are barely hanging on. A storm like we had back in June could wipe them out. The foundation is there for them."

Andrea's voice broke into his thoughts. "Haven't you ever been to the festival? To *any* festival?"

"Not my thing." Zayne didn't like crowds. He didn't like being jostled around. It made him tense, and tension made him do dumb things like…drink. Or take a swing at someone. Or both. So when he'd sobered up eight years ago, he'd learned to avoid trigger situations like noisy festivals.

"So is this corn maze thing *really* that important?" To him, it made more sense to keep the activities in town, like all the other festivals did.

Andrea came over to the saw table where he stood. "The mazes have turned into artwork over the years. It usually gets us featured in the news in Rochester or Syracuse, which brings in more people. We rent school buses to shuttle people, and the bus ride up the hill is half the fun—they have sing-alongs and play games. It's pandemonium…" Her face twisted. "And that is totally *not* a selling point for you, is it?"

Luke had said something similar. He'd also pushed Zayne not to give Andrea false hope. "If you're *not* going to do this thing, you should tell Andrea now instead of leading her on for ten days. I talked to Whitney, who heard from her aunt Helen, who heard from Iris Taggart, who knows *everything*…" Zayne had rolled his eyes at that. This freakin' town. "And the scuttlebutt is that Andrea really needs this festival to be a winner."

Zayne had asked why, and Luke just shrugged. "All Whitney knows is that it has something to do with Andrea trying to get a new job, and also something about her mother. She told Zoey Hartford that—" he made air quotes with his fingers "—'failure is not an option.'"

He looked at Andrea now, standing across from him, her chin high.

"You're acting like this is a quest," he said. "Why is this year's festival *so* important to you?"

Her mouth opened to answer, then snapped shut again. Her forehead wrinkled. "Let's just say I have a lot to prove. I'm the youngest chairperson ever. I don't want to let people down. I don't want to fail."

"You've probably never failed at anything in your life."

She huffed out a laugh. "Boy, do I wish that were true. I'll give you a list of people to talk to about my failures, starting with my mother."

When Zayne thought about Marissa Wentworth, he always thought of sharpness. Not the *smart* kind of sharp, but the dangerous kind. Sharp eyes. Tight face. Sharp words. There was a time when he'd expected Andrea to be just like her. But he'd seen how hard she'd been working this week. He'd seen her swinging Hudson in the air and laughing. Those images were beginning to push the old ones out of his memory.

"I can't imagine you failing at something you put your mind to."

Her eyes brightened. "I've put my mind to getting the maze back, so does that mean…?"

"We made a deal." Despite all the new impressions of Andrea, he had to remember that she'd turned on him before. Just like so many other people in his life. "Finish your part of the bargain and we'll talk."

She didn't look discouraged—she looked defiant. It was a good look on her. She headed back to the desk with a little wave of her fingers. He wanted to trust her. It just wasn't in his nature to forget a slight. He thought of his brother's parting words yesterday.

"You have even more reason to carry a chip on your shoulder than I do," Luke had said, "what with the accident and all. But man, that's a lot of weight to carry around. It's exhausting. I was a better man—a *happier* man—once I gave it up. I highly recommend it."

"MOMMA, CAN I PLAY with Duke?"

"We'll see."

It was Sunday afternoon, and she was *still* working on straightening out the mess that was Zayne's bookkeeping "system." She'd been surprised Friday night when he'd acted as though he was missing Hudson's nonstop questions when he was with her. Zayne looked up now from some weed trimming he was doing. He smiled when he saw Hudson and whistled for the dog.

"Can we play?" Hudson asked. Boy and dog had become fast friends this week.

Zayne nodded. "Just remember that *play* to Duke usually means the same thing as *nap*. But you might get him to fetch a stick a few times first."

The two wandered off together, and Andrea called after them. "Don't leave the yard, Hudson. I want to be able to see you when I come out here."

He didn't look back. "Okay, Momma."

She looked to Zayne and rolled her eyes. "He's four and he's already discovered that *whatever* tone of a teenager. God help me." Zayne followed her into the shop, and she shook her head. "I just need to pick up the last of the files. I promise not to steal anything in here if you want to finish your yardwork."

"I'm not worried about you stealing. I'm just surprised you're still on this. Aren't you done yet?"

Yeah, *she* thought she'd be done by now, too. She'd taken

on a little more than expected. But she gave him a bright smile.

"Almost. Which is good, because my deadline's this week. I'm using an off-the-shelf bookkeeping program, but it will keep track of your scheduling, billing and even your inventory if you want. I'm doing most of the data entry at home—that's the tedious part. All you'll have to do is press a few buttons once I'm done, I promise. It'll even calculate your taxes."

She added that last sentence hurriedly, only because he looked so skeptical. She gathered up the last few folders of orders. These were the most recent and would bring the records up to date.

"I didn't expect you to spend your own money..."

"I consider it my investment in the corn maze. That's why I'm doing this." Her face fell. "You get that, right? This is all about the maze. You promised."

"I promised to *think* about it," he answered.

"I'm going to knock your socks off, my friend." She put as much confidence in her voice as she could muster. "You won't be able to say no."

"We'll see." Her stomach churned at the thought that he was just stringing her along. Or maybe it was churning because she'd only eaten a banana muffin so far today. Or maybe it was because she'd only slept three hours last night, between schoolwork, festival work and Zayne's bookkeeping.

She headed for the door with her armful of folders, fighting her rising anger. "No, *you'll* see. I don't break my promises."

She was outside before she heard his response behind her.

"I seem to recall you doing exactly that."

He followed her to the door. Andrea dropped the folders

on the hood of her car and pointed her finger at him. Would he ever get over that one awful mistake of hers? All these years, she didn't think she cared one way or the other. But now that she'd spent time with him this week, it was important that he forgave her. That he was okay.

"I told you I was sorry about that. I made a mistake when I was seventeen, Zayne. Let it go." Her frustration with herself made her sound annoyed.

"Let it go?" His voice sharpened. "You were always going to be my friend, remember?"

They were glaring at each other when Hudson walked over and took Zayne's fingers in his hand. "Duke fell asleep, Mr. Zayne. Are you talking about when you and Momma were friends? She told me you used to climb a big tree with her. Do you still climb trees? Can you teach me how?"

It only took a beat for Zayne's eyes to soften. He looked down at her son, now leaning against Zayne's leg—his bad leg, if she remembered correctly—staring up at him with nothing but happiness. Her beautiful boy. Seeing Zayne's expression—his gentleness—with Hudson made her chest go warm.

"Your momma told you that, huh?" Zayne looked a little confused. "I wonder… I mean, yes." He glanced her way quickly. "Your momma and I had a favorite tree we used to meet at. It was a willow tree with a big old limb down low—it didn't take much climbing. But once we were up there, no one could see us. We were safe."

Safe. Her breath caught at the word. It must have been a rare feeling for him when they'd first started hanging out in the sixth grade. The old willow was about halfway between her mother's sprawling contemporary home and Zayne's single-wide.

"What did you do in the tree?" Hudson made a face. "Did you kiss my momma in the tree?"

Zayne looked straight at Andrea. "Only once."

It was the summer before senior year. Zayne's dad had just been given what was basically a life sentence. Andrea swallowed hard. And she'd promised him she'd always be his friend. The kiss had been sweet and gentle—sealing a promise she broke two months later.

"I really am sorry, Zayne."

"Sorry for what?" Hudson asked. "Momma, what did you do?"

"I—"

"Nothing, Hudson." Zayne talked over her. "Your momma was a good friend." Until she wasn't. She blinked as he continued. "We both did silly things."

"Can I go find Duke, Mr. Zayne?"

Andrea let out a soft sigh of relief as he took off, no longer interested in them.

"The only thing that saves me from his constant questions is his short attention span." She watched him disappear around the corner of the shop, knowing he wouldn't go any farther than the barn doors, where Duke liked to nap. "Thank you," she said softly. "For not ratting me out to my four-year-old, who doesn't know what a flaming *be-yotcha* I was."

Zayne gave her a half smile, rubbing his left thigh with a grimace. "Truth is, I wasn't exactly a prince back then, either. You were smart to back off."

"It didn't feel smart." She glanced down at his leg. "Is that from your accident?" He gave a quick nod. "I was really sorry to hear about that. You were hurt bad, right?"

He shrugged. "I had a lot of broken bones, but I survived. That's more than Larry Canfield can say."

It had been the talk of the town for a while. They'd been speeding down a country road when their car went airborne, flipping multiple times across a cornfield. Larry died instantly. Zayne had been in the hospital for weeks.

"I should have called or...something." She cringed. "But I didn't, did I? Sorry."

"Let's make a deal," he answered, looking deep into her eyes, freezing her in place. "One that has nothing to do with the maze. Let's agree to stop apologizing. What's done is done."

"Okay." She held out her hand and he took it. Instead of shaking, though, they just stood there. A shiver of sensation shot through her the instant his hand engulfed hers. She wasn't sure what it was, but neither of them seemed to mind. They didn't release each other until Hudson came bouncing around the corner, Duke on his heels.

Two days later, Andrea was in the college office when her head bobbed so hard that it jolted her awake.

"Almost snapped your neck on that one, didn't you?" Tani asked from the conference chair she was curled up in, her feet tucked under her. She was trying hard not to laugh. Tani worked part-time at the college as an administrative assistant, which gave her a discount on classes as she pursued the art degree she'd decided she needed.

Andrea's back straightened. "I don't know what you mean."

Tani just snorted. "O-kay. You need to get some sleep before you crack your head on this table. Why don't you stretch out on the sofa in Pete's office and take a nap?"

"For one thing, it's not Pete's office anymore. And it's not mine, either."

"Not *yet* anyway." Tani leaned forward, her eyes now full of concern. "You can't keep going like this. We're heading into the busiest time of year at the college—students start moving in next week. Why you took on this festival that happens in *September* is beyond me. And now you're revamping Zayne Rutledge's accounting...for free."

"It's *not* for free—it's for the maze, remember?" She crossed her fingers under the table that she could wow Zayne enough to get him to agree. "I can get *lots* of sleep after the festival. And after I get this job." She shuffled the folders in front of her, fanning them out on the table. "And after we make sure these kids have the class schedules and support they need. So...maybe by... Thanksgiving?" Tani wasn't amused. Andrea sighed. "It'll be better after this week. Between admissions and cramming in all this work for Zayne, it's been...a lot. And naturally, my mother has suddenly decided she's too busy to babysit Hudson."

She gave Tani a tired smile. "He won't have to use a rusty old spike to schedule his work anymore. The book-keeping part will be on the computer too, and I'm making it super easy for him." Which didn't mean it had been easy to create. She just hoped it was enough to satisfy him, because she needed to know if the maze was a go or not. If not, she'd have to find a farmer with a cornfield, and she'd have to beg—*really* beg—them to let the festival carve a maze into it somehow. But first, she had one more shot to convince Zayne Rutledge to let her...er...the *festival* succeed.

That evening, as intriguing as she usually found Zayne's company, all she wanted was for him to *leave* so she could finish setting things up and go home to sleep. Hudson was having a sleepover at Mary Trask's home. Hudson and Mary's son Nathan were best pals at preschool. The timing was perfect. She only had to upload the software program and data. Then she could drive home to a quiet house and a comfy bed and sleep for a day.

"You sure you want to stay here on your own?" Zayne was at the door. "If I'd known you were coming this late—"

"I need to get everything ready for tomorrow. And I have a day job, so it's evenings or nothing." She gave her head a little shake, trying to clear it so she could focus and just. get. this. done.

"Are you feeling okay?" Zayne's voice went soft, which totally threw her. She wasn't prepared for soft, caring Zayne.

"I'm fine," she said briskly. "I just want to get this done, so, as you like to say, go away."

"Where's Hudson?"

"He's having an overnight with a friend. I wanted to be able to concentrate on this." She nodded at the computer, hoping Zayne would take the hint and leave.

"Maybe I should cancel this appointment." He glanced at his watch.

"And do what?" Andrea asked. "Stand around and watch me work? Honestly, you'd just be in my way. Besides, didn't you tell me this was a client appointment?"

"Well, yeah, but…"

"*Please* go. It'll take me less than an hour to set this up. I promise I'll turn off the lights and lock the door." She paused. "Where do you want Duke? He's welcome to stay out here with me if it's okay."

The massive dog was stretched out next to the desk, snoring softly. Duke had scared the daylights out of her at first, just because of his un-doglike size. But he'd proved to be a big old softie. She was okay being here alone, but having a dog that weighed more than she did made her feel extra safe.

"He can stay out here if you want." His smile made her feel like he'd read her mind about feeling more secure. "When you leave, just shut him in the screen porch at the back of the house. It's unlocked, and he has a water dish and a bed out there, so he'll be fine until I get home. Just point the way and he'll go. He likes you."

"Do *you* like me enough to go where *I* point?" She pointed at the door. She kept her smile firmly in place and finally gestured with a brushing motion. "Seriously…go."

She got to work as soon as he left, knowing she'd *finally* be able to sleep once she got it done. Her stomach grumbled. She should have eaten before she drove straight here from the college, but she wanted to finish this. She was getting too old to pull all-nighters like she did last night.

She downloaded the software program onto his computer, then plugged in the thumb drive to upload the records she'd been typing at home for the past week. The first spreadsheet began filling with data—numbers, dates, accounts. It was a scrolling, mesmerizing screen of tiny figures.

Whoa. She couldn't afford to fall asleep here in the shop. But maybe if she just put her head down on her arms for a minute to rest her eyes and avoid looking at the data tick, tick, ticking up across the screen…

CHAPTER FIVE

ZAYNE PULLED HIS truck up to the Purple Shamrock and headed inside the local hangout. Bridget O'Hearn ran the family business with her Irish husband, Finn. Her last name had been McKinnon back in high school when she and Zayne became friends. An only child, Bridget had been a bit of an outcast, too, despite all her McKinnon cousins. She'd resented the family pub back then for taking all of her dad's time. She and Zayne had bonded over the chips they carried on their teenage shoulders, hanging out together to make fun of the kids who made fun of *them* for being different. When her dad died a few years ago, she'd come back to save the business with hopes of selling it, but she'd ended up falling in love—with the pub *and* with Finn O'Hearn.

"Hey, Zayne." Bridget slid a glass of ginger ale his way. "You're usually a lunch guy."

He took a sip of soda. "I was hungry, thirsty and lazy, so I figured I'd grab something here on my way home. I had a client appointment tonight up in Geneva. Could be a big job."

"Technically the kitchen closed ten minutes ago, but I'll make you a burger and fries. Seems like you're getting a lot of big jobs lately." She headed toward the kitchen. "I don't know how you keep up with it all."

He didn't. At least not very well. Someone slid onto the bar stool next to his. It was Bridget's grandmother Maura

McKinnon. Maura was one of several women in town who'd done their best to help his family when he was a kid, dropping off food, toys and clothes. At the time, Zayne had resented the charity. He didn't want anyone's hand-me-downs or handouts. But honestly? He'd have barely eaten or been warm without those boxes that showed up on the steps of the trailer.

"I hear you're getting some help with that," she said, eyeing him with curiosity.

"Help from who?" His was a one-man shop.

"Tani told me Andrea Wentworth is setting up some kind of ordering and billing system."

"Oh, that." He shifted in his seat. He hadn't been comfortable leaving her there alone earlier. There'd been a tightness around her eyes he didn't like. A shadow behind her determined smile as she insisted he go. He frowned. He wasn't used to some of the feelings she brought out in him. Like…*caring*. He shrugged a shoulder, not wanting to reveal this unfamiliar sensation. "She offered, and it's not costing me anything, so I figured why not?"

Maura tipped her head to the side, sending her short white hair swinging.

"I thought it was costing you a corn maze."

"I never committed to that." His answer was swift, and a little harder than he'd intended. He cleared his throat. "I mean…the deal was she'd try to organize my process, and I'd *think* about the maze. But you know me and crowds, Maura. One of the reasons I bought the place was the location." The old farm was high on the hill overlooking Seneca Lake and Rendezvous Falls. If more than two cars drove by in a day, it was a lot. "She wants to bring *busloads* of people up there."

"For three days, Zayne. Surely you could grin and bear

it for three days." Maura smiled and patted his hand. "Or at least bear it. Andrea needs this."

"People keep saying that." Zayne nodded his thanks to Bridget when she delivered a mouthwatering plate of food. She leaned against the bar to listen. "I know she wants what she wants, but Jesus…it's just a corn maze for some local fair. And frankly…" He looked at Bridget, who remembered high school just as well as he did. "I'm trying to figure out why I owe Andrea Wentworth *anything*. You know how she treated me in school."

"Zayne Rutledge, how old are you?" Maura asked, a surprising sharpness to her voice. He talked around a bite of his burger.

"Thirty-seven."

"And you're still holding grudges from high school?" She pulled her hand back. "I thought you and your brother wanted people to get over the whole *Rutledge boys* thing, but you seem to be hanging on to it."

"I am not!" He winced. He sounded like a child. "I'm just saying Andrea wasn't the nicest person then." She seemed much nicer now, but she'd broken his heart once. "And besides, it's just a *corn maze*! Why is the town so obsessed with this thing?"

"The festival is important because—"

He interrupted Maura as gently as he could. "I know, I know. It brings in money and the foundation helps vineyards and people love it."

"That's all true, but it's personal this year for Andrea."

Bridget nodded in agreement. "When Marion Hall had to step down from the chairmanship, Marissa Wentworth *fought* the idea of Andrea taking over. You remember how coldhearted the woman always was."

"That's pretty low. I thought Andrea was her most precious possession." That was why he and Andrea had to keep their friendship secret as kids—her mother was so overprotective.

Bridget rolled her eyes. "She always was, and still is, obsessed with *herself*. When Andrea had Hudson without a husband, Marissa took it as a great personal insult to *her*. She's given Andrea a hell of a time."

"That's for sure," Maura agreed. "She stopped paying Andrea's college loan. That's why she needs the festival to go well."

"Why? Does she get paid for it?"

Maura laughed. "Hardly. She's trying to get a management position at the college. Having a successful festival will look good on her résumé."

He took another bite of his burger and thought about that. "Which means she needs the damn corn maze."

"Without it," Bridget said, "her mother and her boss will be able to say they were right about her leadership skills. That's why she's been pulling all-nighters to give you a *free* billing system."

"That's not *my* fault…"

Maura's eyes narrowed. "She has a full-time job. And a *son*. And the festival. She's squeezing in your work on top of all that."

"Okay, ladies." Mike McKinnon walked up behind his cousin Bridget, giving Zayne a sympathetic nod. "Quit ganging up on the guy. I think you've made your point."

The conversation rattled around his head all the way home. She'd been working to get a new job. A raise. To make a better life for the son she clearly adored. And he'd been a jerk about it.

He pulled the truck into the driveway and saw the lights on in the shop. He looked at the dash—it was after ten o'clock. She'd probably forgotten to turn them… Wait. Her car was still parked by the door. She'd said she only needed forty-five minutes, and that was over three hours ago. He parked next to her car and went inside.

Duke sat up when Zayne came in. The dog was right next to the office chair where Andrea was slumped forward—her head on her arms, eyes closed, sound asleep. Zayne knelt at her side, calling her name and stroking her shoulder, brushing her hair back. It felt like satin through his fingers. He was beginning to fear she was unconscious when she finally let out a soft moan and moved, her eyes fluttering open. Her eyelashes were a mile long, framing her caramel-colored eyes.

"Oh…" she sighed, blinking and trying to straighten. "I fell asleep. Sorry. I'll go home…"

"You're not going anywhere like this. You're barely functioning."

Being this close to her, he could see the grayish pallor beneath her freckles. Her gaze was unfocused. She pushed herself upright and went to stand.

"I'm fine. I'll just go home…" Her legs refused to hold her, and he swept her up in his arms to keep her from hitting the floor.

"I've got you, girl. When did you eat last?" He looked around the desk. "Have you had anything to drink?"

She curled up against him. Something very weird happened inside his chest when she did that. She mumbled something, then he heard "…not drunk…"

"I know you're not drunk. But you're probably dehydrated." He nodded for Duke, who looked as worried as Zayne felt, to head to the door. It wasn't easy to lock up the shop with Andrea in his arms, but he managed. Her eyes opened briefly as they passed her car.

"I can drive…"

He just chuckled, shaking his head. "I think not. Go to sleep."

He got her into the house and laid her on the sofa, covering her with the throw blanket his brother's wife had given him for Christmas. Duke plopped down on the floor right in front of the sofa that was often Duke's bed. The dog didn't seem to mind loaning it to Andrea. Zayne sat in the armchair and stared at the woman, now back in a deep sleep. Her pale pink lips were slightly parted, her breathing slow and steady.

Should he tell somebody she was here? She said Hudson was at a sleepover, so there wasn't a sitter waiting. He'd grabbed her leather bag from the desk, and cautiously went through it to find her phone. It was locked, but there was a text message on the home screen from Zoey Hartford.

Z: Thought you were stopping by tonight? Call me.

Zoey and her new boyfriend, Mike McKinnon, had been a few years ahead of Zayne and Andrea in school. Zoey had taken over her late father's appliance repair business, and she'd done an emergency repair on his band saw motor a few months ago. He *knew* her, but it wasn't as if they were close friends. Still…she might be able to give him some guidance. He dug out his own phone and called, walking into the kitchen so he wouldn't wake Andrea.

There was a long beat of silence after he explained the situation to Zoey.

"She's asleep. On your sofa," Zoey said slowly. "And you're thinking of leaving her there. All night. In your house."

"What else am I supposed to do?" he asked, raking his fingers through his hair. "She can't drive like this. And I think it would be creepier to take her home. Besides, I don't know if she should be alone. What if she's actually sick or something?"

Another beat of silence.

"Mike's sister, Mary, told me that Andrea's been burning the candle at both ends lately. Students are moving in at college, so it's wildly busy there, and then she has the festival and Hudson…" She paused. "And rumor has it that some total asshat challenged her to create a complete billing program for him for *free*."

"Hey, that was *her* idea, not mine." He was beginning to realize a lot of people in town were unhappy with him. There was a time when he wouldn't have given a damn, but—as everyone kept pointing out—he wasn't a sullen teenager anymore. He rolled his eyes, sharing the decision he'd reached at the Shamrock earlier without even realizing it. "She's going to get the damn corn maze, okay?"

He had no idea how he was going to make that happen, or how he was going to tolerate it, but there it was.

"Really? Oh, Zayne, that's great news." Zoey chuckled. "That makes me feel better about advising you."

"What do you mean?"

"If I thought you were still taking advantage of her, I'd be a lot less keen on you letting her sleep there."

"I was never…" He realized his voice had risen, so he brought it down to a near whisper. "She offered to barter for the maze and I took her up on it. I mean, come on, Zoey." He felt a need to defend himself. "In high school, she was—"

"In high school, *you* were a grubby-looking troublemaker who spent half his time in detention for fighting and talking back." She wasn't wrong. She also wasn't done. "Didn't you steal one of the teacher's motorcycles and drive it down the hallway to class? And didn't you call the principal a jackass…in the middle of your own graduation ceremony?"

"Sounds about right." He wasn't proud of his behavior as a rage-filled kid. But damn, he'd had his reasons. "What's your point?"

"You know what my point is," Zoey answered. "If people judged *you* based on your younger years, you wouldn't be drowning in orders for your new business. No one would trust you in their home. That farm you just bought would be nothing but a pipe dream." There was a pause, and he heard her muffled voice asking someone—probably Mike—for a refill.

"Look," she started again. "I'm not saying you're wrong about High School Andrea. I got my share of her snooty looks and comments. But that was High School Andrea— she was still under her mother's obnoxious thumb. So maybe you should cut Grown-Up Andrea some slack." Zoey paused. "And for God's sake, let her get some sleep. I'll let Mary know what's going on and ask her to keep Hudson during the day tomorrow—she can take him to preschool with Nathan."

He went back to the living room and tucked the blanket more tightly around Andrea before sitting in the armchair again. It was a little after midnight when she made a face and mumbled something, her eyes sweeping open. She looked around the darkened room, but before she could ask any questions, he handed her a bottle of water.

"Drink this. You're dehydrated."

She did as he asked, taking a sip at first, then downing most of the bottle before letting out a deep sigh. She looked around.

"Am I in your *house*?"

She started to stand up, and he moved to stop her. She wobbled on her feet and sat back down, bringing him to the sofa with her. "Damn," she muttered. "What's wrong with me?"

Somehow she'd ended up in his arms, leaning against his chest as if *he* was the sofa. She didn't seem to have noticed, resting her head against his shoulder. His arm tightened around her, holding her close. She was warm. And soft. She smelled like flowers, with a hint of sawdust from the shop. He knew that because he'd buried his nose in her hair.

"Gotta go… Hudson…" Her voice was low.

"Go to sleep. Hudson is at Mary's. She knows where you are. So does Zoey."

"Hmm…" She burrowed closer, as if seeking more of his warmth. Right now he had plenty of heat to spare. "Gotta upload software…"

"You did that already. Go to sleep." He shifted his weight. If he was going to be stuck here, he could at least stretch out and get some sleep himself.

"S'okay. Just need to finish student files…"

"It'll wait," he whispered against her skin.

He thought she'd finally gone to sleep, but she had one last worry on her mind.

"The corn maze…" she breathed. "Need a plan B…"

"No, you don't. Go to sleep, girl."

He stayed as still as possible until he knew she was actually sleeping. Then he slowly worked himself under her so she was stretched out on top of him. He pulled the blanket up over her shoulders and closed his eyes.

It wasn't as if he hadn't been with women through the years—he did okay for himself. Women loved being with a bad boy, although they rarely wanted to spend time cuddling.

But this woman was different. This woman was clinging to him as if she needed him. Wanted him. *Trusted* him. That was a new sensation.

He liked it.

A lot.

CHAPTER SIX

ANDREA USUALLY WOKE up with a jolt, even without an alarm. She'd always been the sort to just go from sleep to fully awake. Out of bed. Start the day. But right now she was in a delicious half-awake state, and she wanted to stay in this soft, hazy place for as long as possible. She must be dreaming, because she was surrounded by warmth. A blanket over her. A warm body breathing deeply beneath her. Something strong around her waist, making her feel safe. What a nice dream.

But that sound… Was that *panting*? That didn't feel very dreamy. She tried to hang on to the dream, but the sound of heavy breathing wouldn't stop. She finally gave up and opened her eyes. And stared right into the face of a giant brindled grizzly bear, just inches from her face. She flinched backward with a cry, which made the warm body beneath her—wait, there was *actually* a warm body beneath her—move and mutter something. Whatever had been holding her relaxed, which started her sliding toward the giant bear, which was now whining worriedly. She grabbed for purchase to stop sliding, and the muttering under her turned to a yell of pain. But something caught her waist to prevent her fall.

Where was she and whose body was under hers?

She started to panic, pulling away as the dog—okay, it was a dog, not a bear—jumped backward. Wait…was that *Duke*? Which meant…

"Zayne? What the…"

"Whoa, easy, girl. I'm trying to hang on to you."

"Yeah? Well, you'd better let go of me right the hell now."

"Okay…" He loosened his grip, and she began to slide again. She swore, and Zayne sat up in one smooth motion, catching her and bringing her upright with him.

"Jesus. Do you always wake up this salty?"

"What the *hell* is happening right now? Am I in your *house*? Were we just sleeping together?"

She looked around the dark room. The only light came through the door from the kitchen, but she could see the living room was cozy and neat, with a large fireplace and lots of leather furniture. A man's home, for sure, but comfortable.

Zayne scrubbed his hand down his face. "What time is it? Two? Ugh…go back to sleep."

"I will *not*." She stood, doing her best not to stumble over Duke, who was watching with a great deal of interest.

"Be careful…" Zayne's voice sharpened, and he reached out to hold the hem of her blouse. "Oh, you're standing on your own. Good." He smiled up at her. "You weren't doing too well at that when I got home and found you passed out at the desk."

She remembered sitting at his desk, thinking she'd just close her eyes for a minute as the data loaded. That was at seven. That was *hours* ago. She covered her burning cheeks with her hands. Fragments came back. Being carried? She heard herself saying she could drive, and Zayne's responding laughter. He gave her water at some point. She took a deep breath. At least they were both still fully dressed.

"I am *so* sorry. I have to go home…"

"It's two in the morning. Lie back down and get some sleep. I'll move back to the chair." He stood, stretching with a loud groan. "Do you want more water to drink? Something to eat? When was the last time you ate?"

"I don't know. A bagel at lunch?" She grimaced. "I was going to eat when I got home, but…"

"But you'd barely slept in twenty-four hours, you were dehydrated and you basically passed out." He brushed her hair behind her ear. "You need to take better care of yourself."

His hand stopped moving when his fingertips touched her skin. Her heart stopped moving, too. Zayne Rutledge was touching her, and she didn't want him to stop. It didn't make sense, but when had desire ever made sense in her life? And this was definitely desire coursing through her veins. It was exciting. Terrifying. And oh, so tempting…

She reached out and flattened her hand on his chest. *He* was why she'd felt so warm and safe and happy when she woke up. *His* arm had been holding her tight and secure, *his* breath moving in perfect rhythm with hers…just like it was now. She looked up and met his hooded gaze. His fingertips began moving against her skin, and she lifted her face toward his.

"Andrea…" Was he warning her away? Or begging her to come closer? His hand moved to cup her cheek.

"You carried me up to the house," she said. It wasn't a question. "You took care of me. You held me." She curled her fingers to grab his shirt directly over his heart. "That's a lot of caring for a guy who says he doesn't."

Zayne's eyes went dark, the desire in them making her tremble. She hadn't been celibate since Hudson was born, but it had been a while. Long enough to make her feel every sensation with more intensity. His fingertips were setting off sparks against her skin. And those sparks were floating through her body and settling like embers deep and low in her belly.

"When I care," he answered, "I care one hundred percent." One hand still cupped her cheek, and his other moved to the back of her head, pulling her closer. Their mouths were nearly touching now.

Zayne's eyes fell closed, shutting off a little bit of the heat. His forehead touched hers, and his head rolled back and forth.

"You need to eat something, Andrea."

That was *not* what she wanted to hear. It didn't sound as though he liked that option any more than she did, but he wasn't wrong. As if to put an exclamation point on the idea, her stomach grumbled loudly. His eyes opened, ocean blue again. She smiled.

"Food wouldn't be my first choice, but I won't say no to a sandwich."

Zayne straightened, stepping free of her. She had to force herself not to pull him right back. He turned toward the kitchen.

"I think I can do better than a sandwich."

"I don't doubt it." She hadn't really intended to say that out loud, but there it was, out in the room. He definitely heard it because his body froze for a second before he moved on into the kitchen.

She found the bathroom and freshened up. She ran her fingers through her tangled hair the best she could, tucking it behind her ears. She splashed some water on her face. Her stomach rumbled again, propelling her out to the kitchen.

Zayne was sliding a perfectly folded omelet onto a plate as she walked in. The long, narrow kitchen was clean and neat. The walls were a dark gold. The cupboards were vintage, painted bright white. The floor was vintage, too—

white hexagon tiles interspersed with occasional black hexagons. The round table was of gleaming cherry wood, and that was where he set her dish as he gestured toward one of the wooden chairs.

"Sit. Eat. Juice? Or do you want coffee?"

"Juice is good. Coffee at this hour would end all hope of getting more sleep." Of course, sleep wasn't what she wanted anyway. He made his own omelet as she started eating, then joined her at the table. She looked up, talking around a mouthful. "Thish is so good!"

"Thanks. I'm good at small meals—just don't ask me to feed a crowd."

They ate in relative silence. Duke had joined them, clearly concerned that they might drop a tasty morsel. Zayne tossed a piece of sausage in the air and Duke snapped it up.

"Where did you get this beast?" she asked with a laugh.

"One of my first clients raised mastiffs." He scratched Duke's head, which was now resting on Zayne's thigh. "This guy was just a pup, all legs and head and goofiness. He just…" He looked at her. "He made me smile."

"And not many things do?"

"Are you psychoanalyzing me?" He stood, taking their dishes to the sink. He returned to the table, reaching for her hands and pulling her to her feet. There was a surprisingly playful gleam in his eyes. She gave him a one-shouldered shrug.

"I'm just observant."

"Yeah? And what are you observing right now?" His arms slid around her waist, and those internal embers roared back to life.

"I'm observing a man who really wants to kiss me."

The corner of his mouth lifted and he pulled her close, speaking quietly against her cheek.

"A man who knows he probably *shouldn't* do that. So what do you think should happen next?"

This was the moment—kiss or…don't. She pressed against him and his nostrils flared. He wanted this as much as she did. And she wanted it very much.

"Well…" She looked straight into his eyes. "I think we should stop talking and kiss."

She rose up on her toes to make first contact. She told herself she was doing it out of curiosity. The instant their lips touched, nothing in the world existed but her and Zayne. No festival. No farm. No kitchen. Just the two of them, mouths moving against each other. Tongues moving against each other. Breaths mingling. Zayne let out a deep growl, his hand moving under her blouse to flatten against her lower back.

Her arms wound around his neck, and she pulled herself higher on his body. Their mouths never parted as he slid his hands under her bottom and lifted her like a feather. Her legs wrapped around his hips. She couldn't get close enough. Their teeth clicked and Zayne snorted a short laugh.

Don't stop. Don't stop. Don't stop.

He was walking somewhere with her wrapped around him like a blanket. She didn't care as long as he kept kissing her. He stumbled, jostling her. His mouth only moved away enough to be able to growl at the dog.

"Get the hell out of the way, Duke!"

He went back to kissing, taking a few more steps before halting again. Holy sweet God, they were in his bedroom. Or at least in the doorway to it. Her back was against the doorframe, legs still around him, and he was staring hard into her eyes. His chest rose and fell in deep breaths, which was the only sound in the small space.

"I presumed a lot by coming this far," he said. His face and voice were solemn. "I want to go all the way..." The corner of his mouth curled upward. "No pun intended. But I'm not taking another step until I know this is what you want. I mean...we can stop anytime, but do you want to see what happens with fewer clothes between us and a comfortable bed beneath us?"

"Uh...*yeah*, I do." She grinned. She wanted to be skin to skin with him more than anything. "But—this is not us starting a relationship or anything. This is..." She dropped her forehead against his, staring into his cobalt eyes. "It's a one-night thing. But saying that reminds me that it was a one-night thing that gave me Hudson, so *please* tell me you have condoms handy that aren't ten years old."

Zayne huffed out a low laugh, his eyes softening. "I'm not *that* much of a hermit. We're good."

She lifted her head, nodding toward the large bed in the center of the room.

"Then why are we still in the doorway?"

CHAPTER SEVEN

ZAYNE DIDN'T NEED to be told twice. He pulled her close and walked to the bed, kicking the door closed behind them. He lowered her before he gave her a little drop. She let out a squeal when she bounced onto the mattress. Her red hair fanned out onto the sheet like flames.

Everything about her made him think of fire—her fingers set off sparks like match strikes, her eyes smoldered and burned, her kiss… Hell, kissing Andrea was like kissing nitroglycerin—it made him wonder if he was about to explode. It set every nerve on high alert.

He yanked his T-shirt over his head and knelt on the edge of the bed, crawling over her before lowering himself down for a kiss. She welcomed him with open arms, sliding her hands down his ribs and around his back. Skin on skin. He wanted the same, so he took the hem of her blouse and tugged it up. Andrea shifted her weight to help him drag it up and over her head.

Her bra was pale pink satin, with a tiny bow in the center, right between those perfect breasts. He bent down and kissed the skin right above the bow. Her back arched and he licked his way along the edge of the bra up her left breast. Then he reached under her and unfastened it. If he thought her breasts were perfect *in* the bra, they were even better now that they were free of it. Ample and soft, with rigid peaks he needed to kiss. He went back and forth between the two, kissing and nibbling and pulling until she was writhing beneath him.

Her hands fumbled for his belt, yanking it free and unbuttoning his pants. He slid off her and pulled them off, while she wriggled out of her shorts and panties. He dropped onto her and plunged his tongue into her mouth, holding her face with his hands.

She seemed as frantic as he was. She gave an urgent moan and her hands traveled up and down his body. Then they wandered lower and gripped him. He mumbled a curse into her mouth. He was already rock hard, and her touch threatened to undo him before he ever got inside her.

He pulled away from the kiss just long enough to grab a condom from the nightstand, rolling it on and immediately getting himself between her spread legs. He felt like they were both racing right now, and as much as he didn't want to stop, he didn't want this to get out of control. She let out another needy whimper and his body jerked against her in response. Her eyes were closed, her lips parted.

"Look at me, Andrea." His throat was so full of emotion that he could barely form the words. Her eyes swept open. He'd stopped moving, but it still took a moment for her gaze to focus.

"What are you waiting for?" Her words came in a gasp, telling him all he needed to know. She wanted this. Wanted *him*. He intended to make this slow and sexy, but her expression as she watched him... Well, she undid his control. Undid any connection to a world where *slow* had any meaning.

He drove himself into her and she cried out. He kept moving, knowing he wasn't going to last long inside her tight warmth. They moved together like pistons in an engine, rocking the bed so hard the headboard slapped against the wall. She whispered a word. *"Ready..."* And that was that.

They came together, both crying out as he kept driving. Her fingernails dug into his back and the pain propelled him further over the edge until the world went pure white behind his closed eyes. He collapsed on her, knowing he was probably crushing her, but unable to make himself move. His muscles were jelly. Very weak, happy jelly.

"Oh my God..." she breathed. "That was..."

"Intense. Very, very, very intense." He groaned, trying to move, but...jelly. "Push me."

"What?"

"Push me off you. I can't move. I know I'm crushing..."

"Hey, if this is how I go out of this world, I'm okay with it." Her laughter was soft and whiskey rich.

He relaxed, tracing a line of kisses along her jaw.

"You are so beautiful. So sexy." He nibbled her earlobe and smiled when she trembled beneath him. "It was over too fast. I'm sorry. I..."

"Don't you dare apologize for giving me the best sex I've ever had in my life." She patted his shoulder, then gave a weak push. "But you *are* crushing me, and I've decided I want to live."

Best sex I've ever had... He smiled against her, and she shoved his shoulder again.

"Seriously, Zayne. Move."

He immediately slid onto his side, gripping her tightly in his arms. She didn't seem to mind his bear hug, turning onto her side and putting her back against him.

"Much better," she said. There was a pause before she spoke again. "Wow."

"Yup." He kissed the back of her neck. He'd never been

this much of a kisser, but he couldn't seem to keep his mouth off her silky smooth skin. "That was a *wow* alright."

They lay like that, back to front, every available inch touching each other, for a few long, peaceful moments. But something she'd said before was bugging him.

"What did you mean before, when you talked about another impulsive night that got you pregnant?"

She twisted her head to look back at him. "Do I really need to explain the bees and the birds to you? Do you not know where babies come from?"

He rolled his eyes. "I understand that, but..." There was no good way to have this conversation, no matter how curious he was. "Never mind. None of my business."

She studied his face, then turned away, resting her head on his arm. "I love my son more than anything, but he came from an ill-advised one-night stand. Alcohol was involved. And an ancient box of condoms I had in my nightstand."

"Did he take advantage of you?" The thought made his jaw tighten.

"No. I wasn't *that* drunk. I'd just been dumped by the guy I'd been dating for years and assumed I was going to marry. I was depressed and desperate, sitting alone in a bar. A friendly guy smiled at me, and that was pretty much all it took. Not my finest moment, but because of Hudson, I can't regret it."

Zayne thought back to the years when he'd had lots of one-night stands. Some he could barely remember. He supposed it was possible there was a kid out there somewhere with a Rutledge family connection. "Does the father know about Hudson?"

"Of *course* he knows." Her voice sharpened. "He just doesn't care. Turns out he already had a wife and kids he forgot to mention. He offered me money to *take care of things*. When I told him I was having the baby, he thought it was some kind of shakedown and suggested he wasn't the father. I told him he was welcome to sign away his parental rights, and he did it without a second thought." She paused. "This is so *not* the after-sex conversation I was expecting."

"Sorry. I'm not very good at the after-sex stuff." He tended to just…go. They were rarely in *his* home. Or in his arms.

"Well, you are very good at the *during*-sex stuff." She patted his forearm lying across her stomach.

"Thank you, ma'am. You're not so bad yourself." He buried his face in her hair again, inhaling the scent of her. A scent that would be forever tied to this night in his memories. Her fingers traced slowly back and forth on his arm. He closed his eyes, knowing these memories would visit him every night for a very long time.

When he opened his eyes again, Andrea was gone. He sat up, trying not to panic. Had she *left*? Before he had a chance to make love to her again? To explore every inch of her…to make her cry his name? He glanced at his phone on the nightstand and blinked. Holy hell, it was six thirty. He swung his legs out of the bed, and he heard something. Was that…*singing*?

He stepped into his shorts and followed the sound to the bathroom. Duke was lying on the floor right outside the door, which was cracked open a few inches. He could see Andrea's reflection as she brushed her hair. She was singing something to herself—slightly off-key, but with great enthusiasm. She was wearing the T-shirt *he'd* been wearing earlier, and it hung down to her thighs.

Duke let out a loud groan, sounding irritated that Zayne was disturbing his watch. The dog had definitely embraced having a woman around the place. Zayne realized he could get used to the idea, too. At least with *this* woman.

She glanced at the doorway at the sound and dropped her hairbrush when she saw Zayne.

"Oh! How long have you been standing there, you creeper?"

He pushed the door open. It was warm in there, and her hair was still damp. She'd taken a shower. He stared at the tub, knowing he'd never take a shower without imagining her standing in there, naked and wet.

"How can I be a creeper in my own house?"

"Easy—spy on your female guests while they're in the bathroom." She turned back to the mirror with a smile.

"You showered." He glanced at his watch. "It's early."

She ran the brush through her gleaming hair again. "Not for me. I fell asleep twelve hours ago, remember?" She turned to face him. "I thought I'd make us a second breakfast. Interested?"

"Second breakfast? Like the hobbits did in *The Lord of the Rings*? Yes, please."

Her eyes widened. "You know those books? I can't wait to read them to Hudson when he's a little older."

"I started reading a lot once I stopped drinking. I had to do something while I was sitting around by myself." He stepped back to let her walk by. Duke leaped to his feet, following Andrea down the hall toward the kitchen. If she was going to walk around all morning in just his shirt, Zayne was going to want more than food.

ANDREA STRETCHED HER arms over her head in the Adirondack chair, letting out a long, contented sigh. The view from Zayne's porch was impressive. The valley. The lake. The old red barn. The fine view of his ass as he bent over and pulled at some weeds at the base of the steps. He had shorts on, but still—it was a damn fine view. She gave herself a mental shake. She couldn't be ogling the man when he was teaching her son how to know weeds from flowers.

"Some people say weeds are just flowers that someone hasn't loved yet," Zayne was saying. "But they can also be kinda pushy, so we have to make sure they don't choke out the real flowers."

Hudson looked up from where he was kneeling, his little eyebrows crunched together. "But why are *those* flowers more real than the unloved flowers, Mr. Zayne?"

His mouth opened, but he didn't have an answer. Andrea finally came to his rescue.

"They're not more real, honey. But weeds grow anywhere and everywhere. The flowers that Mr. Zayne is trying to save were planted there on purpose."

Hudson's face brightened. "They're special!" It was one of his favorite words.

"Yes, sweetie. They're special." Zayne looked at her over Hudson's head and mouthed *thank you*. She winked in return, taking a sip of her iced tea.

It had been two weeks since she'd spent her first night with Zayne. For all of her protests that the night was a one-time thing and *not* a relationship, things were definitely feeling like a relationship now. She'd only had two other all-night sleepovers, including last night, when Hudson had spent the night with her mother. Andrea had picked him up that morning and brought him to his new favorite place—Mr. Zayne's farm.

Even without many sleepovers, she and Zayne captured every stolen kiss they could whenever they were together, nearly feverish with their need to touch each other. They both agreed that it couldn't possibly last. That the level of intense desire had to be some sort of fluke. They'd have fun with it, but it was just sex. Sex was fun.

Except…she was pretty sure it wasn't just sex. She watched as Zayne shook a soil-filled root in her son's direction, sprinkling him with dirt. Hudson laughed and tried to do the same, but he got more dirt on himself than Zayne, which only made him laugh harder. He'd need a bath before dinner. Zayne was going to grill burgers and veggies for them.

They'd been having a lot of dinners together, the three of them. Almost like a family. She frowned. It was probably a mistake to let Hudson become so attached to Zayne. So used to having him around. But the little boy seemed to be as good for the big man as the man was for the boy.

The dirt fight had subsided when Zayne realized how messy it could get. Instead, he'd put Hudson on his back so Zayne could run around the yard with the screeching boy clinging to him. Duke followed with a wagging tail, wanting to join the fun, but having no idea what was happening.

Same, dog. Same.

After dinner, Hudson curled up on the porch swing and fell asleep. Zayne sat in the same chair she'd occupied earlier and patted his knee. She didn't hesitate to crawl onto his lap and curl into his arms. Her favorite place to be.

He nuzzled her hair, his breath on her ear, voice low.

"Happy?"

"Very. It's been a great day." She looked over at Hudson and grinned. "I'll need help carrying him to the car, because I'm pretty sure he's out for the night."

"This house has three bedrooms upstairs. Why don't I just carry him up there later?" She hesitated.

"I think it's too soon for a family sleepover. I need to be

careful with him, Zayne. He's bought into this relationship wholeheartedly, and I don't want him confused or hurt."

Zayne pressed his mouth to the top of her head, leaving a kiss before answering. "I don't want that, either. For him *or* you. So we're calling this a relationship now?"

"Well, it's not a one-night stand anymore, so it's a relationship of *some* kind." She twisted so she could look up at him. "Where do *you* see this going?"

He stared out over the porch rail. The sun was setting behind them, sending a looming shadow down the hill toward town.

"I don't have any experience at building a relationship that lasts more than a few nights." He looked down at her. "I like having you and Hudson here. It makes me feel good. Makes me feel like I want it to keep going. Can't we do that—just…keep it going?"

She looked over to Hudson again. "If it was you and me, sure. Taking things a day at a time would work. But it's *not* just the two of us. He already adores you."

"And that's a problem?" There was a defensive edge to his voice.

"Only if he thinks we're becoming an insta-family. You and I agreed to have fun while it lasts, but he'll be hurt if…" She hated to think about it. "If things change. Right now we're here in our little bubble, but that can't last. People are going to know, and some will have opinions."

Her mother would *definitely* have a few to share. But there was nothing left for her to take from Andrea, other than a mother's love, which had never really been part of their relationship anyway. She realized Zayne had gone very quiet.

"Hey, are you okay?"

"I've never been a fan of other people's opinions."

She cupped his cheek with her hand. "I know. You've heard more than your share of them through the years. But we don't have to listen..."

"Then why bring it up?" A tiny muscle pulsed in his cheek.

"I honestly was thinking of myself. My mother. Other people who think they have the right to judge my choices with Hudson or anything else." She gave a little shrug. "You're not the only one who gets judged in this town."

"You think people won't want you with a Rutledge." He stated it as a fact, not a question, and she bristled.

"Oh, please. You're not *a Rutledge*. You're the man I care about. The man my son cares about. The man who makes me very happy." He was the man she was falling for... like, head-over-heels falling for. "I'm sorry I mentioned opinions. I'm trying very hard to not be my mother, but I stumble once in a while."

"She doesn't know about us?"

"*No one* knows about us yet."

He frowned. "Are you ashamed—"

"Whoa, stop right there." She sat up, still in his lap but facing him. "Don't you even *think* that for a second. I was just trying to respect your desire for privacy." She glanced down at the maze below them and smiled. "At least until I start bringing buses of people up here in a few weeks."

They both relaxed, easing away from the tricky topic of how people might react to them as a couple. The social-ite's daughter and the convict's son. She could hear her mother now.

Zayne made a face. "Owen Cooper is coming over this week with some equipment he thinks can tackle the mow-ing. Once we get the grass chopped down, the maze should reappear. It might be a little more ragged than usual, but people will still get lost in there."

She'd feel a lot more confident once that mowing was done. Right now, no one would get *anywhere* in that field. "I want to talk to Owen about getting some pots of flowers to scatter around the farm that weekend. You know, to spruce it up a little."

"You think my place needs sprucing up?"

"Just a little." She held up her hand, pinching two fingers together. "It needs a woman's touch, that's all."

He held her closer and chuckled, his voice rough and sexy. "I need a woman's touch, too. *Your* touch, to be specific."

She was more than happy to oblige, wrapping her arms around him. This was definitely a relationship, and it was one she didn't want to lose.

CHAPTER EIGHT

"Momma! I'm in your tree!"

Hudson was laughing, but he also had a tight grip on Zayne's hands, holding him steady. They'd driven over to Darby Road to show her son the tree where she and Zayne had spent so much time as kids. The old willow tree along the side of the road had lost some limbs over the years, but it was still standing.

"It's like being in a secret room, Momma!"

"That's what your mother used to say." Zayne smiled over at her. "She called it our secret place. We weren't quite as little as you are, but still—once we were up inside, it was hard to spot us."

"We had a lot of long conversations up there, didn't we?" She rested her hand on his waist and he nodded quietly.

She remembered meeting him at the tree and talking for hours. Or just sitting in silence. It was before mobile phones and texting, so sometimes one of them would show up and just be there by themselves, hiding inside the draping willow branches. It wasn't just a secret place—like he'd said before, it was also a safe place.

When Zayne's father got in trouble with the law over and over. When her father died. When his mom was "sick," which was what they'd called it when she was too drunk to take care of her children. Zayne and his big brother, Luke, had done their best to make sure there was food every day—even if they had to steal it.

"Who'd have ever thought back then that we'd be standing here now?" she asked, grinning at Zayne. "Look at how far we've come…especially you. I'm proud of you."

His rough cheeks went ruddier than usual at the compliment. "You haven't done bad, either. Raising a son, running a fancy-dancy festival like a diva."

She laughed. "A *diva*? I beg your pardon? I'm running that fancy-dancy festival like a *businesswoman*." The festival was less than two weeks away and was consuming pretty much every moment of her life these days. That was why Zayne had insisted she take a few hours off to spend with him and Hudson. He said the spectacular September day was too good to waste staring at her computer screen.

"Have you heard anything on the job front?" he asked, swinging Hudson back to earth and letting him go to explore the crumbling stone fence.

She shook her head. "I don't expect to hear until October, which is perfect because it will be after the festival. Hopefully they'll be so impressed with my leadership skills that they'll have to give it to me and my sterling reputation."

They walked along the quiet road back toward his truck, keeping an eye on Hudson's adventures near the stone fence.

"Does your reputation really matter, as long as you have the skills?"

She shrugged. "Probably not, but you know how this town is. You don't want to be on the losing side of any gossip." She took his hand. "I think I have enough people in my corner, though."

ZAYNE DIDN'T RESPOND. He was definitely in her corner, but sometimes he couldn't help worrying that it may not be a good thing for Andrea. Over the past few weeks, it seemed the more he fell for her—and he was falling hard—the more he fretted about that.

This was all so new for him. A committed relationship with a woman. With a single mom. Trying to be a good public citizen, despite the anxiety it brought. He was a businessman now—another brand-new experience. Thank goodness Andrea had created that bookkeeping and sched- uling system for him, because his workload seemed to dou- ble every month.

The business was making money. *Good* money. He had a beautiful woman who said she wanted to be with him. Life was good, but he couldn't shake the feeling there was a shadow out there, waiting just for him. That was pretty much the story of his life, and there was no reason to think that had changed, despite his recent successes in business *and* in life.

She'd asked him a few times if something was bothering him, but he didn't want to add to the stress of the upcom- ing festival by telling her he was getting more and more anxious about their future. He *wanted* her. Hell, he *loved* her, although he hadn't said the words out loud yet. Every time he thought about telling her, he remembered how dif- ferent they'd always been. She was Little Miss High Soci- ety, running events and working at the college. While he was…well, he was one of *the Rutledge boys*. Anyone local knew exactly what that meant.

That night, after Hudson fell asleep on the sofa, the two of them went out to the porch. They talked about the work Owen was doing in the maze, trying to save it. He'd got- ten lost the day before and had to scramble up on top of the tractor seat to see how to get out. They chuckled over that story, then talked about Hudson for a few minutes before an easy silence fell. Andrea put her head back and closed her eyes with a contented sigh. It was the best view on the farm.

Owen's fiancée, Lucy, had come over for dinner last night, and the four of them had sat around the old firepit Zayne had cleaned out and put back to use. His brother, Luke, had brought his wife, Whitney, and their baby, Anthony, over for dinner on the weekend. It felt like he and Andrea, and Hudson, of course, were turning into a family.

She'd mentioned being nervous about an *insta-family*, but Zayne was enjoying it far more than he ever expected. Despite that little shadow of fear he was trying to quell, he wanted more. And he was going to tell her tomorrow. Her mother was going to watch Hudson all night. He and Andrea were going to hike to the top of the hill behind the house, where Cliff Thompson had supposedly built a platform of some sort overlooking the valley from the highest point on the farm. And once they were up there, complete with a surprise dinner he had planned, he was going to tell Andrea that he was falling in love with her. That he wanted more with her—more time spent together, more lovemaking, more Hudson, more laughter and more nights like this, where they sat on the porch together without saying a word.

Zayne walked into The Spot diner the next afternoon and waved to Evie behind the counter. "Can I get a couple stuffed burgers to go? With shoestring fries and two vanilla shakes?"

Evie gave him a conspiratorial grin, letting him know that *she* knew who he'd be sharing his dinner with. "Sure thing, Zayne. I'll even toss in a couple of Andi's favorite chocolate chip cookies for you."

He found himself grinning back. He'd been doing more of that these days. He took a seat at the counter to wait, accepting a glass of ginger ale from Evie.

"Mr. Zayne!" Hudson's high-pitched greeting had everyone turning to see the little redhead run up to Zayne, reaching his arms high. "What are you doing here? Where's Duke? Did you build more ginjah-bed today?"

Zayne's smile was even more quick this time. He lifted the boy up onto his lap, looking around for Andrea. "Hi, kiddo! I'm picking up some food. Duke is sleeping at home. And yes, I carved some gingerbread pieces this morning for a house here in town."

"Put him *down* this instant! How dare you touch this child!"

The harsh words came from an older woman who'd just come through the door. Her hair was blond, but it was the brazen sort of blond that came from a box. She was slender, well-dressed and heavily made-up, particularly for The Spot. She grabbed at Hudson, who was still sitting on Zayne's thigh.

"Let *go* of my grandson before I call the authorities!"

"But, Mimi, Mr. Zayne's my friend!"

Marissa Wentworth pulled Hudson away from Zayne and set him on his feet, her hands gripping his little shoulders like claws. Zayne went cold all over, quelling his anger the best he could, but only because of Hudson's eyes on him. Andrea's mother's eyes were golden brown, but just as cold and lifeless as a chunk of metal. She was still glaring at him.

"This man is not your friend, and you need to stay away from him—"

Evie slapped her hand on the counter a couple of times to get everyone's attention, her eyes narrowed on Wentworth.

"That's *enough*, Marissa. Take a breath, take a step back and lower the volume." Evie pointed. "Or take that door right back out of here."

"No, Mimi!" Hudson looked up at her, confused. "Mr. Zayne's my friend! Momma and I go to his farm all the time, and he has a giant dog named Duke and he builds stuff with wood. He's making a corn maze for Momma and I know she likes him because she holds his hand a lot and I saw them kiss…" Hudson's voice trailed off when he saw Zayne give a quick shake of his head.

Marissa's eyes went wide. "Andrea's with…*you*?" Her voice dripped with disgust. It had been a while since anyone used that tone to his face, and it brought back plenty of memories. None of them were pleasant. He thought of what his brother said a while back—that being mad at the world was exhausting. But this feeling? Being treated like shit? That was exhausting, too. He shook his head slowly, trying to balance his response. He was in a public place. And Hudson was right there.

"Good to see you, too, Mrs. Wentworth," he said evenly.

Evie snorted from her side of the counter before walking away, asking Hudson if he wanted a chocolate milkshake. He pulled free from his grandmother and happily followed Evie to a counter stool far enough away to give them privacy. Zayne turned back to Marissa. "And yes, Hudson and I are friends. His mother and I are also…friends." Anything else they were was none of her business.

Marissa deflated as if someone had popped her with a pin. "Oh my God. Andrea's choice of men just keeps getting worse and worse. First she humiliates me by having a child out of wedlock by some married deadbeat stranger, and now she's…" Her face twisted. "She's with…*a Rutledge*. I thought I got you out of her life back in her senior year." She rolled her eyes. "She has to be doing this to me on purpose, but to stoop this low…"

Sure, her words stung his pride, but more than that, they made him angry on Andrea's behalf.

"Andrea's a grown woman, making her own decisions and living her own life. Instead of bad-mouthing your only daughter, you should be proud of what she's done for herself."

"He's right, you know." Vickie Pendergast stopped next to Marissa on her way out the door with Gordy Lexiter. "Andrea's putting together a stellar festival, and because of it, I hear she's under serious consideration for the director job at the college." Vickie's eyes met Zayne's. "And if she and Zayne are falling for each other, you should be happy for her." Vickie winked, then left, taking Gordy's arm.

Zayne appreciated the support, but it rankled that anyone thought it was necessary to defend him. He couldn't move past Andrea's mother referring to him as *a Rutledge* as if she was saying *a disgusting troll*. He frowned, thinking of something else she'd said.

"What did you mean when you said *you* got me out of Andrea's life?"

She waved a hand dismissively, talking as matter-of-factly as if she was discussing grocery shopping. "I told Andrea I wouldn't pay for her college if she remained friends with you, and that was all it took."

He went silent and still. They'd declared their love for each other at sixteen, and she'd turned on him a year later because of a bribe. His face felt tight as he wrestled with the anger and hurt boiling inside him. Anger with Marissa, yes—but also with Andrea. At the worst point of his life, with his dad going to prison and what felt like the whole school mocking him, she'd walked away and let him face it all alone.

Marissa sighed dramatically. "I wonder what I'll have to bribe her with this time."

"What?" He blinked a few times, trying to remember his more recent encounters with Andrea. Laughing. Loving. Sweet. Hot.

"I *said* I wonder what I'll have to bribe her with this time. I can't let her ruin her life—and Hudson's life—by getting involved with you Rutledges." Her voice dropped even lower, so only he could hear. "She keeps talking about rebuilding her reputation in this town, but how can she do that with you? What will people think? Any chance she had for a promotion at the college will disappear. You will erase anything good she does. You will ruin her."

Evie came out with Zayne's order, but he shook his head at her, dropping a twenty on the counter. "Give it to someone else. I gotta go."

"Zayne, don't…" Evie's face fell, then she glared at Marissa. "Not because of her."

He'd never thought much about Marissa's opinions, but in this case she was probably right. He'd ruin Andrea. He'd spent a lifetime ruining things, so why would he think their relationship would be the exception? Enough people thought like Marissa Wentworth that Andrea would always have a cloud around her if they were together. What kind of judgment would she be showing if she stayed with a guy like him?

Not to mention that Marissa could just bribe her to turn her back on him the way she did years ago. Andrea had walked before. It would break him if she walked again. No, it had to be him deciding this time. He left the diner, ignoring Hudson's little voice calling out to him. He'd been a fool to think he could create some fairy-tale family on that farm.

He'd been a fool to think loving Andrea would be anything but a disaster for them both.

CHAPTER NINE

ANDREA LOOKED AT the text for about the twentieth time in the past hour.

Z: Can't do the hike tonight. Don't stop by. Busy with stuff.

"Sweetie, do you think the words are going to change if you keep checking your screen?" Tani raised an eyebrow at her. They were sitting at the bar at the Purple Shamrock. Andrea had texted Tani to meet her for a drink and for help interpreting this new development.

"I just don't understand. He's the one who was so excited to go check out the old deck Cliff Thompson supposedly built." She scowled at her phone. "He was going to bring dinner. I sent Hudson to stay with Mom for the night. I don't care if we don't walk up the hill, but him saying *don't stop by* bugs me. And he's not responding to my calls or texts."

"Maybe he had a family emergency, or he doesn't feel well and he's sleeping, or, you know, he's actually *busy*." Tani nudged Andrea's shoulder. "Girl, you've got it bad for this guy, don't you?"

She chewed her lip for a moment before replying. "It sounds crazy, but I think I'm falling in love with him, Tani. Like…for *real*."

Her friend's expression went soft. "Good for you. Have you told him yet?"

"Not in those exact words, no. But we've been so great together." She grinned. "And I'm not just talking about the sex. Even if I'm just sitting in the shop watching him work, it's…great. We talk, although sometimes we don't say a word. We're just together and it feels…"

"Great? Yeah, I'm getting that." Tani took a sip of her wine. "But does *he* feel the same way?"

"I thought he did." The way he smiled when she walked in. The gentle touches—and the scorching ones. The fire in his eyes when he held her. The way he was with Hudson, teaching him how to put spindles together in patterns, laughing when he set him high on his shoulders as they walked around the farm. His lips on her skin… "I'm *sure* he did. *Does.* I mean… I really thought we had something going."

"You still *might*, Andrea. It's one lousy text. It is way too soon to assume he's ghosting you. Especially if nothing happened between you—no fight? No weird conversation?"

"No! Hudson and I were at the farm last night for dinner, and we worked on a puzzle afterward, and it was all so relaxed and happy. I wonder…" She paused. "I wonder if it scared him a little. Maybe we're moving too fast…"

She tapped out another text to him.

A: Call me when you want to talk.

Tani chuckled. "Maybe what's scaring him is you stalker-texting him every five minutes. I'm going to take that phone away…" She looked over Andrea's shoulder. "Oh, hi, Vickie."

Andrea turned to see Vickie Pendergast standing beside her at the bar. She didn't know Vickie as well as some of the other book club matchmakers, like Maura McKinnon.

She remembered that when she was a child, Vickie and her mom had been friendly rivals for a while. Two Rendezvous Falls socialites trying to outdo each other with their garden parties. Then something had happened, as it often did with Mom's many short-term friends, and Vickie wasn't part of their life anymore.

"I know this sounds a bit forward," Vickie started, "but have you talked to Zayne today?"

"Um, yes. This morning. Why?"

"But not since then?"

Andrea shook her head, not wanting to share the date-busting text he'd sent two hours ago.

Vickie looked away, her eyes squinting as if she was arguing with herself. Then she sighed and looked back to Andrea. "He and your mother had a bit of a...*scene* at the diner this afternoon."

Oh, no. She straightened. "Define *scene*."

"Apparently your mother didn't know you two are... involved. Hudson ran to jump in Zayne's lap and Marissa lost her mind. She treated Zayne like he was some monster and yanked Hudson away."

"Oh, shit," Tani muttered.

"Exactly," Vickie answered. "It wasn't pretty. Evie got Hudson away from them with a milkshake, but your mother was...well, she was Marissa. All about *her*, and how your life choices have affected *her*, and basically just me, me, me, as always."

"Sounds like good old Mom." Marissa's world had always centered on Marissa. "How did Zayne react?"

Vickie smiled, putting her hand on Andrea's arm. "He defended you, of course." Andrea felt a blossom of warmth in her heart, but Vickie's smile faded. "Not that your mother listened. She's still hung up on who the Rutledges used to be. What their father did. How rough they grew up. I don't know how Zayne kept his cool."

"How did it end?"

"Gordy and I left while they were still…uh…talking. I put in a good word for you and Zayne, but…"

"Mom didn't listen to you, either."

Vickie looked uncomfortable. "No. I talked to Helen Russo after—you know her niece is best friends with Evie, right?" Andrea nodded. "Well, I wasn't hunting for gossip or anything. I was just worried… Anyway, Evie told Whitney that Marissa said some things Evie couldn't hear, and Zayne left in a hurry. Didn't even take the two take-out meals he'd paid for."

"Uh-oh," Tani said. "Forget what I said about giving him space. You need to find out what line of nonsense Marissa fed him." Andrea was already sliding off the bar stool. Tani pointed to the door. "I've got the drinks. Go. And text me later to let me know your mother didn't drop a bomb into things."

There was no doubt that was exactly what Mom had done. The only question now was how bad the fallout was. The shop lights were on when she drove up the hill, so that was where she parked. She knocked on the door, then walked inside when there was no answer. She could hear machinery running.

Zayne was standing at the band saw, head down, shoulders hunched over whatever he was working on. He was concentrating on the piece of wood in his hands, turning it carefully. He had his safety glasses on, but not his earplugs that she could see. She called his name. Instead of looking up, he just stopped, pulling the carved wood back slowly before reaching down to hit the switch that made the machine wind slowly down to silence. Even then, he didn't look up right away. This was not a good sign.

"Look at me, Zayne." He wouldn't. "I know what happened with my mother." That got his attention. His blue eyes hit her like an iceberg. "I don't know all of it, but I know she did her Marissa Wentworth thing all over you."

He gave a brief nod. "She did."

Andrea started toward him. "Why did you cancel our plans?"

"I just think we need to…" He looked away. "I'm no good for you, Andrea." She stopped next to the table but didn't touch him. She had a feeling that would be a mistake.

"What the hell did she say to you?" She held back the panic pushing at her heart. "I don't want us to end."

"She said she bribed you to turn on me back in school."

She sucked in a breath. "Yes. But we were seventeen, Zayne. She told me I'd never go to college if I didn't do what she said. I've already told you how sorry I am. Why are we still talking about this?"

He stared at her, and she stood there, hoping he could see straight to her soul to know how sincere she was. But something he saw must have bothered him, because he blinked and looked away.

"She said she'd do it again, to keep us apart now."

Andrea barked out a laugh. "She said she'd *bribe* me again? With what? She has nothing more to take from me. It failed with Hudson and it will fail with you."

His head snapped back. "What do you mean, it failed with Hudson?"

She swallowed hard, emotion choking her again. Her mouth opened, but she held back the words, ashamed.

"Andrea?" Zayne took her hand, his voice suddenly tender. "What do you mean?"

"Let's just say… Hudson's father wasn't the only one who offered to pay for him not to be born. When I refused, she withdrew the financial support she'd promised when I quit *you* in high school. She said she'd pay off my college loans, contribute to my expenses, all kinds of broken promises."

His mouth fell open. "But she…she takes care of him. He's with her tonight."

"Well, how would it look if she didn't? Remember, my mother is all about appearances. Once Hudson arrived, she had to be the doting grandmother." She thought for a moment. "To be fair, I think she *does* care about him." She gave Zayne a crooked grin. "I don't think she'll be offering to babysit much now that she knows about us."

"There isn't an *us*, Andrea." He grimaced. "At least, there shouldn't be."

She stepped closer, putting her hand on his chest. "There *is* an us. Right here. Right now. Can't you feel it?"

He put his hand over hers. "I *can* feel it, but of all the miserable things your mother has said and done, she said something very true today. I can't get past it."

"What was that?"

"You want to get this new job. You want to run more festivals. You want to show your mother how much you can accomplish on your own." He took a deep breath and stepped away from her, making her heart constrict at the loss of his touch. "You can't do that sleeping around with a Rutledge."

He probably thought he was being noble and wise. But in reality, he was being incredibly selfish. Her panic changed to rage, and she slapped him across his cheek.

ZAYNE ABSORBED THE blow in silence, but inside he was breaking. He'd hurt her. But he was doing what needed to be done. Marissa Wentworth was right. He was bad for Andrea. He was a Rutledge. He'd spoil her future.

"You are so full of bull." Her eyes narrowed and she stabbed at his chest with her forefinger. "You're not 'a Rutledge'! You're not your last name, damn it. If that were true, I'd be 'a Wentworth,' and I refuse to believe that." She poked him hard again. "And if I can do that, so can you."

Zayne linked his hands on top of his head and stared up at the ceiling. "There will always be people—your mother's not the only one—who will never see me as more than that name. It's not the same as you—your mom's a snob. My dad died in *prison*. I'll always be a Rutledge." He looked back to her, his hands falling to his sides in defeat. "And that will stain *you*. I can't do that. I won't." He wanted to take her hands, but touching her was more than he could handle right now. "I love you too much to do that to you."

She stood frozen, staring at him. There, he'd said it. He wanted her to know. After what seemed like an eternity, she shook her head, tears spilling down her cheeks. "Oh my God. You're just like her."

"Like who?"

"You're just like my mom. Thinking of no one but yourself."

"I just told you I *loved* you. How is that not thinking of you?"

She wiped at her cheeks with the back of her hands and moved farther from his reach. "If you loved me, you wouldn't be chased off by a few words from a woman who doesn't think *anyone* lives up to her precious standards." Her voice continued to harden. "You're just as afraid of what people think as she is. So afraid that you can't see what's right in front of your eyes."

She hit her own chest with the flat of her hand. "I'm

standing here, loving you—*really* loving you. And all you can think of is some faceless, nonexistent mob out there and what *they* might think—instead of what *I* think. Instead of what your friends think." She took a shaky breath, the hardness falling from her voice…replaced with sorrow. "Bad things happened in your youth. I know that. But I'm loving you *right now*. My mother controlled my entire world twenty years ago, and I was a coward. But I outgrew that. Now it's your turn."

"I'm not a coward." The words felt false as soon as he spoke them.

Andrea shook her head, pity filling her eyes. That hurt far more than her anger. "You've just been waiting for me to remember you're a *Rutledge*, expecting me to leave you as soon as that happens." He shook his head, but they both knew she was spot-on. "Look how happy your brother is these days, and Luke had the same hard start that you did." She gestured around the semi-dark shop. "You have a successful business. You bought a freakin' farm. You have a dog. And my son adores you." Zayne's mouth twitched at that. He adored Hudson right back. Then he remembered how Marissa had snatched Hudson out of his arms at the diner.

"Your mother isn't happy about that."

Her eyes flared in renewed anger. "I don't care what my mother thinks about who I love. And my four-year-old is a far better judge of character than his grandmother is."

She'd just said she *loved* him. He wanted to believe they could be happy.

"I don't know." He scrubbed his hands down his face. "It's not that easy to shake off a lifetime of…being less in people's eyes. Maybe I'm imagining *some* of it, but…" He looked at her, realizing she'd been exactly right about him being selfish. "Yes, I do it to protect myself."

She pursed her lips, nodding slowly. "I know. But I don't want to be constantly wondering when you're going to do this—when you're going to hear something and just…panic. If you're going to love me—*really* love me—you're going to have to leave the past in the past." Her eyes glistened with fresh tears, each one a razor slice on his heart. "You once said that when you care, you care one hundred percent. That's what I need from you. One hundred percent. Can you give me that?"

"I can. I just don't know if I *should*. You deserve better."

Silence hung in the shop like a heavy, smothering blanket.

"And there you go," she finally said softly, "retreating again. Call me when you're ready to give your all. Because *that's* what I deserve."

CHAPTER TEN

"You *SLAPPED* HIM?" Tani blew out a breath. "That's one way to knock some sense into him." She handed Andrea more tissues. "I take it that didn't work, though?"

Andrea took the tissues, blowing her nose while shaking her head. They were sitting in a corner booth at the Shamrock, far from curious eyes. She'd come straight here from Zayne's, after calling Tani and learning she was still at the pub. Tani had called in reinforcements, so Andrea was now crammed into a booth with Tani, Bridget and Whitney.

Andrea didn't know Whitney all that well, but she understood why Tani had invited her. Whitney had married "a Rutledge" and knew what kind of baggage that could bring. But she'd been quiet so far, murmuring a few words of sympathy as Andrea wept, but that was it. Andrea looked across the table at her.

"It was a slap, not a slug, Tani." She shifted in her seat. "Whitney, was Luke as screwed up as Zayne?"

Whitney's eyebrows rose. "Oh, honey—Luke was a giant ball of anger when we met. He didn't trust *anyone*, least of all his boss's niece. He assumed everyone he met was out to screw him over. Except Aunt Helen, of course." She smiled, taking a sip of wine. "The fact that he cared so much about her showed me there was a heart in there under all that resentment." Her smile faded. "Then he thought I doubted him. And that was all it took—*bam!*—the walls went right back up."

"Yes!" Andrea leaned forward. "Those damn Rutledge walls! How did you get rid of that?"

Whitney shrugged. "I didn't. What happened to that family caused some deep damage. But I basically staged a public intervention to prove to him how many people cared about him in this town. Even then, I had to fight to keep him from walking away. It was touch and go there for a while. That hurt, but I can be just as stubborn as Luke—"

"I'll vouch for that!" Evie laughed.

Tani agreed. "Girl, the two of you were like two mountain goats going at it. No one knew *what* was going to happen!"

Whitney straightened, flipping her dark hair back playfully and preening a little. "Oh, *I* knew what was going to happen. I was gettin' my man. And I did." The others laughed, but she looked at Andrea. "It still took a while for him to relax into loving me without thinking he was 'bad for me' or whatever." She'd made air quotes with her fingers for the *bad for me* part.

"That's what Zayne is worried about. I told him he was a coward, but I think he really is worried his name will hold me back somehow."

"I'm sure he is," Whitney said. "Those kids grew up with no stability at all. Their dad was in and out of prison. Their mom was often zonked out on booze. All the people who were supposed to love them…*left* them. Their trust and abandonment issues run really deep. You've got to be ready, because it never fully goes away."

Evie waved her hand between Whitney and Andrea. "Your big gesture of community love won Luke back. And that was at a Blessing of the Grapes Festival, right? Maybe Andrea could…"

Bridget shook her head. She'd been friends with Zayne for years. "A public *anything* won't work with Zayne. He hates crowds. Hates attention. That's why he fought against the corn maze so hard."

Tani's eyes went wide. "Oh God—do you think he'll pull the corn maze from the festival? It's only a week away. What should we do?"

"We should have a festival without a maze." Andrea shrugged. "He never wanted it. We'll survive."

Evie sat back with a wry smile. "Well, look at you—*not* worrying about a pretty big glitch in your festival."

Andrea thought for a moment before answering. "I guess I've realized it was never *my* festival to begin with. I'll make it the best I can, but the world will not come to an end if there's no corn maze."

"And if there's no Zayne?" Bridget asked quietly.

Andrea turned her glass, frowning at the table. "My world would be very empty." She looked over at Whitney. "I love him."

Whitney nodded with a smile. "Then find a way to love him through his fear."

ZAYNE SAT ON the tailgate of his truck, staring at his phone, trying to decipher the text conversation he'd just had with Andrea. It had been nearly twenty-four hours since she'd walked away from the shop. Away from him.

A: Wanted to let you know the good news ASAP—we're canceling the maze this year.

Z: Why?

A: You never wanted it. The field's a mess. We'll figure something else out.

And then, a few minutes later...

A: I love you.

Those three words were the ones that did him in. She

still loved him. Even after he'd chased her away. There was a crunch of car tires on the driveway, but it wasn't Andrea as he'd hoped. It was his brother, and he looked grim when he got out of his car.

Zayne held his hand up with a sigh. "I'm not in the mood for a big brother lecture."

Luke nodded and joined him on the tailgate anyway. "Okay. How about a big brother ear, then? What happened?"

And just like that, Zayne was telling his brother everything. How happy he'd been with Andrea. With Hudson. What Marissa Wentworth had done and said—not only in the diner, but back when they were all kids. He told Luke about Andrea coming to the shop to confront him. How he'd tried to explain that he was no good for her.

Luke winced. "And how well did *that* go over?"

"She slapped me in the face."

"No shit? Good for her!" Luke laughed.

"Who's side are you on?"

"*Your* side. Always."

They'd had their years of barely speaking—all that Rutledge anger twisted up inside them, keeping them apart. Luke would check in a few times a year, basically confirming Zayne was still alive and functioning.

"Thank you," he said, surprising Luke.

"For being on your side? You're my brother, man."

"Not just now, but…for the past, too. I didn't make it easy, but you kept calling and stopping by, even in my hermit years."

Luke chuckled softly. "There were a few times when I drove up that dirt road to the old trailer that I half expected you to greet me with a shotgun." He paused. "I'm proud of how you've turned things around in the past few years. It took Whitney to pull *me* through, but you did it on your own. Found a job you loved. Built a business. Bought a place." He looked around. "I told you I was on your side, and that's why I gotta tell you—none of this matters without love in your life. And you *have* that."

"I know. But—"

"No *buts* when it comes to love. We're the Rutledge boys, remember? When we find a woman who doesn't see *that* before she sees *us*... Well, we need to hang on to that woman. You need to hang on to Andrea."

Zayne winced. "I want to, but her mother managed to turn her against me before." If he gave her his heart completely, it would crush him to lose her.

Luke leaned forward, looking up into Zayne's eyes. "You can't live in fear of what *might* happen—especially something as unlikely as that. Our upbringing made us one way, and *her* upbringing made her another. We've all had a chance to evolve in twenty years." Luke clapped his hand on Zayne's shoulder. "Take it from me—a woman's love can heal a lot of wounds, brother."

"But what if I've already blown it?"

Luke chuckled. "We *really* need to work on that cheery disposition of yours. Stop defeating yourself before you've started. Did she tell you what it'll take to win her back?"

Call me when you're ready...

"She wants me to give her my all."

"So...do it."

Zayne nodded, staring down the hill. To the maze. Which was still a raggedy mess. They'd managed to get the design roughly mowed, but it was hardly the smooth pathways everyone said Cliff had provided. The festival was a week away. He looked around. The whole farm looked...tired.

He pulled his phone out again, and his brother sighed.

"Her text isn't going to change."

"Maybe not." He started to dial. "But her plans are about to."

CHAPTER ELEVEN

IT WAS THE opening morning of the Blessing of the Grapes Festival, and Andrea was running down Main Street in a panic.

"Tani!" she shouted, waving a fistful of brochures in the air. "What *is* this?"

"What is *what*? Slow down!" Tani excused herself from one of the festival's vendors, who was setting up a food tent in the expansive park near Brady College. "And stop yelling," she hissed. "You're gonna freak everyone out."

"Well, *I'm* freaked out." She stopped to catch her breath. "The brochures still say there's a corn maze! You said you were going to cover that up with stickers or something. What happened?"

Tani pressed the tip of her tongue to her top lip as she took a brochure. "We must have missed a few. It'll be fine."

"It's *not* fine. This says there are going to be shuttles to the maze like every other year."

"Wait—didn't you say you weren't going to be bothered if we didn't have a maze this year? That Zayne's happiness was more important than the festival?"

Andrea put her fists on her hips. "I never said his happiness was more important. I just didn't want him *un*happy. Even if we're not together…"

Her voice trailed off. She hadn't spoken or texted with him in a week. Not since she told him there wouldn't be a maze. She'd just have to figure out another way to prove her management skills at the college. Another job would roll around eventually. And she was pretty sure she never wanted to run another festival in Rendezvous Falls.

"Okay, okay." Tani put her arm around Andrea's shoulders. "I'll make sure everything works the way it's supposed to. And no one's going to be disappointed with the shuttle bus rides, since they'll now take them up to Eagle Rock Distillery. That was a brilliant idea on your part."

"But not as family-centered as the maze was."

She had a feeling quite a few parents would get the same earful from their kids that Hudson had been giving her. Although his distress may have had more to do with missing Zayne than missing the corn maze. Her son had been moping around all week, asking to go to the farm. Asking to go see Duke. Asking why Momma didn't like Mr. Zayne anymore.

Whitney had advised Andrea to love Zayne *through his fear*. But first, she needed to know that he loved *her* enough to try. But every day that passed without him reaching out to her made her feel more lonely. She'd been grateful for the festival, because it kept her too busy to think about how much she missed him—at least until nighttime came. But now the festival was here, and in a few days it would be over and then she'd be forced to confront a future without Zayne in it.

"Yoo-hoo! Andrea!" Iris Taggart was walking her way, using the cane that had become a regular thing since the octogenarian broke her hip a few years ago. Vickie Pendergast was with her. They'd both been chairs of the festival multiple times in the past. "Everything looks lovely, dear. You're going to have a smashing success this weekend—I just know it. Even without the corn maze."

And there it was. The first of what would probably be a thousand mentions of the missing maze. Andrea forced a smile. "Thank you, Iris. What has you here so early? The festival doesn't officially start until this afternoon."

"We're here for the traditional first bus ride, of course." Vickie smiled, patting Andrea's arm. "Even if we are going to a different destination this year."

And there was mention number two. Andrea pulled her shoulders back. She could do this. "What bus ride? The festival hasn't start—"

"We know it hasn't started, dear." Iris patted Andrea's arm. "That's the whole point. The festival staff has to make sure the shuttles are operating properly."

She laughed a little, looking at Tani in confusion. "Well, it's not like they're going to get lost driving up the hill."

"It's tradition!" Vickie exclaimed. "And former chairs are always invited. So let's get this show on the road."

She watched the two women walk toward the shuttle area, where, sure enough, there was a yellow school bus waiting. She looked at Tani.

"Did you know anything about this tradition?"

"Not really, but it sounds like fun. Come on, let's join them."

Andrea was going to ask what *not really* meant, but Tani was jogging—*jogging!*—toward the bus. Some other people were boarding, including more seniors like Maura McKinnon and Helen Russo. She was pretty sure neither of them had been festival chairpersons. And was that Whitney Rutledge and Bridget O'Hearn already inside? Bridget waved as Andrea got to the bus.

"Isn't this fun? Come on aboard and let's get this show on the road!"

"But I have so much to do…"

"Nonsense. Get on the bus, Andrea."

Okay, then. Who was she to buck tradition? She sat near the front, but everyone kept asking her questions and telling stories of past festivals, so she wasn't paying much attention to where they were. Until the bus slowed and turned onto a gravel drive. A driveway she knew too well. It was Zayne's farm. She looked out the windshield. Or was it?

She hardly recognized the place. There were flowers everywhere—in hanging baskets, in large planters, on top of wooden wine barrels. The lawn was mowed short and trimmed around all the trees and outbuildings. There were signs pointing to "bus parking." She blinked. What was *happening*?

The bus stopped near the field where the maze was located. There was an ornate wooden archway at the entrance, with lots of gingerbread frills. She knew it was Zayne's work, but…why?

No one stood on the bus. Whitney leaned forward and tapped Andrea's shoulder.

"I think this is *your* stop."

Andrea stood, still not sure what was going on. She went to the top of the steps at the open bus door and gasped. Zayne was standing outside, looking up at her.

"Zayne?" Beyond him, she saw a virtual tower of colorful mums on either side of the maze entrance. The path into the maze was cut short and neat, without a weed in sight. Just beautiful grass and tall corn. "You didn't have to do this. We weren't going to have a maze…"

"*You* weren't going to have a maze," Vickie said behind her. "But Zayne told us the maze was on." Vickie gave Andrea a not-so-subtle push toward the steps. "And we decided to go with Zayne's plan. You should, too."

Andrea walked down the steps. Zayne held out his hand

for her, and she took it, smiling in spite of herself as soon as their fingers touched.

"This was all your idea?"

He shrugged. "Well, doing the maze was my idea. Then I mentioned needing help, and you know how this town is. People came out of the woodwork."

She was staring up at him in wonder. "I thought you weren't a people person."

His mouth slid into a slanted grin. "I'm an *Andrea* person. And if this is what it takes to put that smile on your face, then I can handle it." She looked around the yard.

"But the flowers—I've never seen this place look so pretty."

"You said it needed a woman's touch. Lucy Cooper helped."

She had no idea what to say.

"Why?"

Zayne laughed. The sound was warm and deep and made her feel lighter.

"Because when I care, I care one hundred percent, remember?"

A spark of hope blossomed inside her. This was about more than just a maze. "I remember."

"Well, I care about you. I *love* you." He cupped her face with his hands. "I'll give you all of my heart, Andrea. Right now. In front of…" He looked up at the bus behind her, where everyone had their faces plastered to the open windows. "In front of a crowd of people that are apparently my friends now." There was a small cheer of agreement from the bus. "They don't give a damn about my name or my past or any of the things I was getting so hung up on. And they promised to help *me* not give a damn—" he dipped his head to give her a quick kiss "—about anything other than loving you. Do you think *you* could help me with that, too?"

"I can do that, but, Zayne…"

"Nuh-uh." He kissed her again, lingering longer this time, melting her fears like butter. "No buts in love. Just promise to love me, and we can get through anything together."

She took a deep breath, then held it while she stared into his ocean-blue eyes. Eyes that were full of love. She let out the breath and reached up to touch his cheek with her fingers.

"I can love you through anything."

They kissed again, clinging to each other. He lifted his head and studied her face. "You need to know I love Hudson, too."

"That's good, because he and I are a package deal."

He brushed her cheeks with his thumbs. "Why are you crying?"

"Because I'm happy. Hudson has missed you so much—he already adores you." She giggled. "And Duke, of course."

"Of course," he laughed. He lifted her in his arms and swung her in a circle. "We'll be one big happy family."

* * * * *

Do you love romance books?

Join the Read Love Repeat Facebook group dedicated to book recommendations, author exclusives, SWOONING and all things romance!

A community made for romance readers by romance readers.

Facebook.com/groups/readloverepeat